CIVIL TO STRANGERS

and
Other Writings

Barbara Pym

virago

VIRAGO

This edition published in 2011 by Virago Press
First published in Great Britain in 1987 by Macmillan London Limited

Copyright © the estate of Barbara Pym 1987
Introduction copyright © Hazel Holt 2011

The moral right of the author has been asserted.

A CIP catalogue record for this book
is available from the British Library.

ISBN: 978-1-84408-722-8

Typeset in Goudy by M Rules
Printed and bound in Great Britain by
Clays Ltd, St Ives plc

Virago Press
An imprint of
Little, Brown Book Group
100 Victoria Embankment
London EC4Y 0DY

An Hachette UK Company
www.hachette.co.uk

www.virago.co.uk

CONTENTS

INTRODUCTION

When *A Last Sheaf* was published, several years after Denton Welch's death, Barbara Pym wrote, 'How splendid that we are to be given one more Denton.' When she died in 1980 she left not only nine published novels, but also a considerable amount of unpublished material. So I gathered together Barbara's own last sheaf, a final selection from her unpublished writings.

Barbara Pym was from a generation that disliked waste and was naturally frugal: she made over her old clothes (letting in bands of different colours to achieve a newly fashionable hemline) and devised delicious meals from leftovers. She was equally thrifty in her work. Characters from her early, unpublished work appear in later novels (for example, Miss Morrow and Miss Doggett from *Crampton Hodnet* are later found in *Jane and Prudence*, as well as in the short story 'So, Some Tempestuous Morn'), and when she was unable to find a publisher for *An Unsuitable Attachment*, she salvaged Mark and Sophia Ainger and, especially, Faustina for use in 'The Christmas Visit'. So I am sure she would be pleased that so much of her work that wasn't published in her lifetime is available to be read and enjoyed.

From the beginning of her career as a published novelist in

1950 (though she had been writing novels since the age of sixteen), she had consistently good reviews. John Betjeman described her, in 1952, as 'a splendidly humorous writer' and the chorus of praise grew with each new book until her later novels were best-sellers here and in the United States where she had a growing following. The novelist Anne Tyler wrote, 'Whom do people turn to when they've finished Barbara Pym? The answer is easy; they turn back to Barbara Pym,' and John Updike in the *New Yorker* wrote of her novels: 'A startling reminder that solitude may be chosen and that a lively, full novel can be constructed entirely within the precincts of that regressive virtue, feminine patience.' Best of all was her champion Philip Larkin's assertion that he'd 'sooner read a new Barbara Pym than a new Jane Austen'. In 1977 she was on the shortlist for the Booker Prize for *Quartet in Autumn* (even more prestigious then, when there were few literary awards) and received the popular accolade of appearing on *Desert Island Discs*.

This late success was especially heartening as she had previously had such a blow to her confidence. When Jonathan Cape rejected *An Unsuitable Attachment* in 1963, Barbara tried to place it with other publishers, but in the 1960s her novels were thought to be old fashioned. As one publisher remarked, it was 'not the sort of book to which people were turning'. There followed fourteen years of rejection and frustration until, in 1977, the *Times Literary Supplement* published a list, chosen by eminent literary figures, of the most underrated writers of the century. Barbara was the only living writer chosen by two people: Lord David Cecil and Philip Larkin. She was deemed publishable again.

After her death in 1980 she left behind complete but unpublished novels, half-finished works, short stories and a mass of papers – especially diaries and the series of notebooks where she had noted down odd thoughts, comments, overheard remarks and ideas for novels. It seemed, given the interest her novels had aroused, suitable to publish the latter. *A Very Private Eye: An Autobiography in Diaries and Letters* (published in 1984) caused a minor publishing sensation, giving, as it did, a fuller, and unexpected, picture of her very varied life. It was received with enthusiasm and there seemed to be a desire for 'more Barbara Pym'. *An Unsuitable Attachment* had finally been published in 1982 and received good reviews here and ecstatic ones in the United States: the *Washington Post* commented, 'The publisher must have been mad to reject this jewel. The cut-glass elegance of her precise understated wit sparkles, her understanding of the human heart gleams more softly but just as bright' and the *New Yorker* called it 'a paragon of a novel'. Then *Crampton Hodnet* was published in 1985 and *An Academic Question* followed in 1986.

Civil to Strangers, which appeared in 1987, was the result of requests from the many scholars writing about her novels, who wanted access to her earlier work, but which also proved very popular with all her non-academic readers.

The novel at the centre of this collection was written in 1936, when she was twenty-three, and has all the confidence of youth. She greatly admired the novels of Elizabeth von Arnim, especially *The Enchanted April*, and she seems to have made it the springboard, as it were, for this book. There are several parallels: the selfish, uncaring husband, the apparently submissive wife who, nevertheless, observes life with an ironic eye, and the transformation of a difficult husband by the Romance of Abroad. The style has something of the same cadence – formal, light, elegant, slightly sardonic. But Barbara could never be just an imitator and her own personality comes through early on. Then there are the purely Pym characters: the Rector and his family, Mr Paladin the curate, as well as the splendid Mrs Gower – and no one but Barbara could have written chapter thirteen. This novel is interesting too because it is one of the few in which the heroine goes abroad, and the passages set in pre-war Budapest have the charm and interest of descriptions of a vanished world.

The second half of this book is a collection of novels and short stories, mostly written while she was living at home in Oswestry before or during the war, which show how Barbara was working steadily at her craft. I also included the radio talk she gave, *Finding a Voice*, in 1978. It was part of a series featuring well-known writers (the author before her had been Beryl Bainbridge) on how they developed their own individual style. She was very pleased to be asked to contribute, since it was a confirmation at last of her position as a professional writer, a title especially precious after her years in the literary wilderness. Reading this piece is poignant since we can hear her quiet, rather hesitant voice, summing up with style and succinctness, her thoughts on writing and on 'finding one's own particular voice', ending, typically, on a wry, almost wistful query.

So often, after well-known novelists die, their reputation, high in their lifetime, diminishes over the years. With Barbara, the opposite has happened. Since *Civil to Strangers*, the last of her posthumously issued books, was first published, her reputation has grown. This is most satisfactory, though it is sad to think that, after her rediscovery in 1977, she only enjoyed three years of her hard-won success.

It is remarkable to see how many editions of Barbara Pym's books there have been. In addition, she has been translated into French, Italian, German, Dutch, Portuguese, Hungarian, Russian and Japanese and there are to be new editions published shortly in Italian and Spanish. So it still goes on and all her novels remain in print. A number of books about her work have been published and there seem to be more to come. And she would be delighted to know that she has provided a rich field for students (not all like Larkin's Jake Balokowski) looking for a worthy subject for a thesis, many of whom come to visit the collection of Pym papers in the Bodleian library. Towards the end of her life, Barbara said, with a mixture of pleasure and incredulity, 'I am being *taught* in Texas!' She would be amazed and gratified to know that she still provides material for English literature courses (mostly in America). There are two flourishing Barbara Pym Societies, the main English branch based on Barbara's old college, St Hilda's in Oxford, and the American one in Cambridge, Massachusetts. Both hold annual conferences, both well attended and with distinguished speakers, and they both include a dramatised reading, each time, of one of Barbara's unpublished works.

Once, when she was unpublished and depressed, she wrote to Philip Larkin, 'Here I am sixty-one (it looks worse spelled out in words) and only six novels published – no husband, no children', to which Philip replied sharply, 'Didn't J. Austen write six novels, and not have a husband and children?' – not the first comparison with Jane Austen, but one of the best. The fact is that all Barbara wanted to be was a writer, that was the mainspring of her life. 'After supper,' she wrote in her diary in 1941, 'I did some more writing which quells my restlessness – that is how I must succeed!' She could have had a husband and children (she rejected several proposals of marriage) but the men she really cared for had married other people. As she moved towards her maturity as a writer she looked back on her relationships – recollection, not in tranquillity precisely, but with an amused and affectionate compassion. She knew she could transmute them, by the alchemy that is creativity, into Material, the aim of every writer.

Even though she had such a short time of personal success, she did achieve what she always wanted. That magic year of 1977 she wrote in her notebook, 'Who is that woman sitting on the concrete wall outside Barclay's Bank reading the *TV Times*? That is Miss Pym the novelist.' No one else could have written that. At the end of her radio talk, *Finding a Voice*, published in this volume, she sums it all up: 'I think that's the kind of immortality most authors would want – to feel that their work would be immediately recognisable as having been written by them and by nobody else.' And she adds, in her typically self-effacing way, 'But, of course, it's a lot to ask for!'

But that is the kind of immortality she has achieved. Her voice *is* immediately recognisable; that word includes the whole person – what she thought, believed in and, especially, noticed. Her work is still read not only for the style but for what it says to us, now, as we read it. One of the most remarkable things is the way her name has become a sort of shorthand for a certain kind of person, moment or, even, place. It crops up regularly (sometimes in the most unexpected places) in books, on the radio and television. Truly, as the novelist Shirley Hazzard has said: 'We may now say Barbara Pym and be understood instantly.' 'To say that a moment is "very Barbara Pym"', Alexander McCall Smith writes, 'is to say that it is a self-observed, poignant acceptance of the modesty of one's circumstances, of one's peripheral position.'

It would seem that we are still glad to turn to the author who advocated small, blameless pleasures, to provide us with good books for a bad day.

Hazel Holt, 2011

PART ONE

Civil to Strangers

———————

Civil to Strangers

'Her Conduct Regular, her Mirth Refin'd,
Civil to Strangers, to her Neighbours kind'

John Pomfret, *The Choice*

Note on the Text

This was Barbara's second novel (362 pages), written in 1936, after the first version of Some Tame Gazelle *had gone the rounds of the publishers with no success.*

In May she wrote to Henry Harvey, 'Did I tell you I had started a new novel? I am just beginning to get it into form, although at first I found it something of an effort.' By July 17th she had got as far as Chapter 6 and on the 20th she noted, 'Today I wrote about 8 pages in a large foolscap size notebook. I'd like if possible to get the whole thing done by November. It will be something to work for.' On August 20th she wrote to Henry Harvey:

Adam and Cassandra are getting on quite nicely though I haven't done much to them lately. Adam is sweet but very stupid. You are sweet too, but not as consistently stupid as Adam. But I wish you were here to show me where to put commas and to help me with my novel . . . I am all alone in the house, except for the wireless, which you despise so much. I am writing rather slowly and laboriously and every time I think of something nice to say I stop and consider it well before I put it in.

In October she was revising and typing (on the Remington portable her father had just given her): 'In the morning I finished (typing) Chapter XIV of Adam and Cassandra [the original title]. I have now reached p.170 and think I can finish it. It seems to get better as it goes on, I think.'

The later part of the book, set in Hungary, was inspired by Barbara's own visit in August 1935, when she and her sister Hilary went to Budapest with a group from the National Union of Students. As always she had a lively time, with many admirers.

Civil to Strangers marks a turning point in Barbara's development. The confident but slightly self-indulgent enthusiasm of the first draft of Some Tame Gazelle has been tempered with maturity of style and craftsmanship. Barbara Pym the writer was turning into Barbara Pym the novelist.

Note: the quotations at the beginning of each chapter are all taken from James Thomson's poem 'The Seasons'.

CHAPTER ONE

''Tis silence all,
And pleasing expectation.'

'Dear Cassandra,' smiled Mrs Gower, 'you are always so punctual.' She leaned forward, and brushed Cassandra's cheek with her lips. Cassandra responded with a similar gesture, a little awkwardly, for Mrs Gower was a large woman, and her cheek was rather difficult to reach.

'I always try to be punctual,' said Cassandra with a smile, although the flat, even tone of her voice implied that she had made the remark many times before.

'You have every virtue, my dear,' said Mrs Gower warmly, as they settled themselves on the sofa.

Cassandra sighed, although not loudly enough for Mrs Gower to hear. She knew that she had every virtue, because people were always telling her so. She was twenty-eight years old, a tall, fair young woman, not exactly pretty, but comely and dignified. This afternoon she was wearing a well-cut costume of blue tweed. Her hat and shoes were sensible rather than fashionable. Cassandra could always be relied upon never to wear anything unsuitable to the place she happened to be in at the time.

'I asked Mrs Wilmot and Janie to come this afternoon,' said Mrs Gower. 'I suppose you didn't see any sign of them as you came past the rectory?'

'No,' said Cassandra. 'As a matter of fact I didn't come that way. I had to do some shopping. I'd forgotten some things in the town.'

'What a consolation to know that you are human like the rest of us!' laughed Mrs Gower.

Cassandra smiled a little sadly. People so often raised doubts as to her humanity that she sometimes wondered whether she was not indeed some unearthly being, who had found her way into the small town of Up Callow as the wife of Adam Marsh-Gibbon, a gentleman of means, who wrote a little poetry and a few obscure novels.

Actually, most of the money that enabled Adam to lead this pleasant life was Cassandra's, but she never reminded him of it. Before they were married she had implied that everything she possessed was as much his as hers, if anything more his, for she had been so grateful that he returned her love that she would have done anything for him. After five years of marriage her rapture had died down a little, for Adam was in many ways difficult, but she was still pleasantly surprised when she realized that this handsome and distinguished-looking man was her husband and nobody else's.

'There goes another tree,' said Mrs Gower suddenly. 'The noise they make is quite frightening until one realizes what it is. I'm hoping they'll cut down that big one next. It will make this room so much lighter,' she added.

'Adam loves trees,' said Cassandra. 'He says it grieves him so much to think of these opposite your house being cut down.'

'Oh, well, of course he's a poet,' said Mrs Gower tolerantly, although she had never yet succeeded in understanding his

6

poetry at all perfectly. Nor had she tried very hard, for since she had been a widow it had no longer been necessary to pretend an interest in literature. 'My late husband used to like the open spaces better,' she declared. 'When he was Professor of Poetry at Oxford, we lived at Headington, although our first house in Norham Road was rather shut in ... that must be Mrs Wilmot and Janie arriving now,' she said suddenly.

The door opened and in pattered a grey-haired and grey-coated little woman, accompanied by a dark, slender girl about nineteen years old, who walked meekly beside her.

'Dear Kathleen, I'm so glad you were able to come. And Janie too. Holidays again?' said Mrs Gower, with a kind of vague brightness which she adopted when speaking to all really young people.

Janie smiled patiently. 'Oh, no, I've left school,' she said. 'I'm helping Mother at home.' She was relieved that neither Mrs Gower nor Mrs Marsh-Gibbon went any deeper into the subject. For everyone knew the kind of life that the dutiful elder daughter of the rector of a country parish must lead, and Janie conformed exactly to that pattern. She taught in the Sunday school, helped with the GFS, and spent a great deal of time decorating the church.

'I thought the font was so prettily decorated at Easter,' said Cassandra, remembering that it had been Janie's own particular contribution to the decorations.

Janie looked pleased. 'I'm so glad you noticed it. I was afraid I had put in too much greenery.'

The arrival of tea excused her from the necessity of enlarging further upon the subject, and the conversation turned once more to the trees that were being felled opposite Mrs Gower's house.

'The new tenants of Holmwood can't be very fond of trees,' said Mrs Wilmot. 'I suppose nobody knows whether it really *is*

7

let? I heard that some people had been looking over it, but of course they may not have taken it. It's a very old-fashioned house, and would need a lot of alterations.'

'And Rogers was telling me that if they take a brick out the whole house will collapse,' said Mrs Gower, in tones of melancholy satisfaction, for she had built for herself a large black and white house which still looked very new. When her husband had died eight years ago, she had decided to come back to Shropshire, where she had lived as a girl. Over the front door of her house she had put a slab of stone, with A.D. 1929 engraved on it, but somehow one never imagined the house becoming old, not even in a thousand years' time. Mrs Gower did not mind this newness at all. She liked solid, well-built comfort, with electric light and central heating, better than all the glories of the past.

'Rockingham is wondering if they will be church people,' said Mrs Wilmot rather hopelessly, for the last inhabitants of Holmwood had been wealthy, generous, but, unfortunately, Roman Catholics.

'I do hope they will be,' said Cassandra sympathetically, smiling a little as she always did when she heard the rector's Christian name.

There was a short silence during which they heard another tree fall. This noise was followed by that of a car stopping near Mrs Gower's house. Mrs Wilmot could not resist getting up and going to the window to look.

'Two men have got out,' she said, 'and they're walking up and down the drive, looking at the trees, I think. What *are* they doing? They seem to be putting up a sort of notice.'

By this time the others had risen and come to the window. 'They *are* putting up a notice,' confirmed Mrs Gower. Reading slowly she began to decipher the notice word by word. Everyone agreed that it was disappointing. It merely said 'PEA STICKS &

FIREWOOD FOR SALE. ALSO WOOD FOR RUSTIC FRAMES. APPLY WITHIN. TRESPASSERS WILL BE PROSECUTED.'

'Well,' said Mrs Wilmot in a flat voice, 'so that's all. I wonder what they mean by rustic frames?' she added, brightening up a little, as if it might possibly be something exciting.

Nobody seemed able to enlighten her and there was a depressed silence until Cassandra remarked that Mrs Gower's pink tulips would soon be out.

'They're such lovely things,' she said. 'Adam says that they're the heralds of summer. We always think the weather grows warmer when they come out.'

'A writer must be very sensitive to Nature,' remarked Mrs Wilmot. 'Of course Wordsworth was, wasn't he?' she added uncertainly.

'Oh, yes, I'm sure he must have been,' said Cassandra distastefully, for Adam always quoted Wordsworth at her when he was in a bad temper, so that for Cassandra the great poet of the Romantic Revival was inevitably associated with quarrels with her husband.

'How is your husband's book getting on?' Janie asked Cassandra shyly. She thought Adam Marsh-Gibbon quite the handsomest man she had ever seen and accordingly his writings had an added glamour about them.

Cassandra smiled kindly. 'Well, at present he is working on rather a difficult chapter,' she said.

'I suppose every author gets stuck occasionally,' said Mrs Gower.

'The inspiration flows less easily,' interposed Mrs Wilmot, thinking that it was a more suitable phrase.

Cassandra smiled at both of them. 'That's just it,' she said, making each woman feel that she had said exactly the right thing. 'It's so nice of you to ask after Adam's book,' she said, turning to Janie. 'People are so kind,' she added vaguely, almost

9

as if her husband were an invalid who needed sympathetic enquiries.

'Would you like to see round the garden?' asked Mrs Gower, feeling that there was not much to talk about now that the subject of the new tenants of Holmwood and Adam Marsh-Gibbon's book had been exhausted.

Cassandra sprang eagerly to her feet. 'I should love to,' she said. 'I was admiring what I could see of it when I came in.'

'I'm afraid we must be going,' said Mrs Wilmot hastily, for she disliked walking round gardens in her best shoes. 'Come, Janie ... I always say that the worst of being married to a clergyman is that there's always some good work to be done.'

'But I'm sure that must come naturally to you,' said Cassandra.

Mrs Wilmot smiled and told Cassandra to be sure to wish Adam good luck with his novel.

Cassandra thanked her. She liked the idea of Adam being wished good luck with his book, as if he were rowing in the Boat Race, or had a horse running in the Derby.

When the Wilmots had gone, Mrs Gower and Cassandra walked slowly round the garden, deep in gardening talk. Cassandra was completely happy, and all thoughts of Adam were absent from her mind as she and Mrs Gower discussed the advantages of taking up gladioli in the winter, or of raising aubretia from seed.

When she left, Cassandra took with her a large paper carrier, containing several new plants for her rockery.

'You know,' said Mrs Gower confidentially, 'I can't help feeling that the new tenants of Holmwood are going to be rather interesting. I've a sort of premonition,' she declared, with a glance at the fallen trees in the drive opposite.

'I hope your premonition will come true,' laughed Cassandra. 'I always think it's such a fascinating house with all those queer little turrets. Adam says it reminds him of the Castle of Otranto.'

That must be somewhere in Italy, thought Mrs Gower, but she did not say anything, as Adam Marsh-Gibbon so often meant something one had never heard of.

CHAPTER TWO

'These are the haunts of meditation'

Adam Marsh-Gibbon's study was the nicest room in the house. Cassandra had insisted, and so he was spared the necessity of having to be selfish about it. This was one of Cassandra's special virtues, that she anticipated her husband's wishes almost before he knew what they were. Some men would have been irritated by this, but Adam always pretended that he was so engrossed in his art that he did not have time to think of where he should have his study, or in which chair he should sit in the drawing room after dinner.

On this evening in early spring he was sitting at a table, deeply engrossed in *The Times* crossword puzzle. All around him was a litter of papers covered with his fine spidery handwriting. His new novel was not going very well. Hitherto he had been able to say very much the same things in all of them, with a few variations and slightly different characters. He was proudly described by the admiring inhabitants of Up Callow as a 'philosophical' novelist, but his philosophy, such as it was, was beginning to wear a little thin, and he did not know where to find another. It was over a year since the publication of his last novel, *Things For Ever Speaking*, and already his public was beginning to get impatient, he thought. He was a vain man, and valued especially his reputation in Up Callow, because it was really the only reputation he had. He enjoyed autographing his novels and poems and was always delighted to give a lecture to the Literary Society on The Craft of the Novelist.

Even the rector admired Adam's works, not so much for the ideas expressed in them, which were vaguely Wordsworthian, but because they were fit for his daughters to read. They might be a little above their heads, for the rector had a low opinion of female intelligence, but at least one didn't have to hide them away, like so many of the novels that were written nowadays.

Adam heard the front door open and, looking at his watch, saw that it was twenty past six. That must be Cassandra coming home from Mrs Gower's, he thought. He pushed his novel away from him and took up the crossword again.

Cassandra went upstairs to her bedroom. Her feet made no sound on the thick carpets. This house was always quiet, especially in the evenings when there was no bustle of housework. It was understood that the master liked to get on with his writing after tea. Lily and Bessie looked upon it with some suspicion, but they admired Cassandra and for her sake they put up with Adam's late rising and untidy ways.

Cassandra opened the door of her room, taking care not to let it bang as she shut it. Living with an author had made her almost inhumanly quiet in her movements, so that shutting doors softly came as naturally to her as breathing.

It was a large, pleasant room, decorated in blue and primrose yellow. Adam's room, which led out of it, was much more gloomy, for it had been designed at a time when Adam had ideas about interior decoration. The walls were grey and the carpet black and very thick. The long curtains at the windows were of heavy crimson velvet, so that Cassandra could not help thinking of a super cinema every time she went into the room. On the wall opposite the bed hung a large reproduction of Böcklin's picture 'The Island of the Dead'. It was the first thing that caught his eye when he awoke in the morning, so that even if he had intended to begin the day cheerfully by leaping out of bed at eight o'clock, he was nearly always plunged into gloom again at the sight of it and would sit brooding in bed until lunch-time.

Cassandra went to her wardrobe and took out a plain, black velvet dress. It suited her fairness and she thought a bright colour might jar on Adam if he had been having difficulty with his novel. She put on only the merest suspicion of lipstick and went downstairs looking nice but inconspicuous. In her earlier twenties she had occasionally indulged in scarlet nail varnish with lipstick to match, but now, since her marriage, she had felt less tempted to break out.

She knocked at the door of Adam's study so quietly that he need not have heard if he hadn't wanted to. But as he was stuck both with his novel and the crossword, he welcomed her interruption.

Cassandra went up to him and kissed his cheek. He stood up, smiling rather wearily, and put his arm round her waist. He was slightly taller than she was, a good-looking, thin-faced man, with dark hair and grey eyes. He was thirty-two years old. His elegant clothes were always very much admired, although nobody in Up Callow would have dared to copy his velvet coats and suède shoes. These were the trappings of genius, even if those who had the opportunity of knowing were reminded of a young aesthetic undergraduate.

'It's chicken for dinner,' Cassandra said.

'I could eat a whole chicken, now, at this minute,' said Adam. 'I haven't been able to do much writing this evening and I feel hungry. I don't believe I've had anything to eat since luncheon,' he added.

'Oh, *Adam*,' said Cassandra in a shocked voice, 'surely Lily brought you some tea?'

'I don't remember any,' he said absently.

Cassandra laughed. 'I'll see if Bessie can manage to let us have dinner a bit earlier,' she said.

In the kitchen she said, 'I hope you gave the master a good tea, he gets so hungry when he's working.'

Lily and Bessie smiled tolerantly, for writing was hardly what they would have called work.

'Oh, yes, madam,' said Lily in her precise voice. 'He had a nice boiled egg.'

'And he fancied a bit of that tinned salmon,' chimed in Bessie, eager to show that everything had been done as it should be in Cassandra's absence.

Over dinner, she reminded Adam about the boiled egg and the tinned salmon, wondering how it was possible to forget such a meal. 'Are you sure you were wise to have the salmon, dear?' she asked anxiously. 'You know tinned things don't agree with you. I only keep them in the house because Lily and Bessie like them. When you read about food poisoning cases in the paper, they've nearly always eaten tinned salmon.'

'And tinned apricots and fish and chips and ice cream as well,' interposed Adam, and fell into a gloomy silence.

Perhaps the tinned salmon and boiled egg were already beginning to disagree with him, thought Cassandra detachedly, while she reported the conversation at Mrs Gower's tea party. She asked Adam if he had heard anything about the new tenants of Holmwood, but of course he hadn't, and said that he didn't even know that it was to let.

Cassandra wished he would be a little more worldly at times; it was so tedious having to tell him things that everybody else had known for weeks.

'I hope they'll change the name of the house,' he said. 'Obviously it should be called Otranto, or some other romantic name. Oroonoko would be nice.'

Cassandra reflected that Adam had some very funny ideas about the naming of houses. Their own house, which Cassandra had wanted to call The Grove, or The Poplars, because of the avenue of those trees leading up to the front door, had been named The Grotto, although anything less like one could scarcely be imagined, and when she was first married she had always felt self-conscious about giving the name of the house when she ordered things from shops.

When they were drinking their coffee in the drawing room, she made some tentative enquiries about Adam's new book. 'They were asking about it at Mrs Gower's tea party,' she told him. Adam looked pleased and stood up.

'Shall I read you what I've written, or shall we go on with "The Seasons"?'

'If it would help you to read what you've written today of course I'll listen, but I daresay you would rather do some more before it's ready to be criticized,' said Cassandra. She hoped it was going to be 'The Seasons', as she was always a little embarrassed when Adam read aloud from his own works. It was sometimes difficult enough to understand what it all meant, let alone give any penetrating criticism. And at the back of Cassandra's mind was the uncomfortable suspicion that perhaps there wasn't very much meaning after all, else why couldn't it be put more clearly?

'Perhaps we'd better get on with "The Seasons",' said Adam. 'After all, Spring will not wait for us if we lag behind.'

He sat down on the sofa by her, opened his book and began to read.

It had been their custom ever since they were first married to read together in the evenings. At first Cassandra had been a little frightened by her ignorance of English Literature, but Adam had taken her in hand very kindly, and, smiling with superior love, had introduced her to the glories of *Paradise Lost*.

Her husband's name being Adam made it almost inevitable that Cassandra should find in that poem a motto for her own life. Thus, before she had been married six months, she was continually reminding herself of Eve's words:

> My Author and Disposer, what thou bidst
> Unargu'd I obey; so God ordains,
> God is thy Law, thou mine: to know no more
> Is woman's happiest knowledge and her praise

although, as time went on, she found herself thinking that while the attitude of wifely submission was an admirable one, it was nevertheless just a little absurd.

Now, after five years of such instruction in English Literature, Cassandra felt that she could regard herself as a reasonably cultured woman. Sometimes she was even so bold as to wonder whether she might not have been even *more* cultured and intelligent than her husband, if she had had his advantages, Balliol and the Honours School of English Language and Literature.

Tonight Cassandra tried hard to concentrate on what Adam was reading. She listened attentively to the description of fishing, and even noted the advice:

> But let not on thy hook the tortured worm
> Convulsive, twist in agonizing folds . . .

What funny things the eighteenth-century poets chose to describe in verse, she thought. In spite of the austerity of some of their poetry they were very homely, and she loved them for it. Her attention wandered, although she was still thinking of homely things. She began to wonder whether the loose covers ought to be sent to the cleaners. Spring-cleaning was so difficult with Adam about the house all day. If she chose to turn out a particular room she could be quite sure that he would want to use it just when it was at the height of its confusion. On these occasions he would say that it was impossible for him to write in any other room, and, of course, it was hard to argue with him, for how could ordinary mortals possibly know where an author could or could not write at a particular time?

Cassandra wondered idly how many wives were at this moment having 'The Seasons' read to them. Probably none, she decided, and looked up at Adam with a happy and affectionate smile on her face. It was comforting to know that after five years of marriage he should still be taking the trouble to educate her.

'Do I sound as if I had a cold?' said Adam suddenly.

Cassandra pondered a while. 'Perhaps you do a bit,' she said. 'But how could you have got one?'

Adam looked guilty. 'I was sitting on the bank by the stream yesterday afternoon,' he explained, 'and the grass may have been damp. "Or lie reclined beneath yon spreading ash" – that reminded me of it. I feel rather shivery too.'

Cassandra was at once all concern. 'Oh, darling, you really ought to be more careful. If only you'd had more sense you'd have realized that the grass would be damp at this time of the year. And it's such long grass too.' She laid her hand on his forehead. 'I hope you aren't feverish,' she said anxiously. 'I think you'd better stop reading and go to bed.'

Adam smiled complacently, for he liked being fussed over when he was in the mood for it. 'Perhaps I shouldn't have had that tinned salmon,' he suggested.

'Oh dear,' said Cassandra. 'I'd forgotten about that, but I don't think it can have been anything to do with the salmon. It must have been the damp grass. You must have a hot bath and a hot drink and I'll rub your chest.'

Thus, in the space of five minutes, Adam Marsh-Gibbon was turned from a perfectly healthy man who had perhaps eaten an unwise mixture of things for his tea, into an invalid with a devoted wife fussing round him.

When he was in bed Cassandra brought him a hot, milky drink and a box of biscuits.

'I'm going to rub your chest,' she declared, 'with good old-fashioned camphorated oil. There's really nothing like it.'

He took hold of her hand. 'Where should I find another wife who would look after me so well?' he asked, gazing at her fondly. 'Nobody else would take such care of me when I was ill,' he said pathetically.

'Oh, Adam, don't be so ridiculous. You know perfectly well that if you weren't married to me you'd be married to somebody else,' said Cassandra sensibly. 'There are plenty of people who would be only too glad to be your wife and who would look after you as well as I do.'

Adam smiled. 'Well, yes, I daresay there are,' he said complacently, pleased at the picture of himself surrounded by adoring wives all ministering to his needs.

Cassandra put the cork back into the bottle of camphorated oil. 'There,' she said. 'You ought to be all right in the morning.'

'That's a long way off,' said Adam comfortably, as he kissed her good night.

CHAPTER THREE

'Well ordered home, man's best delight . . .'

The next morning Adam decided that his cold was a little worse. He woke up at about ten o'clock to find Cassandra standing over him with an expression of anxiety on her face. She was wearing a soft grey dress, and held a thermometer in her hand. She seemed relieved when Adam stirred and opened his eyes.

'I do hope you're feeling better, dear,' she said. 'I'm going to take your temperature.'

'How long have you been standing here watching me asleep?' demanded Adam. 'You should have woken me up. My time's too precious to be wasted lying in bed till all hours of the morning.'

'Yes, darling,' said Cassandra meekly, with a little smile on her face. Her time was also precious this morning, for Lily and Mrs Morris, the cleaning woman, were giving Adam's study a thorough spring-cleaning, and she wanted to get back to them as quickly as possible. There were so many things that needed careful handling, and everything must be put back in its proper disorder, so that Adam should not know what had been happening behind his back. As she put the thermometer into his mouth Cassandra could not help hoping that Adam's temperature would be just the tiniest fraction above normal. So much could be done in the house if he were safely out of the way for twenty-four hours.

She put her hand on his forehead. 'It feels rather hot, dear,' she said, and then took the thermometer out of his mouth, holding it up to the light to read it. Practically normal, or as near as made no matter, she decided. But no, perhaps it was just a little *above* normal. Now that she came to look at it again she was sure of it, and so she felt justified in giving herself the benefit of the doubt. Adam must stay in bed today. It was a golden opportunity. Why, they might be able to turn out the drawing room as well. Cassandra bristled with energy at the thought of it.

'I'm afraid it's not quite normal,' she said brightly, 'but I daresay it wouldn't do you any harm to get up,' she added, knowing that it was no use commanding Adam to stay in bed.

Adam drew the eiderdown round his shoulders. 'Well,' he said, 'I don't want to make a fuss, but I certainly feel rather shivery. I dare say I could work just as well in bed too,' he added thoughtfully. 'Perhaps I'd better have breakfast in bed anyway,' he said, looking up at Cassandra for her approval. 'I hope it won't be very inconvenient.'

Cassandra thought that there was no need to remind her husband that never, under any circumstances, did he get up for breakfast, although she was surprised that his recollections of such an important event in his daily life should be so hazy.

Adam explained at some length that although he did not feel completely well, neither did he feel completely ill. Cassandra listened with sympathy and understanding, and not long afterwards returned with a well-laden breakfast tray. 'Feed a cold and starve a fever,' she laughed. 'I hope there'll be enough for you here. If you want anything more, just ring for it. I've brought you *The Times*. I thought you'd like to do the crossword. That poet yesterday was Dryden, not Milton. That was what put us wrong. Is there anything else you'd like to read? The new Crime Club book is one of the best we've had.'

She left Adam happily settled with food, cigarettes, a crossword puzzle and a murder story. He ought to be all right until lunch-time, she told herself, and hurried downstairs, stopping on the way to put on her overall, which she had hung over the banisters. Then she went into Adam's study.

'Please ma'am, what shall I do with all these bits of paper?' asked Mrs Morris, the cleaning woman. 'I can't get at this table to polish it.'

'Oh, leave those to me,' said Cassandra, gathering them up. She sorted the papers as well as she could, and put them in the desk until the room was finished. She wished Adam wouldn't be so extravagant with paper. Some of these sheets had only one sentence written on them. If he didn't like crossing out mistakes, he could use an india rubber, she thought sensibly; he nearly always began by writing in pencil.

After a while Cassandra went into the kitchen to give Bessie the orders for lunch, and then she went back into Adam's study and began to arrange his things exactly as they had been before the great cleaning. She put the books back on the table, taking care to leave them open at the right places, wondering as she did so why he should be reading an article on Wireless in the *Encyclopaedia Britannica*. After she had done this, she thought about her shopping. If Adam were to be kept contentedly in bed he must be treated like a proper invalid, and given specially nice food.

She made out her shopping list and went upstairs. It looked cold outside, so she put on the grey squirrel coat that Adam had given her last Christmas. On her way down she listened for a moment at his door, but could hear nothing but a contented droning sound, which was his way of singing. It was a sign that he was quite happy, and could safely be left for an hour or two.

Cassandra walked down the drive. The grass under the poplars was golden with daffodils. On an impulse she stopped, and picked a bunch of the nicest ones with long golden trumpets. Mrs Wilmot might like to have them, and she would have time to leave them at the rectory.

Adam and Cassandra had no children, at least not *yet*, Cassandra used to tell herself, because she was always hoping that he would see her point of view about it before it was too late. He thought they would interfere with his work, and said that it would make him so old to see a creature growing up in his own likeness. He did not seem to realize that the child might quite easily grow up in the likeness of Cassandra. But she had accepted her husband's decision very philosophically, telling herself that after all Adam needed quite as much mothering as Mrs Wilmot's two girls and three boys, although at the back of her mind there was always the hope that Science might one day prove weaker than Nature.

Cassandra decided to call at the rectory first, so that the flowers could be put in water at once.

Janie Wilmot came to the door. Her dark eyes lighted up with pleasure when she saw the flowers. 'Oh, how kind of you,' she said, 'and such lovely big ones too. Won't you come in? Mother will be so pleased to see you.'

Cassandra followed Janie into the dining room, where Mrs Wilmot was mending a pair of combinations.

'Thank goodness it's the summer term next term,' she said, after the flowers had been admired and arranged in vases. 'Edith will be wearing vests and won't need to take any combs back with her. These are very thin, but they'll do as an emergency pair for next winter.'

'I hear Edith's getting on so well at school,' Cassandra said. 'You must be proud now that she's in the lacrosse team. She's only fourteen, isn't she?' Cassandra was glad that Mrs Wilmot had such good reason to be proud of her second daughter, for she could not help feeling that she was in many ways a disappointed woman. When she had married her husband she had expected great things of him, and had imagined herself at some period of her life directing the affairs of the diocese as the wife of a Bishop or at least an Archdeacon. But the Reverend Rockingham Wilmot had never got beyond being the rector of Up Callow in Shropshire. The living was quite a good one, and he was very much liked in the parish, but Kathleen Wilmot had somehow got it into her head that he had been done out of his rightful heritage.

It was therefore a consolation to her that Edith was doing so well at school. Janie was a nice girl, but not particularly talented in any direction, although she could decorate the church very artistically. The three boys, also away at school, were equally undistinguished, though the eldest showed signs of becoming a fair cricketer, to the delight of his father, whose passion it was.

'I hope your husband is well?' asked Mrs Wilmot as she walked to the door with Cassandra.

'He has a slight chill and is staying in bed this morning,' said Cassandra, 'but there's not really much wrong with him. It's an awfully good opportunity to spring-clean his study. On ordinary mornings he's always wandering about the house, but if he thinks he's supposed to be ill, he'll stay in bed quite happily.'

Mrs Wilmot sighed as she contrasted Adam Marsh-Gibbon's pleasantly idle life with that of her own husband. But she did not complain, for she was a great admirer of Adam's novels, and she supposed that such a life was necessary for their production.

Meanwhile Cassandra did her shopping. When she had ordered all the necessary things she went into the best fruit shop and bought some peaches and some grapes for Adam. In the shop she met Mrs Gower, a mountainous figure in a dark musquash coat.

'Just the person I want to see,' she declared, advancing towards Cassandra. 'My dear,' she whispered confidentially, 'things really *are* beginning to happen now.'

Cassandra looked puzzled and tried to guess what she was talking about. 'Things?' she echoed thoughtfully, and then said, 'Oh, you mean Holmwood?'

Mrs Gower paused a moment, and then said in a low voice, 'A stove was seen going in this morning.'

'A stove?' said Cassandra incredulously.

'Yes,' said Mrs Gower, 'of rather a peculiar design.'

'In what way?' asked Cassandra, suppressing a desire to laugh, for she did not see that there could be much scope for peculiarity of design in things like stoves.

'It seemed to have coloured tiles on it,' said Mrs Gower, 'like those you see abroad. Whatever would the new tenants of Holmwood want with such a thing?'

'Perhaps it's an heirloom, or it may have some sentimental significance,' suggested Cassandra, smiling at the idea of a stove with sentimental significance. 'Or they may even use it,' she added.

Mrs Gower agreed doubtfully. 'Yes, I suppose they may,' she said. 'My late husband used to like keeping to old ways. That's why we always slept in that four-poster bed. It was supposed to have belonged to Bishop Percy, the *Reliques* one, you know. But we always used to find it so hot in summer that my husband usually slept in his dressing-room.'

Cassandra was rather taken aback by this intimate glimpse of the late Professor and Mrs Gower's married life, and did not quite know what to say.

'Shall we be seeing you at Mr Gay's on Friday night?' asked Mrs Gower.

'Oh, yes, I hope so,' said Cassandra, 'and Adam too.'

When she got home she found out by tactful enquiries that

Adam had been in his room all morning and had not rung for anything. She walked upstairs quietly, and could hear him droning some tune of his own composition.

When she went in with the peaches and grapes Adam was lying on his back, looking up at the ceiling.

'I knew you must be awake because I heard you singing,' said Cassandra. 'Look what I've brought for you.'

'Oh, my dear, how nice!'

'Are you better?'

'I don't know. Just about the same, I think.'

'Do you think you'll be well enough to go to Mr Gay's party on Friday?' asked Cassandra.

'Why, of course,' said Adam shortly. 'You talk as if I were really ill.'

CHAPTER FOUR

'While through their cheerful
      band the rural talk,
The rural scandal, and the rural jest,
Fly harmless, to deceive the
      Tedious time ...'

Mr Philip Gay lived by the church, in a large gloomy house called Alameda. He was a bachelor, between fifty and sixty years old, and a disappointed man. As a youth he had not fitted himself for any career, as it had been his intention, from the time he was old enough to know about such things, to make a profitable marriage. He had been convinced that his good looks, which were of the guardsman type, would be enough to win for him any woman he might choose to woo. But unfortunately his efforts had not met with success. It is probable that his proposals lacked the assurances of love and devotion which every young woman expects at such a time, for being of a cold nature Mr Gay had never fallen in love, nor was he clever at acting what he did not feel. If the young women he pursued were sensible as well as rich they had seen what he was after, and had given him to understand that his attentions were unwelcome. None of these rich young women had ever fallen in love with him, in spite of his long eyelashes and handsome, if wooden, features. Nor had he ever had the good fortune to meet a woman who was rich and anxious to get a husband at any price. His later attempts to marry wealthy widows had been no more successful, for those he met seemed to have reached an age when they could no longer be bothered with husbands. As the years went on he still hoped, but lately he had become resigned to what he imagined was a life of genteel poverty.

He spent most of his time pottering about in his conservatory and garden. In the evenings he read novels and sometimes a little poetry, generally Dryden or Pomfret. He was especially fond of Pomfret, although he could never agree with that poet that it was unwise to aspire to riches in excess. It had been one of his happiest dreams, an eligible woman with riches in excess, but now it seemed to have little chance of coming true.

With Mr Gay lived his niece, Miss Angela Gay. She was the daughter of his brother, who had married a Frenchwoman. Both her parents had died while she was a child and Mr Gay, as her only remaining relative, had reluctantly assumed responsibility for her. Apart from their relationship there was another bond between them. They were both disappointed people. For Angela Gay was thirty and still unmarried. She was a small dark woman with a very coy manner, who would have been pretty if the expression of her face had not been so discontented. She disliked Cassandra Marsh-Gibbon more than anyone else in the world, and had once imagined herself secretly in love with Adam, although she was ready to fall in love with any man who came her way.

Mr Gay and his niece occasionally gave an evening party. Perhaps they were still hoping that there was a rich woman or an eligible husband in the town whom they had somehow missed in their search. Certainly there was more hope for Angela than for her uncle, as a new curate had just come to Up Callow. He was twenty-six years old and unmarried, and Miss

Gay had seized upon him almost as soon as he had arrived. Ever since then he had been contriving to avoid her.

On the evening of the party Mr Gay was decorating the hall with potted palms.

'Angela,' he called, 'where are the aspidistras?'

'Oh, we don't want *those*, Uncle,' said Miss Gay sulkily. 'They're such dusty old things.'

'But I polished the leaves with oil only yesterday, and people always admire them so. We must have them in the hall.'

'I think they're in the conservatory,' said Miss Gay wearily. Anyone would think we were entertaining Royalty, she thought, instead of a few couples to bridge and light refreshments. Still, Mr Paladin would be there, and Mr Morrison, a master from the Boys' High School. She had met Mr Morrison several times and knew him to be an efficient bridge player, but a dull and silent young man. Mr Paladin was something of an unknown quantity, and Miss Gay had hopes.

Cassandra had had the greatest difficulty in persuading Adam to go to the party at all. Suddenly at the last minute he had said he wouldn't go.

'I shall be so *bored*,' he said peevishly.

'But you'll be quite as bored here,' argued Cassandra. 'It will be a nice change for you to go out and meet people. Besides, we've accepted, and I don't see what excuse we can make.'

'Tell them I didn't want to come,' said Adam shortly.

'But, dearest, it would be so rude. One simply can't do things like that,' said Cassandra hopelessly. 'There'll be nice refreshments,' she added, feeling ashamed that she should have to coax her husband to fulfil a social obligation by such very childish means. 'And you'll be able to tell people about your new book, and you'll probably win at bridge,' she concluded, and sat down, worn out by her efforts.

'Well,' she said firmly, after a few moments, '*I'm* going to get ready.' She went out of the room and Adam followed her quite meekly. He seemed to have forgotten his reluctance to go to the party. Cassandra had known for nearly five years now that his difficult moods almost always came when he was bored and had not been able to show himself off at one of the town gatherings.

'May I wear my velvet jacket?' he asked as they went upstairs.

'Of course, dear, everyone expects it.'

Cassandra hoped that he would approve of the grey chiffon dress she was wearing this evening.

He looked at her critically. 'Very nice,' he said. 'You look very pretty. You should always wear pale colours.' She did not remind him that the previous evening he had told her that she should always wear black velvet.

On the way, Adam drove with a fine carelessness which sometimes frightened Cassandra, but they had never had an accident yet and so she could not say anything to him about it. Only Adam was allowed to have any nerves. Cassandra had learned to keep hers in dutiful subjection.

'I hope old Philip will like your dress,' said Adam.

'And I hope dear Angela will like your velvet coat,' retaliated Cassandra.

'Oh, she's seen it before,' said Adam seriously, 'but she does like it. She said I looked like Shelley.'

'How ridiculous,' said Cassandra sharply. It always annoyed her when unattached women told her husband he looked like Shelley. She didn't want any ideas put into his head. 'Shelley had fair hair,' she said emphatically, as if that disposed of the matter.

Mr Gay and his niece stood in the hall to receive their guests. They always did this, so that the beginning of their parties had an air of formality which some people found alarming. Miss Gay, wearing a dress of rather too bright a shade of green, was standing nearer the door, and the guests were then passed on to her uncle, a dignified figure against his background of palms and aspidistras.

As she shook hands with Adam, Miss Gay remarked that it was a long time since they had had the pleasure of seeing him.

'Not since last Sunday at the Rectory,' she added. 'Now I wonder what work of genius have you given to the world since then?'

Adam replied shortly that it was hardly possible to produce a work of genius in five days. Cassandra hoped he wouldn't be rude to anyone, or silly. It always made her feel uncomfortable, especially as everyone expected her to take her husband seriously. In places like Up Callow wives did take husbands seriously, in public anyway.

They went into the drawing room and Adam began talking to the rector about cricket. Shortly afterwards they settled down to bridge. There were just two tables without Miss Gay, who had agreed to sit out for a while. Mr Paladin had been delayed and would be arriving shortly.

'Rockingham doesn't believe in his curates being too frivolous,' Mrs Wilmot confided to Cassandra, 'and, as you know, Mr Paladin is young. He needs guidance from an older person.'

Cassandra reflected that poor Mr Paladin was such a serious young man that it was impossible to imagine him even knowing that such a thing as frivolity existed. In any case there would have been little scope for him here in Up Callow. It was Miss Gay who should be watched rather than Mr Paladin.

At this moment the front door bell rang, and Mr Paladin arrived. He was a dark, bespectacled young man, who disliked bridge parties, and would have much preferred to spend the evening in his lodgings reading *Lightfoot on the Galatians*, for he intended to rise above the position of parish priest, and even possessed some of those special gifts which Mrs Wilmot believed her husband had. Mr Paladin had spent his time at Oxford very studiously, and had been rewarded at the end of his three years with a First in Theology.

As he came into the room he saw with horror that of the nine persons there eight were playing bridge, and the one left over was none other than Miss Gay herself. And what made it worse was that in order not to disturb the players she began talking to him in a thrilling whisper which made it necessary for him to do the same. This gave to their conversation a kind of spurious intimacy, so that topics like the weather and the fine aspidistras were somehow pushed aside, and that most horrible of all subjects for nervous young men, *themselves*, was discussed.

'I haven't seen you for so long,' said Miss Gay, pouting a little.

'No, indeed . . .'

'I almost wondered whether you were *avoiding* me.' This was said with such coyness that Mr Paladin drew back visibly.

'Oh, Miss Gay, really . . .'

After more in this strain Mr Paladin made a great effort to drag the conversation back to more reasonable subjects. 'I was admiring your palms, as I came in,' he said in a very impersonal tone of voice.

'Yes, aren't they lovely? But we have some even finer ones in the conservatory. Would you like to see them?' she asked sweetly.

There was nothing Mr Paladin could do now but go quietly, for he had brought it on himself. He vowed that he would never again look on a palm without feelings of loathing, except, of course, the ones used to decorate the church on Palm Sunday, but they were comfortably dead and dried.

The conservatory was very hot and smelled strongly of arum lilies, so that Mr Paladin was appropriately reminded of a funeral.

'Here are the palms I was telling you about,' said Miss Gay, with triumph in her voice.

'But they're exactly the same as the ones in the hall!' exclaimed Mr Paladin indignantly, for when he saw that he had been brought into the conservatory under false pretences, his anger got the better of him.

Miss Gay laughed coyly. 'You men are all alike,' she said, 'so *blind*.' These last words were said in tones of lingering tenderness which were most alarming to a young curate.

Mr Paladin put up a gallant fight. 'I know I'm short-sighted, but I really cannot see any difference,' he said politely. 'Perhaps the ones in the hall have longer leaves though. It would be interesting to compare them.' He made a move towards the door. 'I expect they will be wanting to play bridge,' he said, with a firmness unusual in him.

As they walked back to the drawing room his self-confidence came back to him. He felt like a character in *The Faerie Queene*, one of the characters who has successfully withstood the temptations of the Bower of Bliss, he thought confusedly. He could afford to talk easily about the palms now, and even went with Miss Gay into the hall and solemnly measured their leaves.

Miss Gay felt that she had been snubbed. That was the worst of these inexperienced young curates, she told herself. They always read into one's thoughts and actions far more than was meant. Now a man of the world, like Adam Marsh-Gibbon, say, would surely have made a less blundering escape from the conservatory. Miss Gay glanced angrily at Mr Paladin and went back to the bridge tables, where they played until the light refreshments were served.

As usual, Adam was the centre of attraction, and everyone was asking him questions.

'Now, do tell us what your new novel is about,' said Miss Gay. 'Or is that one of the questions one just shouldn't ask?'

Adam smiled condescendingly. 'Well, I think I can tell you that it is about a gardener,' he said.

There was a short silence, during which, to her horror, Janie Wilmot let out a schoolgirlish giggle. She blushed with shame, for she had been thinking of old Wilkinson their gardener, and how funny it would be to have a novel written about him. What *would* Mr Marsh-Gibbon think? Janie looked down at her shoes, and wished that the carpet with its design of huge brown roses would swallow her up. Then, to her relief, she heard hearty, unashamed laughter. Cassandra was laughing too.

'Oh, Adam,' said Cassandra weakly, 'why can't you be more explicit? It sounds so ridiculous just stated baldly like that. I couldn't help thinking of Rogers and old Wilkinson. My husband is not intending to become a comic writer,' she explained to the company. 'You mustn't misunderstand him.'

'I thought it sounded rather beautiful,' said Miss Gay, coldly.

'It's a very original idea, I should think,' said Mr Morrison doubtfully. 'Something after the style of Mary Webb perhaps?'

'Well,' said Adam, who was really more interested in the refreshments, 'it's rather difficult to explain.'

At this Miss Gay uttered a specially loud sympathetic noise, and directed a venomous look at Cassandra, who was still smiling.

'I am endeavouring to show this gardener is affected by what Wordsworth calls "the beautiful and permanent forms of Nature",' said Adam.

Everyone beamed appreciatively, though not necessarily comprehendingly. This was obviously quite a different thing from mere gardening.

'How will you show this effect?' asked Mr Paladin earnestly. 'If I remember rightly, Wordsworth believed that in humble and rustic life, to quote his own words, "the essential passions of the heart find a better soil in which they can attain their maturity, are less under restraint, and speak a plainer and more emphatic language ..." I was wondering if you thought this too?' he suggested deferentially, for he had never read any of Adam's novels and did not quite know where to place him.

Cassandra was amused and touched by his humility.

'I think there is some truth in it,' declared Adam slowly, and then devoured an egg and cress sandwich in one mouthful. 'Don't you agree with me, Miss Gay?'

'Oh, yes, I do agree. I've often noticed how passionate these rustic people are,' she said seriously.

The rector looked shocked. 'What about the language?' he asked hurriedly. 'Is your novel to be in dialect? I think that would put a great many people off, if I may say so.'

Adam looked at him scornfully. 'It is to be a contemplative novel,' he said impressively.

'But what about the other characters, won't they speak at all?' asked Mr Paladin.

'There is only one character,' said Adam, 'the gardener.'

There was a gloomy silence after this pronouncement, as everyone thought it sounded a dreary novel. Yet in some way they all felt that the presence of an author in their midst, even the author of unreadable novels, gave a certain cachet to Up Callow.

'Give Mrs Marsh-Gibbon some coffee,' said Mr Gay, breaking the silence. He thought Adam Marsh-Gibbon a fool and envied him Cassandra, a rich woman and a charming one too. He sighed and passed Cassandra's cup to her.

Miss Gay was still interested in Adam's novel. 'Only one character,' she repeated thoughtfully. 'That's very unusual, but don't you think that there ought to be a *love* interest?'

'My wife has told me that it would make the novel more human,' said Adam, 'but I feel that it would detract from the main purpose of the book.'

'I'm sure that your wife must be a great help to you in your writing,' said Mrs Gower warmly.

'I'm afraid all I can do is to see that he's well fed,' laughed Cassandra.

'I always think it must be a help to a writer to have a wife who can share his intellectual pursuits,' said Miss Gay.

'I should have thought it was more important to be well fed,' said her uncle. 'I imagine that the proverb about too many cooks spoiling the broth can be applied to writing as well as anything else. The poetical or literary broth is better cooked by one person.'

Cassandra smiled at Mr Gay, delighted at this charming comparison which allowed her to think of Adam's writings as so much Irish Stew or Lancashire Hot-Pot.

'I don't think I really have any intellectual pursuits,' said Adam surprisingly, coming down to earth and being suddenly more human, 'and such as I have Cassandra shares.'

'Well,' said Mr Gay genially, 'what about some more bridge? We want our revenge, you know,' he said, rubbing his hands together.

They played on until nearly midnight, when the rector and his wife got up to go. Janie was feeling very sleepy, and she had been so frightened at having to partner Adam Marsh-Gibbon that she had not been able to enjoy the last part of the evening very much.

'Late nights don't agree with me,' said the rector, glancing meaningly at Mr Paladin who had not yet made any move.

'Now, Rector, I hope you're not going to take Mr Paladin away with you,' said Miss Gay. 'Don't forget that we're only young once!' she twittered.

When Mr Paladin heard this he vowed that, if he could, he would at once forgo all claims to the remaining years of his youth. Pleasure and frivolity had little appeal for him at any time, and at this moment they had never seemed so unattractive. He stood up and began to thank Miss Gay very nicely for a delightful evening. 'No doubt I shall have the pleasure of seeing you at the Choral Society practice on Monday,' he said easily. He judged that he was safe in saying this, for he felt that he had the upper hand now, and could afford to be gracious towards her.

Miss Gay seemed satisfied and made no attempt to detain him. Instead her thoughts leapt forward to Monday, and she planned how he should escort her home from the practice and what their conversation should be about.

With a coy smile she accompanied the ladies upstairs to get their coats. 'Your husband tells me he has been ill,' she said to Cassandra. 'I thought he wasn't looking quite himself.'

'Oh, it was nothing really, just a light chill,' said Cassandra shortly.

'But we can't have our man of genius ill. You should take better care of him,' said Miss Gay jokingly, but with an edge of malice to her voice.

'I do my best,' sighed Cassandra, for she was feeling too tired to joke, and she thought Miss Gay very interfering. 'It is sometimes difficult being married to a man of genius,' she added, with an attempt at lightness.

'I'm sure it is,' agreed Miss Gay sympathetically. 'In fact I think such men shouldn't have wives at all.'

Cassandra looked surprised. 'Then what should they have?' she asked stupidly.

'A great artist needs many women to inspire him,' said Miss Gay evasively. 'Take Shelley, for example,' she said, with a sharp look at Cassandra.

Oh, please don't let us take Shelley, thought Cassandra wearily.

'I expect he will be waiting for me downstairs,' she said. 'It's been such a nice party. I hope you will come to us some time.'

'We must do all we can to welcome the new tenant of

Holmwood,' said Miss Gay, leaving the subject of Adam as a dog leaves a bone, meaning to return to it later.

'Do you know anything about him or her or them?' asked Cassandra with a show of interest.

'*Him*,' said Miss Gay in low thrilling tones. 'I've heard on good authority that it is to be a *man*.'

Downstairs Adam was talking to a weary-looking Mr Gay about his new novel. Perhaps if he were to have his hair cut, thought Cassandra detachedly, people would be less inclined to label him as a Great Artist.

CHAPTER FIVE

'Meanwhile the village rouses
up the fire ...'

'I hear that a foreigner is coming to live at Holmwood,' Mrs Wilmot announced to her husband at breakfast one morning. 'Mrs Gower said so,' she declared, thus putting the seal of respectability on this rumour.

The rector put down his paper. 'We shall see all in good time,' he said. 'In the meantime there are better things to do than gossip.' And he went away to his study to make a list of the village's cricket fixtures for the season.

As the door closed behind him there was a buzz of conversation.

'I do hope we will be asked to tea there,' said Edith. 'Holmwood's got a ripping garden and a field,' she added enviously, 'big enough for a lax pitch I should think.'

'It would be exciting if he really were a foreigner,' said Janie sadly, for she hardly hoped that such a thing could possibly be true. Life here was so dull, and why should God take it into His Head to make it more exciting? she asked herself. Janie had a certain amount of faith in God; she knew that He wouldn't let anything dreadful happen to them, but on the other hand she couldn't imagine that He would stoop to anything like providing someone to fall in love with, at least not the God Mr Paladin preached about. Her father preached more often about The Game of Life, but his God was quite as unapproachable as Mr Paladin's terrifyingly intelligent conception. Janie sighed.

'Then Mr Marsh-Gibbon's nose *would* be put out of joint,' said Edith astutely.

'Oh, Edith,' said Janie angrily, 'you are the limit!'

'I must go shopping,' said Mrs Wilmot.

In the town Mrs Wilmot met Mrs Gower, as she had hoped she would. They met in the grocer's. When they had finished tasting and smelling the butter, an occupation of which Mrs Wilmot was very fond, they walked out into the street. Mrs Gower took Mrs Wilmot confidentially by the arm and almost dragged her into a narrow alley where some children were playing. This was a good sign. Mrs Wilmot bristled with anticipation.

'Holmwood *is* let,' said Mrs Gower in tones of satisfaction, 'and to a foreigner!'

'*Oh!*' Mrs Wilmot gasped. 'Are you sure it's true?'

'Oh, yes,' Mrs Gower replied. 'I saw him coming down the drive. Quite dark and wearing a black hat.'

'Really . . .' mused Mrs Wilmot, a smile stealing over her eager little face. After the black hat there could of course be no doubt.

'And I heard him speaking,' continued Mrs Gower. 'In the Post Office. He asked for a three shilling book of stamps, only he said three sheeling.'

'*Well!*' Mrs Wilmot exclaimed. 'But I expect he will be very nice,' she added as they parted company.

Mrs Gower shook her head doubtfully as she walked away, but very soon she was beaming on Cassandra and telling her the interesting news.

'That would explain the funny-looking stove you saw going in,' observed Cassandra sensibly.

'He was very handsome,' said Mrs Gower in a voice which made Cassandra feel that the ladies of Up Callow might be already turning from their dull husbands to this attractive foreigner.

'Yes,' she said, 'foreigners do seem to have a kind of glamour about them.' But this was said in a matter-of-fact tone which suggested that she was thinking less of the glamour of foreigners than about what fish would tempt Adam's delicate and capricious appetite.

He had been particularly trying lately. He was at work on a difficult chapter of his novel, and it was not going at all well. The evenings were terrible, for Adam would pace about the house, not even sitting down to eat his dinner, and Cassandra would have to listen to long passages which he had written during the day and which had 'something wrong' with them.

'Now, what is the matter with this?' said Adam one evening, as they were drinking their coffee in the drawing room. 'I feel that there's something wrong with it, but I can't decide what. I've tried to show the effect of this particular spring morning on a man who has hitherto found them all alike. At the beginning of the chapter I am quoting "It is the first mild day of March", from Wordsworth, you know.'

Adam began to read and Cassandra's thoughts wandered to Mrs Gower's speculations about the foreigner who had taken Holmwood. It might amuse Adam if she told him. But perhaps, she thought, glancing at Adam's gloomy face, this wasn't the right time to tell him anything amusing. It would have to wait.

'Really, Cassandra,' said Adam's irritable voice, 'I think the least you can do is to *listen*.'

'Oh, Adam, don't be cross! I was listening,' she declared uncertainly, trying to remember what it had all been about. 'I thought the description of the gardener's vision was very nice.'

'Very nice!' repeated Adam in accents of fierce scorn.

'This man is caught in the major experience of his life and you say it's "very nice".'

'If you would like to read again what you have written,' said Cassandra placatingly, 'I'll see if I can think of any more suitable criticism that will help you.'

'Very well.' Adam was a little pacified. He walked twice round the room and then began in a loud and startling voice, '"He stood transfixed upon his spade . . ."'

Cassandra listened patiently. When he had finished there was a long silence.

'I can see that you are impressed by it,' said Adam, coming and sitting on the arm of her chair. 'I think I may have been a little rude to you just now. Perhaps it *is* nice after all. "Very nice",' he repeated slowly. 'I would much rather have a sincere criticism, and if you think it is very nice, then it is better for you to say so than to pretend you think something else.'

He smiled and patted her lightly on the head, as one might a faithful, dumb friend.

CHAPTER SIX

'Thy sober Autumn fading into Age ...'

It was Mr Gay's habit to take a little exercise before tea. This afternoon he thought he would walk through the park and then go past Holmwood, so that he might see the destruction of the elm trees for himself.

It was pleasant in the park. The tulips in the geometrical flower-beds were at their best, and the water-lilies on the pool would soon be out. Mr Gay always felt sad when he passed through the park, although it was only a municipal one, with green-painted iron seats, waste-paper baskets and keep-off-the-grass notices. Nevertheless, it reminded him in a small way of the magnificent grounds he might have walked in had he made a profitable marriage.

He came out at the other end of the park and went up the hill towards Holmwood. From there he could see the great bare spaces where the trees had been. He felt himself becoming a little breathless as the hill became steeper and began to wish he hadn't come so far. After all, there was nothing to see, only a few tree-stumps, and it wasn't as if he were like Angela and those other women, who were flocking round the place simply to get a sight of this foreigner.

At the top of the hill, on the other side of the road, was Mrs

Gower's house. As Mr Gay came up to it, he saw that she was in the garden, doing something with a basket of young plants.

'Good afternoon,' she called out. 'I see you've been looking at Holmwood. Are you thinking what a shame it is?'

'I don't like it. Those fine elms . . .' He was still very breathless.

Poor Mr Gay, thought Mrs Gower. He looked rather tired. He was a handsome man, but how much greyer his hair had gone lately; it was nearly white. She would ask him in to have a cup of tea.

'I wonder if your niece would mind if I asked you to stay to tea? Will she be expecting you back?' she asked, looking up at him from under the brim of her big straw gardening hat, with its embroidery of gaudy raffia flowers.

'Why . . .' Mr Gay was quite taken aback, and the offer of a cup of tea just at this moment when he wanted one so much was too good to be refused. Besides, Mrs Gower was a very nice woman, he told himself. She came of a good Shropshire family, he believed. He opened the gate and walked in, his bearing noticeably more soldierly, even a little jaunty. 'This is *most* kind of you,' he said.

'You must excuse my old gardening clothes,' said Mrs Gower, who was wearing a voluminous jumper suit of sage-green knitted material. The pockets of the cardigan sagged a little, from being filled with packets of seeds and gardening scissors, but if not elegantly dressed, there was, as always, a certain majestic dignity about her, and in its early days the jumper suit had been a very good one.

Mr Gay gave a courtly little bow. 'My dear Mrs Gower, you look charming.' He waved his hand about, searching for a suitable phrase from Dryden or his favourite Pomfret to describe her, but not finding it he let his waving hand rest on one of the stone knobs of the gate posts. Indeed, he thought a few minutes later, as he sat in a comfortable armchair in a nicely furnished drawing room, with the clatter of tea-cups within earshot, at this moment she appeared to be quite the most charming woman he had ever seen.

Over tea and hot buttered toast they talked mostly of the elms.

'It depresses me so,' said Mr Gay. 'What I feel is that we shan't live to see the day when Holmwood is once more surrounded by trees.'

Mrs Gower nodded mournfully and there was a gloomy silence. 'Do have a piece of this mocha cake,' she said at last. 'It is one of my cook's specialities.'

'Well, really, I hardly dare take it,' said Mr Gay uncertainly. 'What I mean to say is that *I* like it very much, but another part of me doesn't,' he added, with an effort at jocularity.

'Now, how funny,' said Mrs Gower, 'it used to be just like that with my late husband, but I wasn't going to have my good cakes wasted, so I found a remedy.' She got up and advanced majestically towards a small bureau in one corner of the room. Here she opened a drawer, and after looking for a few minutes, took out a small bottle of white tablets. 'Here it is. Now *do* try one,' she added in a tempting voice, as if she were offering him a sweet.

Mr Gay looked at the proffered tablets rather suspiciously. He was now feeling ashamed of having admitted his weakness, and could not help wondering whether these tablets were the remains of those identical ones which the late Professor Gower had taken to aid his digestion, and, if so, whether they were still good after all these years.

Mrs Gower quickly set his fears at rest. 'I keep them in here because I occasionally take them myself,' she admitted. 'They're quite fresh.'

She sat down again, and with the little bottle of tablets on the table between them, they attacked the delicious mocha cake courageously. Mr Gay even had a second piece. No cake that his niece or their cook-general made had ever tasted like this.

'Now just two of these little tablets and all will be well,' said Mrs Gower. After this Mr Gay found himself growing quite confidential about his stomach and Mrs Gower responded, so that by half past five each knew just what the other could or could not take.

At a quarter to six Mr Gay thought he ought to go. He was feeling greatly refreshed after the tea, and the rich cake had not so far had any ill effects. Mrs Gower too had been glad of company, and she was really pleased that she had been able to suggest a remedy for his trouble.

As they stood in the hall Mr Gay noticed that in one corner there was an aspidistra on a little table. But when he looked at it more closely the tears almost came into his eyes, for it was such a sad contrast to those fine plants which decorated his hall. There was no gloss on the leaves and one of them was quite withered. He stopped by it and fingered the dead leaf tenderly. Mrs Gower stopped too.

'I'm afraid it isn't nearly such a fine specimen as yours,' she said apologetically, 'but then it's old, and you can't expect them to live indefinitely.'

'With proper care,' said Mr Gay sternly, 'there is no reason why they shouldn't live for ever.'

Mrs Gower smiled as there rose up before her a vision of aspidistras, immortal, everlasting, the only living things in a dead world. 'Now you mustn't scold me,' she said. 'I'm afraid I know so little about them.' Nor did she particularly like them, and only kept this one because it was a relic of that first house in North Oxford.

'A little fertilizer, a little oil,' repeated Mr Gay thoughtfully. 'It's so simple.'

'Then I wish you would show me how to take better care of my poor plant,' said Mrs Gower.

'I will, if I may. It would be a great pleasure. Perhaps I may bring you some of the special fertilizer I use for my own aspidistras?'

'That would be very kind of you.'

'Not at all, Mrs Gower. You have done *me* a great kindness this afternoon, as well as giving me a delicious tea.'

And so, uttering mutual expressions of gratitude they proceeded to the gate. Here they stood for a few minutes regretting once more the passing of the elm trees.

'I wonder why they've left all the fir trees?' said Mrs Gower. But before Mr Gay had time to answer, the sound of a car was heard. It stopped outside Holmwood and someone got out to open the gate. They saw a tall man of about thirty-five, wearing an overcoat of foreign-looking cut and a black hat. When he saw them standing at the gate he bowed and raised his hat, calling out in a deep voice, 'What a beautiful evening!' Then he gave them a brilliant smile and got into his car. They were both so surprised that by the time they had returned his greeting the car was halfway up the drive. Mrs Gower did not know what to say. He was even more handsome than she had remembered, with that lean face and flashing black eyes.

'He's very dark, isn't he?' she said non-committally.

'Yes,' agreed Mr Gay, thinking that he didn't like the look of the fellow.

As he walked down the hill he told himself that all these changes weren't a good thing. But then he realized that he was feeling remarkably fit, that he had eaten two pieces of very rich cake for his tea and they weren't disagreeing with him. Gradually his mood changed, so that by the time he was walking back through the park, in his new-found mood of benevolence, he began to think that it needn't necessarily be a bad thing for this foreigner to come to the town. It might even be a *good* thing.

CHAPTER SEVEN

'Poor is the triumph o'er the timid hare!'

Mr Paladin was writing home to his mother. He sat in his lodgings, crouching over the electric fire, for although he had just said in his letter that the weather was becoming warmer every day, the evenings were still chilly enough to make him realize that the heating of his room was inadequate. He hardly liked to go upstairs to fetch his rug, although it would have been comfortable to sit with it wrapped round his knees. If he did this his landlady might be offended, and it would look so odd if the rector called. Or if anyone else called. Mr Paladin shivered and drew nearer to the glowing bar in the wall which was his fire. Suppose Miss Gay were to call this evening? She had hinted at it after the Choral Society practice on Monday, and the worst of it was that she had an excuse. It was now more than a month since she had borrowed *Paradise Lost*, and she would surely bring it back this evening when he had the misfortune to be in.

He turned once more to his letter. 'I am preaching a course of sermons on God's Presence,' he wrote, and then gave a short account of the first one, which had been on the need to approach God in a spirit of Wonder and Awe. 'I am also continuing my studies in Hebrew, and am finding time to read a little Plato and Homer in the evenings. I was glad of the thicker pyjamas, although I am hoping that the nights will soon be warmer. Now that the cricket season is beginning I expect to be busier than I was in the winter, as the rector is so keen about it and will be playing whenever he can. All my evenings will be taken up with Evensong, Bible Classes for men and boys, and the Lads' Club, and there will be my sermons to prepare ... ' He produced such a formidable list of activities that when his mother read the letter she was quite alarmed and wrote off to her son at once, giving him strict instructions to have milk or Horlicks before he went to bed.

As a matter of fact Mr Paladin had not meant to create the impression that he was overworked. He had been thinking, as he wrote, of all the excuses he could legitimately produce for not seeing Miss Gay or going to parties at her house. He had to admit that he had suffered a setback since the glorious victory in the conservatory. After the Choral Society practice he had not been on his guard, for the singing of Haydn's *Creation* had been very exhausting, so that he had quite forgotten to avoid Miss Gay after it was over. The worst had happened, and he had found himself in duty bound, as a gentleman and clergyman of the Church of England, to escort her home.

'Now, Mr Paladin, I'm going to admit something,' she had said, before they were out of earshot of a group of Sunday school teachers.

'Oh, yes?' He had been polite, interested even, but he had avoided the gaze of her sharp, dark eyes. He expected to hear an admission that she preferred Haydn to Bach, or something else relevant to the evening.

Instead she edged nearer to him so that she nearly pushed him off the pavement, and said in a simpering voice, 'You know, I'm really frightened of the dark.'

'Indeed, that is very interesting.' He tried to raise the tone of the conversation. Instead of adding, 'You have no need to be

49

afraid now that I am here,' he said, 'Now *I* feel quite different. I agree with the poet Young, "Darkness has more divinity for me,"' he quoted. 'Don't you find that sublime thoughts come most often with the darkness?' he said quickly and desperately. 'Is it not possible that your fear is a kind of *wonder*, that necessary *awe* ...' Mr Paladin stopped, feeling rather foolish as he realized that Miss Gay had already heard his sermon. Her next remark was not reassuring.

'I shall never have to feel afraid of walking home by myself now that you've joined the Choral Society,' she said, as they reached the gates of Alameda.

Mr Paladin felt like a prisoner, for she was clinging to his arm and he could not shake her off without being impolite. He had come to the conclusion, regretfully, for he was fond of singing, that he would have to sacrifice those pleasant evenings at the Choral Society. It seemed unfair; all he wanted was to be left alone with his Hebrew, his Plato, and his Homer.

'You and I must talk more about these things,' she said, letting go of his arm. 'I'm sure you could do so much to improve my mind. Oh, and I really must return your *Paradise Lost*, I've had it a dreadfully long time.'

It's only a three and sixpenny Oxford edition, thought Mr Paladin suddenly. 'Perhaps you would like to have it?' he said hopefully.

'Oh, no, thank you, although it's most kind of you. Do you know, I discovered after I'd borrowed it that we had one all the time?' she tittered. 'And now I must go in. I don't know what my uncle would say if he knew how long you'd kept me out here talking.'

Mr Paladin could think of nothing to say in reply to this unjust accusation. It did not occur to him until he was nearly home that he could easily have asked her for the book there and then. He might even have been carrying it under his arm at that moment, the last link between him and Miss Gay. He cursed his stupidity as he sat in his lodgings.

He finished his letter, and then decided that he would meditate on his sermon for a little while. It was half past nine, quite a likely time for Miss Gay to call. Then suddenly he had an idea. If he turned out the light she would come past and see that his room was in darkness, and then she might not ask to see him, but just leave the book and go away. At least it was worth trying. He would turn out the light and the fire too, although it would be cold without it, and he would sit in the corner by the bookcase, so that if Mrs Roberts came into the room to make sure, she would think he was not in.

Half an hour passed, and Mr Paladin was still meditating in the cold and darkness. He had found that his thoughts were inclined to wander from the theme he had set himself, which was 'O worship the Lord in the Beauty of Holiness'. Holiness. What did it mean? What *was* Holiness? He believed in beginning very simply, with a definition wherever possible, and then working gradually upwards and outwards, taking his congregation with him, he hoped, to a broader and yet more subtle interpretation. Mr Paladin's dictionary gave him five definitions of the word Holy, three of which he proposed to use in his sermon: 'pure in heart; free from sin; set apart to a sacred use'. The first two he found he could explain quite simply, but the third was more difficult. 'Set apart to a sacred use': God's ministers, of course, were set apart in this way. Miss Gay ought to realize this. Mr Paladin's meditations were interrupted at this point by the ringing of the front door bell. He felt suddenly colder. Would he be safe? he wondered. He could hear Mrs Roberts open the front door, shut it, and then tap at his door. He crouched in his corner, almost holding his breath. He was beginning to wish that he had been braver now. He would feel so foolish if Miss Gay were to discover him like this.

Mrs Roberts had opened the door now and he could hear her fumbling about for the light switch. Why need she stay so long? he wondered. Couldn't she see that he wasn't in? Suddenly the room was flooded with light, or so it seemed to Mr Paladin, who had been sitting for more than half an hour in the darkness, though in reality the light at Arlington House was very poor.

Mrs Roberts advanced into the room, and looked around.

'Why, Mr Paladin,' she exclaimed, 'what *are* you doing there cowering in the darkness?'

Her stilted phrase, which would otherwise have amused him, now made Mr Paladin feel even more embarrassed. 'Cowering in the darkness'. He supposed that it described his state very well.

He rose to his feet with as much dignity as he could muster and said, 'Ah, yes, Mrs Roberts, I find the darkness conducive to great thoughts.'

Mrs Roberts stared at him uncomprehendingly. 'Somebody brought this for you,' she said, holding out a square parcel.

Mr Paladin knew by its shape that it was *Paradise Lost*. He opened it, and saw that there was a note inside. It was very short. 'Dear Mr Paladin,' it ran, 'here is the book. I am sending Amy with it, as I find I shall not have time to bring it myself. Isn't this weather lovely? Yours sincerely, Angela Gay.'

Mr Paladin crumpled it up and threw it into the waste-paper basket. Why had Miss Gay sent the maid? he wondered. Could it be, he asked himself tentatively, hardly daring to hope, that she had grown tired of him? He speculated on this interesting subject for the rest of the evening, and forgot all about his meditations on Holiness.

The explanation of Miss Gay's conduct, had he known it, was very simple. That morning, when she had been doing her shopping, she had been approached by a tall and handsome stranger in a black hat.

'Excuse me,' he said, bowing as nobody in Up Callow ever did, 'but could you perhaps tell me, is there here an ironware shop?'

'Ironware?' Miss Gay looked puzzled, and then, 'Oh, I expect you mean ironmonger's,' she said. 'Yes, there is one, but it's rather out of the way.' She looked about her doubtfully.

'Thank you so much. Perhaps you will tell me how I can go there?'

'Well, it's rather difficult.' Miss Gay hovered a little, and then said suddenly, 'But I happen to be going there myself, so I can go with you.'

'Oh, but I cannot trouble you so much, you are really too kind.' All this was said with a brilliant smile, and much bowing and flourishing of the black hat.

'But I assure you it's no trouble,' said Miss Gay eagerly.

They started on their way, he taking long strides, and Miss Gay pattering along beside him in her high heels.

'Are you *sure* I do not trouble you?' persisted the stranger.

'It's no trouble at all,' Miss Gay assured him. 'As a matter of fact I have to go there myself to see about a spare part for a Primus stove.'

'Very strange,' said the stranger, his deep foreign voice making this exchange sound far more exciting than it really was. 'I too wish to buy a Primus stove.'

'Such useful things,' murmured Miss Gay, thinking that this was a real bond between them, if not a romantic one. While she was speaking her glances were darting about from one side of the street to the other, to see whether any people she knew were anywhere near to watch her walking with this distinguished-looking stranger. She saw Mrs Gower's broad back disappearing into the fish shop, and they came face to face with Janie Wilmot as they rounded the corner into Market Street, but otherwise the walk was a little disappointing.

'What a charming little town,' said the stranger, 'and everyone is so *gemütlich*.'

'Pardon?' said Miss Gay, surprised to think that the inhabitants of their dull town could possibly be anything that needed a foreign word to describe them.

'Kindly, friendly, what would you say? But how stupid I am. You don't know German, perhaps? You look so much like a Parisian.'

Miss Gay smiled complacently. Her tight black costume and little hat with an eye-veil had at last, for they were both nearly a year old, produced the effect she had hoped for. He wouldn't be saying such things to Cassandra Marsh-Gibbon in her tweeds and brogue shoes. 'My mother was French,' she declared proudly.

'You are very like her, I think,' said the stranger with rather surprising certainty.

'That I cannot say. She died when I was five years old and I can hardly remember her.'

'Oh, how sad for you.' The dark eyes expressed real sympathy. 'My mother also died when I was five.'

Miss Gay was silent, thinking that here was yet another bond between them, and a more beautiful and permanent one than a Primus stove. Perhaps it was a little too much to hope that they would be able to comfort each other for the deaths of mothers long since forgotten, but at least they might be *something* to each other.

Her dreams were interrupted by the stranger remarking that he was sure that this was the shop, yes? Miss Gay looked up, then sighed and shrugged her shoulders, as if she had been jerked away from the contemplation of a beautiful vision by the sight of the buckets and watering cans and Aladdin lamps. 'Yes,' she said, 'this is the shop.'

'It was indeed kind of you to come with me,' he smiled.

'I hope you are settling down in your new house,' said Miss Gay.

'Oh, it is charming!' he declared enthusiastically. 'But how did you know I am coming to live here?'

'News travels quickly in a small town.'

'Specially good news, yes?'

Miss Gay fluttered her eyelashes at him. 'I hope we may call it that,' she said.

'You will see,' laughed the stranger, and having thanked her again, he walked into the shop, and was soon lost in its gloomy interior.

Miss Gay walked away feeling very sprightly, and quite forgetting that she herself was supposed to be buying something.

When the evening came, she remembered that she had intended calling on Mr Paladin to return his book. What a dull book it was, she thought. Why did Mr Paladin like such stupid things?

'Amy,' she called, 'bring me some brown paper and string, and then get your hat and coat on. I want you to take a parcel round to Mr Paladin's lodgings.'

CHAPTER EIGHT

'Come Inspiration! from thy hermit seat,
By mortal seldom found . . .'

'What's all this about a foreigner coming to live at Holmwood?'
said Adam Marsh-Gibbon to his wife one evening.

It was about ten days after Miss Gay had shown the stranger
the way to the ironmonger's shop. The weather had suddenly
become much warmer, and Adam and Cassandra were in the
garden. He was sitting on a seat under the cedar tree, while she
was weeding a flower-bed nearby.

'Really, Adam,' laughed Cassandra, 'haven't you heard about
Miss Gay and the handsome stranger, and how they found they
were soul-mates because of something to do with Primus stoves
and their dead mothers? It was really most entertaining. Mrs
Gower told me, and she heard it from Mr Gay, so it must be
quite genuine.'

'I have better things to do than to listen to a lot of women
talking,' said Adam loftily. 'It sounds rubbish to me.'

'Of course it does,' said Cassandra, 'but I think it's *true*, that's
what makes it all the more delightful.'

Adam had done practically nothing during the last ten days
but pace about the house and garden, complaining about his
inability to write, dust on the piano, buttons off his shirts and

pyjamas, beef too much or mutton too little cooked at dinner, too hot or too cold weather, and anything else he happened to think of at the moment.

'I think you ought to come and help me with these weeds,' Cassandra went on. 'You can't expect to get at the soul of your gardener if you have no practical experience of gardening. Besides, you aren't doing anything at present.'

No, Adam had to admit that he wasn't doing anything at present, but he felt bound to justify himself, and proceeded to do so at some length. 'Why must you always be bothering me?' he said peevishly. 'You bustling women would do well to read Wordsworth. Surely you remember "Expostulation and Reply"?' he demanded, and began to recite in a defiant voice which did not accord very well with the sense of the poetry.

Cassandra was silent. Adam had an unfair advantage over her by being able to finish off so many of their little arguments by quoting suitable poetry to support his point of view. What could she say after two stanzas of Wordsworth? Sometimes she almost wished that Wordsworth had never been born. She felt that he was almost entirely responsible for this tiresome gardener about whom Adam was finding it so difficult to write. If it weren't for Wordsworth, she told herself, we wouldn't be bothering about the beautiful and permanent forms of Nature, and wise passiveness, which, in Adam's case, was simply another name for being lazy and doing nothing.

Cassandra stopped grovelling among the dandelions and looked up at Adam and saw that there was a look of intense concentration on his face. He was very laboriously making paper boats out of the last chapter of his novel. Much the best thing for it, thought Cassandra, suddenly loving him very much indeed.

After working on the dandelions for about ten minutes, she got up, for her back was aching, and sat on the seat beside her husband.

57

'Adam, dear,' she said tentatively, 'don't you think we might give some sort of a party and ask this foreigner and various other people. It's ages since we saw anybody, and I'm sure it would do you good.'

'How do you mean "do me good"?' said Adam uncompromisingly, still making paper boats.

'Well, take you out of yourself.'

'But my dear child, why should I want to be taken out of myself? It's impossible anyway. How can I become any other self but my own self? Tell me that.'

Cassandra sighed. She felt that she was hardly equal to the strain of a philosophical argument at this moment, but she did her best by saying, 'Everyone should occasionally have his attention distracted from a too profound contemplation of his own self.'

Suddenly Adam laughed, and put his arm round her shoulders. 'My poor Cassandra, that was a very nice sentence,' he said.

'Well, Adam, you know you like meeting people, really you do. And I should like to give a party.'

'A sherry party, I suppose?' he said indulgently.

'When would be the best day, do you think?' Cassandra asked.

'Oh, any day will suit me,' said Adam surprisingly. 'What about this foreigner, who is he anyway?'

Cassandra proceeded to give as full an account as she could, for she had not yet seen him herself. By dinner-time Adam was in quite a good temper, and even kissed her in the dining room, saying that he thought perhaps he might have seemed a little irritable of late and had she noticed it? To which Cassandra replied that he had certainly been preoccupied but, of course, that was to be expected, and that if he had sometimes been irritable, it was probably *her* fault. Indeed, when Adam was so nice and good-tempered, Cassandra found herself thinking that perhaps she was to blame for those times when he wasn't.

'Well,' said Adam benevolently, as they were drinking their coffee in the drawing room, 'what would you like to read tonight?'

'I think it would be nice to go on with "The Seasons",' said Cassandra meekly, thinking that it would really be nicer not to have any reading at all, but how much better the reading would be than to have another of those gloomy evenings, with no sound but Adam pacing about the room and into the hall and back again.

'You shall begin, Cassandra,' said Adam. 'You read so nicely.'

Cassandra opened the book and began to read:

> 'Still let my song a nobler note assume,
> And sing the infusive force of Spring on man.'

She hurried a little over these lines, and glanced anxiously at Adam, for she was afraid that he might be reminded of his novel and that wretched gardener. But her fears were soon set at rest. He was lying back in his chair with his eyes closed and a pleased smile on his face. Darling Adam, he isn't even listening. The words pass over him like the waves of the sea, or roll off him like the water off a duck's back, she thought affectionately. When she had read to the end of the passage she stopped.

'Adam,' she said gently, 'I believe you're asleep.'

'Oh, no,' he answered drowsily. 'I was just thinking.'

'What about?' she asked.

'Nothing.'

'How nice,' said Cassandra. 'It's so good for you to think of nothing. I wish you could do it more often.'

'Unfortunately you have to have thought a great deal about

something first of all to make such a pleasant state as thinking of nothing possible,' said Adam intelligently.

Cassandra waited, but he made no reference to the gardener. Perhaps, she thought, he will burn it or tear it up in the morning, or even lay it aside. That would be something.

CHAPTER NINE

'. . . the herds
In widening circle round, forget their food,
And at the harmless stranger wondering gaze.'

Stefan Tilos considered himself a very ordinary man. He was genuinely surprised when so much interest was shown in his coming to live at Holmwood. After thinking about it, he came to the conclusion that it must be because the English were naturally *gemütlich*. They welcome a poor foreigner – Mr Tilos sometimes had rather ridiculous ideas about himself – into their midst as if he were one of themselves, he thought, not realizing that he was not, and never could be, anything so dull as one of themselves. He overlooked the importance of his being a foreigner and a Hungarian. Foreigners are rare in Shropshire, particularly Hungarians. For the inhabitants of Up Callow, Stefan Tilos had about him all the glamour of Budapest, against a background of mediaeval castles, *tzigane* bands and vampires. Above all, he was a single man, so far as anyone knew.

On the morning when he received the invitation to Adam and Cassandra's party, Mr Tilos was sitting at breakfast in his dining room. From his window he could see a group of fir trees. He might almost be living in the middle of a thick forest, a Hungarian feudal lord in the heart of Shropshire. His friends in Budapest had thought he was mad to go and live in England. It was cold, they said, and always raining. London was nice, but the nightclubs were very expensive, though he must be sure to visit Quaglino's. They had heard that Scotland was beautiful, but Shropshire, where was that? There must surely be many wolves in such a wild region. It was unfortunate that his business (something to do with importing and exporting commodities) should have made it necessary to leave the safety of the capital. Stefan would soon be back, they told themselves.

'I'm beginning to wish we hadn't asked this man,' said Cassandra to Adam as they were getting ready for the party. 'After all, we don't really know anything about him.'

'It is really very inconvenient to have invited anyone at all,' said Adam. 'I am so busy, I really ought not to spare the time.'

Cassandra sighed. 'Well, you can always rush out to your study if you're suddenly inspired,' she said, for Adam's inspiration was now coming very irregularly, and one never knew when to expect it. He had laid aside the novel about the gardener, as she had hoped, and was now at work on an epic poem, which was nearly as bad.

The first people to arrive were Mr Gay and his niece. When she greeted them Cassandra could not help exclaiming how well he looked.

'Yes,' said Mr Gay, 'I have never felt better in my life.'

'It's the spring,' said Miss Gay, who knew nothing of Mrs Gower's wonderful tablets. 'Isn't the weather *lovely*?'

'It *is* lovely,' Cassandra agreed, 'and all the flowers are coming out so beautifully.'

Miss Gay seemed very sprightly. Had there been other meetings between her and the romantic stranger? Could it be that they had discovered that they had other things in common besides Primus stoves?

'What a delightful frock!' said Miss Gay, taking Cassandra

aside and speaking in a confidential feminine whisper. 'That shade of blue suits you so well,' she added, thinking how insipid it was.

'When will this man arrive?' asked Adam, coming up to them. 'Will he be in native costume?'

'Oh, Mr Marsh-Gibbon, how charming! But I'm afraid you're going to be disappointed. Stefan is really quite English in his appearance.' She brought out the Christian name with self-conscious pride. In fact, Mrs Gower had told her that she had seen his name on a trunk that was being taken into Holmwood, and Miss Gay had decided to use it. She felt that as she was the only person who had really spoken to him, she was justified in calling him by some more intimate name.

Adam looked at Miss Gay over the top of his spectacles. He often wore them when people came to the house, to make himself seem more learned, but he could not see through them very well as they were intended only for reading.

'Am I to understand that you have got as far as that?'

Cassandra thought that he was getting rather silly and so, evidently, did the rector, for he joined the little group and asked Adam how he was getting on with his novel.

'I have laid it aside,' said Adam. 'Temporarily,' he added, imagining that he detected a look of disappointment on the rector's face, although Cassandra, who had also been watching, suspected that it was relief.

'Oh, but surely you will go on with it?'

'Certainly, but in the autumn. I shall find it easier to write about the spring then. It is always better to recall one's emotion in tranquillity.'

Cassandra smiled, wondering whether, when autumn came, Adam would find that there hadn't been any emotion to be recollected at all. She rather hoped so.

'Then you are taking a well-earned rest?' said the rector.

'Oh, no.' Adam shook his head and a weary smile crept over his face. 'I am at present contemplating an epic poem,' he declared, raising his voice a little so that, as he had intended, all the other people in the room heard, stopped their trivial conversations, and edged nearer to hear more about it. 'Dryden tells us that it is the greatest work of which the soul of man is capable,' he went on impressively.

There was an admiring silence, during which nobody knew what to say. Then Mrs Gower remarked in an indulgent tone, as if she regarded him as a child who must be humoured, 'My late husband once thought of writing an epic poem about King Arthur, but he never wrote more than fifty lines, as far as I can remember.'

'And I suppose that wouldn't be long enough for an epic?' suggested Miss Gay, thinking distastefully of *Paradise Lost*.

'Hardly,' said the rector. 'I imagine that length is an essential qualification, whatever else may be lacking.'

The door opened and Lily announced Mr Stefan Tilos. The stage was set for an impressive entrance. All the occupants of the room were crowded in one corner where they had been listening to Adam, and when the door opened they all turned automatically to see who it was.

Cassandra advanced to meet him. 'I'm so glad you were able to come,' she said.

'It was most kind of you to ask me. But I am late, yes?' He looked around him, smiling at everyone. 'I am so sorry,' he said.

'Oh, not at all . . .'

Cassandra gave him some sherry and began introducing him to people. She tried to do this as quickly as possible, as she had the uncomfortable feeling that Miss Gay was watching her and was ready to snatch Mr Tilos away, should she monopolize him for too long.

'Ah, my Parisian friend,' he said, when he saw Miss Gay.

Mr Gay looked at him sternly. How could this be? Angela had left Paris when she was a child.

The rector cleared his throat. 'I daresay you will find that it is quieter here than in your part of the world,' he said.

'I came here for quiet,' said Mr Tilos, 'and I hope I will find it.'

Surely he isn't writing an epic poem as well, thought Cassandra hopelessly. The town certainly could not hold two authors.

'The country round here is very pleasant,' ventured Mr Gay.

'It is a healthy place, I think,' said Mr Tilos.

'Oh, no,' interrupted Adam, 'it isn't. Not at all healthy,' he declared gravely. 'Too low lying.'

'Perhaps he has come to lie low,' said Miss Gay laughing. 'After all, we know nothing of your past,' she said provocatively looking up at Mr Tilos.

'I must hope you will never discover anything,' he replied in the same strain.

I think we are going to regret this man's presence among us, reflected Mrs Gower. He was far too handsome to be let loose in a small town.

'Are you staying here long?' she asked.

'Oh, yes, I hope that I stay many, many months.'

'I expect you will find it tedious here,' said Adam, 'unless you like walking or riding.'

'I like very much to hunt the wild boar,' said Mr Tilos simply.

Even Adam was impressed by this. He imagined mediaeval castles and spacious forests with great dogs running about. The rector remembered the ceremony of bringing in the Boar's Head at Queen's College, Oxford. Cassandra thought of one of those false boar's heads, made of galantine with a shiny brown surface, decorating a cold buffet table. Nobody knew what to say. It seemed hardly kind to tell Mr Tilos that he was unlikely to be able to indulge in his favourite sport in Shropshire.

He was standing by the fireplace with a happy smile on his face, almost as if he was smiling at some secret. This was, in fact, the case, and he could not very well reveal what it was. Being a susceptible man, he had fallen in love, at first sight, with Cassandra Marsh-Gibbon.

CHAPTER TEN

'An elegant sufficiency, content,
Retirement, rural quiet, friendship, books ...'

'I don't like it,' said Mr Gay, shaking his head, and rubbing the aspidistra leaf vigorously. 'No good can come of it.'

Mrs Gower nodded sympathetically. 'I'm sure you're quite right,' she declared. It was what she was used to saying after many years of life married to a man who was always talking about things slightly above her head. The late Professor Gower had thus had the gratification of knowing that his wife at least was convinced of his rightness when he maintained that Nicholas of Guildford had nothing whatever to do with *The Owl and the Nightingale*.

'It was bad enough when Angela was after young Paladin,' continued Mr Gay, 'but of course every woman goes for a curate.' He said these last words sadly, as if remembering the rich young women of the late Victorian period who had preferred the church to him. 'I wondered if you could perhaps say something to her,' he suggested tentatively. 'You see, Angela has never had a mother ...'

Mrs Gower looked rather alarmed. She did not by any means feel equal to being a mother to a thirty-year-old spinster who was determined to get herself a husband. Yet Mr Gay had been so kind, coming all this way on a hot afternoon to attend to the aspidistra, that she hardly liked to refuse point-blank. 'Of course, *you* are her guardian,' she said, stating an obvious truth to gain time.

'Yes,' said Mr Gay unhappily, for he was in no danger of forgetting. He had already been told by his niece that he had one foot in the grave, and the memory still rankled. In a burst of confidence he told Mrs Gower about it.

'What a cruel thing to say!' she protested indignantly. 'But you shouldn't let it distress you. Anyone can see that both your feet are a long way from the grave yet. You remind me so much of Professor Gower,' she said suddenly.

Mr Gay was aware that this was a compliment of the very highest order, for which any acknowledgement would be hopelessly inadequate, so he did not say anything. Mrs Gower, who read novels, would have described the silence as a pregnant one, but it brought forth nothing beyond the observation from Mr Gay that Angela was no chicken, which made it all the more awkward saying anything to her.

'Why don't you just let things take their course?' said Mrs Gower wisely, although she was really trying to change the subject. 'After all, a woman of thirty should be able to look after herself.'

'Do you think so?' For a moment the expression of Mr Gay's face implied that he doubted whether a woman of any age could look after herself, but this expression was replaced almost immediately by one of mingled gratitude and relief. After all, what could he do? And things always took their course whatever one did, he told himself. He straightened and surveyed the aspidistra. It had become almost sprightly.

'It's quite rejuvenated,' said Mrs Gower. She found her thoughts going back to the house in Oxford. She was ashamed to remember that she had not visited for several days the room which she had filled with her husband's belongings. I'll take Mr Gay to see it, she thought suddenly. He was so sympathetic and understanding, although Mrs Gower was not clear what exactly there was for him to be sympathetic and understanding about, except the death of poor Ernest eight years ago, and she had just been coming to the conclusion that she no longer regretted that. 'Would you like to see some of my late husband's books?' she asked. 'I think you'd be interested in them.'

Mr Gay's face lighted up with pleasure. It was so seldom that anyone took the trouble to show him anything.

They went upstairs, Mrs Gower leading the way. The room was on the first floor, and faced out on to the rose garden at the back of the house. Mrs Gower opened the door, and stood waiting for Mr Gay to go in.

'Why, it's one of the nicest rooms in the house!' he exclaimed, unable to keep a note of surprise out of his voice. It was almost as if he were thinking what a pity it was.

'Why yes, perhaps it is,' said Mrs Gower slowly, as if this had not occurred to her before.

'It must face south,' conjectured Mr Gay.

'Yes, it gets a great deal of sun.'

They went to the window and looked out.

'What a pleasant, peaceful view,' said Mr Gay. 'A lovely prospect. "Fields on this side, on that a neighbouring wood",' he recited a little sadly, for from the windows of Alameda one saw only tombstones, or the dusty monkey-puzzle in the front garden.

Mrs Gower agreed with him about the loveliness of the prospect, although she had no quotation ready. 'I hope they won't build,' she observed sensibly.

Mr Gay looked about him. It was a nice room. Two of its walls and the spaces on either side of the door were taken up with bookshelves. There was a table in the middle of the room, and the large airy windows opened on to a balcony. In front of the window there was a desk, and in the corner to the right of it stood a large cage with a red cloth over it.

'Of course I see that it's dusted,' Mrs Gower remarked confidentially. 'There is such a thing as carrying reverence for the past too far, I think.'

Mr Gay looked puzzled. Surely the late Professor Gower had never lived in this house, or indeed in Shropshire at all?

Mrs Gower must have been reading his thoughts, for she remarked that her late husband had never really occupied this room, as he had died in Oxford, 'But I have always kept his things here, and somehow it saves the trouble of explaining to people who don't know about it. Perhaps it's silly of me.'

Mr Gay felt rather awkward. He turned away and began to examine the cage in the corner.

Mrs Gower went over to it and drew off the cloth.

In the cage was a parrot with bright green and grey feathers.

It made no sound at being disturbed since it had been silent for the last seven years.

Here Mr Gay really forgot himself. He laughed out loud. The bird looked so ridiculous perched there with its silly, staring, glassy eyes. But what a terrible thing he had done! He must surely have offended Mrs Gower for life. He saw himself banished from her pleasant tea parties. What could he say or do to make amends?

'Why, Mr Gay,' she said, 'it does me good to hear laughter in this room. I never thought of it before, but I suppose it *is* funny to see poor Wulfstan stuffed,' she added, almost apologetically. 'Professor Gower was so fond of him. He tried to teach him Old English, but he never got beyond saying *Hwaet!* How he used to startle us with it sometimes!' Mrs Gower was laughing now. 'Poor Wulfstan, he was such a lively parrot. I wonder if I could give him away,' she mused. 'Perhaps the rector knows of some child who would like him.'

'I believe one of the rector's boys collects birds' eggs,' said Mr Gay helpfully.

'But of course poor Wulfstan is rather past the egg stage,' laughed Mrs Gower. In fact she laughed more than was necessary, for she was enjoying the sensation of being able to make fun of hitherto sacred relics. With Mr Gay there didn't seem to be anything wrong in it at all; she almost imagined that poor Ernest was there too, laughing with them. 'Anyway,' she went on, when they had both laughed at her little joke, 'I'm sure the rector would know of somebody. And there are far too many books in this room. I wonder whether the public library would like some of them?'

'I'm sure it would be only too glad of them,' said Mr Gay enviously.

'But of course some of them are too good for the public library. Are there any you would like?' Mrs Gower looked vaguely about her at the ancient calf-bound volumes.

'Oh, but Mrs Gower, I really couldn't . . .'

'Well, anyway you must come and help me sort them out one of these days. I know so little about books, and I've only kept these out of sentiment. I don't like the old ones – I've never been able to get used to their horrid smell.'

As they went downstairs Mr Gay could not help wondering whether it was not perhaps wrong of them to begin disposing of the late Professor Gower's possessions like this. He felt vaguely responsible, although he could not have said in what way. He felt that he ought to say something, and yet it wasn't any business of his what Mrs Gower chose to do, although if he hadn't laughed about the stuffed parrot it might not have occurred to her. He was standing on the doorstep puzzling about this when his attention was distracted by something across the road. Mrs Gower, who had been pointing out her flame-coloured lupins, stopped in the middle of a sentence, and they both stood still in the middle of the path and stared.

Mr Tilos was walking down the drive of Holmwood, carrying the largest bunch of Madonna lilies that either of them had ever seen. As he came nearer they looked at each other questioningly. Could it be that they were imagining things? For it seemed to them that Mr Tilos was singing.

They both felt rather embarrassed as he drew near. They did not know what to say and were relieved when he took no notice of them. He seemed so happy and engrossed in smelling the lilies that he did not even see them, but walked quickly down the road, almost tripping in his haste.

'Well, *well*,' said Mrs Gower, 'I wonder what lucky person is going to have those beautiful lilies.'

'I expect they are for the church,' said Mr Gay sensibly.

Mrs Gower looked disappointed at this simple explanation. 'I suppose they may be,' she admitted reluctantly, 'but I can't help feeling he may be taking them for your niece.'

'Oh dear, I hope not. I don't know where Angela would put all those flowers. Besides, it would make things even worse,' he added unhappily. He had not wanted to be reminded about Angela, and now this wretched foreigner with his lilies had quite spoilt the afternoon.

CHAPTER ELEVEN

'At first the groves are scarcely seen to stir
Their trembling tops . . .'

Mr Tilos would have been most concerned if he had known that he was spoiling anyone's afternoon. He had been so happy when he gathered the lilies from the conservatory, and when he walked down the drive and into the road, he had burst into song almost without knowing it.

He was surprised at the amount of attention he seemed to attract as he walked through the town. People even turned round to stare at him, for he was already being pointed out as the new tenant of Holmwood and a foreigner. His only fear was that the lilies might droop or their juicy white petals become bruised before he reached his destination. He had to walk a long way, but he felt that it was more suitable to arrive on foot, carrying his offering, than to drive up to the door in his car.

This must be the house; he remembered the stone gateposts and the long avenue of poplars. He marched boldly up the drive and then, not wishing to ring the bell if he could help it, he walked cautiously round to one side of the house. Here he stopped, for he heard sounds coming from an open window on the ground floor. Somebody was reciting poetry. Mr Tilos caught a fragment:

'And this those other eyes of mine had seen
That still a boundless . . . '

but the rest was lost to him as the reciter, who was pacing about
the room, had walked over towards the door. Mr Tilos wondered
for a moment what 'other eyes' were and what it was they had
seen. That must be the husband, he thought. He felt he must
look again to make sure, but just as he was going to press his face
as near to the glass as he dared, he was startled by the sound of
crunching gravel behind him.

He turned round suddenly, and saw Cassandra standing on
the path with a small fork in one hand and a basket of weeds in
the other. She had been standing there for some time, rooted to
the spot by the sight of Mr Tilos with a huge bunch of lilies in
his arms, looking through Adam's study window.

Mr Tilos had not intended their meeting to be like this. The
look of consternation on his face when he saw Cassandra standing there was so pathetic that she smiled kindly as he walked
towards her.

'I have brought you some flowers,' he said simply.

'Oh, how lovely they are!' exclaimed Cassandra. 'But surely
you can't mean them for *me*?'

'Beautiful flowers for a beautiful woman,' said Mr Tilos
bowing, although with some difficulty as the flowers were in his
way.

Cassandra received the compliment as gracefully as she could,
for she had never felt less beautiful in her life. She knew without looking at herself that her face was shining and unpowdered,
her hair untidy, and her hands and nails caked with earth. Her
old blue gardening skirt and jumper concealed rather than set
off her nicely rounded figure, while her sensible-sized feet looked
even more so in their inelegant galoshes.

Unconsciously she moved out of range of Adam's study

window, and led Mr Tilos towards the seat under the cedar tree. 'Let's sit down,' she said. 'It's so hot this evening, and you must be tired after your long walk. But did you want to see my husband?' she asked, for it had just occurred to her that the flowers might not, after all, be the main object of his visit.

'Oh, no, I saw him through the window, I think,' laughed Mr Tilos. The idea of Stefan Tilos coming to see the husband was quite the funniest thing he had heard since coming to England.

'I've been doing some gardening, as you can see,' said Cassandra. 'I'm afraid I'm terribly dirty and untidy,' she said, glancing down at her hands.

'You have charming hands,' said Mr Tilos, 'and why do you complain when you look so nice? I don't care that you are dirty and untidy,' he said emphatically.

'Don't you?' said Cassandra, unable to think of any other reply, and realizing at the same time that it was hardly Mr Tilos's business to care or not care how she looked. On such a short acquaintance it should have been a matter of indifference to him. And yet it had been so kind of him to bring the lilies. 'I'm so fond of flowers,' she said, 'and lilies are some of my favourites.'

'You looked so much like a lily the day I first saw you,' said Mr Tilos.

'I had them in my wedding bouquet,' said Cassandra firmly, thinking that it was time she made some allusion to her married state, as Mr Tilos seemed to have forgotten it.

'And when I am dead you will send some to my funeral, I hope,' he said simply, taking her earthy hand in both his and raising it to his lips.

Cassandra hardly knew what to do, especially as out of the corner of her eye she could see Adam coming out on to the lawn. 'There must be lovely flowers in Budapest,' she said loudly.

'The gardens there are beautiful,' said Mr Tilos. 'In the moonlight they are so romantic.'

Then, before Cassandra had time to disengage her hand or say anything more about the gardens, Adam came up to them, and after bidding Mr Tilos good evening asked him if he would like a glass of sherry before dinner. He then sat down on the other side of Cassandra and began a cordial conversation about the weather, in which Mr Tilos joined him.

Cassandra thought that Adam might at least have shown a little surprise at seeing her and Mr Tilos sitting there with a huge bunch of lilies spread out on their knees. They must have looked peculiar, to put it mildly. And then surely an English husband ought to think it forward of a strange foreigner to be kissing his wife's hand when he had only met her on one previous occasion?

'Mr Tilos brought me these lovely flowers,' she said to Adam. 'I must go and put them in water.' She got up and, after thanking Mr Tilos again, went into the house.

She arranged the lilies carefully in large glass jars and bowls, and put some on the table in Adam's study, thinking that they would be a reproach to him every time he saw them. Then she went up to her room to change for dinner.

When she came down again Mr Tilos was just going. He and Adam had been drinking sherry, and she heard Adam say in very cordial tones, 'You must let us show you the countryside some time. There are some charming villages round here.'

Cassandra smiled as she imagined them all together in the car, Adam and Mr Tilos sitting in front, while she sat demurely in the back with the picnic basket, in which would be tasty sandwiches, made for them with her own hands. She was glad that Mr Tilos had been able to see her looking really nice in her black velvet dress. Not that she particularly wanted him as an admirer, but she had some natural feminine vanity, and she liked him to see that although his compliments were ridiculous when she was in her old gardening

76

clothes, there was at least some truth in them when she was respectably dressed.

'I think he's quite an interesting man,' said Adam patronizingly, as they sat down to dinner. 'He was telling me that he walked all the way here.'

Cassandra did not think much of this as a specimen of his intelligent conversation.

'Perhaps he has fallen in love with you. I don't very much care for this fish. Is it plaice?' Adam lifted up a piece on his fork and sniffed it suspiciously. 'Do you think it's quite good?' he asked.

Cassandra looked at him. It saddened her to think that her husband could be more concerned with the goodness or otherwise of a piece of plaice than with the possibility of a rival for his wife's affection.

'Do you think it's quite *good*?' repeated Adam urgently, for he had already eaten nearly all of his.

'Of course it's good,' said Cassandra sharply, almost wishing for the moment that it wasn't. 'It only came this morning and has been in the refrigerator since then. You've got too much imagination.'

'An author naturally has imagination,' remarked Adam with dignity.

'Don't the lilies smell lovely?' said Cassandra, feeling unequal to a debate about the author and his imagination.

'I believe you like Mr Tilos,' declared Adam. 'It would be something for Up Callow to talk about if you fell in love with each other.'

'You seem very calm at the prospect of losing an excellent housekeeper,' said Cassandra evenly.

'You talk as if being an excellent housekeeper were something derogatory. It is really extremely important. I know you're too sensible to fall in love with anyone else. Besides, do you suppose

77

that even if you wanted to your faithful, tender heart would let you? You know you are much more to me than just an excellent housekeeper,' he declared kindly. 'Although I'm not quite sure about this fish,' he added, as he finished up what remained on his plate.

CHAPTER TWELVE

'Oh! knew he but his happiness, of men
The happiest he ...'

'The Marsh-Gibbons seem to have taken quite a fancy to that foreigner, or is it the other way about, do you think?' said Mrs Wilmot to her husband one Sunday evening after church. She always felt that this was a good time to introduce any subject which bordered on the frivolous, for with all the worries of Sunday behind him, her husband was usually in a good mood, and as he was more fond of cold beef than of hot, Sunday supper was nearly always the most pleasant meal of the week. Tonight Janie had made a nice potato salad, and everything was very peaceful because the younger children had gone back to school.

'He seems quite a good fellow,' said the rector. 'He's promised a subscription to the Cricket Club although he doesn't play, which is very sporting of him. I was glad to see him in church this morning. It shows the right spirit.'

'He sat just behind the Marsh-Gibbons,' observed Mrs Wilmot. 'Did you notice how he stared at Cassandra?'

'You can hardly expect me to have noticed how Mr Tilos was occupying his time during Divine Service,' he said sternly. 'I hope he comes to church for better reasons than to stare at a young married woman as respectable as Cassandra.'

79

'Oh, yes, it would be hard to find anyone more respectable than Cassandra,' observed Mrs Wilmot in a flat voice, which hinted that she might almost have been more pleased had it not been so.

'If only we could get someone like that for Paladin,' mused the rector. 'That young man needs a wife.'

'Oh, but Rockingham, he's so young,' said Mrs Wilmot.

'Every man should have a wife,' declared the rector firmly. 'A single clergyman is the prey of every spinster in the parish. He should marry for safety, if for no other reason.'

Mrs Wilmot looked up from her cold beef in surprise. Could it be then that Rockingham had married her for *this* reason, and not because he considered her a worthy partner to share with him that high position which must of necessity await one with his exceptional gifts?

'We shall have to see what we can do for Mr Paladin,' she remarked. 'What about Miss Gay?'

'She might put ideas into his head,' said the rector darkly. 'We couldn't have that.'

'No, of course not,' agreed Mrs Wilmot, who would have liked to know what sort of ideas her husband meant, but felt she could hardly ask. 'But surely all women put ideas into men's heads?' she suggested, with a suspicion of coyness in her manner.

'Of course, of course, and quite right that they should,' said the rector heartily, 'but we must remember that Miss Gay hasn't had the advantages of a good upbringing and a healthy family life. Also, she has lived in France ...' Here the rector made a sweeping gesture with his hand, for he had just remembered that Janie was at the table, and he judged that a sweep of the hand was the wisest conclusion to his sentence.

Mrs Wilmot nodded wisely, and began to serve out the blanc-mange.

'A healthy and normal family life is of great importance in

the formation of character,' said the rector, thinking that it was time the conversation took a more general turn. 'We should do all we can to preserve it, shouldn't we, Janie?'

'But surely Mr Paladin is very clever?' ventured Janie.

'Oh, yes, undoubtedly. But a First in Theology needs to be leavened with a great deal of experience in the School of Life before it can be expected to bear fruit,' said the rector.

Mrs Wilmot looked up in surprise. Rockingham was not usually like this on a Sunday evening. 'Well, well,' she said brightly, as her husband rose from the table, 'we must find Mr Paladin a wife.'

'Yes, he would go far if he had some good woman at his side,' said the rector. 'I think I shall go and oil my cricket bat,' he said, and with that he left the two women alone.

I wonder if I'm a good woman, thought Janie, or just a nice girl? She liked Mr Paladin, and if he was going far that meant that he wouldn't remain in Up Callow all his life. Surely it was obvious that being a nice girl was the next best thing to being a good woman?

'I really think you had better be Mrs Paladin,' said Mrs Wilmot, almost as if there were nothing else for it. 'Nobody could say that you would put ideas into his head,' she declared proudly.

'No, Mother, he would put them into mine,' laughed Janie. 'But not the sort of ideas Father meant when he was talking about Miss Gay.'

'I think Miss Gay must have Mr Tilos, if it can be managed,' said Mrs Wilmot. 'After all, she did see him first.'

'But what about Cassandra Marsh-Gibbon? Remember what Mrs Gower told us about the lilies.'

'Yes, dear,' said Mrs Wilmot, suddenly realizing that Janie was only a young girl, and that she herself was the rector's wife. 'I expect it is a foreign custom to send flowers to your hostess after you have visited her house.'

Janie got up, rather disappointed. She could not help thinking that it was time something interesting happened in the town. And Mr Tilos had certainly been to The Grotto many times in the last ten days.

He had, in fact, been so many times that if Cassandra heard the bell ring now she knew just what to expect. He always brought something with him, flowers, photographs of Budapest, specimens of peasant embroidery, even bottles of Tokay and peach brandy, which Cassandra was expected to taste solemnly in the drawing room. Because of this, even Adam had taken quite a fancy to him. He noticed that Mr Tilos was attracted by Cassandra, but he treated the whole thing as a joke, and was always teasing her about it, at the same time priding himself on being the one love of her life. This annoyed Cassandra because she knew that it was true. She found herself wishing that it wasn't. Adam might be shaken out of his complacency if he found that he was in danger of losing her.

One fine afternoon she was sitting in the garden thinking that she was too devoted to Adam, and gave in to him too much.

Into the midst of these thoughts walked the rector. He often paid an afternoon call at The Grotto, which was particularly pleasant in the summer, for, if he timed his call for about half past three or a quarter to four, they would not have been talking long before Lily would bring tea out into the garden. This afternoon he saw that Cassandra was busy with some embroidery. He fingered it rather clumsily and asked what it was.

'A firescreen. I'm making it for the Sale of Work,' explained Cassandra.

'Oh, but it's too nice,' the rector said, remembering the useless and ugly things that usually cluttered up the stalls. But then, recollecting his duty as rector of the parish, he added, 'I mean, it will far outshine anything else that we shall have.'

'Oh, I'm sure it won't,' Cassandra protested.

'But your embroidery seems to be so much better than any-body else's. I wonder why that is?'

'I'm sure it isn't. Mrs Gower does lovely work,' said Cassandra. 'But I think some people don't put in enough stitches, so that the rich effect is lost and it looks rather thin. I like to put in as much as I can, so that everything looks really well filled.'

The rector looked thoughtful. 'Yes, that must be it. Some people don't put in enough stitches,' he repeated, half to himself.

Cassandra looked at him with a surprised look on her face. No doubt he would feel better when tea arrived. 'Mr Tilos was showing me some of the Hungarian peasant embroideries the other day,' she said. 'They really put my efforts to shame.'

'Ah, Tilos. A nice fellow, as far as one can judge,' said the rector cautiously, remembering what his wife had said about him staring at Cassandra during the service.

'Oh, yes, he's quite nice,' said Cassandra indulgently, as if she were speaking of a child or a friendly dog. Indeed, that was just how she felt about Mr Tilos. It would have been far more excit-ing if she could have regarded him as someone to fall in love with.

'I hear that he is altering the name of Holmwood,' said the rector.

'Yes, I believe he is calling it Balaton, after a lake in Hungary,' said Cassandra. 'Personally I think it's ridiculous. But of course *we* can't talk,' she smiled. 'You couldn't find a much sillier name for a house than ours.'

The rector could hear Lily approaching with the tea.

'Will the master be in to dinner?' asked Lily.

'Yes, Lily,' Cassandra said, looking up from her work, 'but he may be a little late. I don't know which train he is getting. I'll

83

have mine at the usual time.' She turned to the rector. 'Adam has been in Oxford for a few days, working in the Bodleian Library.'

It must be very trying, thought the rector, to have a husband who was an author. Certainly Cassandra looked much more cheerful and relaxed when he was away.

Cassandra began to pour out the tea. 'Help yourself to a scone, or a sandwich,' she said. 'They're cream cheese and walnut, I believe.'

'My favourite ones,' the rector beamed.

'I'm so glad,' said Cassandra, 'take two. Bessie is splendid at remembering just what people like. I expect she saw you arrive.'

She composed herself to listen to the rector talking about the Mothers' Union. 'I'm sure it must be a good thing,' she said, trying to appear interested.

'It makes one realize what a blessing marriage is,' observed the rector.

Cassandra said that marriage was certainly a blessing, although one could have too much even of a blessing.

'A fortunate young woman like you has hardly the necessary experience for speaking of those less happy,' he ventured.

Cassandra sighed. She should have realized that she would never be allowed to be anything but fortunate. 'I suppose nobody in the world has everything he wants,' she remarked flatly.

'No, of course not. Perhaps even you must sometimes feel that you have missed something. I mean,' the rector gazed at the walnut and cream cheese sandwiches, as if expecting them to help him, 'do you not sometimes long for the presence of a third person in the house? A little person,' he explained, just as Cassandra had been contemplating the idea of Mr Tilos as a paying guest.

'I'm afraid children would disturb Adam writing his epic poem,' she said with a laugh.

When he had gone Cassandra went into the house. She was feeling depressed. The rector had not cheered her up at all. If she had let him go on, he would have added that children are such a bond between two people. One always knew just what he was going to say. Only he didn't know that she and Adam wanted a bond between them at this moment.

Cassandra had dinner by herself. Adam will expect me to have waited, she reflected, but the thought did not give her much pleasure.

After dinner she went into the drawing room and took up her embroidery. As the clock struck eight, she realized that Adam's dinner would be getting spoilt. Serve him right, she thought with unnecessary intensity. She became tired of the embroidery and thought that she would like to read. She went to the bookshelves and took down one of Adam's early works, a small volume of poetry, most of which had been written to her. It was not very good, but it reminded Cassandra that she was justified in thinking that there had been what one might call a falling-off in Adam's love for her. This evening she felt that she wanted to be justified.

At that moment the door opened, and in rushed Adam, carrying an important-looking document case. 'Cassandra, darling, I shall never forgive myself if you've waited dinner for me.' Adam came over to the sofa where she was sitting, and kissed her. 'And what has my Cassandra been reading?' He took the book out of her hand. 'Her husband's poems. Could anything be more suitable?'

You weren't my husband when you wrote them, thought Cassandra reproachfully, feeling annoyed that he should have discovered her reading them. But she could not say it. It was all wrong. Adam ought to have been in a bad temper after his journey, and because he hadn't had any dinner. He ought to be forgetting to say how glad he was to be with her again, instead of kissing her, and saying in between the kisses that an hour with his dear Cassandra was better than a whole week reading in the Bodleian Library. So I should hope, thought Cassandra indignantly, but there again she couldn't say it and she found herself laughing at the comparison, and feeling pleased because Adam was so nice.

'I'm afraid your dinner will be horrid,' she said. 'I had mine at half past seven.'

'Oh, that doesn't matter. I'll just eat what there is.'

So they went hand-in-hand into the dining room to eat Adam's nasty dinner. It was really even worse than Cassandra had hoped, but it made no difference to Adam, who just ate everything without looking at it.

Cassandra began to think that she was a wicked wife. And yet Adam *wasn't* always as nice as this, she told herself stubbornly. Lately he hadn't been at all nice, but cold, neglectful, argumentative, sarcastic – all these things.

'Cassandra, why are you so serious? Aren't you glad to have me back, or do you prefer to be without me? Or have you perhaps fallen in love with somebody else?' he persisted.

Cassandra gave him a startled look, suddenly alarmed at the prospect of being able to fall in and out of love in as short a time as two days. 'No,' she said. 'Why, have you?'

'My darling, you know quite well I would rather have a wife than anything else,' said Adam complacently. 'Doesn't that please you?'

Cassandra realized that it was no use arguing that 'a wife' didn't necessarily mean her. So she said that yes, it pleased her very much, and she was not sorry to spend the evening being a devoted wife to a devoted husband.

CHAPTER THIRTEEN

'Held in the magic chain of words, and forms,
And definitions void . . .'

The rector was pleased with the sermon he preached that Sunday. He had managed to work everything in rather well, and the central idea was most original. He began by talking about the Parable of the Talents, going on from there to the question, the challenge, almost, 'Do we make the most of our lives and opportunities?'

'Last week,' he said, 'I had tea with an old lady.'

There was, of course, nothing extraordinary in this. Rectors and vicars all over the country were having tea with old ladies every day. Especially, perhaps, in small country towns where old ladies are predominant.

'When I came upon her,' continued the rector, 'she was engaged in doing some very beautiful embroidery. Jacobean embroidery, I believe it is called, although I am not very well qualified to speak of such things,' he added deprecatingly, almost with a smile, or the nearest to a smile that was allowable in the pulpit.

'I remarked how beautiful her work was, how much more beautiful than any I had ever seen before.'

Who was this old lady? wondered some of the female members

of the congregation, for they did embroidery, and the rector had not had tea with any of them last week. And yet whose work could be more beautiful than theirs? It was each one's private opinion that her work was much too good for the Parish Sale. One only did it because of the Good Cause and the dear rector. Mrs Wilmot sat quite complacently, thinking what a clever preacher dear Rockingham was. Who would have thought of bringing the everyday things of life into a sermon as skilfully as he did? The embroidery reference did not trouble her at all, as the only needlework she ever had time for was mending her husband's socks and the children's combinations.

The rector continued. 'She told me what she considered the secret of good work. I wonder if I can give you her exact words; I thought she expressed it so well. "Some people don't put in enough stitches," she said, "so that the rich effect is lost, and it looks rather thin. I like to put in as much as I can, so that everything looks really well filled."'

Cassandra started from her pleasant day-dreams and realized that she was the old lady. There was something pleasing about the idea of being really old – say between seventy and eighty, but not infirm or a nuisance to anybody. To have money and leisure to sit in a lovely garden, enjoying the sunshine and doing Jacobean embroidery; to be a comfortable widow, not recently bereaved, but one whose husband had been ten to twenty years in his grave and whose passing was no longer deeply mourned, would not this be a delightful existence? Cassandra asked herself. She imagined herself visiting her husband's grave under the yew trees and putting seasonable flowers on it. She glanced guiltily at Adam, sitting so meekly beside her. One would not have thought to look at him that he had been dragged to church only after much argument and unwillingness. She sighed as she realized how very far she was from being a comfortable old widow. Forty years and more, she thought. But it was nice of the rector to have suggested to her what peace and comfort the far distant future might hold.

'Some people don't put in enough stitches,' repeated the rector, in a slow emphatic voice. 'Isn't that true of many of *us*?' He leaned forward. 'Aren't our *lives* pieces of embroidery that we have to fill in ourselves? Can we truthfully say that we always put in enough stitches? Are there not in all our lives some patches that look thin and not properly filled? Think of the richness of some beautiful piece of embroidery – the design, the colours, the fine stitchery that has been put into it, the labour that has gone to make it what it is. "A thing of beauty is a joy for ever", the poet Keats tells us, "its loveliness increases; it will never pass into nothingness."'

There was quite a stir in the congregation, as the rector had never before been known to quote so much as a line of poetry in a sermon. Adam thought that as it was the first time such a thing had happened, Wilmot might at least have quoted from the local poet, Marsh-Gibbon, and began to rack his brains for something suitable from his own works.

The rector waved his arm in the direction of the altar frontal and the various banners which stood near the altar, so that some of the church workers who had been feeling disgruntled about the unknown old lady regained their good temper as they recognized a reference to their own work. 'Do we not all wish our lives to be like that?' said the rector. 'Rich and finely coloured, each corner well filled and bearing witness to the labour and effort we have expended upon *living*? I think,' said the rector more seriously, 'that if we look upon our lives as we would upon a piece of embroidery, we shall find many bare spaces, or spaces that might have been more beautifully filled. We shall discover places where we should have used a different stitch or a different colour ...'

Janie was whiling away the time by staring at Mr Paladin. He was the only person she could see, except for her father and the choir. I wonder if he really *will* go far, she thought anxiously. She had heard that some clergymen remained curates all their lives. He wasn't really plain-looking, and if he wore horn-rimmed spectacles instead of those ones with gold pieces at the sides he would be quite distinguished. At that moment she saw that Mr Paladin was returning her stare. She blushed and looked away, only to catch the eye of Mrs Gower's gardener, who sang bass in the choir.

The rector is repeating himself, thought Mr Paladin; trying to gain time and overworking the idea. Not really a bad idea, he thought condescendingly. The old lady with her embroidery had been a godsend to a man with the rector's limited intelligence; an idea for a sermon given free, with tea thrown in. Mr Paladin's thoughts were always bolder than his conversation. He generally agreed with everything the rector said, even when, rather surprisingly Mr Paladin thought, he had suggested that he would be better off with a wife. 'Some good woman', the rector had said, by which Mr Paladin had understood 'not Miss Gay', because somehow, nobody seemed to think of her as being a good woman. Who then? His eyes roved round the unpromising congregation. His glance met Janie Wilmot's, and she looked away with becoming modesty. She was hardly old enough to be called a good woman, thought Mr Paladin, but she was quiet and sensible and didn't run after him or say silly things. Also, she was pretty.

Mr Tilos, who had not taken his eyes off Cassandra for a moment of the service, was thinking how agreeable it must be to have a wife. Not a Hungarian wife, although his fiancée Ilonka was a pretty, lively little thing, but an English wife. Someone tall and fair and dignified, who looked charming in the oldest clothes and yet would attract glances of admiration if one walked with her down the *Andrássy-utca*. A nymph, a goddess, in short, Cassandra Marsh-Gibbon.

Surely English women were pre-eminently intended to be delightful wives? Why had nobody ever told him this, and why hadn't he met anyone else like Cassandra? If she were typically English, why weren't there dozens of unmarried Cassandras from whom he could take his choice? He supposed it must be because such charming creatures were all married. Mr Tilos realized that it was unfortunate that he should have chosen to fall in love with the respectable and respected wife of the most important man in the town. But he was not easily put off by trifles. Such an amiable trifle too. Mr Tilos would really have been more at his ease had Adam Marsh-Gibbon been less amiable. He smiled at the recollection of them all sitting in the drawing room, sipping Tokay and peach brandy. Perhaps it was a characteristic of English husbands that they were amiable to their wives' suitors. Or perhaps the husband didn't regard him as a suitor, for Mr Tilos realized sadly that he hadn't done very much to show that he was one, beyond kissing Cassandra's hand and bringing her gifts.

The sermon finished, and the last hymn and prayer were got through quickly. As they walked out, Mr Tilos found himself by Miss Gay. He was afraid that he had neglected the Parisian lady since meeting the nymph of The Grotto. Being naturally a polite man and a braver one than Mr Paladin, he therefore stopped to talk to her, and even accompanied her as far as her front gate. The congregation thus had the satisfaction of seeing Mr and Mrs Marsh-Gibbon walking home to their Sunday roast beef like any respectable English husband and wife. There was no dangerous foreigner lurking near.

The rector was glad of this, and when he saw Mr Tilos and Miss Gay together, he told himself that this was how it should be. For although he was not one to listen to gossip, it did seem as if this Hungarian had been hanging round The Grotto rather too much.

'Your admirer has forsaken you for another,' said Adam to his wife as they walked home.

'No such luck,' said Cassandra complacently. 'He's sure to be round this evening bringing – well, I really don't know what there is left for him to bring.'

'I'm sorry you're tired of him so soon,' said Adam.

'Oh, but I'm not,' said Cassandra, remembering that it would be better policy to pretend some interest in Mr Tilos, 'only I wish he was a little more secret about his love.'

'All right, I'll go for a long walk whenever he seems likely to call,' said Adam. 'Will that suit you?'

'I daresay we could arrange something more convenient than that, especially as you hate going for walks,' said Cassandra vaguely, feeling unequal to finishing what she had started. It was going to be difficult to pretend to be more interested in poor Mr Tilos than she really was, but something was certainly needed to make Adam realize what a real treasure his wife was.

He had done no work for several days since his return from Oxford. He said he was assimilating the knowledge he had acquired about Wordsworth, with a view to considering his novel about the gardener.

'Why can't you write about something of more universal interest?' suggested Cassandra.

Adam wrinkled his nose in distaste.

'Why not write about a husband and wife? Everyone is interested in husbands and wives.'

Adam had to admit the truth of this. 'But what would I write about them?' he asked.

'You could draw on your own experience,' said Cassandra boldly.

'My dear, you must admit I could hardly write a novel about *us*. It would be so dull.'

'It is never dull to record the vicissitudes of love,' declared Cassandra.

> '"By many deeds of shame
> We learn that love grows cold."

A hymn, you know.'

Adam looked at his wife in surprise. 'But our love hasn't grown cold, or at least, not as far as I know. Surely,' he repeated, 'I should have had some idea if our love had grown cold, shouldn't I, my dear?'

'I suppose so,' said Cassandra vaguely. 'I didn't mean *cold* exactly, perhaps lukewarm is a better word. Like the church at Laodicea.'

'But, Cassandra, you know quite well that, as Johnson so aptly puts it, "the pleasures of sudden wonder are soon exhausted and the mind can only repose on the stability of truth." Isn't it nice to think of us reposing on the stability of truth?'

'Yes, dear, very nice,' said Cassandra. 'I don't know if I meant that exactly, though. I'm so bad at explaining myself.'

She supposed that Adam and Johnson must have the last word. There was really nothing more to be said on the subject.

CHAPTER FOURTEEN

'... while heard from dale to dale
Waking the breeze, resounds the blended voice
Of happy labour, love, and social glee.'

During her walk home from church with Mr Tilos, Miss Gay discovered that he played bridge.

'Often in Budapest have I played bridge,' he declared.

'Are you quite sure you don't mean *whist*?' said Miss Gay doubtfully, for it seemed impossible that one could play the same game in Budapest and in Up Callow.

'Please? I do not know that word. What a charming dress you are wearing!' He flashed a brilliant smile at her.

Just at that moment they were passing the Marsh-Gibbons. One in the eye for Cassandra, thought Miss Gay with schoolgirlish glee, for Mr Tilos's voice was loud.

By the time they arrived at the gate of Alameda it was decided that Mr Tilos really did play bridge, and Miss Gay was already planning a bridge party. This time she meant to invite only young or fairly young people. 'You know you're not really keen on bridge,' she said to her uncle. 'It would do you good to go to bed early for a change. When you're getting on, you must take things more easily, you know.'

Mr Gay, who did not fancy the idea of bed at eight o'clock on a light summer evening, bristled with indignation, but he merely said quietly, 'Yes, my dear, it will be nice for you to ask some of your friends in. As it happens, I have an engagement for the evening you mention. I have arranged to take Mrs Gower to the cinema.'

Miss Gay devoted her mind to thoughts of a new dress for the party. Cassandra Marsh-Gibbon was sure to have something new.

As it happened, Cassandra had decided, for various reasons, that she would appear as a sober matron and chose to wear a navy crêpe-de-Chine patterned with little pink daisies, which was in its second season as a bridge-party dress. She realized her wisdom when she saw that Miss Gay was dressed in a brand new creation of plum-coloured cloqué, with a spray of artificial gardenias at the neck.

'Cassandra, how charming you look.' Miss Gay blinked her eyelashes, which were so stiff with mascara that Cassandra stared at them, fascinated. 'I've always liked that dress so much,' said Miss Gay brightly.

'Isn't Tilos coming?' asked Adam, as they were arranging themselves at the bridge tables.

'Oh, he's always late,' said Mrs Wilmot. 'I don't believe he can read the time by English clocks,' she added obscurely.

'I expect it is because he knows he's going to be the centre of attention and likes to keep people waiting,' said Adam.

Poor Adam, thought Cassandra affectionately. He hadn't put on his velvet coat this evening, and looked just like an ordinary English husband.

'Well, you four can start without him. I don't think he'll be long,' said Miss Gay confidently.

So the four, which consisted of Cassandra, Janie, Mr Paladin and Mr Broome, a young man who worked in the bank, started to play and Miss Gay, Adam and Mrs Wilmot made desultory conversation.

When Mr Tilos arrived, there seemed to be a great deal of laughter at everything he said, whether it was funny or not. Mr Tilos, although he had some idea of the game of bridge, had his own individual way of calling and playing. He enjoyed himself immensely, doubling whenever he could, and laughing like a child when he and his partner were badly down. As his partner was Miss Gay it didn't really matter, but Mrs Wilmot wondered whether, as the oldest person present, she ought not to do something to restrain him.

She looked anxiously towards the other table where Janie was playing, partnered by Mr Paladin. It would be splendid, thought Mrs Wilmot, if Janie and Mr Paladin were to take an interest in each other. An interest would be quite enough to begin with, as they were both so young. He looked quite handsome tonight. That young man would go far, in Mrs Wilmot's opinion, for she was inclined to rate a First in Theology higher than her husband did. Besides, he had influential connections.

Everyone knew that Mr Tilos was always going to The Grotto and taking presents for Cassandra, but this evening he was taking no notice of her at all. The town was beginning to be full of interesting and complicated relationships, thought Mrs Wilmot; and she thought it again when, just before eleven o'clock, Mr Gay came in with Mrs Gower and announced that they had been to the cinema together.

'I do hope we haven't disturbed your bridge,' said Mrs Gower, beaming at everyone, 'but the picture finished rather early and Mr Gay said there might be refreshments here.' She laughed.

There were certainly refreshments and, as Mr Tilos seemed to have presented Miss Gay with a case of Hungarian wine, they were all very merry.

'You like this wine, yes?' said Mr Tilos raising his glass. 'Then you will like Budapest. There you must visit the wine cellars at Budafok. Budapest, Queen of the Danube, is flowing with wine.

And all so cheap for the English. You will get there many *pengö* for your pound.'

There was a silence after this speech. Mr Tilos said such unexpected things.

This is really most unusual, thought Mrs Wilmot. But what delicious wine it was; it was making her feel quite sleepy.

Janie, whom the wine had made a little bolder than usual, asked in her clear voice, 'What are *pengö*?'

'*Pengö* is the root of all evil and the secret of happiness,' said Mr Tilos solemnly.

'Oh, I see,' said Janie, 'it's money.'

'How disappointing,' said Mr Broome, making his first contribution to the evening's conversation. 'I thought it was going to be something much more exciting.'

'Fancy not thinking money exciting,' laughed Miss Gay, 'but then you see so much of it every day.'

'And I daresay it has no more influence on you for good or evil than the beautiful and permanent forms of Nature have on most of the Cumberland rustics,' declared Adam.

'I don't think anybody ever gets tired of *spending* money,' said Cassandra, seeing that Mr Broome was looking at Adam with an expression of alarm on his face, 'but I expect you get tired of seeing it, and being surrounded by it every day.'

'Well, yes, I do really,' said Mr Broome gratefully, thankful that he was not after all required to carry on the conversation about Cumberland rustics. He was pleased at the idea of himself as a financial magnate, surrounded by piles of money, when in reality he was the most junior of all the clerks.

'I don't think it's the whole secret of happiness,' said Mr Gay slowly, thinking that although she was one of the nicest and most comfortable people he had ever met, Mrs Gower hadn't got nearly as much money as some of the young women he had unsuccessfully wooed in his youth. 'Although, as Pomfret puts it, "a genteel sufficiency" is almost a necessity if happiness is to be built on a lasting foundation.'

'The eighteenth-century poets say some very sensible things,' remarked Adam benevolently.

'So does our great Hungarian poet also!' interrupted Mr Tilos.

'What is his name?' asked Adam condescendingly. 'I can't say that I've heard anything about him.'

'What! You have not heard of our Petöfi Sandor?' Mr Tilos's tone became so indignant that Cassandra instinctively moved nearer to Adam.

'Well, after all, Hungary is a remote country to us and, unfortunately, very few English people know its language,' she said, anxious to keep the peace. 'You must remember that the average Englishman has not heard of very much outside his own country,' she added, wondering how Adam would like being described as an 'average Englishman'.

Apparently he had not noticed for he went on to support what she had said by adding naïvely that his second book of poems sold only just over a hundred and fifty copies.

This pronouncement silenced everybody, and shortly afterwards the party broke up, following the lead of Mrs Wilmot, who thought she had better go home before the wine made her feel any more sleepy.

Adam and Cassandra offered to take Mrs Gower and Mrs Wilmot home in their car. Cassandra was glad to go. Somehow, she told herself, she hadn't enjoyed the party very much, although there had been amusing moments. Could it be that she was disappointed because Mr Tilos had taken so little notice of her?

Mrs Wilmot was not too sleepy to be pleased at hearing Mr Paladin offering to take Janie home.

'It's a beautiful night, and the walk will do us good,' he explained to Mrs Wilmot, whom he had imagined raising objections.

But she merely smiled, and said that there was a lovely moon. It was nice for young people to walk together in the moonlight, she thought, especially if the young people happened to be Janie and Mr Paladin. What was his Christian name? she wondered. Edward, or Edmund, she couldn't remember which.

Janie was still feeling quite bold, and they had not walked many yards before she took Mr Paladin's arm. He made no attempt to free himself, as he had done when Miss Gay did the same thing. It seemed right and pleasant that they should walk arm-in-arm, and, as Mrs Wilmot had said, there was a lovely moon.

CHAPTER FIFTEEN

'Their colours burnish, and, by hope inspired,
They brisk advance . . . '

'Now that the weather is so nice,' said Adam to Cassandra one morning, 'I think we ought to show Tilos some of the beauties of the countryside.'

'Yes,' said Cassandra doubtfully. 'When do you want to go?'

'When? Oh, any time.'

'How would tomorrow do, if it's still fine?'

'Of course when I say *we* it will probably be *you*,' said Adam, 'because I doubt if I shall be able to spare the time. I'm very busy, you know, and the man would much rather have you as a guide.'

'But, Adam, I couldn't possibly take him by myself, it wouldn't be proper, and I don't know all the legends and dates of things, and styles of architecture, and names of hills, and things like that.'

'You can make them up. Ring him up and suggest tomorrow, about twelve. Say we'll call for him in the car. I may come if I feel like it.'

After hesitating a little, Cassandra went to the telephone and asked for Mr Tilos's number. When Mr Tilos heard her voice he was delighted and relieved. What if Cassandra hadn't minded being ignored at the party? He had just been thinking of renewing his attack by rushing to The Grotto with more lilies. Cassandra's voice sounded cordial. It would be *so* nice if he could come. Mr Tilos was well satisfied.

The day they had chosen for their expedition was bright and sunny. At first Adam had raised some objections but Cassandra managed to persuade him that the air would do him good. As she had anticipated, Cassandra sat demurely in the back of the car with the picnic basket.

'I thought we'd go to Milton Amble,' said Adam. 'We'll see most of the pleasantest villages that way. We can go through Boulderstones and perhaps make a loop through Down Callow and that other place, I can't remember the name but it's charming. Quite typical too. You've nothing like it in Hungary,' he declared, with a positiveness which was all the more startling as he had never visited that country and knew absolutely nothing about its villages. 'You'll find the houses rather mixed,' he went on. Like a tap turned on, thought Cassandra, who was sure poor Mr Tilos wasn't understanding half of what he was saying.

'Now we must find a place to have lunch,' Adam said when they arrived on the outskirts of the village of Milton Amble. After a great deal of argument between Adam and Cassandra and some unheeded suggestions from Mr Tilos, a suitable grassy place was found and Cassandra spread the cloth and laid out the rugs for the picnic. She busied herself ministering to their needs, offering them sandwiches and pieces of veal and ham pie and filling their glasses with beer.

'"Unsavoury food perhaps to spiritual natures",' she said gaily to her husband, interrupting his dissertation on Milton, of whom Mr Tilos had apparently never heard, but Adam took no notice of her. It was Mr Tilos who kept glancing in her direction and smiling secret smiles at her. Cassandra wished he wouldn't stare, as she found it difficult to be continually avoiding his glance. It annoyed her that Adam should sit there so calmly reciting *Lycidas*, completely unaware that Mr Tilos wasn't listening to a word he was saying.

It would serve Adam right if she went off with Mr Tilos. Cassandra amused herself by toying with this idea for a few moments, but then decided that it was impracticable, for apart from any moral considerations there was the important fact that she had no desire to go anywhere with Mr Tilos. But to run away alone, to go for a holiday by herself, that was a very different matter. People could see too much of each other, she thought. *Change*, that was the secret. What if she were to go away by herself for three weeks?

'Cassandra,' said Adam, 'isn't there anything more to eat? I'm still hungry.'

'Of course, dear, look in the basket.' Cassandra's calm voice gave no hint of the plans she was making.

'Oh to live always in the open air,' said Adam, stretching himself luxuriously on the grass and lighting a cigarette, 'to have no cares, not to have to worry about tomorrow ...'

'And to have no cigarettes, and not to know where the next meal's coming from, and to have to sleep on damp grass or prickly bracken,' laughed Cassandra.

'Cassandra, you have no imagination, no poetry,' said Adam in a displeased voice.

'A woman does not need to have such things, it is enough that she is beautiful,' said Mr Tilos, solemnly gazing at Cassandra.

Cassandra looked to see how Adam was taking this remark, but he was stretching and yawning and saying that he had eaten too much and thought he might just have a little nap.

'Do you want to go to sleep too?' she asked Mr Tilos.

'I? Why no.'

'Then let's go for a walk, I feel energetic. Adam,' she said loudly, for his eyes were already closed, 'we're going for a walk.'

'Very well,' he replied drowsily. 'Meet me by the car at three o'clock.'

Mr Tilos gave Cassandra a boyish grin as they walked away from Adam. He was filled with excitement and anticipation at being alone with her. He took her arm and was pleased to notice that she made no attempt to disengage herself.

'Let us find a nice place to sit down,' he said, when they were out of Adam's hearing.

'Well you can if you like,' said Cassandra briskly, 'but I'm going for a walk. I want to go into Milton Amble and see how they're doing up the old cottages, and you might buy something for your house at the antique shop there.'

They walked on for some time without speaking. Mr Tilos still had Cassandra by the arm, although as they came into the village she made some attempt to break away from him. It was quiet in the village and there was very little traffic, but suddenly a car came into sight. Cassandra gave one look at it and, pulling Mr Tilos with her, rushed into a shop they happened to be passing.

'They've some charming hand-woven things in here,' she said in some confusion. 'Let's look around, shall we?'

Mr Tilos found himself forced to pretend an interest in a wooden loom at which a stout young woman in a blue smock was working. Cassandra went over to a table by the window and began to examine some scarves and lengths of home-spun material, peering out surreptitiously, waiting for the car to pass. When it came by she saw that she had been right, for in it was Mrs Gower and the driver was almost certainly Mr Gay. They went past slowly, but were obviously not stopping in the village. Cassandra was glad of this, for although there was nothing wrong in what she was doing, she thought it better that two respectable inhabitants of Up Callow should not see her walking arm-in-arm with Mr Tilos. She was certain that they had not seen her, because they had been too much interested in each other. How nice for two people of their years to find pleasure in each other's company, thought Cassandra benevolently. She was glad the weather was nice for their drive.

When the coast was clear Cassandra and Mr Tilos managed to slip out without attracting the attention of the woman at the loom. 'I didn't want to buy anything,' explained Cassandra, 'everything is so ruinously expensive, although they're handwoven.'

'Yes,' said Mr Tilos, not wishing to make conversation about an occupation which he considered fit only for peasants. 'Do you not feel tired?' he asked hopefully.

'No, I'm still full of energy,' said Cassandra, 'but it will take us all our time to walk to the car. We've quite a long way to go.'

'You know I admire you!' declared Mr Tilos suddenly.

'Hush! People will hear you,' said Cassandra in agitation, for his voice was embarrassingly loud.

'I would want all the world to know,' he declared.

'Don't be silly,' said Cassandra firmly, thinking that it wouldn't matter the whole world knowing as long as the people in Up Callow and thereabouts did not.

They walked on, with Mr Tilos preserving a gloomy silence.

'Here's the car,' said Cassandra with some relief. 'Adam is putting the picnic basket in.'

'Have you had a nice walk?' he asked.

'Lovely. Have you had a nice sleep?'

'Yes. But only quite nice. The ground isn't such a comfortable bed as I thought it would be. But all the same, about twenty more lines of the epic came to me.'

'How lovely,' she said and smiled to herself as she arranged the rugs in the back of the car.

'Cassandra, what are you smiling at?' asked Adam, for he had just been telling Mr Tilos about Milton's three wives and he didn't see anything particularly amusing about that.

'I don't know,' said Cassandra weakly. 'I think it's just been a funny day.'

CHAPTER SIXTEEN

'Endeavouring by a thousand tricks to catch
The cunning, conscious, half-averted glance
Of their regardless charmer ...'

'Mr Tilos seems to have dropped the Marsh-Gibbons,' said Mrs Wilmot to her husband one morning.

'What did you say, dear?' The rector looked up from his paper.

'Oh, I was only saying that Mr Tilos seems to have dropped the Marsh-Gibbons,' said Mrs Wilmot, feeling silly at having to repeat her sentence.

'Well, my dear, I don't see how you can say that,' declared the rector. 'It is hardly in the power of a new resident like Mr Tilos to "drop" anyone of such standing as the Marsh-Gibbons.'

'I am expecting Paladin,' he added, getting up from the table. 'I shall be in my study.'

Mrs Wilmot began aimlessly piling the plates together. She was a little depressed this morning but her face brightened and she felt more cheerful when she saw Mr Paladin coming up the drive.

Since the night of the Gays' party she had begun to think of him as 'dear Edmund', and was already regarding him as a member of the family. Mrs Wilmot glowed with satisfaction as she imagined for her daughter that future of which she herself had been cheated. It was known that the Bishop thought very highly of Mr Paladin, and it was only a matter of time before he would start out on a brilliant ecclesiastical career. Janie had always been a good girl, and that she should fall in love with someone eminently suitable was only to be expected. Mrs Wilmot liked to think that her good upbringing had had something to do with this. She was a little inclined to forget that Janie was only nineteen, and that Mr Paladin was so far the most eligible suitor, indeed the only suitor of any kind, who had presented himself.

In the study the rector was talking to Mr Paladin. His manner was almost that of the genial father-in-law, and yet it was not so marked as to be in any way frightening to a young man; he did not call Mr Paladin 'my dear boy', he was merely kinder and more interested than usual. 'Your last week's sermon was excellent,' he said, 'but don't overwork yourself. Get out into the country sometimes. You can take the afternoon off when you've nothing important to do and I hope we'll see you here for tea sometimes. The children will be home in July. You will see no happier family than ours anywhere. Marriage is a great blessing, and companionship with people of our own age with whom we have tastes in common is a happy preliminary to that state . . . ' The rector paced about the room, flinging out stray sentences, while Mr Paladin stood and listened in respectful silence.

'I know what it is to be young,' continued the rector. 'Yes, I know what it is to be young,' he repeated, as if Mr Paladin might not believe him. 'We want to be with young people when we are young. Janie is staying with her aunt, but she is coming back tomorrow. I am glad that you have become friends. I hope you will go into the country together now that the weather is so good. Janie is very interested in Nature,' he added, and then went on hastily to talk of cricket, as if he had said rather more about Janie than he had intended.

Mr Paladin now joined in the conversation, which took a

more parochial turn, and shortly afterwards went away. Mrs Wilmot watched him out of a bedroom window; he saw her as he was mounting his bicycle, and waved his hand. He rode slowly into the town, smiling to himself, as people in love often do. The inhabitants of Up Callow were now quite used to seeing a smiling Mr Paladin. They smiled too, and there was not a single person who did not think that the young people were admirably suited to each other.

Mr Paladin rode on. He knew he would have to write a sermon some time today, but the thought did not trouble him. Nowadays his sermons got written as if by magic, or even Divine Aid, thought Mr Paladin reverently, for whereas a month ago he had been continually thinking of sermons, his head was now filled with fragments of poetry and other thoughts more suitable and certainly more natural to a young man in love. He passed Miss Gay, but there was no embarrassment or sourness in the smiles they gave each other. Mr Paladin had forgotten his fear of her, and Miss Gay was happy in the knowledge that Mr Tilos had dropped in for tea yesterday, and was taking her to the cinema this evening. He had been most attentive during the last fortnight.

Mr Tilos had not been near The Grotto since the day when Adam and Cassandra had taken him to see the countryside. He had thanked them very charmingly, but had refused their invitation to stay to dinner afterwards. He had been disappointed in Cassandra, for he had imagined her falling into his arms and telling him that her husband did not love her. Mr Tilos thought that perhaps he would not see her for a month. Then he would try again. In the meantime, as he did not care to stay in his half-furnished house all the time, he had taken to calling on Miss Gay.

But he did not find it easy to forget Cassandra or to enjoy himself in Miss Gay's company. Her dark complexion reminded him that Cassandra was delicately fair, her arch manner that his nymph of The Grotto was tantalizingly aloof. Miss Gay accepted his presents greedily and yet casually, as if they were only what was due to her. Cassandra had always been surprised and pleased. But he must not even see Cassandra, and so he was condemned to spend long hours sitting among the aspidistras with Miss Gay, or in the dark intimacy of the three shilling seats at the cinema.

When they sat among the aspidistras they had long, tedious conversations, generally about Love. Miss Gay imagined that Love was making him tongue-tied and she would begin to make advances to him, which he rejected with great skill. If she ever hinted that he ought to be more demonstrative, he would make pretty little speeches about good things increasing in goodness if they were kept, and quote some Hungarian equivalent of 'before, a joy proposed behind, a dream', feeling desperately bored and unhappy, and smiling more and more stiffly, until his face felt as if it would crack.

The object of all this was to make Cassandra jealous. News travelled quickly in a small town, he believed, especially news about people and their love affairs. He did not realize that by calling so often he hardly gave Miss Gay a chance to impart the news of her good fortune to Cassandra. As yet Miss Gay had not found any suitable opportunity. She had met her once in the fishmonger's, but their conversation there had been about fish. It was rather a big jump from filleted plaice to Mr Tilos, and Miss Gay did not feel equal to making it. After all, she was top-dog now, and could afford to be kind to poor Cassandra.

Cassandra was annoyed with Mr Tilos for dropping her so completely. She knew that everyone in the town thought it funny, but nobody had dared say anything about it, with the exception of Mrs Gower. She had taken the opportunity of saying that she thought it a good thing that Mr Tilos had given up calling at The Grotto so much.

'Yes, he has quite forsaken us,' said Cassandra laughing. 'I hear he is courting Miss Gay.'

'Well, I hardly think he is courting her, although he goes to see her a great deal, and may have put some silly ideas into her head.' She paused and went on in a more serious tone. 'I think his coming here has not been a good thing on the whole. He has been made too much of a fuss of. Still, we soon get tired of these little novelties,' she added, as if Mr Tilos were a mechanical toy. 'I think we shall be better when we have settled down for the winter,' she said in a firm tone of voice.

Cassandra liked the definiteness of this last remark. She imagined the evenings drawing in, fires in the morning, and autumn leaves falling untidily over the garden, Mr Tilos back in Budapest, and the events of this disturbed summer behind them. Then she saw that the lupins were out and that it was only June. There was a great deal to be got through before October. She sighed and Mrs Gower sighed too, perhaps out of sympathy or for some reason of her own. Cassandra suddenly felt glad of the stability of things, of the pattern of her life in Up Callow, and the nice solid people who knew and respected her.

Cassandra was annoyed at Mr Tilos's behaviour mainly because he had been an important part of her plan. Although Adam had not shown any signs of being jealous of him, there was always the hope that he might be.

As the days went by Cassandra's thoughts became very confused and she could see no clear solution to her problem, nor even a problem at all, when she thought about it a little longer. Only one idea stood out in her mind. She must go away, abroad, and by herself. She would tackle Adam about it. She chose one evening when, as far as she could tell, he seemed to be in a fairly good temper.

She put her plan into action.

'Poor Adam,' she added, 'you look so tired. I think you need a nice holiday.'

His face lit up at this suggestion. 'Yes, Cassandra, I really do believe I need a holiday. I haven't been at all well this spring. I was beginning to wonder whether there was something really wrong with me,' he went on more happily, 'but perhaps it's only because I need a change.'

Cassandra encouraged him to talk of holidays but did not make any mention of her own plan, except to make him admit that a change was good for everyone.

'I think I shall go to Oxford,' said Adam.

'But won't it be very hot? Oxford's a terribly enervating place.'

'Yes, terribly enervating,' agreed Adam, almost with pleasure. 'In the mornings I shall work in the Bodleian. I might even edit some manuscript. I used to be quite a good palaeographer.'

'I'm sure you're awfully good,' said Cassandra fondly, trying to remember what palaeography was. 'I don't think I shall come to Oxford with you. I should only be bored when you were working, and I've seen all the colleges,' she added simply. 'I think I shall go abroad, for a fortnight,' she said firmly.

'But, my dear child, you couldn't go abroad by yourself. I imagined you'd be staying here.'

'Surely you're not going to leave me alone in Up Callow with Mr Tilos?' said Cassandra pathetically.

Adam evidently hadn't thought of that. Cassandra was pleased to see that he looked rather worried.

'Oh well, then we may as well go somewhere together,' he said.

'Just as you like,' said Cassandra tactfully, 'but I thought your idea of going to Oxford was such a good one. It must be so restful working in the Bodleian, and rest is what you need. But I want to see Budapest. I've heard so much about it. Mr Tilos said it was the City of Love, so perhaps we ought to see it together,' she added, whether hopefully or not she was not sure.

Adam looked puzzled. Cassandra had been harping so much on love during the last few weeks. It was surely unnecessary in a woman who had been happily married for five years, he thought. But then Cassandra was like that, very much apt to clutter up her mind with trivialities. And if she wanted to go abroad by herself, why shouldn't she.

'You would certainly be very bored here without me,' he declared simply.

'I should have Mr Tilos,' she reminded him, 'but I would rather go away.'

'Very well, darling, you shall go away. I daresay the City of Love would be more congenial to you than the Bodleian,' said Adam.

'I suppose it would be,' Cassandra agreed, but she did not sound as certain as she had been. She had won her victory so easily that she felt rather flat. Adam had been so nice about it. Perhaps there wasn't any need to go, after all.

CHAPTER SEVENTEEN

'... the sudden starting tear
The glowing cheek, the mild dejected air,
The softened feature, and the beating heart,
Pierced deep with many a virtuous pang ...'

As the days went by and the arrangements were made, Cassandra began to feel more excited about her holiday. She was really going to Budapest. She almost wished she could tell poor Mr Tilos of her plans so that he could advise her, but she had more faith in her respectable travel agency. She certainly did not want Mr Tilos to know where she was going. Perhaps at the back of her mind was the picture of him leaping on to the end of the train as it moved out of Up Callow station. She knew that this was ridiculous, especially as he had taken no notice of her for three weeks now, but she decided that it was safer to say too little than too much.

Adam fussed around her while she was packing. 'You'd better take your fur coat,' he said. 'It's sure to be cold on the train. I expect you'll be terribly sea-sick. Take some Mothersill and drink plenty of mineral water ...'

So with her ears ringing with Adam's well-meant advice, Cassandra was taken to the station. At the last moment Adam began to wonder if he ought to come to Budapest with her. Cassandra rejoiced to hear his voice so full of concern, and to see his forehead so wrinkled with anxiety, even if most of it was on his own account.

'Do take care of yourself, Cassandra. I shall be nothing without you, absolutely nothing,' said Adam gloomily. 'And what about my food? Have you told them about my food?'

She might have been leaving a pet dog behind her instead of an able-bodied husband, but she kindly reassured him that she had made every arrangement for his comfort. 'I shall only be away for a fortnight,' she reminded him, 'and, besides, you're going to Oxford, and you'll have a lovely time.' She kissed Adam rather tearfully. Now that the moment had come she would rather have been doing anything else in the world than going away.

When the train had pulled out she sat in her corner trying to read, but she could not concentrate because she felt tears pricking at her eyes. To distract her mind she looked out of the window. In the distance she could see Milton Amble church. She looked for it again, but she could no longer see it, as a man passed in the corridor and blocked her view. He looked into the carriage, and the next minute he was inside, exclaiming in a voice that sounded genuinely surprised, 'Oh, Mrs Marsh-Gibbon! This is very nice. You are going away? But of course, *selbstverständlich*.' He looked up at her suitcases and read the labels. 'Köln, München, Salzburg, Wien,' he recited, and then with a cry of delight he pronounced the final name, 'Budapest!'

Cassandra wondered why his way of saying Budapest made it sound such a sinister place. She was glad that he was keeping up a flow of conversation, for she found herself quite incapable of saying anything.

'Why, this is delightful, is it not?' he said, with an anxious little glance at her. 'I too am returning to Budapest. My business requires that I shall go there,' he added, as if Cassandra had doubted the honesty of his intentions.

But Cassandra was past feeling anything so subtle. Seeing Mr Tilos at this moment was altogether too much for her. She tried to pull herself together and make suitable conversation but it was no use. 'Your business?' she said faintly, and then burst into tears.

Mr Tilos moved across and sat down beside her, full of concern.

'What is the matter?' he enquired.

'It sounds ridiculous,' said Cassandra, trying to collect herself, 'but I think I must be home-sick already!'

'You are sick? Oh I am so sorry!' Mr Tilos dived into his pocket and brought out an assortment of things – a bottle of aspirin, some sea-sick tablets and a small bottle of smelling salts.

Cassandra began to laugh uncertainly. 'It isn't that kind of sick,' she managed to say.

Finally, she recovered herself, after Mr Tilos waved the bottle of smelling salts vaguely under her nose and took a large green silk handkerchief from his pocket to dry her tears.

'Thank you,' said Cassandra, hardly knowing where to look in her embarrassment.

'I did not know that the English were so emotional,' said Mr Tilos, in a pleasant conversational tone.

Cassandra was glad of his casual manner. It gave her back some of her self-assurance. 'I'm so sorry,' she said, smiling. 'I'm really terribly ashamed of myself.'

'Do not trouble yourself. I think you would like some tea? Yes?'

'Tea? I'd love some,' said Cassandra. 'But there isn't a restaurant car on the train until we get to Birmingham.'

'But I have tea. Wait a minute, please.' Mr Tilos produced a little basket with handles, just the sort of basket a sensible aunt might have, and inside were two thermos flasks, two cups and some packets wrapped in greaseproof paper.

Cassandra was deeply touched at this.

Mr Tilos handed her a jam sandwich. 'It is plain food,' he said, 'but healthy I think.'

'It's lovely,' said Cassandra warmly, 'and I'm sure it must be healthy. It's making me feel so much better.'

What an excellent and useful man Mr Tilos was, she thought, and what a pity he spoilt things by embarrassing her with his protestations of affection.

And then she wondered, did anyone in Up Callow know that Mr Tilos had got on to this train. If they did, then there would no longer be any doubt about it. To all intents and purposes, she had gone off with Mr Tilos.

CHAPTER EIGHTEEN

''Twas friendship heightened by the mutual wish'

'I wonder where Mr Tilos can be going?' said Mrs Gower, looking over her garden wall on the day when Cassandra left for Budapest. 'He seems to be going away somewhere. He's wearing a hat and carrying an overcoat; he has a suitcase too, and a basket, but there doesn't seem to be any more luggage in the back of his car. Can you see him, Mr Gay?'

'No, I can't see him, and I'm much too comfortable here to get up and look. But you've given me such a good picture of him that I feel I've missed nothing,' said Mr Gay, smiling. He often smiled nowadays, and even laughed sometimes. On this sunny morning he was sitting in a deckchair in Mrs Gower's garden. He was finding that her garden and her company were much pleasanter than his own garden and his niece's company.

'I daresay he is going to Birmingham,' said Mrs Gower, still on the subject of Mr Tilos.

'Yes, perhaps he is,' said Mr Gay lazily. 'Let us be thankful that *we* are not going there.'

'And yet I don't see why he should be taking a heavy overcoat to Birmingham in June.'

'You never know what these foreigners will do,' said Mr Gay, giving the fact of Mr Tilos taking his overcoat to Birmingham in June a deep, almost sinister significance.

'Well, I suppose he *must* be going to Birmingham,' said Mrs Gower reluctantly and was just about to leave the matter when Mr Tilos saw her and came over to the wall.

'I go to Budapest,' he said. 'My business requires that I shall go there.'

'Your business?' said Mrs Gower uncertainly.

'Yes, my business,' repeated Mr Tilos firmly. 'I go only for a few weeks,' he said reassuringly. But Mrs Gower was not reassured.

'Well,' she said when Mr Tilos had gone, 'we now know that he is going to Budapest. On business.'

'I never knew that he *had* any business,' said Mr Gay.

'Wasn't Cassandra Marsh-Gibbon going to Budapest today?' said Mrs Gower, trying to make her voice sound light and casual.

'Was she?' Mr Gay looked doubtful. 'Perhaps it was some place that sounded like it. Belfast,' he said uncertainly. 'Or Bucharest. That would be more likely.'

'I don't think it was either of those places,' said Mrs Gower. 'They aren't really the sort of places one does go to, are they? I'm sure Cassandra said something about going to Budapest. We've heard so much about it lately, of course. But fancy Mr Tilos going there too, on the same day and on the same train. That seems rather funny, doesn't it?'

'Yes, but I don't suppose there's anything in it,' said Mr Gay. 'Do you?'

'No, certainly not,' said Mrs Gower emphatically, but as her eye caught Mr Gay's she knew that he was thinking the same as she was.

'I suppose it must have been them in Milton Amble that afternoon we went out for a drive,' he said.

'Yes,' said Mrs Gower. 'They were arm-in-arm, weren't they?'

'Yes,' said Mr Gay, 'they were arm-in-arm.' He was equally definite.

'What a pity,' said Mrs Gower, almost as if walking arm-in-arm in Milton Amble were worse than going off and leaving one's husband. 'Cassandra's so nice too. And we've always thought her such a model wife, so devoted to her husband.'

'Yes, they always seemed to be so happy. I wonder what Marsh-Gibbon will do now? Of course he will be a broken man.'

'I suppose he will.' Mrs Gower nodded gloomily.

It seemed as if there was nothing more to be said about it. It did not occur to either of them to doubt that Cassandra had gone off with Mr Tilos.

'I thought Mr Tilos had been to *your* house a great deal lately,' said Mrs Gower tentatively.

'Yes, I don't know what Angela will say about all this,' said Mr Gay. His face clouded over at the thought of facing his niece when he got home.

'I can't believe that it can be true,' said Mrs Gower. 'Dear Cassandra, she was always such a nice girl.' Already she was being spoken of in the past tense, with sad shakings of the head.

Mr Gay went home, wrapped in gloomy thoughts. He dreaded going into the house. Angela was in the drawing room, sitting on a hard chair by the window, doing nothing. She did not look up or say anything when her uncle came into the room, but this was not unusual. It was not their custom to greet each other more than was necessary. Still, Mr Gay felt that there was a certain delicacy about the subject. He could not bring himself to say, 'Have you heard that Cassandra Marsh-Gibbon has gone off to Budapest with Mr Tilos?' because they were not absolutely sure that she had. And yet there seemed no doubt about it. He tried to think of something else. There was a funny smell, like something burning, but as it was summer there was no fire in the room, or, indeed, in any of the rooms except the kitchen.

'Angela,' he said, 'do you smell a peculiar smell?'

'No more than usual,' she replied curtly.

'I think there must be something burning.' Mr Gay got up and went into the kitchen. 'Amy,' he said to the maid, 'do you smell something burning?'

'Oh, it must be that knitting of Miss Angela's,' said Amy, quite unperturbed.

'Knitting? Where?'

Amy pointed towards the fire and Mr Gay saw a green woolly mass smouldering among the coals. Some of it had burnt away, but there was no need for him to ask what it was. He recognized it as a pullover that Angela had been knitting for Mr Tilos. So she did know, after all. And she had burnt what was more or less a perfectly good pullover, for it had been nearly finished. He stood for a while looking pensively into the fire.

'I didn't put it there, sir,' said Amy, in an aggrieved tone of voice.

'Oh, I'm sure you didn't,' said Mr Gay hastily, and went out of the kitchen. He crept quietly up to his bedroom, and sat there filing his nails until half past seven, when he came down to the dining room. Supper was a gloomy meal. Angela must have decided that although she was, to all intents and purposes, a woman scorned, she would not show it in the orthodox way. If she had felt fury surging within her, she had evidently worked it off by throwing the pullover into the fire. By supper-time she seemed to have become Patience on a monument, smiling at grief, so that Mr Gay was profoundly irritated. She was a woman of thirty, he told himself, and she was making herself ridiculous. 'Come, Angela,' he said shortly, 'surely you're going to eat more than that bit of dry toast? This macaroni cheese is excellent.'

'No, thank you. I can't take food.'

'Don't be silly. I can't think why you're making such a fuss. Mr Tilos has gone to Budapest on business. He told us so himself; he said he was coming back in a week or two. And anyway, it isn't as if you'd been engaged to the fellow.'

'I have had a great shock,' she said. 'I think you might realize that.'

'But he'll soon be back and in the meantime it won't do you any good to go without your supper.'

'No, he won't come back,' said Miss Gay, as if she had made up her mind, and really preferred it to be so.

After supper Mr Gay found that he was still unable to settle to his reading, so he went for a walk. After a while he found that he had arrived at Mrs Gower's house. Quite soon he was sitting in her drawing room.

'Come to the fire,' she said. 'I always like one in the evenings. Just because it's June it doesn't mean it can't be chilly.'

Mr Gay gave her a grateful look. What an excellent woman she was! They never had a fire in the summer in his house. The fireplace was ruthlessly filled up on the first of May, wet or fine, with a large and hideous Victorian firescreen.

He drew his chair nearer the fire. Mrs Gower did not seem to think it at all strange that he should be calling on her at half past nine in the evening. It seemed quite natural that they should be sitting there together. Lucky Professor Gower to have had such a wife! What matter if she had been bored by *Epipsychidión*, and known nothing of Middle English? Good sense and kindliness, a little money if possible – for Mr Gay was now growing more modest in his demands – surely that was all one wanted in a wife? The idea of spending the rest of his life with Mrs Gower was suddenly the nicest thing he could think of. With all the disturbing happenings of the day, Cassandra going off with Mr Tilos, Angela burning the pullover in the kitchen fire and refusing to eat macaroni cheese of which she was usually so fond, Mrs Gower seemed to be the only stable thing left in a changing world. 'What a sensible woman you are,' he said aloud. It was, perhaps, a curious thing to say, but Mrs Gower did not appear to think so.

'Well, I try to be,' she said calmly. 'I've come to the conclusion that it's really the best thing to be at our age.'

'But chiefly let her humour close with thine,' thought Mr Gay. How well suited they were to each other! 'I think you and I agree on all subjects,' he said tentatively, for after all it would not do to take too much for granted. Just because Mrs Gower had given away the stuffed parrot it didn't necessarily mean that she was willing to take a second husband.

'Yes, we do,' said Mrs Gower. 'I have noticed it more and more lately.'

'Then I believe we could be happy together. Laura, will you marry me?'

'Yes.'

This, thought Mr Gay, must be the most sensible and satisfactory proposal in the history of the world. No insincere raptures, no coy refusals not meant to be taken seriously, just the necessary question and the answer, a simple affirmative.

'I am happy to know that you feel as I do,' said Mr Gay. 'You must have seen that I am very fond of you.'

'Yes. Mr Gay, Philip, we cannot expect to be passionately in love at our time of life, but I think we shall make each other very comfortable.'

'Very comfortable.' How nice that sounded. Wasn't it, after all, what everyone wanted to be? Especially when they were nearing what the rector called 'the autumn of life'. It made Mr Gay think of a pleasant drawing room, with a fire on the chilly evenings, well-tended aspidistras, tea and toast in the winter ...

'Shall we be married soon?' he asked.

'Yes, quite soon, don't you think? After all, we mustn't forget that we each have one foot in the grave and may not have many more years left to us.'

Mr Gay laughed. This time having one foot in the grave was a pleasant joke, but it reminded him of Angela, and a shadow crossed his face at the thought of her.

Mrs Gower must have known what he was thinking, for she took his hand in hers, and said with a positiveness that was completely reassuring, 'Now, Philip, you are not to worry about Angela. We will find her a husband.'

CHAPTER NINETEEN

'From look to look, contagious through the crowd
The panic runs, and into wondrous shapes
The appearance throws ...'

'Well, so you're a lonely man,' said the rector heartily, as he met Adam Marsh-Gibbon in the town one afternoon.

It was the day after Cassandra's departure, and the news that she had gone to Budapest with Mr Tilos was already being eagerly discussed. Even the rector had heard it, but he thought it best to make some reference to Cassandra's absence, if only a joking one. It might seem pointed to avoid the subject altogether.

'Yes. My wife has left me,' said Adam simply.

'I'm sorry to hear that,' said the rector, trying to infuse a mixture of flippancy and concern into his tone, as he never knew whether to take Adam seriously or not.

'Yes,' agreed Adam. 'I am going to Oxford to read in the Bodleian, but she has chosen Budapest, which is the City of Love, according to our friend Tilos. Perhaps she has chosen the better part. I really think she has,' he said thoughtfully.

'Well, she will have nice weather,' said the rector hastily, changing the subject. His voice was now rather stern. What right had Tilos to talk to a respectable married woman about things like Cities of Love? And was it not frivolous and unbecoming of her husband to mention it as if it were a thing of no importance? Or perhaps, thought the rector glancing quickly at Adam, he did not consider it important. Adam's face told him nothing. He was looking as he generally did, handsome and pleased with himself. Well, there was no knowing what these modern writers thought, decided the rector, sliding out of the difficulty easily; it was not for him to make any comment. It was much better to leave well alone sometimes. Everyone was saying that Cassandra Marsh-Gibbon had gone off with Tilos, but judging from her husband's manner it couldn't be true.

'Where is Tilos these days?' asked Adam calmly. 'He hasn't been near us for weeks.'

The rector gaped. 'He's gone away,' he said hurriedly.

'Oh, really? It hasn't taken him long to get tired of us. Where's he gone?'

'Europe, I believe,' said the rector feebly, but somehow he could not bring himself to say Budapest straight out.

Adam laughed. 'I expect he's gone to Budapest. He'll be able to take Cassandra about,' he declared calmly. 'She can't speak a word of anything but English and she always misses the things she ought to see if she hasn't got a reliable person with her.'

'I'm sure that Mr Tilos would be an excellent guide,' said the rector dubiously, but one could hardly describe him as a reliable person, he thought.

Adam walked slowly back to The Grotto. So Tilos had gone to Budapest as well. He must have been on the same train as Cassandra, although it was funny that they hadn't seen him. Nor had Cassandra mentioned him on her postcard, which Adam had received that morning. She said that she had had a pleasant journey, quite uneventful. She had ended, 'Take care of yourself, darling. All my love, Cassandra.'

Cassandra had spent a long time writing her simple postcard. She had had Mr Tilos's company from Milton Amble to

Paddington, and he had behaved just like a nice maiden aunt all the time, except that he was much more efficient at dealing with taxis and luggage. He had seen her to her hotel, where she was to stop overnight, and then left her. They would meet next morning, when he would come in a taxi to take her to Victoria. When she came to write to Adam, Cassandra found herself in the difficult position of not knowing what to say about Mr Tilos, or even whether to mention him at all. She felt that he needed explaining, and yet there was no room on a postcard to tell Adam, at such length as would convince him, that she was still his faithful and loving wife. Eventually, as there was little time and she did not feel up to writing a letter, she made no mention of Mr Tilos. After all, it was improbable that anyone knew that he was going to Budapest as well, she thought hopefully, and she didn't want to start any rumours that might be misinterpreted.

As Adam walked about Up Callow he noticed that people seemed awkward in their manner to him, even sympathetic so that with all this and the postcard, Adam began wondering whether Cassandra *had* left him after all and he was the only person who didn't know it. But Cassandra was sensible and business-like. If she had intended to go off with Mr Tilos she would certainly have told him, or at least have informed him on a postcard or left a letter behind. But Cassandra had left no letter on her dressing table, or on her pillow, or in any place where an eloping wife might be expected to leave such a thing.

Adam glanced distastefully at the papers spread about his desk. They were all muddled. The novel about the gardener and the beginnings of a Hungarian romance had somehow got mixed up together, and the epic poem was nowhere to be found. He took up his pen and wrote down a good phrase that had occurred to him, but apart from that he was uninspired. He smoked a cigarette and then went to look for something to eat.

In the dining room Lily was laying the table.

'Dinner will be ready in a quarter of an hour, sir. Or I could give you a snack now, but it would only spoil your dinner.'

'Yes, I suppose it would,' said Adam meekly and went away to brood over his crossword until Lily called him.

During dinner he sat with his elbows on the table and his spectacles on, and stared down at his plate. He ate everything that was put before him, doggedly but gloomily.

After dinner he felt bored and depressed with nobody to talk to. He opened a book but it did not interest him. At last he decided to go out and call on somebody. Perhaps there were other people similarly depressed. They might all cheer each other up, he thought hopefully.

Adam had no really close friends in Up Callow, or, indeed, anywhere. He had his writing, his local fame and a charming and loving wife. As long as he was admired he was quite content. But this evening he found himself wishing that he had some intimate friend to whom he could go and in whom he could confide his troubles.

He walked until he came to the church. It looked very picturesque in the half-light, with its setting of yew trees and tombstones. Adam contemplated the scene for some time and began to feel the charm of philosophic melancholy. He climbed over the low wall. Perhaps he would find comfort and inspiration here. The eighteenth-century poets certainly seemed to have found both in churchyards, he reflected. How Blair must have enjoyed writing his poem 'The Grave'. 'Midst skulls and coffins, epitaphs and worms', thought Adam, deciding that in future he would spend more time here. He might even write an epic poem, on Judgement Day. He could not remember that many had been written lately, and it was the kind of subject, he thought mistakenly, that would be greatly appreciated in Up Callow.

'Why, Mr Marsh-Gibbon. All alone in the churchyard!'

He turned and saw the dim shape of Angela Gay standing beside him. His pleasant eighteenth-century-graveyard mood vanished.

'And what are *you* doing here?' he asked her rather rudely.

'Oh, I might as well be here as anywhere else. There is nothing left for me now.' She smiled her Patience on a monument smile, but it was dark and he did not see it. He merely thought that she sounded rather strange. It occurred to him that he was feeling rather cold.

'I see there is a light in your drawing room,' he said. 'I think that I might enjoy a cup of tea.'

Miss Gay was looking at him with something that might almost have been compassion, but he did not see that either. He quickened his step and was glad to be in the lighted drawing room of Alameda. Here a happy domesticated scene met his eyes. Mr Gay and Mrs Gower, or Philip and Laura as they now were to each other, were sitting side by side on the sofa, Mr Gay holding on his hands a skein of wool which Mrs Gower was winding. It was just like the happy evenings he used to spend with Cassandra, thought Adam sentimentally, ignoring the fact that he had never held wool for her to wind. Cassandra knew better than to expect it.

'We are going to have some tea,' said Mr Gay. 'I hope you will join us. Or would you rather have some whisky?'

'I'm sure he'd prefer tea,' said Miss Gay rather scornfully, piqued that Adam had not turned to her as a fellow sufferer.

'Yes, thank you, I would,' said Adam. But as he made desultory conversation he thought that there was nothing for him here. The old lovers were happier by themselves and he certainly didn't want to be comforted by Miss Gay. Tomorrow he would go to Oxford. There he could be tolerably happy. A writer and a scholar, working in the Bodleian.

CHAPTER TWENTY

'The choice perplexes. Wherefore should we choose?'

As soon as they were comfortably settled in the train at Ostend, Mr Tilos stopped behaving like a maiden aunt. Cassandra had been wondering when it would happen and had hoped that he would not drop this comfortable attitude until they were on Hungarian soil, or even in Budapest itself, when she could more easily escape.

During the crossing from Dover to Ostend she had tried to find out, as tactfully as possible, whether anyone in Up Callow had known that Mr Tilos was travelling on this train and going to the same place as she was.

'Oh, no,' he said, 'only the old woman who lives across the road, Mrs Gower. I told her that I go to Budapest and her friend Mr Gay who was with her in the garden.'

Cassandra was doubtful if Mrs Gower and Mr Gay would be able to keep this fascinating piece of news to themselves, and since Mrs Gower knew that she was going to Budapest she could hardly be blamed for putting two and two together and making quite the wrong number.

Mechanically she made pleasant conversation on general subjects, looking out of the window of the train and remarking on the flatness of the Belgian countryside, the clemency of the weather and the likelihood of its being hot in Budapest, but as she talked she was wondering how she could escape without creating a scene that might draw attention to them. She wished desperately that there was some other person in their railway carriage, especially when Mr Tilos seized her hand and cried, 'Why do you not look at me? Do you not care for me at all? Why, then, do you go to Budapest?'

'I certainly do not,' said Cassandra firmly, 'and I am going to Budapest for a holiday. I had no idea that you were going too.'

Such forthrightness was, she decided, the best way to deal with the situation. Mr Tilos became silent and, releasing her hand, sat hunched in his corner looking out of the window. Cassandra glanced at him and saw that he was likely to go on sulking for some time and thought that this was a good opportunity to escape into the corridor and find more congenial travelling companions.

All the third-class carriages seemed to be full. Many of the occupants were eating, playing cards, and even singing. There seemed to be a party of students on the train, and Cassandra came across groups of them in the corridors, smoking and talking in loud excited voices. They all looked kind and friendly, but Cassandra was making for another party she remembered seeing on the boat at Ostend, a group of middle-aged, respectable-looking people, with a tall clergyman who seemed to be their leader. She was beginning to think that they must have stayed behind in Ostend, when she heard a voice calling. It was a fluty, cultured voice, the voice of an English spinster of uncertain age, Cassandra decided, just the sort of voice she wanted to hear. The sound of it was music in her ears after Mr Tilos's gentle but sinister foreign accents.

'Canon Coffin! Canon Coffin!' called the voice.

Cassandra, who had been standing looking out of the window, turned to her right and saw a grey-haired woman hurrying down the corridor. She was small and efficient-looking, and wore pince-nez. In her hand she had a pencil, and a piece of paper that looked as if it might be a list. From a carriage just beyond where Cassandra was standing there emerged the figure of a tall clergyman. This must be Canon Coffin, thought Cassandra. In spite of his depressing name he had a kindly face, beaming with smiles. Cassandra recognized him as the man she had seen on the boat.

'Oh, Canon Coffin, here's the list,' said the woman. They stood talking in the corridor, so that Cassandra was able to hear all their conversation.

'Thank you, Miss Edge,' said the clergyman. 'All those on the list will be taking dinner when we get to Brussels, I presume?'

'Yes. Miss Lomax and Miss Fye are dining with friends. And Mrs Dewbury won't be with us at the Pension Flora tonight. She has a nephew at the Embassy, and is staying the night with him and his wife.' This information was given in a slightly scornful tone, which was at the same time a little aggrieved. It was as if Miss Edge had heard too much about the nephew at the Embassy, and had hoped for an invitation to meet him which had not been forthcoming.

Cassandra's heart warmed towards these people. She felt that she would be at home among them. She hoped that they would like her too. She did not think they could disapprove of her, for although she was more smartly dressed than in Up Callow, in a blue suit with silver fox furs, her face was made up quite discreetly, and she had natural-coloured polish on her nails.

She walked along a little way, hoping that Miss Edge might speak to her when she had finished her business with Canon Coffin. She was not disappointed. In a few minutes she heard the fluty voice saying, 'Excuse me, but are you with *us*?'

How comforting that *us* sounded, thought Cassandra. She

turned round and smiled. 'No, I'm not,' she said, 'but I'd very much like to be. I'm all by myself,' she lied, 'and I'm longing for someone to talk to.'

'Oh, you *must* join us,' said Miss Edge enthusiastically. 'We're quite a lively party.'

'You're very kind,' Cassandra smiled.

'That was Canon Coffin I was speaking to just now. He's our leader. His wife is with us too, but she doesn't *travel* well, if you know what I mean, so I'm doing all the secretarial work on the journey, but of course I really enjoy it. I run the St Monica's Guild at home.'

She chatted on until Cassandra felt that she knew a great deal about the party and its members. There were seventeen of them, three clergymen and their wives, three widows and eight spinsters, all inhabitants of a West Country cathedral town. They were making a fortnight's tour of South Germany and the Austrian Tyrol.

Cassandra said that she had left her luggage further up the train, but that she would go and fetch it and then join Miss Edge and her companions in their carriage.

'I'm sure Canon Coffin would go along with you and help you carry it,' said Miss Edge.

Cassandra, remembering his kindly face, was sure that he would, but then he would see Mr Tilos and everything would be spoilt. 'Please don't trouble him,' she said hastily. 'I've only a dressing case – I sent the rest of my luggage on in advance.' She marvelled at how adept she was becoming at lying.

Cassandra found Mr Tilos sitting just as she had left him, still sulking in his corner seat. He showed some interest when she came in and looked up hopefully.

'What are you doing with your case?' he asked anxiously.

'It has all my make-up things in it,' said Cassandra. 'I am going to have a wash and tidy myself up.'

She made her escape from the carriage, hoping that he would not come searching for her. She had had to abandon her big suitcase and hoped he would look after it for her. It was labelled with the name of the hotel in Budapest, so she trusted that he would see that it arrived there safely. She would be joining it in her own time.

She almost ran down the corridor and was relieved to see Miss Edge standing by the carriage door, obviously waiting for her.

'Oh, good,' she said. 'There are four of us in here, plenty of room for another,' and she introduced Cassandra to Mrs Dewbury, Miss Lomax and Miss Fye.

Mrs Dewbury was sitting in a corner by the window, and looked rather defiantly at Cassandra, as if expecting that she might have to give up her seat and being determined not to. She was a plump woman who looked about sixty-five. She wore an assortment of gold chains round her neck, from one of which hung a pair of eyeglasses. Her fingers were loaded with old-fashioned rings, set with diamonds and turquoises.

Miss Lomax and Miss Fye were much younger. Cassandra would have said that they were in the late thirties. They looked very much alike, rather dim and faded, with wispy brown hair, and sensible brown tweed costumes. They both looked up at Cassandra with quick, friendly smiles, and made room for her on their side of the carriage.

'I do hope I'm not disturbing you,' said Cassandra.

'Not at all,' said Miss Lomax and Miss Fye together. 'We're glad to have you with us.'

Cassandra learned after more experience that they nearly always seemed to make their remarks in chorus. She sat down, and glanced at Mrs Dewbury, who had not as yet shown any signs of welcoming her. 'I suppose I ought to introduce myself,' she said shyly. 'I'm Mrs Gibbon.' She had decided to leave out the 'Marsh', in case people should ask if she were any relation to the author of that name, although she was not at all certain that Adam's fame would have reached the inhabitants of a remote West Country cathedral town. Still, it was better to be safe, and Mrs Gibbon was a good plain name without actually being an assumed one.

'Where are you travelling to?' Miss Edge enquired.

'Budapest,' said Cassandra, trying to look like a seasoned traveller.

'*Alone?*' asked Miss Lomax and Miss Fye in sympathetic chorus.

'Well,' Cassandra hesitated, and then realized that she would have to say something. 'I'm meeting my husband there.' How she wished that it was true.

'Are you going straight through, or are you spending the night in Brussels?' asked Miss Edge.

'I would like to spend the night in Brussels,' Cassandra said, thinking of her escape from Mr Tilos. 'But,' she added, trying to sound pathetic, 'I'm not sure where ...'

'I don't like to think of you wandering about Brussels on your own,' said Miss Edge, with a worried frown. 'You hear of such things ... Now, I wonder ...'

Cassandra sat back and listened contentedly. Obviously Miss Edge was the sort of person who was used to arranging things and loved it. For although she could perfectly well have gone to a hotel, she would feel much safer from Mr Tilos if she spent the night at the Pension Flora.

'Of course,' said Miss Edge tentatively, 'you would have to share a room with one of us. Would you mind that?'

Cassandra felt that she would rather share a room with all the eight spinsters and three widows than be in the same town alone with Mr Tilos. So she thanked Miss Edge and smiled at everyone and asked what to do about paying.

'Oh, that will do later, dear,' said Miss Edge. 'We can settle that on the train going to Frankfurt.'

It was very comforting to be called dear and to know that she was to be safe until they reached a place as remote as Frankfurt. Cassandra leaned back against the hard clean wood of the carriage and thought of Mr Tilos, sulking in his cushioned second-class luxury.

As the train drew into Brussels, Canon Coffin came down the corridor and warned people to get ready and collect their luggage. Miss Edge introduced Cassandra to him and he beamed kindly on her, which made her feel like a wolf in sheep's clothing, which was quite a new experience for her.

While the group was bustling about on the platform fussing with their luggage, Cassandra moved up the platform to where Mr Tilos was surrounded by his own and her luggage.

'I am staying the night in Brussels,' she said pleasantly. 'With some friends,' she added, indicating the three clergymen, their wives, the three widows and the eight spinsters. 'Do you think you could very kindly see to my luggage for me? I will only need my dressing case,' and she gave him the name of her hotel in Budapest.

For a moment it looked as if he was going to protest, and she held her breath. But then he bowed coldly and said something in Hungarian which, fortunately, perhaps, she was not able to understand. He was upset and annoyed, but, thought Cassandra resentfully, I certainly never gave him any encouragement, so it's all his own fault.

She felt a mixture of guilt and annoyance and was glad to be interrupted by Canon Coffin, raising his voice to command the attention of the group. 'Now come along everybody. The luggage is going to the Pension Flora, so will you please leave it over here in a pile? Then we can all go to the restaurant where we are to have dinner.'

The party moved off the platform and Cassandra joined them quickly. As she went she turned her head and saw Mr Tilos still standing there amid the luggage, looking very forlorn.

'Now are we all ready?' came Canon Coffin's voice, and they filed out of the station. Cassandra marched happily between Miss Edge and a tall thin woman called Miss Crump.

In the restaurant, when they were arranging themselves at their tables, a clergyman sat down heavily next to Cassandra.

'I think this is the best place,' he said rather anxiously, looking around him to see how far he was from the door. 'Since my recent illness it is quite fatal for me to sit in a draught. Quite fatal,' he repeated, so that she should realize the gravity of the situation. She was somehow reminded of Adam and for a moment she felt quite melancholy, until Canon Coffin addressed the clergyman cheerfully.

'Well, Langbaine, we certainly couldn't have that! Now then, everybody, what are we all going to drink?'

'Water,' said one of the spinsters firmly.

'Oh, you can't have ordinary water,' said Miss Edge. 'I believe it isn't fit to drink, but I believe you can get some very nice *mineral* water, non-alcoholic, of course.'

'Personally, I think some wine would be nice. It would revive us after our long journey,' said Canon Coffin, making it seem quite respectable.

'Well, perhaps it *would* be rather nice,' ventured another of the spinsters. 'It isn't as if we *often* have it.'

Cassandra smiled. While the question of the drink was being settled she was able to observe her neighbour.

The Reverend William Langbaine was a tall man of about forty-five. He was dark and going a little bald. He had a thin pale face and wore horn-rimmed spectacles. Cassandra noticed that he was wearing a thick grey hand-knitted pullover under his jacket. She wondered whether it had been knitted for him by some devoted lady of the parish, but decided that he did not look like the sort of clergyman who would inspire such devotion and that it had probably been made by his wife.

'I think I will have some mineral water,' she said. 'I think it would be more refreshing than wine.'

'I believe it is delicious,' said Miss Edge. 'Mrs Dewbury told me that they always have it at the Embassy. Is your wife not well, Mr Langbaine?' she asked, putting on her pince-nez and giving him a sharp glance.

'No. Ethel is a poor traveller,' he said carelessly, 'so she has gone straight to the Pension. Mrs Coffin has gone with her, I believe. She will be taking a little Bovril in bed. Much the best thing for nausea,' he said with authority.

After dinner they all trooped off to the Pension Flora. A few of the bolder spirits had gone sight-seeing in the dark, but Cassandra was feeling tired after her full, exciting day. She found that she was to share a room with Miss Edge. The proprietress of the Pension, a grim, dark-haired woman, showed them into a room papered in dull crimson damask, with heavy red velvet curtains and massive furniture. She indicated with a sweep of the hand what were its advantages and amenities, and shut the door behind her.

Cassandra was relieved to see that there were two beds, very high, with ornately carved wooden headboards and covered with strange plumped-up feather quilts.

If the shocked inhabitants of Up Callow could see her now, she thought, as Miss Edge made polite remarks about wardrobe space, how surprised they would be, perhaps even a little disappointed, that instead of being with Mr Tilos she was sharing a room with the secretary of the St Monica's Guild.

CHAPTER TWENTY-ONE

'Books are but formal dulness, tedious friends.'

In his lodgings in Oxford Adam finished his breakfast quickly and hurried out to work. He was not at all sure what that work was to be, but he thought he would start by going to Balliol to call on his old tutor.

In the lodge the porter remembered him. This pleased Adam and made him feel more cheerful. This mood did not last, however, for when he enquired for his tutor he was told that he had died the previous month.

'But he wasn't an *old* man,' said Adam, half to himself.

'Well, no, sir, but he wasn't young. He was in his fifties.'

'I shall be in my forties quite soon,' said Adam despondently and he turned and walked out of the lodge and along Broad Street to the Bodleian feeling very depressed. It was ridiculous to be plunged into gloom by the death of his tutor, a man he hardly ever thought of, but this and the fact of Cassandra's absence induced in him a mood of melancholy, so that by the time he was walking up the steps of the Bodleian he had almost resigned himself to never seeing Cassandra again.

He walked into the Picture Gallery and then through into the English Reading Room. He set out his things on a desk and began walking vaguely round, looking at the books on the open shelves. Eventually he took down de Selincourt's edition of 'The Prelude', thinking of Cassandra's impatience with Wordsworth. After trying to read for a few minutes, Adam began to feel impatience too.

He shut up the book with a bang and looked around at his neighbours. One was busily writing an essay, another was engrossed in Emerson's *Middle English Reader*. Adam saw that he was writing down all the unfamiliar words in a notebook.

Outside, the clocks began to strike eleven. At once the Reading Room was full of movement. It seemed as if everybody had an eleven o'clock lecture. Then he suddenly remembered that it wasn't that at all; it was the coffee hour. This depressed him still further. It made him feel old to see all the young people going off to Elliston's to drink coffee, eat chocolate biscuits and criticize the people around them. He saw them putting PLEASE LEAVE notices on their piles of books and going out together. He decided that he was at least ten years too old for this place. He got up quickly and walked out. It had been just the same in Mr Gay's drawing room, but there it had been old people. There was nothing for him here either.

After lunch, Adam found himself walking round the Botanical Gardens. Here it was very pleasant and he began to feel a little less gloomy. The sun was out, the rock-garden and borders were ablaze with flowers and there were some orchids in the tropical houses. How Cassandra would have loved it!

Adam felt so much better after tea that he decided to give the Bodleian another chance. He would go and work in Duke Humphrey. There, enshrouded in history, he would find peace and contentment. As he walked up the stairs, he met a crowd of minions clattering down to their tea. The library was quiet and deserted. Adam walked up to the Selden End, looking into the little alcoves as he passed. Eventually he chose a seat by an old man who had his back to him. He seemed to be a clergyman and he wore a suit that looked quite green with age. The top of his head was bald and fringed with greenish-grey hair. He took no notice of Adam but went on reading in a large calf-bound volume.

Adam began to write odd lines of his epic poem and then wandered about looking at various books and reading the *Dictionary of National Biography* to see if he could detect any mistakes in it. Then he went up to the Catalogue to look up several books he might want to read. He also looked up his own novels and poems and, for some reason, made a note of them. After that he leaned on a radiator and read several volumes of the *University Calendar*. Finally he went back to his seat and began a letter to Cassandra, but he found it difficult to write, as he really did not know what to say. He was glad when the bell tinkled, for this meant that all readers must leave the library, which closed at seven.

Adam got up and put his things together. He had had quite a successful evening's work, he thought, and decided to visit the library again in the morning. The clergyman beside him turned round and without any preamble addressed him.

'I wonder, when you are working here, have you ever given a thought to all those who have died in Bodley's Library, or as a result of working there?'

Adam was forced to admit that he had not.

'You should, you know. It is quite an education.'

'It would surely do one more good to concentrate on one's work,' said Adam austerely.

'That is my work,' said the clergyman simply. 'I am preparing a thesis on that subject for the degree of Bachelor of Letters.'

Adam said nothing, but looked at him in some surprise.

'Since my wife died,' said the clergyman, 'I have thought much of death. And your wife?' He looked suddenly at Adam. 'You have a wife?'

'She is not with me here,' said Adam, hypnotized by the old man.

'No, she is not with you here, but,' his voice rose, 'you must believe that you will meet again, that she will be waiting for you, in that other life, perhaps?'

'She is in Budapest,' said Adam shortly.

'Oh, well, that's another pair of shoes, isn't it?' said the clergyman surprisingly.

'Is it? I don't know,' said Adam, in sudden fear.

They crossed over into Market Street. Why had he let this depressing old man get hold of him, Adam wondered. And supposing he was right? Supposing Cassandra was waiting for him, not in Budapest, but in Heaven? All the misery of the day without her suddenly weighed heavily upon him. The clergyman droned on.

'We may be taken at any time. Do you read Anthony à Wood? I have often thought that he and I would have been friends. Only this evening I came across a passage that I often remember when I am eating. "In the beginning of this month I was told that Harry Marten died last summer, suddenly with meat in his mouth, at Chepstow in Monmouthshire." Well, here we are. I shall go into Lyons for supper. I can get a delicious meal for one shilling – fried egg, sausage, chips and baked beans, with bread too and a cup of tea. Excellent! Where are you going?'

'Budapest,' said Adam, and bidding the clergyman a hasty farewell, he was off down the Cornmarket.

CHAPTER TWENTY-TWO

'Ye prudes in virtue, say,
Say ye severest, what would you have done?'

When the party arranged itself in the train next morning, Cassandra found herself in a carriage with Canon and Mrs Coffin, the Reverend and Mrs Langbaine, and Miss Edge. It had all come about quite easily, this taking her place among the leaders of the party, and Cassandra was pleased by its easiness. It was a proof that she belonged here. She was a respectable married woman once more, and the party had accepted her as one of themselves without question. She was meeting her husband in Budapest, he wrote books, but they had probably never heard of them, for he was not exactly what one could call famous. Cassandra, now known as Mrs Gibbon, lived in Shropshire.

'I don't suppose you've ever been there,' she added hopefully, and was grateful to see half-apologetic smiles hovering on the faces of her companions, as they admitted that they had never actually *been* there.

'It's really very remote from us,' said Canon Coffin. 'We must make that our excuse for never having visited your county.'

Cassandra gave a little sigh of relief. She had half-expected that he would know the rector of Up Callow or some other

Shropshire clergyman. She looked round the carriage with a happy smile. She had quickly made friends with Mrs Langbaine this morning and had been very sympathetic about her indisposition of the night before, and sorry that she had had to miss the cheerful dinner and retire to bed with nothing but a cup of Bovril to sustain her.

Mrs Langbaine was a lively little woman. She was teasing her husband about his 'having taken a fancy to Mrs Gibbon'.

'It's really a good thing that Willie has a lawful wedded wife,' she said comfortably. Obviously such things as Mr Tilos or his female equivalent were something quite unknown to her and the circles in which she moved.

Then, thought Cassandra, I suppose I can feel quite safe because Adam has a wife and Cassandra has a husband. It was a comfort to her to realize that one could, after all, consider marriage as something that really bound people together, so that even though Adam was working in the Bodleian and Cassandra was in a train somewhere between Belgium and the German frontier, they still belonged to each other. O blessed marriage! thought Cassandra. Poets really should write about it more often. Here she was, making this wearisome journey to Budapest in order to convince Adam that things must be different, and now she had discovered that she wanted nothing better than to go on as before, reposing on the stability of truth.

What was she going to do in Budapest when she got there? Now that she had given Mr Tilos the slip, she was eloping all by herself, as it were. How would she fare in the City of Love? She would no doubt find a good tourist guide, but how much less trouble it would have been not to have come at all.

The train was approaching Frankfurt and she had to say goodbye to her friends and go on by herself, but she felt quite happy about it now that she knew that Mr Tilos was no longer around.

'Goodbye everyone,' she said, 'and thank you so much for your kindness to me. I have so much enjoyed travelling with you,' she said with complete truth. Miss Edge grasped Cassandra's hands. 'Goodbye, my dear. Remember, if you are ever near St Monica's do drop in and see us. And I hope you enjoy yourself in Budapest.'

The train started to move out of the station and she heard Canon Coffin's voice saying, 'Now we are all going on a bus to the Hotel Schweizerhof . . .'

CHAPTER TWENTY-THREE

'Together down they sink in social sleep;
Together freed, their gentle spirits fly
To scenes where love and bliss immortal reign ...'

Cassandra was a little disappointed to find no letter from Adam
awaiting her at the hotel, although she was relieved to see that
her luggage had arrived safely, thanks to poor Mr Tilos. How
long would she have to wait for Adam himself, she wondered,
for she had quite made up her mind that he would follow her
here. She did not want to sit in the hotel all day, although she
had no doubt that she would make friends with somebody if she
did. There were several elderly English ladies and an English
couple with two rather plain-looking daughters, whom she had
noted in case of future need. All the other people seemed to be
foreigners. There were at least half a dozen who looked exactly
like Mr Tilos and a number of blond, sunburnt young people,
who might have been German or Austrian.

Cassandra was hardly surprised when, on her first morning in
Budapest, she found herself in a motor coach, setting out for a
tour of the city. Usually she preferred looking at shops to sight-
seeing, but, after all, she thought, she had done the wrong thing
in coming to Budapest, so she could at least make amends for it
by doing the obviously right thing on her first day here. Besides,
Adam would have been pleased, and she liked to think that she

was pleasing her husband, even if he wasn't there to know about it. It was depressing to think that you could probably please a husband far more when he wasn't with you than when he was.

Cassandra enjoyed the sightseeing tour more than she had thought she would. It was very hot, but not unpleasantly so. The sunshine only seemed to make the radiant city more beautiful. Cassandra thought she had never seen happier or more handsome-looking people walking about the streets. She was sure they were happier and more handsome than the Cumberland rustics, who were in touch with the beautiful and permanent forms of Nature, and wished that Adam had been with her, so that they could have had a nice argument about it. Everyone was so friendly, too. At the Angol-Magyar Bank, where Cassandra changed her money, a smiling Hungarian in shirt-sleeves wished her a pleasant holiday, and told her that she must be sure to visit the Angol Park.

'The Angol Park?' asked Cassandra, rather puzzled. She supposed that as the word 'Angol' occurred in both names the Park must have something to do with the Bank, although it was difficult to see how this could be.

'Yes,' said the Hungarian, smiling. 'Angol means English. That is why you must go to the Angol Park. You will like very much the amusements there, I think.'

So it was an amusement park. Cassandra thought it would have been more suitable if the Hungarian bank clerk had urged her to visit the János-Hegy, or the Royal Palace, or some building of historical interest, but on second thoughts she decided that it was much nicer to be told about the places you might like to visit rather than the places you ought to visit. She was glad that she had been taken for the sort of person who would like very much the amusements at the Angol Park.

She smiled at the Hungarian as she folded the ten *pengö* notes into her bag. How nice Budapest was! There was a bank where the English could change their money and an amusement park where they could spend it. A sort of Hungarian Blackpool to make the English feel at home. She hoped that Adam would take her there when he came.

But when would he come? Would he come at all? After she had been in Budapest a day and a night, Cassandra became more and more conscious that Budapest was indeed the City of Love, and that she was alone in it. A City of Love, surely, suggested a place full of well-matched and happy, though not necessarily married couples. The main point was that there should be couples; that was obvious. Cassandra felt that she was not getting her money's worth, although, when she came to think of it, it was quite right that she should find herself alone. She wondered what Adam would be doing now. Perhaps he was still working in the Bodleian, watching the rain pouring down outside. He must be bored, she thought with satisfaction.

At that precise moment, Adam was on the Vienna–Budapest boat, engaged in conversation with a middle-aged American lady, who had, by some extraordinary chance, read all of his books. It was the lady who was conversing, for Adam was merely listening happily, with a smile on his face, feeling the hot sun piercing right through to his bones.

When she had finished telling him all about his novels, Adam began to tell her about Shropshire and Up Callow. He described The Grotto, with its beautiful garden and avenue of poplars, and the cedar tree on the lawn. Warming to his subject, he introduced the pleasing picture of himself, reclining on the bank by the stream, meditating on an epic poem. He even began to quote a little poetry, not his own, because he could think of nothing suitable, but the ever-useful Wordsworth.

The trip down the Danube had been hot and pleasant and Adam congratulated himself on his decision to come this way. The country was green and wooded and there had been a remarkably fine sunset which made the river look red and gold. Actually, the best thing had been the ice-cream that tasted of fresh peaches, but when one had reached Adam's age things like ice-cream are too childish to be mentioned among the attractions of the journey. All the same, he thought, Cassandra would not have hesitated to say that she preferred the ice-cream to the sunset if she really did.

Dear Cassandra, he thought, as it grew dark and lights began to twinkle on the shore and the stars in the sky. How would he find her? Would Tilos be with her? The more Adam considered the idea of Mr Tilos, the more ridiculously impossible it seemed. No, Cassandra would be alone, he decided, pathetically alone. She might even be crying.

As they approached Budapest and he saw the city in all its floodlit glory, Adam began to feel really excited. The place he was coming to looked like fairyland. It was impossible that it should be real. His journey took on an air of fantasy and became a dramatic adventure. He even forgot to ask which side of the river was Buda and which was Pest, as he would undoubtedly have done if Cassandra had been with him. The taxi took him from the landing stage to the hotel so quickly that he hadn't time to think of what he was going to say.

Cassandra was sitting in the corner of the lounge, looking almost beautiful in a white chiffon dress, and she was drinking not Tokay, or peach brandy, or even coffee or any of the other things that she ought to have been drinking in a foreign land, but tea. And quite strong, English-looking tea.

She did not look up until Adam was near enough to call her name. And then, when she saw Adam standing by her, wearing a navy-blue pin-striped suit, and looking far more English than he ever did in Up Callow, she sprang up from the table and crying, 'Adam, darling!' flung her arms around his neck and kissed him, not once but several times. This scene was watched

148

with great delight by János, the nice Hungarian waiter who had brought Cassandra her English tea, and had decided that she was much too charming to be alone. They were a perfect couple, she and the handsome Englishman, he thought. Perhaps they were running away together, for although the English lady wore a wedding ring, the man who had joined her did not look at all like an English husband, nor was her greeting the one which wives usually gave to husbands, thought János, whose mind worked on very much the same lines as that of Mr Tilos.

Adam and Cassandra were now sitting down, holding each other's hands, and looking into each other's faces to see that there could be no mistake.

'Well, my love,' said Adam, indicating the tea, 'this isn't quite how I expected to find you.'

'Did you think I'd be at a night-club?' laughed Cassandra.

'No, not exactly. I didn't expect to find you drinking tea, that's all,' he said.

This seemed to Cassandra a very small point compared with their being together again, and yet perhaps it was a little disappointing for Adam to come and find her like this, having a cup of tea before she went to bed, just as she did at home. Obviously something more was expected of her. She looked up into his face and thought she detected a look of disappointment there. Poor Adam, he was only a child, and he must feel as if he had been deprived of a treat. She must make amends for it as quickly as she could.

'Adam, dearest,' she said gently, taking his hand, 'I've been so silly.'

'No, darling, I've been silly,' said Adam, so firmly that Cassandra glanced at him in amazement to see if she could have heard aright.

But he was quite serious. He even repeated it. 'Let's go out,' he said. 'I think I like this place, although it's a little overdone.

How clever of you to have thought of coming here. I should have been bored in Paris, and depressed in Vienna. You do everything so well, darling, just like ordering things for dinner,' he added.

'Yes, I suppose it is like that,' said Cassandra, as they walked down by the river. She was glad that the place she had chosen for her elopement should please her husband in the same way as a well-ordered dinner. She supposed that she had put the finishing touch of perfection to it by not having any lover here to spoil it.

'Adam, darling,' Cassandra said suddenly, with a note of concern in her voice, 'you look awfully thin. I can feel all your bones. Have they been looking after you properly at home? Have you had any lunch or any dinner?'

'Well, I'm not sure,' said Adam, becoming a little more himself. 'I can't remember having had anything except some ice-cream on the boat, but I daresay I had some dinner.'

'Oh, Adam, you are hopeless! Why didn't you tell me?'

'I don't know,' said Adam simply. 'I suppose I was too excited at the prospect of seeing you to think about things like dinner.'

Cassandra was very much pleased and touched at this, but she did not let it turn her head and really, when she came to think of it, she was more at ease seeing to her husband's welfare than listening to him paying her compliments. It had been her business for five years now, and she did not think she wanted it changed. They were very soon sitting in the hotel, and Cassandra was watching Adam eat a good meal.

As he ate, Cassandra remembered what Mr Tilos had said about going to Budapest with a husband. 'You do not see the moon and the river. You are thinking only of what you shall eat. Your *gulyás* . . . ' Perhaps it was true, and yet there was nothing wrong or even sad in acknowledging its truth. For, after all, eating nice things with a nice person in a gay foreign hotel was quite as romantic as looking at moonlight and rivers, and far more suitable for a man and a woman who had been married for five years. Cassandra was so happy just to have Adam sitting opposite her that she wouldn't have minded if he had said nothing about being glad to see her again.

CHAPTER TWENTY-FOUR

'A delicate refinement known to few,
Perplexed his breast and urged him to retire.'

'Oughtn't we to be going home, darling?' said Cassandra to
Adam when they had been in Budapest for a week. 'I mean,
what will people in Up Callow be saying? They probably still
think I've eloped with Mr Tilos, and you are still working in the
Bodleian.'

'Could anything be less like the Bodleian than this?' said
Adam lazily.

Cassandra agreed that nothing could. After a moment's contemplation of the sunburnt bodies around her she lay back with
a contented sigh. They were sunbathing at the St Gellért Hotel,
watching the artificial waves in the swimming pool. Even Adam
was enjoying these simple pleasures. He had raised no objections
to Cassandra's desire to visit the Angol Park, saying rather
naïvely that, after all, even if it was a sort of Blackpool, it was
at least a Hungarian one, and it was unlikely they would meet
anyone they knew.

'Don't you think we ought to send the Wilmots a postcard?'
persisted Cassandra. 'They would surely be interested to see a
picture of Budapest floodlit at night.'

'They will be very disappointed to find that you are just with your husband instead of Mr Tilos, but you choose a nice postcard and we will write something suitable on it.'

'Do we have to explain everything?' asked Cassandra. 'There won't really be room on a postcard.'

'Let's go into the water,' said Adam.

Hand in hand they walked down the steps, and sat down by the green marble lions' heads which poured warm water on to their backs.

'Why, look!' said Adam suddenly. 'There's Tilos.'

Before Cassandra had found him among the crowd of laughing, foreign faces, a voice was shouting, *'Jó reggelt!* Hallo!'

'I wondered when we should meet again,' said Cassandra, feeling that her greeting was inadequate, but not knowing how to better it.

He held her hand for rather too long, and then introduced two men who were with him. 'My brother, Tilos Béla, and my uncle, Hunyadi Ferenc.'

Tilos Béla was almost exactly like Tilos Stefan, except that he looked a great deal younger and less sophisticated. The only English he seemed to know was 'thank you', which he pronounced 'senk you'. Uncle Ferenc was a stout, good-looking man in the middle forties. He spoke English well, and was very high-spirited.

They were soon all sitting at a table in the outdoor café, drinking coffee and iced water, and eating peaches.

Cassandra decided that Mr Tilos was very much more attractive in his own land than he had been in Up Callow, because here his gaiety fitted in with the sunny atmosphere of the place and did not seem at all ridiculous. She had imagined that when they met again there would be a great deal of awkwardness between them. It was surely fitting that there should be between the parties in an unsuccessful elopement, even though one of the parties had not been eloping at all.

It was all over. He looked at her and seemed about to say something. She smiled at him uncertainly.

'You will both come with me to visit my aunt at Siófok?' he asked surprisingly.

'Oh, *yes*,' said Cassandra, overcome with relief, 'oh, yes, we'd love to.'

'Is your uncle married?' asked Adam idly.

'Yes, he has had one wife only, but she is dead,' replied Mr Tilos. 'He is the younger brother of the aunt you shall meet at Siófok. He is a rich man because he has no wife to keep.'

Cassandra smiled, thinking that something might be done about it. 'It would be nice if he would visit you in Up Callow,' she said.

'Ah-ha! Ferenc, old boy,' said Mr Tilos, leaning across the table, 'you have made a conquest. Cassandra asks that you shall visit me in Up Callow.' He pronounced it as one word, Upcalloe.

'It would be delightful,' said Uncle Ferenc, bowing low over the table.

Adam, who had been carrying on a conversation in German with Béla, looked up in surprise.

'You would see our beautiful Shropshire countryside,' said Cassandra firmly, for she was suggesting this visit for purely unselfish reasons. It had occurred to her that, given propitious circumstances, Uncle Ferenc might do as a husband for Miss Gay. She felt that it would be a great triumph if she could return bringing with her a husband for Angela, especially if that husband were a rich, Hungarian widower. The inhabitants of Up Callow would no doubt overlook all they imagined they had to overlook in her conduct of the past week or two. She told Adam of her idea when they were back in their hotel. He agreed that it was a good one.

'Only I'm afraid that as he's seen you he won't think anything of her,' he added affectionately.

They were going to Siófok in Uncle Ferenc's car. Adam sat in the front with him, while Cassandra was squashed into the back between the Tilos brothers. They were just like children, she decided. Béla was a baby who had not yet learned to talk, for as he knew no English he could only smile and nod and utter an occasional 'senk you', whenever he felt the context demanded it. Cassandra tried to teach him the names of things by pointing at them and saying the appropriate English word. She felt she would like to adopt him, or keep him as a pet. Stefan kept up a brilliant and ridiculous conversation about the differences between the English and Hungarian countryside. He seemed to be mimicking Adam, though whether consciously or not Cassandra could not decide.

'You have nothing like this in England.' He smiled, indicating the fields which stretched on either side of the hot, dusty road. They were very flat, and the grass was burnt yellow by the sun. Along the sides of them grew masses of pale blue cornflowers. When they stopped at a village, Béla picked a large bunch of them for Cassandra, and presented them to her rather shyly, saying 'very pretty', which was a phrase she had just taught him.

Cassandra felt like a royal personage receiving a bouquet from a child.

'I should be so happy living in a small house here,' said Mr Tilos, 'just digging in the earth, with a goat or pig to give me food. And then in the evening a glass of *tokaj*, and the music of the *tziganes* ...'

'Yes,' said Adam seriously, 'that is the best kind of life. I think I should enjoy it in this sunny country.'

Cassandra suppressed a smile at the idea of Adam and Mr Tilos living together in a little cottage somewhere in the middle of the Hungarian plain. 'It would certainly be nicer than living in Milton Amble,' she said, 'not nearly so damp. I think I should

like it too. I've always wanted to wear that pretty peasant costume, and of course I couldn't in England without everyone
thinking me mad.'

'But the English are all mad,' said Uncle Ferenc tolerantly.
'That is why we love them.'

They arrived at Siófok in time for lunch. Cassandra had half
expected that Mr Tilos's aunt would live in a mediaeval castle
on the edge of a cliff, but she realized as they drove through the
flat, sunny country that she had been too hopeful. There was no
cliff and no castle. Instead they drove up to a large white house.
Its architecture was of a type common in the wealthier suburbs
of big German towns. Cassandra thought it looked exactly like
a wedding cake. Its elaborate stucco decorations gleamed as
white as icing in the brilliant sunshine. The window boxes were
gay with pink and purple petunias.

To Cassandra's surprise Mr Tilos's aunt was exactly like her
own Aunt Beatrice, who lived in Tunbridge Wells and was a
typical English spinster of gentle birth.

Miss Hunyadi was a small grey-haired lady who spoke English
in a quiet sing-song voice. In features she was slightly like her
brother Ferenc, but otherwise she was exactly the kind of person
that Cassandra had thought only existed in England. Hungary
was the last place in the world where she had expected to find
her Aunt Beatrice's twin.

The room into which they were taken had a high white ceiling, was elegantly papered in silver grey and had an elaborate
marble mantelpiece festooned with leaves and flowers. The furniture was substantial and made of mahogany, the horsehair
sofas draped in antimacassars and there was a screen embroidered in faded wools with a design of parrots against a
background of what looked like tombstones. In one corner of
the room stood a large, tiled stove, very like the one that Mrs
Gower had seen being taken into Holmwood.

'It is so nice for me to talk to English people,' said Miss Hunyadi.

'You speak our language very well,' said Cassandra. 'Have you been in England much?'

'Not for many years.' The little woman paused, and a sad, far-away look came into her eyes. 'I spent some happy months in Leamington Spa with my dear friend Miss Mildred Baker. She was governess to a very noble family in Budapest before the war. She was my great friend . . .'

Cassandra nodded sympathetically. She could imagine it all.

'She has been dead for some years now,' went on Miss Hunyadi. 'I should be a lonely old woman, but I have my young people,' she added, with a smile in the direction of the others. She seemed to include her brother Ferenc among the young people, which was not really surprising, as by his behaviour one would have thought him even younger than Béla. Cassandra felt that she too would like to be one of Miss Hunyadi's young people, although she was not sure that she could hope to be quite as young as the Hungarians.

'You must come to England again,' she said. 'My husband and I would be very pleased to welcome you to our house,' she added, in the rather stilted manner she did not seem to be able to avoid when speaking to foreigners. 'You would like Up Callow, and we still have some summer left, I hope,' she laughed, 'but I expect you know our English climate.'

'Yes, I know it and I love it,' said Miss Hunyadi. 'Here there is too much sun, I think. For young people it is good, but when you are old, the autumn and winter are more sympathetic. I liked it in Leamington when the leaves were falling from the trees, and dear Mildred would go to her cupboard and take out her fur stole and muff, and we would be walking to the pumping-room and drinking the waters there. And in the evening we would sit by the fire, the beautiful English fire that you can *see*, and we would be knitting socks for the young pastor, the curate. He was so cold always . . . ' She paused, overcome by her reminiscences.

How lost this little woman must feel in gay, sunny Budapest, thought Cassandra. She was sure that there were no curates in Siófok, although she believed that there were plenty of what Miss Hunyadi called pumping-rooms.

Before they left she gave them real English tea, and presented Cassandra with a picture of 'your dear Queen Victoria', which she had worked in coloured wools.

The night was starry as they drove home. This time Cassandra sat in the back with Adam and Mr Tilos. He and Béla sang German and Hungarian songs, while Cassandra leaned her head on Adam's shoulder and thought what a lovely and strange place Hungary was. She had never before been so happy anywhere. Dear Mr Tilos, she thought sentimentally, she owed him so much. She hoped that he, too, would find happiness soon.

Mr Tilos felt that she had looked at him, but he did not turn his head. He was, at heart, a practical man, although given to flights of romanticism, and he decided now that he would marry Ilonka, the girl his parents had picked out for him, his fiancée, in fact, who would, he knew, be perfectly willing to marry him tomorrow. Besides, he needed a housekeeper for his big English house, since he still needed to live there for some part of the year. Also, and this was most important, being married would be a protection against the attentions of the Parisian Lady in Upcalloe.

CHAPTER TWENTY-FIVE

'Meantime a smiling offspring rises round,
And mingles both their graces.'

'They're back! They're back!' cried Mrs Wilmot in an excited
voice, coming into the dining room at the rectory.

It was a fine summer evening, about ten days after Adam and
Cassandra had visited Mr Tilos's aunt in Siófok. The rector was
standing by the window with his hands in his trouser pockets.
The trousers were white flannels and there was a pleased smile
on the rector's face, for they had had two weeks of uninterrupted
fine weather and the cricket season had really begun.
Consequently he did not check his wife's enthusiasm.

'Who?' he asked.

'Why, Cassandra and Adam Marsh-Gibbon, and Mr Tilos
and a young man who looks as if he might be his brother, and
a girl, and a jolly-looking dark man, about fifty, I should think.'
Mrs Wilmot paused for breath. 'I saw them at the station. I'd
been taking round the parish magazines,' she added, anxious to
make it clear that she had not been hanging round the station
from idle curiosity. 'Oh, Rockingham,' she burst out, 'Adam
Marsh-Gibbon must have gone with her all the time.' Her voice
betrayed her disappointment, but she brightened up as she

remembered the strangers. 'Such a jolly party they all looked, I wonder who they were?'

The jolly party which had travelled from Budapest consisted of Adam and Cassandra, Mr Tilos and Béla, Uncle Ferenc and, most important of all, Ilonka, the wife whom Mr Tilos had married in Budapest. Miss Hunyadi was not with them, but hoped to visit Cassandra some time in the autumn, when the leaves were falling from the trees and she could spend the long evenings knitting and remembering the past.

Adam and Cassandra had both been surprised at the hastiness of Mr Tilos's marriage. He had not mentioned a fiancée and, thought Cassandra indignantly, he had most certainly not behaved like an engaged person. But, perhaps, that was how things were done in Hungary. It really was the best possible thing that could have happened, thought Cassandra, for she had become quite fond of Mr Tilos, now that he was no longer embarrassing her with his attentions and now that she no longer needed him to make Adam jealous. She would enjoy befriending Mrs Tilos and telling her which were the best days to buy fish in Up Callow and where to get a really reliable charwoman.

Mrs Wilmot's news soon spread all over the town. It was known that Adam and Cassandra had arrived home together with a crowd of Hungarians, including 'that Mr Tilos and his wife'. There were naturally many people who did not believe that Ilonka was really Mrs Tilos, but they grudgingly admitted that she *might* be when they received invitations to a garden party at Balaton. Even the most conventional and disapproving people were forced to accept out of curiosity, to see if Mrs Tilos wore a genuine wedding ring, and how Mr Tilos and Cassandra would behave towards each other.

'Of course, I can't possibly go,' said Angela Gay to her uncle, when they received their invitation. She had spent the weeks of

Mr Tilos's absence mooning about Up Callow, looking wronged. She had taken to reading poetry and sometimes sat in the churchyard with the *Oxford Book of Victorian Verse* in her hand. It would obviously not be in keeping with her new character to appear at this garden party.

Mr and Mrs Tilos stood on the lawn to receive their guests. He was making friendly remarks about the weather, while his wife, a pretty girl with auburn hair, smiled brightly, as she knew very little English. Both looked as if they thought the whole thing a tremendous novelty, like some funny English game.

Mr Gay took Mrs Gower's arm – for everyone knew that they were soon to be married – and moved over to where Adam and Cassandra were standing.

'And was it *very* lovely in Budapest?' Mrs Wilmot was asking in a bright but wistful voice. Her tone was hopeful, as if she expected to hear more than a mere 'Oh yes, it was lovely'.

Cassandra sensed this and began to tell her all about the flood-lighting and the strange food and how nice it had been to be there with Adam. 'It was like a second honeymoon,' she said, trying not to catch Adam's eye. Mrs Wilmot seemed satisfied and made a sort of purring noise, while she asked Cassandra if her dress, such a lovely shade of turquoise, had been bought in Budapest.

'Yes,' said Adam, 'Cassandra was frightfully extravagant. She was always wanting to go shopping instead of sitting quietly in the hotel trying to learn Hungarian, as I wanted to.'

'I think they did not learn much,' said Mr Tilos, 'except my name. You know, Mrs Wilmot, when you go to Budapest, you will see *tilos* written up in public places. Cassandra will tell you.'

'Oh, really?' said Mrs Wilmot, wondering if Mr Tilos could be some sort of a king or dictator in his own country.

'Yes. It means *verboten*, forbidden, you know. That's true, isn't it, Adam, old boy?'

If it were the meaning of his name it was really quite appropriate, thought Mrs Wilmot daringly. But fancy Mr Tilos being so familiar with Adam Marsh-Gibbon; and the curious thing was that Adam did not seem to mind at all. He smiled, and said, 'Well, Stefan, we have only your word for it.'

So they were Adam and Cassandra and Stefan to each other, thought the rector, who had just joined the little group. That was all right, splendid in fact. 'I expect you found Tilos an excellent guide,' he beamed, thus bringing it all out into the open.

'Oh, yes, marvellous,' said Cassandra. 'He was so helpful and told us what to see and what to eat. He took us to see his aunt at Siófok. We had a lovely day there.'

'He took us to see his aunt ...' If there were any doubts remaining in the minds of the inhabitants of Up Callow they were dispelled by this simple statement. Everything had been quite all right.

The rector moved on to talk to Mr Gay and Mrs Gower, who were laughing with Uncle Ferenc. There did not seem to be any special joke, unless it were Uncle Ferenc himself, who was wearing a white linen suit and a straw boater he had bought that morning in the town.

How splendidly he would do for Angela, thought Mr Gay wistfully.

'Where is your niece?' asked the rector. 'I hope she is not ill?'

'Not exactly,' said Mr Gay unhappily. 'She had a slight headache, and the sun is so hot ...' He tailed off rather weakly.

'The sun is hot, yes,' said Uncle Ferenc, 'but under the trees there is cool. I shall go to your house to tell her, yes?'

The rector looked at Uncle Ferenc in surprise, Mr Gay in gratitude. It was surely a little unconventional, but then as the fellow was a Hungarian one could perhaps excuse him for not knowing what was or was not done in Up Callow. Besides, how wonderful it would be if ... He caught Mrs Gower looking at him. There was a hopeful smile on her face. Angela could be very nice sometimes, and this Hungarian seemed a good, simple sort of fellow, who might be led unresisting to the altar. All these thoughts passed through Mr Gay's mind as he hesitated and said, 'Well, I hardly know . . .'

But Uncle Ferenc wanted something to do. Stefan had told him about Miss Gay and had made her sound very attractive. Perhaps he too had been thinking that a match might be made between them to the advantage of everyone. Uncle Ferenc had been looking forward to meeting her this afternoon, and her non-appearance had stimulated his eagerness. He was not going to be disappointed if he could help it.

A few minutes later he was seen going down the drive in his car. On second thoughts he had decided to take some sandwiches and cakes and two bottles of Tokay with him. One never knew. If we do not like each other, we will like the wine and food, thought Uncle Ferenc simply.

Meanwhile the rector was moving about the garden, with a vague idea that he was putting things right between people. He felt that he had established Adam and Cassandra as respectable husband and wife once more, although he was not sure how; he had sent Uncle Ferenc in search of Miss Gay, and now he thought he had deserved his tea. His own young people did not need him this afternoon, he thought happily, with a glance to where Janie and Mr Paladin were sitting on a rustic seat, trying to make some sort of conversation with Tilos Béla. The rector recalled with pride the announcement which had recently appeared in *The Times*. Janie had only had her engagement ring a week and she still couldn't help looking at it surreptitiously to see the diamonds flashing in the sunlight or in the dim light of the church during evensong. It gave her confidence, so that she no longer felt apologetic when people spoke to her patronizingly and asked whether she wouldn't like to do a course of shorthand

and typing. 'Oh no,' she would say with a gracious smile. 'You see, I'm going to be married.'

'Now, you young people,' said Mr Tilos, coming up to them and using a phrase he had heard the rector employ, 'you have nothing to eat.' He pushed a plate of little cakes into Janie's hand, smiled benevolently at them and turned to look for Adam and Cassandra.

But they were nowhere to be seen. They had hidden themselves away in a little summer-house at the bottom of the garden, with several plates of sandwiches. It had, of course, been Adam's idea. He said he was tired of telling people about Budapest. 'Besides,' he added, 'I'm so hungry that I would prefer to eat in private. I don't believe I had any lunch.'

'Oh, Adam, you know you did. We had salmon.'

'Well, perhaps, but it was a long time ago.'

'Wasn't everyone pleased to see us so very much Adam and Cassandra once more?' Cassandra said.

'Yes,' he replied, 'we are quite an institution. Like Héloïse and Abélard.'

'Oh, no,' said Cassandra positively. 'I'm sure we are not like them.'

'I suppose you'd rather I said Romeo and Juliet?'

Cassandra laughed. 'Well, I only said that being in Budapest was a second honeymoon because Mrs Wilmot seemed to expect it and I don't like to disappoint people, if I can help it. But it *was* a second honeymoon, wasn't it, darling?' she added, gazing sentimentally at her husband, who was eating sandwiches at an alarming rate.

'Why all this talk?' he asked idly.

'Because I've got something to tell you. Something exciting.'

'Is it about Tilos?' asked Adam, for like everyone else in Up Callow, he was inclined to believe that everything exciting must have something to do with Mr Tilos.

164

Cassandra laughed. 'Well, I should hardly like to say that, although in a *very* remote way it has something to do with him. It's simply that Science has proved weaker than Nature.'

'Science *is* weaker than Nature,' said Adam positively. He looked as if he were about to quote Wordsworth, but Cassandra stopped him in time.

'Oh, Adam, you are *stupid*,' she said. 'I'm trying to tell you that I'm going to have a baby.'

'You, going to have a baby?' Adam stared at her in amazement.

'Are you annoyed with me?' said Cassandra, taking his hand. 'It won't be for a long time, because it's only just started,' she said apologetically, as if to make it more acceptable.

'Annoyed? Why should *I* be annoyed. It is you who will have all the bother. I'm delighted. Besides,' he said in an aggrieved manner, 'you know perfectly well that I have always wanted us to have a family.'

Cassandra gave a little sigh and spread out her hands in a gesture of hopelessness. 'You always said you didn't want any children,' she reminded him.

'Well, if I did, it was only because I was afraid you might die or something. Yes,' he added, now quite convinced that that had been his only reservation, 'that is what it was.'

'Oh, Adam, how *sweet*!' said Cassandra passionately. 'I always thought it was because you thought that they would disturb your work.'

Adam looked alarmed. 'Well, I wouldn't have to have them in my study, would I?'

'Of course not, darling,' said Cassandra soothingly.

They walked up the path arm in arm.

'I'll start writing my novel about Budapest,' said Adam suddenly, 'and by the time little Adam is born the novel will be finished and he shall have it as a birthday present. That will be nice, won't it?'

'Very nice,' said Cassandra guardedly. She was thinking that it would be safe to bet that little Adam – it was to be a little Adam, of course – would win the race by months, or even years, but she did not want to damp her husband's enthusiasm.

PART TWO

Finding a Voice

Gervase and Flora

Note on the Text

This work (216 pages) was written in 1937–8. A diary entry for January 1st 1938 reads: 'Wrote about 8 pages of my Finnish novel now at about p.256'. It began as a series of letters to Henry Harvey when he was teaching at the University of Helsingfors [Helsinki] and she later developed these into a full-length novel, mainly for the entertainment of her friends.

Flora is, of course, the young Barbara and Gervase is Henry. The character of Ingeborg was based on her idea of Elsie Godenhjelm, whom Henry married in December 1938, but whom Barbara had not, at that time, actually met. Because of Henry, Barbara read all she could about Finland, and the details she acquired from books, as well as the descriptions in Henry's letters, give her novel a certain authenticity of background. She read translations of the literature and even tried to learn the languages. Since Finland used to be part of Sweden and is still bilingual (though the Swedish ascendancy is less than it was in the 1930s), Fru Lindblom and Ingeborg speak Swedish. In December 1937 Barbara was jokingly pretending to be a Finn when Denis Pullein-Thompson introduced her to his friends at Oxford as Päävikki Olafsson.

But although Barbara enjoyed the fun and novelty of setting her novel abroad, it is the English characters who are the strongest and there is a great deal of 'pure Pym' in this early work, notably the first appearance of Miss Moberley, her generic name for all such autocratic and difficult old women.

Note: the editor would like to thank Henry Harvey for his helpful suggestions on this novel.

Gervase and Flora

'Now, Rhoda, my nephew Mr Harringay is coming tonight. He will be here for dinner, so we must have something specially nice, mustn't we?'

'Yes, madam,' said Rhoda in a respectful, colourless tone, thinking that her mistress managed to find an excuse to have something specially nice every night of her life.

'I think we will have mushroom soup, made with *fresh* mushrooms, Rhoda, you know I can't take anything tinned, and then sole, lightly steamed with a cream sauce, and then a bird. A bird . . . ' Miss Emily Moberley paused, considering the bird.

'Yes, madam, a bird,' said Rhoda firmly. 'And the sweet?' She stood in the doorway with her hands folded in front of her – the perfect picture of an elderly English servant, with a hard face, grey hair and an immaculately starched apron. 'The sweet,' she repeated with a hint of impatience in her voice, although she made no movement.

'Yes, the sweet. Nothing heavy of course. I have to be so very careful. I think we will have a Charlotte Russe. Gervase is so fond of it,' she added calmly, and all the more surprisingly as she had not seen her nephew for ten years and knew nothing of his tastes. In any case it was not in her nature to consider what other people liked.

But Rhoda was not taken in. She had served Miss Moberley for over twenty years.

'Be sure that you get the finest sponge cakes, Rhoda,' continued Miss Moberley. 'Last time we had it I came across something that looked very like a bit of that *cake* Mrs Barlow brought us.'

The expression on Rhoda's face did not alter as she informed her mistress that she never used anything but the finest sponge fingers for making Charlotte Russe. 'Will there be anything further, madam?' she asked, making a slight movement towards the door.

'No, Rhoda, unless we have a savoury. Mr Harringay might like it. I shall try to eat it myself, although I can't take a heavy meal at night, something light and nourishing is all I require. Still, I don't want my nephew to think I'm an old *crock*, do I?' She laughed the little laugh that always accompanied the use of what she considered a slang expression.

Rhoda smiled dutifully, a bleak smile that soon faded.

'I will arrange about the savoury, madam,' she said.

'Very well. Now hurry down to the market for the fish and a nice bird and mind that you are back by a quarter to eleven. I must have my Ovaltine punctually.'

'Very good, madam.'

'And the cream, Rhoda, don't forget the cream for the Charlotte Russe.' Miss Moberley's voice rose as Rhoda left the room.

Miss Moberley sat beside the roaring fire and unfolded the *Church Times*. She placed her pince-nez on her long, pale nose, and turned the pages. She was a big, sheep-like woman, with a thick white skin and pale blue eyes. She had a long upper lip and long teeth. Her hair was faded and scraped away from her large ears with an arrangement of combs. She was about sixty-five years old.

The room in which she sat was furnished with heavy Victorian mahogany and cumbrous red hangings, which looked as if they would be dusty, but, thanks to Rhoda's ministrations, were scrupulously clean. There were a great many small tables dotted about the room, which the daily woman who came in to help was not allowed to dust since they bore a number of precious objects. A silver table stood against one wall and near the window there was a fine collection of native weapons, beads and other handiwork, presented to Miss Moberley by her cousin the Bishop of Nybongaland, who had thought it an excellent opportunity of getting rid of some junk. The other tables were covered with photographs of clergymen and dowdy-looking women in silver frames. It was, somehow, a very English room. If you had suddenly been transplanted there you would have thought you were in a drawing room in Tunbridge Wells or North Oxford. You would never have imagined that you were in Finland. But the address was 12, Kalevalagatan, Helsingfors. Not that this made any difference to Miss Moberley, who always spoke of her house as The Close. This name dated back to the days when her father, the Reverend Edgar Moberley, had been English chaplain at Helsingfors. When he died she was already the acknowledged head of the English colony and had gathered about her a circle of dull compatriots who respected and disliked her.

Rather than return to England, after her father's death, and become merely a nameless spinster in some cathedral town, Miss Moberley had chosen to remain in Helsingfors where she still retained a considerable position in the English community. She had now reached the stage when it was no longer necessary to explain to visitors that the gentleman on the mantelpiece was Archdeacon Hyacinth and that the bearded man with the tennis racket was Bishop Grote, a kinsman of her mother's, and that the ladies whose photographs stood on the small tables were all connected with the oldest families in England and were, of course, her relations.

It was a pleasant state to be in, reflected Miss Moberley complacently. She went to the window and looked out. Rhoda was hurrying back with her basket. She did the marketing every morning, and by some mysterious means, since she spoke only English, she always contrived to get the best of everything.

When she heard Rhoda come in Miss Moberley called out, 'Now, Rhoda, are you sure it is a *young* bird?'

'Yes, madam. I chose it myself.' Rhoda's voice was flat and patient.

'And the sole, Rhoda, where is the sole?'

'Mr Axelström said he'd be sending it later, madam. He's good about sending,' she added grudgingly. 'And now, madam, if you'll excuse me, it's time for your Ovaltine.'

'Yes, Rhoda, I've had a tiring morning.' Miss Moberley sagged into her armchair and began once more to turn the pages of the *Church Times*.

Gervase Harringay wondered if the boat was ever going to reach Helsingfors. He had come out to be a lecturer in English to the Finns at Philadelphia College, which had been founded by a rich American who had visited Finland some fifty years before and had been very much displeased because the Finns had not understood him when he asked for things in shops. The college was a result of this displeasure.

Gervase began thinking very conscientiously about the lectures he had prepared. He was to do Milton with his students this term. He thought they would appreciate *Paradise Lost*. They might recognize in it some of the grandeur of their own *Kalevala* he thought hopefully. He began to assemble his things and make himself tidy. He looked young and schoolboyish in his navy blue overcoat. He was good-looking, fair and thin with attractively dark eyes. He had come out to Finland straight from Oxford, where he had taken a First in English. He was twenty-four years old.

'We are approaching Helsingfors,' said the Finn with whom he had made friends on the boat.

'A new city,' said Gervase, half to himself, 'a new, clean city.'

'Yes,' said his companion. 'But the Finns are old. We have known much sorrow. There in the lakes and forests of Punkaharju where my home is, you will find things older than civilization itself. These things are the heart of Finland ...' the flat voice droned on. He sounded as if he were speaking to himself and did not mind whether anyone listened or not. Gervase had been listening in the hope of being told what these things were that were older than civilization itself, but when he realized that no explanation was forthcoming, his attention wandered, and he found himself gazing at his companion's dark blue hat. It made him dissatisfied with his ordinary brown one, although it was new.

'You speak English awfully well,' said Gervase when there was a moment's pause.

'Oh, that is nothing.' The man shrugged his shoulders. 'My daughter could speak English fluently by the time she was ten. She also speaks German, French and Italian.'

Gervase felt very depressed by this and was glad that in the confusion and bustle of their arrival he was not obliged to admit that as well as having no Swedish or Finnish, his French and German were merely adequate.

Over dinner at his aunt's he was questioned about various mutual acquaintances in England. Miss Moberley was never happier than when talking about people whose good family and distinguished connections were well known, though she delighted even more in discovering some secret disgrace.

175

'How is Canon Palfrey?' she asked. 'I used to know him very well.'

'Oh, did you,' said Gervase, thinking that this was something of a disadvantage, for Canon Palfrey was vicar of the small town where he lived and somehow people who had known him since childhood never seemed to appreciate him as he deserved.

'His wife was a kinswoman of Bishop Ogg, you know, and his daughter, I seem to remember, was a charming girl.'

'Oh, yes, Flora.' He turned his head away to hide a smile. It was the tolerant, slightly scornful smile of a young man who is loved by a girl for whom he feels no more than friendship. Flora Palfrey had been in love with Gervase Harringay since she was nineteen, and her passion had thrived on its diet of a cooling and pretty constant neglect.

'I heard that she was very like her mother,' said Miss Moberley. 'A very handsome woman.'

'I suppose Flora is quite comely in a hearty, English way' – Gervase's taste in women was rather more sophisticated than this – 'she's very lively and does a good deal in the parish since her mother died.'

Miss Moberley continued. 'Nowadays it is increasingly difficult to meet the right people,' she said. 'Even Helsingfors is *very* different from what it was thirty years ago.'

'I expect you know a great many interesting Finns,' Gervase ventured.

'Finns?' Miss Moberley sounded surprised that he should ask such a thing. 'In the old days, when your grandfather was alive, we knew some of the oldest aristocratic families, but I have never cared for foreigners and during the last twenty years I have kept very much to myself and my own circle of friends. Nations were not meant to be friendly,' she declared firmly. 'The best we can do is to set them an example of behaviour.'

Gervase was silent for some time. He looked round the room

and became depressed by its Victorian atmosphere, which seemed to stifle him. He hoped it would not be long before he was settled with some Finnish family, who would give him conversational practice in the language. He intended to look for such a family as soon as possible.

At half past nine Rhoda brought in Miss Moberley's Ovaltine and a small plate of biscuits.

'Would Mr Harringay like some tea or coffee?' she asked.

'No, thank you, Rhoda,' Miss Moberley said. 'Young people have no need of stimulants.'

Rhoda went out, closing the door quietly behind her. After that there was no sound in the room but that of Miss Moberley sipping her Ovaltine.

It was a grey sunless morning and Gervase sat learning his Finnish vocabularies. It was bitterly cold outside, but Gervase felt that he would have enjoyed the sensation of shivering after living in Miss Moberley's overheated house. He turned to the preparation of a lecture for the afternoon. His work at Philadelphia College was easier than he had expected, and he had only to give five lectures a week, besides taking tutorials. He found that his students had a good command of the English language, but that their critical faculty was undeveloped. He was thus able to talk brilliantly, pacing to and fro as he rolled out long and seemingly endless sentences, only to stop short and bring them to an end when the Finns were least expecting it. He hoped that they understood him, for their bland faces were devoid of emotion, although some of the young women could be seen smiling at each other and passing little notes when the lecture was in progress. But Gervase was not displeased, for some of them were very pretty, although he had not as yet studied them in detail. He was leaving all that sort of thing until he was settled somewhere away from his aunt. Today, indeed, he was to visit a Fru Lindblom, who, he had been told, might take him as a lodger. After his lecture, then, he took a tram to the street where she lived. He was rather frightened of the trams, as they were of the kind that shut up their steps when they were ready to go and the female conductor did not understand him when he spoke in halting Finnish. Eventually he found the right address and came face to face with a green door from which the paint was peeling in large flakes. It stood open so he boldly went in and found himself in what seemed to be a hall. The inner door had a design of flowers and birds carved on it. He knocked rather timidly, but as there was no answer he knocked more loudly until finally he was almost banging and the carvings were hurting his hand.

'Come in,' shouted an emphatic guttural voice at last.

Gervase went in. He found himself in a vast high-ceilinged room. The walls were bare except for an elaborate piece of tapestry hanging on one of them, and there was a great deal of furniture scattered about – a low fender seat, a large round table, several chairs and a massive chest all carved with designs of flowers, birds and animals. The only window had rough linen curtains half drawn across it and at first Gervase found it difficult to see. Finally he discerned the figure of a woman sitting in the darkest corner of the room. She was perched on a high wooden stool, plucking the feathers from a large bird, which looked like a seagull, though this hardly seemed likely.

The sheet on the floor round the stool was covered with a steadily growing pile of feathers. The woman did not look up when Gervase approached her, but she said in the same emphatic voice, 'So you are here.'

Gervase felt that there was no reply to this so he stood holding his brown hat in his hand while she went on plucking the bird, as if he were a prospective servant waiting to be interviewed.

'I hope I haven't come at an awkward time,' he said at last.

There was no reply, but as the bird now looked almost naked Gervase felt that some conversation might soon be forthcoming.

Suddenly she came towards him, carrying the plucked bird in her hand.

'Oh, it is so *immensely* unfortunate that you should come here today,' she said, her voice taking on a wailing quality.

'I'm awfully sorry. I thought any time this afternoon would do. I should have telephoned first.'

'Oh no, it is not that. I am so glad that you should have come. No, the fact is that Helmi, our servant, has gone today – quite suddenly – and I do not know where we shall find another one. And now that you have seen that we have no servant you will not be wanting to come to us,' she added, her voice becoming deeper and more despairing.

'How well you speak English,' he said awkwardly.

'Yes.' Fru Lindblom was calmer now and had put the bird down on the table. 'I spent many years at a school for the daughters of clergymen in the North of England. I taught them how to carve in wood. It is an old Finnish craft, you know. I do not know what use it was, though,' she added sadly.

Gervase murmured something about the lovely carving in the room. 'A thing of beauty is a joy for ever,' he ventured, but not very comfortable to sit on, he thought, shifting uneasily in his carved chair.

'I do not mean that the carving was no use,' said Fru Lindblom impatiently. 'It is always of use to learn some craft. I was speaking of my stay in England.'

'Well, you learned another language,' said Gervase helpfully.

'My life has been *immensely* unfortunate,' continued Fru Lindblom, 'but you have not come for that. You have come to be a lodger.'

She began to gather up the feathers in the sheet. This simple action seemed to dispel her reminiscent, melancholy mood and she became brisker and more businesslike.

'You could have a pleasant room here,' she said, 'with sunny aspect. You need not have your meals with us unless you wish. Ingeborg, my daughter, lives here with me. It will be easy to arrange that when we have another servant. I will show you the room. It will be cheap, because we shall be glad to have someone to talk English to. I wish my daughter to become more proficient. Here is the room. It is clean,' she added simply, with no attempt to enumerate any other advantages the room might possess.

Gervase saw that it was large, although smaller and lighter than the one they had just left. There was a divan, not of carved wood, he was relieved to see, although the table and chairs were. By the window was a large modern desk of black and cream Finnish birchwood and there were plenty of bookshelves. Gervase imagined himself working at that desk and looking out of the window through which he might get a glimpse of the harbour.

There was a silence which was broken by the sound of someone banging on the carved wooden door on which Gervase had hurt his hands. Was there no bell in this curious place? he wondered.

'Excuse me, please, that is my daughter. I must attend to her.'

Fru Lindblom went out of the room closing the door behind her. Gervase could hear the murmur of voices. This seemed to go on for a very long time, then after a while there came the sound of weeping. Gervase saw himself a prisoner in this house until the tears were dried. Resolutely, though with some embarrassment, he opened the door and went into the other room.

Mrs Lindblom was sitting at the table weeping. Her hand was resting on the body of the plucked bird. Ingeborg was standing beside her mother, her face buried in her hands and her shoulders shaking. She was wearing a heavy coat of some coarse, long-haired fur, which looked to Gervase's inexperienced eye very much like a hearth-rug. On her head was a black velvet cap edged with fur. Her feet were clad in heavy snow-boots and her legs and the hands which were hiding her face were very thin. When Gervase came in she raised her head and looked at him for a moment. She had a thin, delicately modelled face and long straight flaxen hair. When she had taken Gervase in, she covered her face with her hands and went on weeping. Her whole body drooped and she seemed to sway. Gervase ran forward and, putting his arm around her furry shoulders, supported her to a seat beside the table. He then placed himself between the two weeping women and, turning first to one and then to the other, tried to find out what was the matter. But he could make out nothing clearly. Fru Lindblom seemed to have forgotten her excellent English. It was *immensely* unfortunate. So much he could have guessed. Perhaps it was something to do with the bird, for Fru Lindblom kept laying her hand upon it from time to time as if the feel of it under her fingers gave her some obscure sort of comfort. He made a move towards the door, but that caused Fru Lindblom to break into fresh lamentations and it was not until he had promised to return the next day that she would let him go. Outside, he looked at his watch and saw that it was four o'clock. O blessed four o'clock, tea-time. He hurried gratefully back to his aunt's house where such good English customs were still observed.

Gervase stood examining a faded sepia photograph of a sickly-looking young man in a high clerical collar. He nerved himself to speak. He was annoyed to find that his manner had lost something of its firmness and that his voice sounded almost timid.

'I have found lodgings with a Finnish family and I will be moving in at once,' he said.

To his surprise his aunt seemed almost relieved at his news. Indeed she had begun to find the presence of a young man in the house slightly disruptive of her comfort, and so she merely said graciously that she would always be pleased to see him at her At Home days and the matter was settled.

Gervase had telephoned Fru Lindblom the evening before and she had told him, in a voice mercifully free of tears or any other sort of emotion, that the room would be ready for him the next day.

As the days went by Gervase became quite at home. He liked Fru Lindblom, in spite of her melancholy manner, although he could make little of Ingeborg. She seemed to be a negative personality, sitting in the room busy with an interminable piece of knitting in an ugly shade of fawn. Gervase hoped it was not for him, though its shape did not look like that of any known masculine garment. It was probably something for herself, for she was not at all elegant in her dress although she had a graceful, slender figure and pretty flaxen hair. She did not often smile and Gervase had never heard her laugh. She went to an art school, studying some mysterious form of art, but not wood-carving. She and her mother had never repeated the curious and distressing scene that had taken place on the day of his first visit, but Gervase was always rather nervous of a repetition and went hastily out of the room when they began talking together vehemently in Swedish.

Gervase's first visit to his aunt was not on her At Home day since he felt more able to cope with her on her own. As he went into the drawing room he sensed a decided air of excitement and she made several references to a surprise. As they drank their tea Miss Moberley kept smiling to herself as if she had a secret that was amusing her. Conversation, though, was much as usual, dealing as it did with the better families, in England and in

Helsingfors, that Miss Moberley had known, so that Gervase, who had not been listening very attentively, was taken by surprise when Miss Moberley announced that she was expecting Flora Palfrey to come and visit her.

Gervase felt himself going hot and cold. A net was closing round him. An English girl of good family was being brought out to Helsingfors to marry him. Miss Moberley, Flora herself and, in all probability, Canon Palfrey as well had decided that it should be so.

The day came for Flora's arrival and he went reluctantly to tea at his aunt's, part of the welcoming party. Flora was a tall, big-boned girl with a fresh complexion and large, bright, intelligent grey eyes. Her mouth was broad and she was always laughing or smiling. She had light brown hair with golden streaks in it. Most people described her as handsome or comely. Had she been smaller and older, her manner might almost have been bustling, but as it was she was energetic and cheerful, a jolly girl. Gervase thought she was alarming, never more so than at this moment when she almost bounded into the room, a green tweed figure with a silver fox over one shoulder, its glassy eyes staring out from her breast.

'Aunt Emily! I can call you Aunt Emily?' Flora had a clear, pleasant voice. 'I have imagined this moment for three weeks, and now it's really here!' She embraced Miss Moberley firmly, towering above her.

'Well, dear Flora,' Miss Moberley sounded slightly overwhelmed, 'you must have some tea and toast.'

'Oh, thank you. I'm simply exhausted. A cup of tea will revive me beautifully.'

Whatever would a revived Flora be like? Gervase wondered. After tea Miss Moberley made some excuse to leave them alone together and Flora turned to Gervase. 'Well, this is nice, isn't it?' she said, her voice losing a little of its certainty.

'Of course it is,' said Gervase heartily. 'I'm extremely glad to see you.' He took out his cigarette case and offered her one. He stood over her with a match. There was a pause while she took a light from it.

'Oh, Gervase,' she said, keeping her hand on his, 'why didn't you answer any of my letters? You could at least have sent a postcard of the Hauptbahnhof if there is one.'

'Oh yes, indeed, it's quite celebrated. But you know that I'm a bad letter writer,' he said lamely. Could one also claim to be a bad postcard writer? he wondered.

'It would have been much nicer coming here if I had thought you wanted to see me,' persisted Flora.

'But I *do* want to see you,' said Gervase, putting his arm around her shoulders. 'You know I do.'

'Well, perhaps you do.' Flora did not sound convinced, but then neither had Gervase.

In a few days Flora knew everybody and was going everywhere. She was a great success with the English colony, some of whom even went so far as to hint to Gervase that he was a lucky man. Flora herself was, however (or *Gott sei dank*, as she would have said), less trying than he had feared she would be. After her display of affection on their first meeting she had more or less ignored him, or at least made no special attempt to seek his company. She was even learning Swedish and Finnish and knew more than Gervase did, which annoyed him considerably.

One evening Gervase was getting ready to go out to a social evening at the Reverend Augustine Boulding's – he was the English chaplain in Helsingfors and, as such, constantly criticized by Miss Moberley, who made a point of remembering how much better everything had been done in her father's time. Gervase had promised to meet Flora there, feeling that there would be safety in numbers. As he dressed he heard the sound of raised voices in Swedish, but he took little notice since it was not unusual.

Suddenly the door of his room opened and in rushed Ingeborg. When she saw Gervase tying his tie she stopped and stood in the doorway with a wild look on her face. She was dishevelled, with the tears still wet on her cheeks.

'What is it?' asked Gervase.

'Oh, I wish I were *dead*,' she moaned. 'I cannot stay here, it is unbearable!'

'Why, what is the matter?' Gervase took her hand. Although he saw little of her he was fond of her and wanted to comfort her. She was so weak and dependent, and yet somehow aloof.

'Oh, I am so *immensely* unhappy.' This was a favourite expression of both mother and daughter and they said it so often that Gervase had learned not to attach very much importance to it. But now Ingeborg began to cry again.

'Take me away, please, take me away *now*. I cannot stay here,' she sobbed.

'Where shall I take you, Ingeborg?' asked Gervase gently, getting out his handkerchief and wiping away her tears.

'Oh, take me away anywhere. Where you are going tonight, take me there.'

He stroked her hand. It was thin and rather rough.

'You can come with me to Augustine Boulding's if you like. It might take your mind off your troubles.'

'Augustine Boulding?' repeated Ingeborg in a wondering tone. 'What is that?'

Gervase laughed. 'You'll see,' he said. 'Hurry up and get ready.'

Ingeborg went quickly from the room. In an amazingly short time she was back again, wearing a black lace dress. She was very pale and had put on neither rouge nor lipstick, but Gervase thought that she looked curiously beautiful. Just as they were going out Fru Lindblom came in from the kitchen. She had quite recovered her equanimity.

'It is kind of you to take Ingeborg out,' she said. 'An old woman is not a good companion for a young girl. We know that young girls like to be with young men. I am glad to see you together.'

Ingeborg looked rather uncomfortable and moved towards the door. As they walked along she said, 'Must I speak English tonight? It is so difficult.'

'Well, I'm afraid the people we are going to meet will not be speaking much Swedish,' said Gervase.

The first person they saw on entering the room was Flora, sitting by Miss Moberley, who examined Ingeborg carefully.

'I think that must be Fru Lindblom's daughter,' she said. 'She looks a quiet, genteel sort of girl, no paint or powder and quite a plain black dress.'

Flora advanced to greet them.

Ingeborg smiled at her and blushed nervously. 'I don't speak English much,' she said.

'Flora is learning Swedish,' said Gervase unkindly.

Ingeborg at once began talking rapidly in her native language while Flora stood by with a bewildered expression on her face.

'I really don't understand very much,' she said.

'Oh, I'm sorry,' said Ingeborg. They both laughed.

Flora took her arm. 'Come and have something to eat,' she said. 'No, Gervase, I think we will go by ourselves. Ingeborg and I will prefer to talk on our own.'

'What about?' asked Gervase suspiciously.

'Oh, *Herz und Schmerz*,' said Flora lightly.

'*Dichtung und Wahrheit*,' continued Ingeborg, who had now quite brightened up.

*

After a while Gervase went over to Flora and Ingeborg.

'Have you had your talk?' he asked indulgently.

'Yes, we have become great friends,' said Flora in a clear penetrating voice. She turned to Ingeborg and wished her good night. Gervase heard them arranging to meet for coffee one afternoon.

'Oh, I like Flora,' said Ingeborg enthusiastically, as they were driving home in a taxi. 'Oh, fancy that I should find such a friend!' She had quite recovered from her brooding unhappy mood of earlier in the evening. Now it was Gervase who was brooding. He resented Ingeborg's high spirits. He wanted them to be together in their unhappiness.

Flora sat up in bed and untied the turquoise blue ribbon which was supposed to keep her hair tidy during the night. But the bed was so comfortable that it was some minutes before she could bring herself to get out of it. When she put her feet on to the floor the carpet was thick and warm. Everything in the room was solid and heavy and good. The same adjectives could be applied to the pictures, Flora thought. There were a great many rich oil paintings of unknown places, but her favourite was a portrait of the late Bishop Burton, which hung, rather curiously she thought, over the bed.

At breakfast Miss Moberley was in a minatory mood.

'Your father has had a hard life,' she declared surprisingly. 'I know that you, his daughter, the apple of his eye, are not going to disappoint him.'

Flora murmured something about hoping so too.

'There is a responsibility resting on you, as there is on every daughter. I think you should realize that a young girl of good family has to be careful whom she encourages. People of good family stand out in a foreign town. Their example will be followed.'

'Oh, Aunt Emily, do you mean that *I* have been setting a bad example to the Finns?'

'Well, dear, that may be putting it rather strongly, but you should not let them take advantage of your good nature. Rhoda told me that a Finn had called here yesterday and asked for you. You can be quite civil to him when you meet, but don't encourage him to seek your company.'

'His name is Ooli Ruomini-Forstenborg. He is a student of Gervase's and of *very* good family. I met him at Mr Boulding's. Perhaps Mr Boulding would be a suitable match for me?'

Miss Moberley spoke of Mr Boulding with carefully modified rapture. He was a good-living man, sound in his views, an able preacher *but* he was not *quite* good enough for their dear Flora.

'I must be very wonderful,' said Flora rather bitterly. 'Is there anyone who is good enough for me? I feel that there may not be. I feel that I may be condemned to keep myself to myself all my life.'

'Now, Flora,' said Miss Moberley archly, 'I'm sure you don't need me to tell you what is suitable and what is not. I have already told Gervase of my feelings in the matter. He understands.'

Oh, *poor* Gervase, thought Flora. 'You must let things take their course,' she said lightly. 'Now that you have drawn such a flattering portrait of me, I feel I could do *better* for myself. Ingeborg Lindblom had a proposal of marriage from a German Baron. I'm not going to be outdone!'

'Then she is engaged?' asked Miss Moberley.

'Oh, no, she refused him. Her mother was furious with her and never lets her forget it. She makes Ingeborg's life a misery.'

'Poor Mrs Lindblom,' said Miss Moberley, 'what a terrible thing.'

'Poor Ingeborg!' said Flora indignantly. 'It is hard for her to be called an undutiful daughter simply because she refused to marry a man she didn't love.'

Flora's eyes grew bright and sentimental.

Flora often wondered what would become of her. She had been in love with Gervase for so long that she could not imagine a life in which he had no part. Nor, on the other hand, could she imagine a life in which he returned her love. That would somehow spoil the picture she had made of herself. It was an interesting picture, very dear to her, and she could not bear the idea of it being spoilt. Noble, faithful, long-suffering, although not without its funny side, it was like something out of Tchekov, she thought. The first two years were the worst, she reflected calmly. She could tell any young woman that. But it was really no use entering upon an unrequited passion unless you were prepared to keep it up for at least five years. Seven years was best. There was something very noble about loving a person for seven years and getting nothing in return.

Flora stood looking out of the window. She liked watching people in the street. She was always hoping that flowers would arrive for her from an unknown admirer. She saw Gervase hurrying along towards the house. He was wearing his blue overcoat (now lined with fur) but he looked cold and in a bad temper.

'What have you been doing all morning?' he asked as she let him in.

'Oh, I have had breakfast. I have talked a great deal. I have tidied my room and manicured my nails. I have read a poem by Cleveland. Oh Gervase.' She put her hand on his arm. '"Not one of all these ravenous hours, but thee devours." That was Cleveland's message to me this morning.'

'A very solemn thought,' said Gervase, looking down at her rosy nails against his coat sleeve. 'You shouldn't read Cleveland in the morning. I'm not sure that he's worth reading anyway.'

'Aunt Emily and I had a talk this morning about marriage and marrying people you didn't love.' Flora paused. 'Did Ingeborg tell you about her German Baron?'

'No. She never confides in me,' said Gervase rather evasively.

Flora told him the story.

'So that's why the mother and daughter are always quarrelling and weeping,' said Gervase. 'Well, well, it would surely have been much simpler if Ingeborg had married him.'

'Oh, Gervase, what a sordid attitude towards marriage!' Flora linked her arm through his.

'I have no "attitude towards marriage" as you call it,' he said. 'I simply said that because it seemed to me the simplest way out of a difficulty. Indeed, isn't it usually that?' he added, disengaging Flora's arm as tactfully as he could.

'Well at least you agree with St Paul that it is better to marry than to burn,' persisted Flora.

'One isn't usually offered the alternative,' said Gervase, 'and, anyway, I am not in the habit of agreeing with St Paul.'

Flora felt suddenly depressed. This afternoon she was having tea with Ingeborg. It would be nice to see her again, but what else could their meeting be but an outpouring of sorrow on both sides?

Flora was feeling more cheerful as she walked to Fazer's where she had arranged to meet Ingeborg for tea. She saw some nice fur shoes in a shop window. Were they made of reindeer skin? Should she buy them? It was lovely being in a really Northern country. You could walk about in a fur coat, snow-boots and a fur hat and feel perfectly natural and at the same time like something out of a Russian film.

Ingeborg was waiting for Flora when she arrived at Fazer's, having wandered through many rooms. How gay and interesting it all was. How different from England! And Ingeborg, in her hearth-rug coat, looked just like Garbo. She was standing up, drooping rather, her hands in her pockets. She had taken off her hat and her fair hair hung down almost to her furry shoulders. She looked tired and pale, but her face brightened when she saw Flora.

'I must try to speak to you in English this afternoon,' she said carefully, as if she had prepared this opening sentence beforehand. 'I must practise. Mama is angry because I do not learn more.'

They drank their coffee and ate their cakes and their talk was light and feminine. Flora promised to knit Ingeborg a jumper.

'I like to have some knitting on hand. I should like to make it in a bright colour,' she said. 'You would look marvellous in jade green!'

'Oh, you are kind. I shall have what you say. I always buy something grey or black or brown. I look plain always, I know.'

'But Ingeborg, you're beautiful, much better looking than I am,' said Flora sincerely.

'Oh no, Flora. I am so flat and thin,' said Ingeborg simply, looking down at her chest.

Flora laughed. 'Well, I am neither flat nor thin,' she said, 'but I don't know what happiness my curves have brought me. How curious it is,' she continued, 'to be sitting in a café in Finland. To realize that life is still going on at home.' She paused reflectively. 'This afternoon I would have been at the working party for the Olde Tudor Fayre, which is being held in May in aid of the new Parish Hall. I am making a tea-cosy for it. In England I am a vicar's daughter and over here I am supposed to be a companion to Miss Moberley, but I suppose what I really am is a young woman in love.'

Ingeborg had been listening to Flora with an expression of bewilderment on her face. Tudor Fayre, tea-cosy, Parish Hall, all these words were unfamiliar to her. It was like coming to the end of a dark forest to hear the word Love. Ingeborg was now able to take an intelligent part in the conversation, able, indeed, to adorn it with a quotation from Goethe.

'"*Und lieben, Götter, welch ein Glück!*"' she exclaimed enthusiastically, her eyes shining and her cheeks quite pink.

'Why Ingeborg,' said Flora, 'are you a young woman in love too? *Do* tell me. Wouldn't it ease your sorrow to have some comfortable female friend to confide in? I know you will tell me some time, people always confide in me. "Dear Flora is so sympathetic," they say. I used to be proud of it, but now there is more resignation than pride in my attitude. It probably means that I shall find friends rather than lovers.' Flora heaved a rather exaggerated sigh. 'I don't know which I'd rather have.'

'A friend is better than a lover,' said Ingeborg.

'I think I should like another cake,' said Flora suddenly. 'Come and choose some.' They got up and went towards the counter where there was a display of rich cakes. Flora and Ingeborg discussed the merits of each one before they made their choice, or, at least, Flora discussed and Ingeborg listened. As they ate their cakes Ingeborg fell silent and sat brooding. As Flora mentioned Gervase's name, casually, in the course of conversation, she started and grew pale. So *that's* what it is! Flora thought. Ingeborg is also in love with Gervase.

'Shall we go home now,' she said gently, 'or would you like to come and choose the wool?'

'The wool?' repeated Ingeborg, looking at Flora with a dazed expression. The tears in her eyes looked as if they might spill down her face at any moment. 'Yes, we will choose the wool,' she said, obviously making an effort to pull herself together.

Oh, poor Ingeborg, thought Flora, taking hold of her arm, what can I say to her? I can't tell her that the first two years are the worst. There was nothing she could say, Flora decided; all she could do was be kind to her. She would say nothing for the present, but she would do all she could to help her to win

Gervase's love. Flora felt noble and suddenly happy when she had made this resolution.

'Oh, Ingeborg,' she said enthusiastically, 'you must have this bluey-green, it brings out the colour of your eyes!'

Ingeborg looked pleased and smiled. 'Oh, Flora, you are *so* kind,' she said. They turned and looked at each other, holding the skein of wool between them.

'I have some number ten needles,' said Flora. 'I shall have to get some eights, though.' I'll begin the jumper tonight, she thought. That will be something.

'I am glad that you are going with Gervase to this party tonight,' said Miss Moberley. 'He needs a steadying influence.'

Oh dear, thought Flora, is that what I am. If only Aunt Emily would see how hopeless it was trying to bring young people together when one was so determined not to be brought.

'I must go and get ready now,' she said. 'I shall look very English in my black velvet dress.'

When they were in the taxi she asked Gervase, 'Why didn't you bring Ingeborg?'

'My dear Flora, why should I? You seem very devoted to her. I can't think what you can have in common.'

Flora laughed. 'More than you could possibly imagine,' she said. 'Don't you like her?'

'Like her?' Gervase sounded startled. 'I simply don't feel anything about her. She's just there in the house.'

As they arrived at the party, Gervase whispered, 'A lot of them are my students. You'll find them very intelligent.'

'Oh, good. I shall quote Cleveland at them and expect their faces to light up as they supply the next line.'

'We are doing Milton this term,' explained Gervase, as if it were impossible that the students would know anything but what he had taught them.

'I think Milton is a bloody fool,' said one Finn shortly. He was fair and slender with intelligent greenish eyes. His name was Ooli and he had already, at their previous meetings, shown himself to be most attentive to Flora. She noticed that his voice sounded very like Gervase's.

'You speak like Herr Lektor Harringay,' she said.

'Only when we are drunk,' laughed Ooli.

'I wish *I* could have such powers given to me when I was drunk,' said Flora, as if she had considerable experience of that state. As the evening wore on and the whisky flowed and the Finnish students proved more and more agreeable, Flora was pleased to see that she was able to enjoy herself even if Gervase did not love her.

Just before the party was over, Ooli turned to Flora and bowed.

'I am giving a party next Friday. It is to be held at the same time as Herr Gervase's colleague Herr Lolly is giving his lecture on Milton's *Areopagitica*,' he said, turning towards Gervase. 'We really did not think we could bear to hear such a lecture, so we are having a tea instead. We hope that Herr Harringay will come. And you, Miss Flora.' He turned and took both her hands in his. His green eyes were sparkling. Flora felt quite weak as she looked into them. 'Perhaps you will come too?'

Flora thanked him, smiled and stood up. For a moment the room with its bronzes, birchwood furniture, flowers, Finns and whisky swam about her, but she soon steadied herself and she was able to walk with dignity to the cloakroom where she made up her face and put on her coat. I believe I am a little intoxicated, she thought, as she looked at her reflection in the mirror. It had huge eyes and a mouth that would keep breaking into smiles.

The next morning after breakfast she slipped out of the house to get a little fresh air. By chance she met Ingeborg in the market.

Ingeborg was more talkative than usual and kept asking Flora about the party.

'It must have been very entertaining. Mr Harringay did not come home until very late. I heard him come in. I was awake.'

Flora looked at her with compassion, then went on hastily to speak in general terms about the party.

'How lovely to have been there,' said Ingeborg, 'and with your own particular man – he *is* your man, isn't he?' Ingeborg looked at Flora piteously.

'No, he isn't,' said Flora evasively. 'We are quite friendly, that is all. I can perfectly well do without a man, and I certainly don't need Gervase Harringay.'

'If only I should be able to say that! But you are my friend and I will say the truth to you. I cannot live without Gervase Harringay!' Ingeborg stopped suddenly in the middle of the market. She obviously expected Flora to stop too, stunned at her revelation. But Flora took Ingeborg's arm and led her away from the rows of shining codfish around them.

'Oh, Ingeborg, I knew it,' she said. 'I guessed it that afternoon. How glad I am to know the truth. Everything will be so much easier now.'

But would it? Flora's tired and still rather fuddled mind saw many difficulties. Suppose Gervase didn't love Ingeborg? Then there would be two unhappy young women. Flora herself was used to this particular kind of unhappiness and was already beginning to realize that Gervase could never be hers now. But was Ingeborg strong enough to stand such misery? And what about Miss Moberley? Nobody who didn't know her could realize what a formidable obstacle a rich, elderly aunt could be.

'I love him. I cannot live without him,' said Ingeborg simply. 'It is terrible when I must be alone with him. I do not speak. And he does not speak. We sit together in the room and I am sewing and he is reading a book. Oh, it is terrible, the silence!

And Mama says I am stupid and how can Mr Harringay love me when I am stupid. You are so clever and so beautiful, Flora, and can say so much . . .'

'Oh, Ingeborg, I'm sure everything is going to be all right. You must be patient, simply that.' You may have to wait five years, she thought, but judged it more tactful not to say so now.

'Oh, *fancy*!' Ingeborg's face lit up with joy and she looked beautiful. 'Oh, if it should be true! I will wait until I am as old as Mama if he will love me one day.'

'I don't imagine you will have to wait as long as that,' said Flora wryly. 'You know, men are just a bit stupid about love. Yes, men are often *very* stupid,' she added. Suddenly she did not feel strong enough to comfort and advise. Later, when she had had time to think about it, she would arrange everything. Gervase and Ingeborg would be married. Flora might even be chief bridesmaid.

As she went back towards Miss Moberley's she met Gervase.

'How did you enjoy the party?' he asked. 'And what did you think of my students? I could see,' he said in tones of surprise, 'they were charmed with you.'

'I simply adore Ooli,' said Flora, enthusiastically.

'You adore Ooli!' Gervase was astonished.

'He's so intelligent and amusing and he has such beautiful green eyes!'

'Well, there's no knowing what women will like,' said Gervase with a shrug of his shoulders. 'First me, and now Ooli,' he added.

Flora gave him a startled look. He had put it into words before she had even thought of it. She didn't like it. She wanted to cling to Gervase's arm – a thing he hated her to do – and say, 'Not yet, please, not yet. Let us stay the same for a little longer. Let me stay in the unhappiness I'm used to rather than start out on a new one which may be even worse.' There was something familiar and comforting about Gervase, walking two or three paces in front of her on the pavement of a strange Northern capital. Flora was sure that there could never be anything comforting about Ooli, even if she were to fall in love with him. But she said none of these things. They could not stand still.

'First you and then Ooli,' she said thoughtfully. 'Now, is that a step forward or a step back?'

'I like to think that it is a step back,' said Gervase laughing, 'but I must be honest and tell you that Ooli is a much better catch than I am, if you can land him. He is a Count, he has plenty of money, he is very intelligent and he can be charming when he likes.'

'I think that it will be out of the frying pan and into the fire,' she laughed. 'Poor Flora, caught between the Devil and the deep green sea!'

'I like to think that I am the Devil,' said Gervase.

How splendid it would be if Flora were to marry Count Ooli Ruomini-Forstenborg. She was really such a nice girl and would make an excellent wife for some lucky man. Gervase felt that he would have given anything to see her happily settled with somebody else.

Gervase sighed and flung the novel he had been reading on to the sofa. He knew that he ought not to be reading a novel at all. He should be preparing a lecture on *Samson Agonistes* or at least be writing an intelligent letter to one of his far-away, unreal Oxford friends. The only reality nowadays was Finland and the Finns and even Flora, the most English of people, seemed to have taken on a curious quality, so that she said and did things she would never have done at home. He never opened a book now, except to divert himself with a novel or to look up a reference for a lecture. He had given up learning Swedish and Finnish. It was so much easier to speak English with Fru

Lindblom and to be silent with Ingeborg. Somehow he didn't need words with her. There was a curious bond between them, he felt, almost as though they could see into each other's minds and knew that what was there needed no explaining. What actually was there Gervase didn't know. He might be in love with her, he supposed idly. Gervase was a great believer in letting sleeping dogs lie. He had no idea that Ingeborg was in love with him. He thought that simply being a Finn was the reason for her strange, almost abrupt manner, her fits of moodiness and her fondness for reading Heine. But although he did not know that she loved him he had some understanding of her. He knew why she longed so passionately for spring. He was beginning to feel the effects of the Finnish climate upon himself. He wondered how it affected his aunt. He did not imagine that Miss Moberley would have enough sensibility to be affected by it. She would see it only as weather. She might dislike the rain – it had done nothing but rain for the past month – but she would miss altogether the curious leaden quality of the air, which Gervase felt was stifling him. Perhaps one grew used to it in time, though. He must remember to notice the people at Mr Boulding's tonight.

This evening he was taking Ingeborg with him again. When they arrived they found Mr Boulding surrounded by the usual group of spinsters, including Miss Moberley, who was annoyed because Gervase had come without Flora. It almost seemed as if there might be something between him and the Lindblom girl. She would have to speak to him about it. Her temper was not improved when Flora arrived with Ooli, although she modified her disapproval when she discovered that he was a Count.

Flora took Ingeborg away into a corner and began a low murmured conversation with her, and Ooli went over to Miss Moberley, who made room for him upon the sofa where he sat very demurely with hands folded while Miss Moberley graciously asked him questions about his family. Glancing across the room,

Flora was pleased to see that Miss Moberley was looking positively affable. If she were to take a liking to him she might easily come to regard him as quite a suitable successor to Gervase when she finally admitted that it was extremely unlikely that he and Flora would make a match of it.

Gervase came up to take Ingeborg away to speak to Mr Boulding and Flora sat alone in her corner. The whole scene before her became unreal. The English colony, the room with its portraits of former chaplains, the food on the long table. All this must surely be a dream and she must really be in the drawing room at the vicarage, listening to the wireless, knitting, cutting out a dress on the floor, reading the new *Vogue*, or even Young's *Night Thoughts*.

Lorenzo of the *Night Thoughts* might have looked like Ooli Ruomini-Forstenborg – thin, sharp features and bold green eyes. Flora saw that Ooli was smiling at her across the room. There was triumph in his expression. Flora went over to them in time to hear Miss Moberley say, 'Now Count, or Ooli, as I am going to call you, do not forget to drop in to tea. Any Tuesday. I do like to be in touch with young people.'

Flora stared at her in disbelief which increased when Miss Moberley reappeared, ready to go home in her long musquash coat with a skunk collar, and smiled archly as Ooli kissed her hand and bowed. He took Flora's hand and held it, smiling at her but saying nothing.

In the taxi going home Gervase drew Ingeborg to him and said, 'Now, Ingeborg, be reasonable. Flora wants us to be happy, I know that. Anyway, she has fallen in love with Ooli,' he added, hoping that he might be speaking the truth. 'She doesn't love me any more. She was never *really* in love with me – it was simply an over-developed imagination and the boredom of being a girl in an English country vicarage. She always dramatizes herself and sees herself as leading a life of absorbing interest. No doubt she has told you that she has been in love with me since she was nineteen, and made so much of it that you were afraid to hurt her. I know Flora far better than you do. She can just as easily fall in love with somebody else – it's her nature.'

'Oh, *fancy*,' said Ingeborg, who had been following this with some difficulty, 'fancy that you should say such things about Flora! Oh, what should Flora say if she hear you?'

What indeed should Flora say to hear the noble passion, the devotion of the best years of her life, dismissed in a few phrases? Gervase realized that he was hardly doing her justice, but he felt that this was no time to be thinking of Flora. They went into the flat. Fru Lindblom's wood-carving tools were scattered over the table in the corner, but she had obviously gone to bed.

'Ingeborg,' said Gervase, 'do you love me? I want to hear it.'

Ingeborg turned away from him. 'I know you want to hear it, because you want that all should love you. Flora, my dear friend . . .'

'No, Ingeborg,' Gervase spoke urgently. 'I've never loved anyone until now, I swear it. I want only you.'

Ingeborg raised her head and looked at him. Her eyes were shining. She looked as if she were about to say 'Oh, *fancy*', but love seemed to give her a command of language and she began to talk rapidly in a mixture of English and Swedish to a fascinated Gervase who could only hold her and gaze at her in wonder.

'Ingeborg,' he said fondly, 'whatever sort of wife will you make?'

'A wife?' said Ingeborg in amazement. 'Oh, fancy, if I should be a wife!'

'Well, some day you will be my wife,' said Gervase, doubt creeping into his mind at the thought of the many obstacles that might stand in the way of their marrying.

*

One morning a few days later Flora and Miss Moberley were sitting together in the drawing room. It was nearly Christmas but neither Flora nor Gervase was going back to England. To Flora the idea of a real white Christmas in a northern land was irresistible, though she felt guilty at the thought of all her parish duties at home. Miss Moberley, too, was busy with thoughts of Christmas, and had already unearthed a large collection of useless presents, which could only have come from a bazaar or sale of work, presumably held by the English community, for where else in Finland could one have bought such pincushions topped with china ladies, organdie lavender bags and leather-covered bridge markers? They were obviously presents which Miss Moberley herself had received in past years. It seemed that at this season Miss Moberley had a large number of mysterious friends in England to whom she sent some 'little token'. When Flora expressed a polite interest, albums of faded sepia photographs were produced and clergymen with jam-pot collars and women with top-heavy hair, wearing tailored blouses and long smooth skirts, were pointed out and their histories told.

As they were thus engaged, Rhoda came in holding a card in her hand.

'There is a young Finnish gentleman to see you, madam,' she said in tones of considerable surprise.

Miss Moberley's expression of suspicion changed to one of cordial welcome as she read the name.

'Tell the Count that I shall be pleased to see him, Rhoda,' she said.

Ooli went over to Miss Moberley, bowed and kissed her hand. He was smartly dressed in a dark suit and carried an elaborately beribboned box which he presented to her with a ceremonious gesture. She gave a cry of delight and began to untie the ribbons. In no time at all they were seated together on the sofa chatting most amiably and eating the crystallized fruits which Ooli had brought.

'Won't you have one, Flora?' asked Miss Moberley, peering into the box.

'No, thank you,' said Flora, 'it's too soon before lunch.'

'Now isn't that like a young woman?' said Ooli. 'I suppose she is afraid of spoiling her figure.'

Miss Moberley smiled. Her figure, upholstered in rich brown marocain, had long ceased to bother her. A gentlewoman was a gentlewoman whatever her dimensions. After some more talk and a great deal more smiling, it appeared that Ooli wanted to take Flora out to lunch. After the crystallized fruit and the charming behaviour Miss Moberley could do nothing else but give her permission. 'Run along and get ready, Flora dear,' she said.

'There is plenty of time,' said Ooli. 'I have allowed her half an hour. It is known that women are always painting their faces and their finger nails, and that takes much time, I think.'

'My canvas is already complete,' said Flora. 'I shall be ready in five minutes.'

They walked along the street companionably until Flora's attention was attracted by a shop window and she stopped and exclaimed, 'Oh, what a heavenly dress! I must look.'

'I cannot think why women waste so much time looking in shop windows,' said Ooli patiently. 'I do not look in shop windows. If I want something I simply go into a shop and ask for it.'

Flora laughed. 'What admirable technique! And does it always work?'

'Why naturally,' said Ooli in a surprised voice.

'But suppose you want something that isn't there? I don't mean material things. One can see that material things can *somehow* be got, but there are other things that seem completely unattainable. Do you know the poem

The desire of the moth for the star
Of the night for the morrow . . .

I think that's what I mean.'

'Women seldom know what they mean,' said Ooli indulgently. 'I suppose you are thinking of some perfect man you would like to marry, and naturally you find that he is unattainable because he doesn't exist.'

'I don't want a perfect man,' protested Flora. 'I want somebody fairly tall and good-looking, who is comfortably off, kind and tender and fond of the eighteenth-century poets,' she added. 'It doesn't seem much to ask.'

'You mean Herr Lektor Harringay?' asked Ooli.

'Oh no!' cried Flora. 'He isn't fond of the eighteenth century and he hasn't enough money.' Nor is he kind and tender, she thought desolately, at least, not to me. She turned her face away because she suddenly felt that she might cry.

Ooli made no comment and began to speculate as to where they should have lunch. 'I will take you to some very nice place,' he said, 'so that people will see me and say, look, there is Helga's youngest boy with a beautiful English girl. I suppose she has not seen Lars and Akseli because if she had she would not be going out with Ooli.'

Flora laughed. 'Are your brothers nice?' she asked.

Ooli shrugged his shoulders. 'Lars is quite handsome, if that is what you mean. He does not like Helsingfors so he lives always in the country and manages the estate. Akseli is clever, he lives much in Paris and has an Italian mistress.'

'Do you consider it clever for a Finn to have an Italian mistress?' asked Flora.

'I think it would be more clever to have a beautiful English wife.'

Flora felt she should change the subject. 'Oh, I am so hungry,' she said as the waiter came up with some *voileipajpoyata*. 'I can eat the whole lot!'

'If you were in love with me,' said Ooli sadly, 'you would not be able to eat even one little fish.'

'I never show by any outward signs when I am in love,' said Flora primly.

'I do,' said Ooli, stretching out his hand and squeezing Flora's fingers.

Flora was grateful for the affectionate gesture, but as the lunch proceeded she became more melancholy, thinking of Gervase. She knew now that he had never really loved her, not as she had loved him, and she had come to feel a sisterly responsibility for Ingeborg. If she couldn't have Gervase herself, Ingeborg must have him.

'What is it, Flora? You look so sad. Have you eaten too much?' asked Ooli solicitously.

Flora came out of her reverie. 'No, I've had a lovely lunch, thank you. I was just remembering that I promised to help Aunt Emily with her Christmas cards this afternoon.'

'But I want you to spend the afternoon with me,' said Ooli.

Flora smiled with what she hoped was a mixture of sadness, firmness and sweetness. 'I'm sorry,' she said, 'but I must go now.' She felt suddenly that she wanted to be quite by herself, away from all complications, of which it seemed that Ooli might well turn out to be the most important.

'Well it is good for me to be disappointed sometimes,' said Ooli. 'But you might have fallen in love with me by five o'clock.'

'I might simply have been wanting my tea,' laughed Flora.

'Women are always wanting tea,' said Ooli, but there was more affection than scorn in his voice and he stood for some seconds, after Flora had gone in, gazing regretfully at the closed door of Miss Moberley's house.

*

It was Christmas Day and Gervase was to have two Christmas dinners, one at Fru Lindblom's and another at Miss Moberley's in the evening. He lay back in his chair – a new comfortable one, bought especially for him – smoking a cigarette and thinking idly of Fru Lindblom. He was particularly interested in her now that there was every chance of her becoming his mother-in-law. He was not sure if she realized that a new understanding had sprung up between himself and Ingeborg, although he was sure that she would be very pleased when she did.

'After dinner we shall give out the presents,' said Fru Lindblom, coming into the room. 'I have kept all the parcels and we shall open them together. The goose is ready, Greta is just bringing it in.'

Gervase had contributed a bottle of sherry and some port to the festivities. After the sherry, Fru Lindblom was polite and grateful, but after her second glass of port she called him her dear son and her tongue was loosed in a flood of reminiscences.

Gervase began to open his presents, which were mostly cigarettes and books. His heart gave an absurd leap when he saw a parcel addressed to him in Ingeborg's large pointed writing. It was a book of German poems. 'Now I shall treasure this,' he said softly.

'Why here is something for Ingeborg in Herr Harringay's writing,' Fru Lindblom exclaimed, holding a small parcel in her hand.

Ingeborg drew back as she saw the radiant look on her mother's face, but Gervase took the parcel and pressed it into her hand. Ingeborg went over to the window and opened it.

'Oh, *fancy*,' she cried joyfully, 'that I should have this beautiful thing!' She turned to her mother and began talking rapidly in Swedish, holding in her hand a thin platinum chain set with pearls.

Her mother took it from her and admired it, looking first at

Gervase and then at Ingeborg with a questioning expression on her face.

'Mr Harringay,' she said, 'this is a very fine, expensive present that you have given my daughter. She has never had any jewellery before.'

'Well, all the more reason why she should have some now,' said Gervase in a hearty, avuncular tone to hide his embarrassment.

'You are very kind,' said Fru Lindblom. 'It is natural that a pretty girl should have jewellery, but you cannot give it to her,' she added in a low voice.

'But Fru Lindblom,' said Gervase in a reasonable tone, 'why shouldn't I give Ingeborg a present? I'm very fond of her.'

'It is not right that you should give her jewellery,' said Fru Lindblom firmly.

Gervase took the pearl chain and fastened it around Ingeborg's neck. The sight of her face moved him so greatly that he suddenly found himself saying in a firm, clear tone, 'Fru Lindblom, I love Ingeborg and I think she loves me. I am going to marry her.'

He had said it now. For a moment he experienced a feeling of panic. He, the cautious Gervase Harringay, who would never hold Flora's hand in the cinema at home in case someone who knew them might be sitting nearby. But this feeling lasted only for a second. When he saw Ingeborg fingering her necklace and smiling at him through her tears, he knew that even if he could have escaped he would not do so now for anything in the world.

The effect of this announcement on Fru Lindblom was wonderful. She rushed to where Gervase and Ingeborg were standing and tried to enfold them, both at once, in her arms, calling them her dear son and daughter.

'Oh, my dear Gervase,' she said, her voice trembling with

emotion, 'as soon as I saw you I knew that you could be a dear son to me. And I have watched you two children together. I have seen it coming and now it has come. Oh, this wonderful Christmas Day!' And with her eyes shining and her head held high she stalked from the room like an actor making a triumphant exit.

When Gervase arrived at his aunt's house everything seemed very English and normal. Rhoda wished him the Compliments of the Season in a respectful, colourless voice as he gave her the present which Flora had helped him to choose. He paused outside the drawing-room door, took a deep breath and went in. Flora rushed to greet him, and it looked as if she only just managed, by a great effort of will, to stop herself flinging her arms around him.

'Oh, Gervase,' she said, 'a *very* happy Christmas. Now everything is complete.'

She went prancing around the room in great excitement when she had unwrapped Gervase's present to her, which was a brightly coloured Finnish scarf of printed wool which suited her admirably. She wrapped it around her shoulders like a shawl and hugged the ends to her breast, as if she wanted to keep it as close to her heart as possible.

'I'm glad you like it,' said Gervase. 'It looks very nice on you.'

'Did you choose it all by yourself?' asked Flora fondly, raising her eyes to his.

'Yes, I am proud to say that I did,' he replied, returning her glance. For a moment they stood looking at each other. Flora was the first to look away because she suddenly found her eyes filling with tears. She went over to another corner of the room and began re-arranging the ornaments on the Christmas tree. When she had collected herself she said, 'I have got a book for you,' handing Gervase a parcel, 'an anthology. I hope you will be able to find comfort in it for many years. I've been reading it myself for the past week.'

'And did it bring comfort?' asked Gervase awkwardly.

'Comfort!' Flora suddenly became very bright and sparkling. 'I don't need comfort, do I, Aunt Emily?'

'I should think not,' said Miss Moberley. 'Have you shown Gervase your presents yet?'

'No, I don't really think he'd be interested,' said Flora quickly.

'Wait until you see what Ooli has given her,' said Miss Moberley archly.

'I don't see why Gervase should be made to inspect my presents,' said Flora rather sulkily. She rolled up her left sleeve and held out her wrist. On it was an elegant platinum watch set with diamonds. 'There!' she said defiantly, but as she looked at it she could not resist a pleased smile.

'Good Heavens!' said Gervase. 'Did Ooli give you this? I had no idea things were that serious.'

'One must expect an attractive girl like Flora to have other strings to her bow,' said Miss Moberley. 'The Count sends her flowers every day. He really is a charming young man. One of the oldest families in Finland, but of course they live on their estates in the country, which explains why I haven't met them before. Now, Gervase, you know who your rival is,' she said.

'Well, I'm afraid I have no chance against a rich attractive Finnish Count,' said Gervase smoothly. 'All I can do is retire at once.'

Flora flung him a contemptuous glance. How gracefully he did things and how she hated him for it.

'Am I to meet my rival tonight?' asked Gervase.

'No, he's in the country with his family,' said Flora.

'Then I am afraid you will have to put up with second best,' said Gervase. 'I never thought the Finns would be robbing me like this – and one of my own students, too,' he added comfortably.

The evening was to be devoted to the entertainment of Miss Moberley's circle, the English community who attended her At Homes and expected to be invited for the more prominent festivals of the Church.

Flora, who had gone to change, came into the room. She was wearing a white dress with some of Ooli's scarlet carnations pinned at the waist. The new watch shone proudly on her wrist.

'Flora,' said Gervase, 'you look marvellous!'

'Thank you, Gervase,' said Flora brightly. She *was* feeling marvellous now.

After the guests had finally departed Miss Moberley went to bed, leaving Gervase and Flora by themselves in the drawing room. Gervase lit a cigarette and slumped into an armchair. Flora put her feet up on the sofa and lay with her head dangling over the edge and her hair streaming down like seaweed. She looked at her new wristwatch and yawned.

'*Die arme Flora,*' she said.

'Why?' asked Gervase in a tired voice. 'Why is it always Flora who is poor?'

'*Weg ist alles, was du liebtest,* or something like that,' said Flora languidly.

'You mean, someone you love isn't here?' said Gervase cautiously, a hope rising and taking possession of him.

'I suppose I may have meant that, but at this very instant I feel quite happy in this room with you.' Flora roused herself and looked at him. 'There you are, Gervase Harringay, sitting in a chair doing nothing, saying nothing, just looking nice.'

'But that isn't enough for you,' said Gervase firmly. 'You know it isn't.'

'Yes, I do know it is not enough,' said Flora in a careful tone as if she were repeating something she had learned by heart. 'I want more.'

'And you'll get it,' said Gervase, looking pleased. 'You and Ooli are in love with each other, aren't you?'

'The Count and I are good friends,' she said.

'Well, friendship is a great thing,' said Gervase, standing up. 'And you never know which way it will turn. I must be going now.'

Flora stood up too and linked her arm through his. 'Do you realize, Gervase,' she said in a calm level tone, 'that this may be our last Christmas together?'

'What do you mean?' asked Gervase irritably. He hoped Flora wasn't going to be difficult.

'Well, things will probably be quite different by this time next year,' she said.

'Things, as you call them, generally are different from one year to the next,' observed Gervase shortly.

'Oh, Gervase, don't pretend not to know what I mean. You might at least face things as I am doing. You're always so cowardly,' she said passionately.

'Hush, don't make such a noise,' he said nervously. 'What have I to face anyway?'

Flora dropped down into a chair and covered her face with her hands. 'It sounds so silly if I have to put it into words,' she said, her voice breaking, 'especially as it obviously doesn't mean anything to you. Losing Flora, that is what you have to face. Poor Flora, fancy thinking you would need courage for that!'

He sat down beside her and put his arm round her shoulders. 'Flora,' he said in a gentler tone, 'you know we shall always be friends, whatever happens.'

'Friends? What's being friends?' said Flora, turning her head away.

Gervase gave a barely perceptible sigh. 'But have we ever been more than friends?' he asked. 'Very good friends, I admit, but not more than that.'

'You don't understand,' said Flora desperately. 'I can't ever make you understand, I can see that. You're too afraid of facing any sort of finality, even if it doesn't touch you. You haven't the courage to put me right out of your life as I would put you out of mine.'

'But Flora,' said Gervase in a puzzled, exasperated tone, 'it isn't necessary. Why should I face things I don't have to face? All this putting each other out of our lives,' he added with an indulgent smile. 'We can always be friends. Poor Flora – it seems a pity that I can't . . .'

Flora began to laugh; she seemed quite herself again. 'Poor Gervase,' she said, 'but there is one thing you can do. Give me a cigarette, please.'

Gervase took out his case and offered it to her.

'Now go home. It's very late. Aunt Emily will think you have been proposing or something! Give my love to Ingeborg.'

Gervase smiled. 'I will,' he said. He stood looking at her for a moment before he turned and went out of the room.

When he had gone Flora went up to her room and began to undress for bed. She hung up her white dress, put the carnations in water and the new watch in its velvet case. She removed all the make-up from her face, brushed her teeth, set her hair and put out the clothes she was going to wear in the morning. Then she knelt by her bed and prayed rather mechanically for all the things she had been taught to pray for when she was a child – parents, relations, people she liked – this was a long list constantly being revised and added to. She prayed for the work of foreign missions, peace in countries where there was war and many other things. Finally she prayed for herself, that she might be good and kind and helpful and unselfish and self-controlled and brave. That was plenty, she thought with a sigh.

Her prayer finished, she stood up and, going to the dressing table, she tied a ribbon round her hair and rubbed some skin-food into her face. And now what, she asked herself. A good cry was supposed to make things better. There was something almost soothing about the idea of being drowned in a flood of warm tears. But then she was firm with herself. If tears came spontaneously and couldn't be avoided, that was one thing, but it was not right to work yourself up into such a state. Perhaps if she put her misery away at the back of her mind and left it there she might one day be able to bring it out into the light and smile at the idea of its ever having had the power to hurt her.

She got into bed, holding in her hand the letter she had had from Ooli that morning.

'This is the first letter I ever wrote to you, darling Flora. I know you would like me to say this because women make so much of beginnings and endings and even you cannot deny that this is the beginning of something . . .'

She stretched out her hand and turned off the light. Then she curled over on to her side still holding the letter. She rested her cheek on it, but the paper was stiff and crackly, so she laid it lovingly to rest under her pillow. That was the traditional place for a love-letter, and like so many traditional things, it was the most comfortable.

Home Front Novel

Note on the Text

This unfinished novel (195 pages) was written mostly in 1939 while the events it depicts were actually happening in Oswestry, where Barbara was living at home, engaged in voluntary War Work like so many unmarried girls of her age and class. She wrote in her diary:

> *October 1st. Church full of evacuees and some soldiers. Made notes for a war novel.*
>
> *October 9th. Busy in the morning sewing sheets sides to middle. Wrote quite a lot of my Home Front novel.*
>
> *October 10th. Cross with the children [evacuees] – they were all running about like Bears in the kitchen. Too tired to write my novel.*
>
> *November 22nd. Did about 5 pages of my novel. Very dogged and slow.*

She then seems to have left it for a while and gone back to revising her North Oxford novel, Crampton Hodnet. She took it up again briefly in 1940 but then started her spy novel, leaving this one unfinished.

Certain characters are echoed in other novels: Amanda Wraye is another version of Lady Beddoes and Agnes and Connie had already made their appearance (as Edith and Connie) in Some Tame Gazelle. Flora Palfrey, however, although she shares the same name, is an entirely different character from the heroine of the Finnish novel.

In the late 1960s, feeling that a novel about the war might be more acceptable to publishers, she took the manuscript out again. But she became involved in writing The Sweet Dove Died and did no more work on it. It is tantalizing to think what she might have made of it if she had worked over the carefully observed wartime detail (supplemented by very full diary entries for the period) at the height of her mature powers as a novelist.

CHAPTER ONE

Canon Palfrey walked up the vicarage drive and looked in through his drawing-room window, hardly knowing what he might see there. He had learned to expect anything on a Monday evening between the hours of six and eight when the ladies of the parish had their Red Cross lectures. He remembered the first occasion very vividly and his shock at seeing a skeleton dangling in front of the large still life painting of the Dutch school, which had been given to them by an aunt of his wife. But this evening an even more alarming sight met his eyes. Miss Connie Aspinall was lying in a bed in his drawing room. As he watched, the door opened and his wife Jane came in carrying a blanket over her arm. Her pleasant face was flushed and her fair hair untidy. She hurried towards the bed and gave the blanket to Nurse Stebbings who seemed to be in charge. Then Miss Agnes Grote and Miss Beatrice Wyatt began to roll the clothes off the bed, leaving Miss Aspinall exposed to full view, tugging ineffectually at her shapeless grey flannel skirt which was riding up to reveal a pink celanese slip. Her helpless body was rolled from side to side while Nurse Stebbings briskly demonstrated different ways of changing sheets.

Excellent women, thought Canon Palfrey, always busy doing something. At present they were preparing for the war that everyone prayed would not come.

'Have they finished yet?'

The canon turned to see his curate, Michael Randolph, standing behind him. The two clergymen stood looking into the big, shabby, comfortable drawing room.

'There's something very soothing about watching a lot of busy women,' said Michael. 'It's like reading Jane Austen.'

At that moment Jane Palfrey saw them and waved. 'Come in!' she shouted. 'We want to practise bandaging.'

The vicar sighed. 'Oh well,' he said, 'we can't expect to be detached from it all. But I will not be bandaged by Miss Grote,' he added firmly.

As they went in Agnes Grote advanced remorselessly, holding a bandage. 'I'm going to do a capeline on you, Vicar,' she said. 'It ought to be easier on a bald head.'

The vicar looked helplessly about for his wife but she was still busy by the bed, where another woman was lying now, Connie Aspinall being occupied in bandaging her own leg in a corner of the room.

Michael Randolph sought out Beatrice Wyatt, a pleasant woman in her early thirties. She was practising hospital corners with the sheet and he tapped her on the shoulder.

'Do bandage me,' he said. 'I should like one of those elaborate cap things that Miss Grote is doing on the vicar.'

Beatrice laughed. 'Oh, I haven't got to that yet,' she said. 'Miss Grote is quite an expert, she's done a lot of this before.'

'Agnes always knows everything,' said a long-suffering voice from the corner of the room. Connie Aspinall was Agnes Grote's cousin and lived with her in a neat little house near the church.

'Well, do another one,' said Michael. 'You shall choose what you do.'

'I shall do you a broken jaw,' said Beatrice seriously. 'Sit down here and shut your mouth firmly.'

How nice she is, he thought, feeling her cool capable hands on his jaw, tall and fair and amusing and yet somehow appealing and shy.

'How is your mother?' he asked when the bandage had been completed and then removed.

'Oh, as well as she ever is.' Which is perfectly well, selfish old woman, thought Michael savagely.

'Poor Mrs Wyatt,' said Jane Palfrey vaguely. 'I must come and see her some time. Beatrice, do tell your mother that I'm coming to see her.'

'Yes, I will,' smiled Beatrice, 'thank you.' Mrs Palfrey had been coming to see her mother ever since she could remember.

'There, Vicar! You won't be able to get *that* off very easily,' said Agnes Grote triumphantly. 'Come and look, everybody.'

How like Agnes to behave as if *she* were the one giving the lecture, thought Connie, staying obstinately in her corner.

'I expect you will be glad to have Flora back,' she said to Mrs Palfrey, who didn't seem very interested in the bandaging either. 'Is it tomorrow that she comes?'

'Yes. She's been staying with my sister-in-law, who has a rather depressing house in Bayswater,' said Jane. 'Still, young people like being in London.'

'Come along, Connie, it's time to go!' Agnes's strident voice cut into the conversation.

'And I must go too,' said Beatrice. 'Mother will be getting impatient for her supper.'

'Poor thing,' said Jane, 'I suppose meals are all there is to look forward to when you are an invalid. Well, Tom,' she addressed her husband, who had finally managed to free himself from the bandage, 'perhaps you and Michael will help to move this bed. I don't want it cluttering up the drawing room.'

The two clergymen stood uncertainly at either end of the bed while the women collected their belongings and trickled out of the room in little groups.

'I do think that the men might take some part in Red Cross and ARP preparations,' said Agnes Grote rather loudly as they walked down the drive.

'They do seem to stand about and mock,' laughed Beatrice.

Agnes and Connie disappeared into Balmoral Lodge and she went on to her own house further down the road. As she took off her coat in the hall a querulous, rather guttural voice called out from upstairs.

'All right, Mother, I'm just coming,' she said, trying to put into her voice a brightness that she did not feel.

Mrs Wyatt lay in bed reading. She was handsome and hard-faced, with complicated plaits of grey hair swathed about her head. She had been a good-looking, lively woman, but after her husband's death ten years before, she had adopted the role of an invalid and now spent most of her time in bed, having decided that there was no longer anything worth getting up for. Beatrice was an only child, who had been born late in their married life. Although not without personality of her own, she had somehow drifted into a sort of subjugation to her strong-minded mother.

'Well,' demanded Mrs Wyatt, 'tell me all about it. Who was there?'

'Oh, it was only the usual Red Cross class. The same people who are always there. The vicar and Mr Randolph came in later.'

'Mr Randolph, he was there?'

Beatrice found herself going rather red and was glad that Alice, their maid, came in at that moment with her mother's tray.

'Look,' she said quickly, 'here's your supper! I wonder what Alice has brought you.'

'Cook thought you might fancy some cold chicken,' said Alice, 'and there's some mushroom soup.'

'I think I will have a glass of wine,' said Mrs Wyatt, making no comment on the rest of the meal. 'Now,' she said, through a mouthful of cold chicken, 'tell me the gossip.'

Beatrice racked her brains. 'Flora Palfrey's coming home tomorrow,' she said at last. 'She's been staying with an aunt in London.'

'She will be getting married soon, I think,' said Mrs Wyatt.

'Oh, I don't think so,' said Beatrice doubtfully. 'Who could she marry? There isn't anybody here.'

'Mr Randolph, the curate,' said Mrs Wyatt, with a sharp look at her daughter. 'He is a nice young man.'

'He isn't very young,' said Beatrice, hardly knowing why she didn't want him to be so described. 'He is quite old for a curate. He must be thirty-five or -six.'

Mrs Wyatt took up her chicken bone in her fingers and began to gnaw it. Her manners were Victorian, even eighteenth-century. There was a knock at the door and Alice put her head round.

'Please, Miss Beatrice, there's a gentleman here to see about the evacuees,' she said disapprovingly.

'I'll come down,' Beatrice said.

'No, no, bring him up here,' said Mrs Wyatt, still busy with her chicken bone. 'I want to see him.'

'It will be Mr Bonner, the history master from the High School,' said Beatrice. 'I believe he is the billeting officer.'

Alice came back into the room followed by a pale, nervous young man with an untidy sheaf of papers.

'Good evening,' he said, shooting a terrified look at Mrs Wyatt in bed. 'Good evening,' he said to Beatrice as if appealing to her for support. 'I'm sorry to bother you like this, but I wonder if you will be able to take any evacuees.'

'Oh, I'm sure we could manage somebody,' said Beatrice cheerfully. 'I don't think we could manage children, though. It is rather difficult with my mother being an invalid.'

Mrs Wyatt smiled complacently and dug her spoon into a quivering mound of orange jelly.

'We will take one grown-up person,' she said.

'Splendid,' said Mr Bonner. 'I will put you down for one of the school teachers. There will be a certain number coming with the children.'

'Yes, that will be easier,' said Beatrice. 'We have quite a nice room for her.'

Mr Bonner thankfully made his escape and paused outside to consult his list. Balmoral Lodge next, Miss Grote and Miss Aspinall. He walked up to the front door and rang the bell.

Agnes and Connie were in the kitchen washing up the supper things. As usual Agnes was washing while Connie dried. Connie would have liked to wash sometimes but Agnes never suggested that she should. Somehow they had just got into a routine and it seemed impossible to make even small changes. Agnes was a positive virago at the sink this evening, bending over the hot soapy water with the usual cigarette jutting from her square jaw.

'Hurry up, Connie!' she said. 'You're so slow!'

Connie seized another dripping plate, but for every one that she dried three or four more appeared on the draining board. It was hopeless, like Hercules and the dragon's teeth, she thought vaguely. It had been like this four times a day for the twenty years she and Agnes had lived together. Connie began to calculate in her head how many times that would have been, when the door bell rang.

'Bother!' said Agnes. She wiped her hands, soft and red from the hot water, and strode out into the hall. Connie followed her, feeling a little defiant, for she knew that Agnes would have expected her to finish drying the dishes first.

'Oh, Mr Bonner, do come in,' Agnes led him into the small chintzy drawing room, furnished in an arty-crafty way with too many barbola-framed mirrors, wool embroideries and water-colour landscapes. Agnes was talented in many directions and liked to have evidence of it around her. Connie was no good at anything like that, though she had rather a pretty singing voice which Agnes regarded with good-humoured contempt.

'Have you come about the children?' asked Connie eagerly.

'Yes, about four hundred are to be evacuated here, you know.'

'Poor little things,' said Connie sentimentally.

'How many spare rooms do you have, Miss Grote?'

'Two,' said Agnes, 'not counting the boxroom.'

'Would you be able to take four, then?'

'Four children, no teachers. I'm good with children. Know how to manage them. If necessary Connie could move into the boxroom, couldn't you, Connie? She has a nice big room that could easily take two.'

Connie's enthusiasm for the children diminished.

'If it comes to that, *you* could move into the boxroom, Agnes. After all, my room's just been done up.'

'My dear Connie, you could hardly expect me to have children on my Turkey carpet!' retorted Agnes sharply.

'Well, I'm sure you will be able to make the necessary arrangements,' said Mr Bonner, rising hastily. As Connie went with him to the door, Agnes's voice came from the kitchen, strident and irritable. 'Why, Connie, you haven't finished drying the dishes!'

Connie went meekly back to her uncompleted task.

'It will mean a lot of extra work, having evacuees here,' said

Agnes. 'I think I'll tell Dawks tomorrow to dig up the front lawn.'

'Whatever for?' asked Connie.

'To plant vegetables, of course. Now, let me see. The vicarage has a very big lawn and there is that herbaceous border at the Wyatts'.'

By the time they had finished their work in the kitchen, Agnes had already, in imagination, commandeered all the gardens in the village and planted them with vegetables. 'Oh, God,' prayed Connie that night, 'don't let there be a war.' But at the back of her mind was the thought that a war might be rather exciting. It would certainly make a difference to the days that were so monotonously the same.

CHAPTER TWO

When Beatrice Wyatt woke up on the morning of September 1st she had her 'anything can happen' feeling. She often had it at the beginning of a new day, especially, she did not know why, on a Friday. She had first met Michael Randolph on a Friday. And today was a Friday too, and the beginning of a new month. September was a lovely month, neither summer nor autumn, and it had begun with brilliant sunshine. She allowed herself to think about Michael Randolph. Their friendship had progressed considerably lately, especially in August when most people had been away. They had had some walks together and he had even taken her to the pictures once. Not wearing his dog-collar. Beatrice smiled as she remembered it. And they had lent each other books – there were some of his on the shelves in her room. Novels by Miss Compton-Burnett, mixed up with the blue Phoenixes, the Aldous Huxleys of her youth.

After breakfast she read the papers, trying hard not to be depressed by them, but they left her feeling the need for some occupation to take her mind off the news they brought. I'll do some ironing, she thought.

The sun was streaming through the windows of the morning room where she did her dressmaking and ironing. The iron slid smoothly over the surface of her pale blue nightdress in the most satisfactory way. When that was finished she took up a vest of flowered artificial silk and tried the iron tentatively on the lower edge. Immediately the stuff frizzled up and stuck to the iron in a brown sticky mass. The room was filled with the smell of treacle toffee.

Too hot, thought Beatrice philosophically, going to switch it off. I shall know another time.

'Why are you making toffee in here?' asked Michael Randolph, suddenly appearing at the french windows.

'Good morning,' she said, feeling hot and untidy. 'Do come in.' She swept a pile of garments into a drawer. Surely it was odd of him to come through the window without any warning.

'I wondered what you thought about the news?' he said, looking serious.

'What news?'

'Oh, Beatrice, surely you heard the ten-thirty news bulletin – Germany has started to invade Poland.'

There was silence.

Beatrice, she thought. It had been Miss Wyatt before. Then she suddenly realized what he had said.

'It seems like war for all of us.'

'It seems impossible on such a beautiful day ...' She looked helplessly about her.

'It may not be so bad ...'

There was silence again.

Michael took up the burnt vest from the ironing board and examined it.

'Is this what was burning? I wonder if it is totally spoilt. Perhaps you could put a patch on it,' he added helpfully.

'Well, Beatrice, this *is* grave news,' said a loud cheerful voice and Agnes, wearing a djibbah and sandals and looking almost radiant, came in through the french windows followed by Connie, who trailed rather resentfully behind.

Does no one ever use the front door, thought Beatrice, feeling suddenly irritated.

'Oh, hello, Agnes,' she said.

'Good morning, Miss Grote,' said Michael, still holding the vest unconcernedly in his hand. 'It is, as you say, grave news.'

Beatrice could feel Agnes's eyes on the garment and saw her raise her eyebrows in surprise. It was perhaps an unusual situation in which to find a clergyman.

'I've burnt a hole in my vest,' she said lightly, almost merrily. 'It smells just like treacle toffee.'

'The Germans have invaded Poland,' said Agnes in a loud clear tone as if Beatrice might not have known what the grave news was.

'Yes. I must go now,' said Michael. 'The children and the teachers will be arriving soon. There will be a lot to do.'

'Yes, it will be quite a change for you, won't it,' said Agnes bluntly.

'Oh, Agnes, wasn't that rather rude!' said Connie, when Michael was out of earshot.

'Well, we've all got to be busy now. We can't afford to be idle for a moment,' she added with a sharp glance at Beatrice.

'I must see about getting our evacuee's room ready,' said Beatrice, resenting the implication that she had been idle. 'And I must do something about the blackout curtains. Fortunately most of ours are thick and dark.'

'Oh, we did ours *months* ago,' said Agnes airily and inaccurately. 'I saw this coming.'

'Goodness, isn't it awful? I can't *realize* it.' Beatrice pushed back a lock of hair from her face. 'It's going to make a lot of changes,' she said inadequately.

'It will affect all of us,' said Connie with a hint of excitement in her voice. 'We shall none of us be the same a year from now.'

'Well now,' said Agnes. 'Do you want any help with your blackout?' She examined the curtains critically. 'I really don't think these will be thick enough. Still, you won't be using this room in the evening, so we can just take the light bulb out. I'll do it for you now.' And before Beatrice had time to protest she had climbed on to a chair and taken it out.

'There,' she said. 'You can take the one out in the downstairs lavatory too – that will be one thing less to worry about. Your mother's room has very big windows, hasn't it? We'd better go up and see what can be done.'

Beatrice and Connie followed her out of the room obediently.

'I hope your mother will feel equal to seeing us,' said Connie timidly.

'Mother is equal to anything,' said Beatrice absently. Her mind was not on blackout curtains. I wonder if I will feel able to call him Michael? she thought.

'Well, Mrs Wyatt, how are you?' said Agnes in the bright, distinct and rather patronizing voice she reserved for invalids, children and tradespeople.

'I am afraid there will be war,' said Mrs Wyatt, as if she and not Agnes were the bringer of news. 'I have listened on the wireless.' She indicated a portable set beside her bed. 'Beatrice, I think I should like a glass of stout and some biscuits.'

Agnes was at the window. 'These curtains should be thick enough.' She sounded quite disappointed and then, brightening up, she said, 'I think I will go and see how they are getting on at the vicarage. I believe they are having five children. I'm sure they will need a helping hand.'

'They ought to have this border dug and planted with cabbages,' said Agnes, as they walked up the vicarage drive.

226

'Aren't you going to the front door?' asked Connie as Agnes marched boldly across the lawn and round to the side of the house, as she had at the Wyatts'.

'I think I'll surprise them,' said Agnes, and this was, indeed, a habit of hers.

She arrived at the french windows of the dining room to be confronted by the vicar's legs at the top of a step-ladder. Mrs Palfrey was sitting at a table drinking coffee and their daughter Flora, a frown of concentration on her face, was carefully lacquering her nails with orchid-coloured polish.

'Good morning!' said Agnes brightly to as much of Canon Palfrey as she could see, but before she was able to say anything else, a pall of black casement cloth suddenly fell down over the window, blotting out the occupants of the room.

'*That's* not thick enough!' said Agnes triumphantly. 'They'll have to use it double, unless they've another curtain they can line it with.'

'Hullo, Agnes,' said Jane Palfrey, pushing the curtains aside and coming out. 'You find us as usual in absolute chaos. Isn't this war sickening!'

'Good morning, Miss Grote.' Canon Palfrey came creaking down from the step-ladder. 'Well, this *is* a business, isn't it?'

'Flora seems to be the only one who doesn't find things any different,' said Agnes acidly.

Flora waved one hand in the air to dry the polish.

'One can't just go to pieces,' she said. 'One must be groomed.'

'I was just having a cup of coffee,' said Jane hastily. 'Will you have one?'

'No, thank you, I never take anything in the morning,' said Agnes virtuously, before Connie could reply.

'A cigarette, then.' Jane produced a silver box and opened it hopefully. By some miracle there was one cigarette rolling about forlornly inside. Agnes took it.

'As you see,' said Jane, 'we are busy trying to do our blackout.'

'Do you think the German planes will get this far?' Connie asked nervously.

'That isn't the point,' said Agnes.

'One rather feels,' said Jane, 'that if one does the front windows, the back ones don't matter.'

'Well, I just came to see if I could help,' said Agnes, who had not actually made any such offer, 'but I see you're getting on all right.'

'Oh, yes, we'll muddle along somehow,' said Flora wearily. 'So far the most ingenious arrangement has been to use an old cassock of father's to black out a sky-light.'

Connie looked rather shocked.

'Of course, *we're* having four evacuees,' said Agnes, 'but I've got everything ready. Come along, Connie, we must get on with the shopping. They say there's likely to be a shortage of bacon.'

'I hear Sir Lyall and Lady Wraye are down here,' said Connie, her voice taking on a reverent quality, as it always did when she spoke of their MP. 'I suppose Edward will be going into the army.' She looked archly at Flora, who said with an assumed air of nonchalance that she supposed he would.

After Agnes had hustled Connie away, the Palfreys spent the rest of the day moving furniture and making arrangements for the evacuees, so that by the evening they were so tired they felt they had actually been at war for months.

CHAPTER THREE

What a waste, thought Amanda Wraye, uncovering the silver dishes on the side-table and gazing at the scrambled eggs, kidneys and bacon which were revealed. She never ate more than a grapefruit and a piece of toast for breakfast and yet the servants, in spite of her vague instructions, persisted in cooking enough for several hearty breakfasts. They knew what was suitable to the household of a Member of Parliament even if their mistress did not. Oh well, she thought, if there is a war we will have to economize.

Lyall Wraye came in briskly and sat down at the table. '*Sunday Times* not come yet?' he grunted, looking around the table and even under it as if the servants might have departed from their usual routine.

'It's always late in the country,' said Mandy helpfully. 'Isn't it a lovely day? One hardly seems to notice it in Eaton Square.'

'Well, it's a good thing you appear to be so fond of nature, since you are likely to be down here a good deal now,' said Lyall, dipping his spoon into a grapefruit. 'If we are to have these evacuees you will have to be here to supervise things or the servants will leave. I shall be going up to town tonight,' he added. 'I have to go to the House.'

He went on talking and Mandy's thoughts drifted to how different it was all going to be, when she suddenly heard him say, 'Of course Eleanor will have to come here.'

'Oh, Lyall, surely not. I mean, *must* we?' Eleanor, Dowager Countess of Nollard, was Lyall's elder sister and she and Mandy had never got on. Since her husband's death she had had to give up her large house in Hill Street and live in a comparatively pokey flat in a new block near Bryanston Square. She was continually lamenting the change and recalling all the brilliant entertaining she had once done, the sort of entertaining that Mandy should be doing so that Lyall could become a Cabinet Minister.

'Oh, Lyall, must we?' she repeated. 'After all there will be the evacuees and Edward will be here,' she said hopefully, trying to fill the house with people.

'Edward will be with his regiment.'

'Yes, of course.' Her voice trailed away as she thought of Edward. He had been such a dear little boy until he went away to school. And now he was a nice young man with charming manners who called her by her Christian name and made fun of her in an affectionate way and didn't need her any more. Nobody does, she thought wistfully, not even Lyall. Certainly not Lyall, she added to herself as he got up purposefully from the table.

'I have work to do and I don't want to be disturbed.'

'Don't you want to hear the news?'

'I can hear it in my study.'

'It's rather a historic occasion,' said Mandy, her voice becoming rather shaky. 'We didn't have the wireless last time.'

Lyall, rather surprisingly, put his arm round her and patted her shoulder. He looked as if he might be going to say something, but evidently thought better of it and went abruptly out of the room.

They had breakfasted late and Mandy was in the morning room waiting to hear the eleven o'clock news when Rogers, the old parlourmaid who had been with them for twenty years, came in with the Sunday papers.

'Sit down with me, Rogers,' said Mandy, 'and listen to the news. I expect you would like to hear Mr Chamberlain.'

Rogers sat down rather uncertainly on an upright chair.

'Sir Lyall is going to listen in his study,' Mandy said, as if sensing Rogers's uneasiness.

They sat quietly listening, Mandy in her smart dress of black crêpe-de-Chine printed with small cerise flowers and Rogers very stiff and starched in her uniform. As Mr Chamberlain spoke, Mandy felt the tears welling up in her eyes and Rogers had turned her head away, so that Mandy would not see her weeping.

'Jane Palfrey isn't here.' Agnes's penetrating whisper irritated Connie. 'I should have thought that she would have been here today of all days.'

'I expect she wants to hear Mr Chamberlain,' said Connie in a reverent tone, more suitable for conversation in church.

'Aren't you too hot in that fur?' said Agnes, looking at Connie's old grey fox tie. 'I should take it off if I were you.'

There was only a small congregation today. Canon Palfrey felt very bleak as he walked up the aisle behind Michael Randolph, three choir-men and a handful of choir-boys. Jane and Flora were still busily preparing for the evacuees who were due at any minute. He hitched his red hood over to the middle of his back and settled down to pray. The congregation was less critical today; their minds were on other things, evacuees, rationing, whether their sons would have to fight, if there would be air-raids. The vicar seemed to be just one of themselves this morning. They understood that there was not much that anyone could say, and the very ordinary things that he was saying, as well as the familiar form of the service, were somehow reassuring.

'Not many people in church today,' Canon Palfrey said to Michael Randolph as they walked along after the service. 'I suppose it will be different later on.'

'Yes, people will come now. And there will be all the evacuees. There will be great opportunities in this war . . .'

'Opportunities?' Canon Palfrey turned over this rather novel aspect of the situation. 'Yes, I suppose there will be. Sunday schools and all that sort of thing.' He liked a comfortable Sunday afternoon, with a good sleep. He was not sure that he really welcomed these opportunities.

'A good many of the children will be Roman Catholics, I hear,' he said hopefully.

'Gladys looks upset,' said Flora, after the maid had brought in the chicken at lunch.

Jane sighed. 'Yes, we will have to humour her. I'm afraid she *may* be difficult about these children coming.'

'Oh well, you'll just have to get someone else if she leaves,' said Canon Palfrey easily.

'But we shan't be able to *get* anyone else,' explained Jane patiently. 'They'll all be going into the forces or off to make munitions like they did in the last war.'

'Oh, don't let's talk about it,' said Flora, appalled at the thought of being stuck at home doing housework for as long as the war lasted.

They went on eating their lunch quite calmly, although Jane kept putting down her knife and fork and saying, 'Supposing they came *now*. What on earth should we do?'

Canon Palfrey poked at the carcase of the chicken helplessly. 'Not much there,' he said.

But the meal passed without anything happening and it was not until after tea that Flora came rushing into the drawing room with the news that a police van was going down the road shouting something. They all went to the front gate, but they could not make any sense of the booming, unintelligible sounds that it made.

'It must be the children coming,' said Jane. 'It can't be anything else.'

Then Flora, who had been leaning over the gate, saw a troop of people in the distance, moving towards the vicarage like an invading army.

'They really *are* coming,' she said. 'I can see them.'

'Well, we're all ready for them,' said Jane, but there was in her voice, as there had been in Flora's, a note of amazement. And they both realized that up till now they had never quite believed that the children would come.

'The King's due to speak in a few minutes,' said Canon Palfrey quickly. 'I think I'll just slip into my study and hear him on the portable.'

'Yes, there's no point in you being here as well,' said Jane soothingly. 'They might be embarrassed if they saw a clergyman standing at the gate.'

Her husband slunk gratefully away.

Mr Bonner with a crowd of children and a few adults stopped at the vicarage gate. The children all carried gas masks and an assortment of luggage, satchels, little cardboard suitcases and cretonne bags, and Jane felt a sudden pricking of tears in her eyes.

'Well, here we are,' said Mr Bonner in a forced hearty tone. 'Now you are taking five, I believe. Miss Stoat,' he said, turning to a thin-faced woman with frizzy bobbed hair, 'which five shall it be? Oh, this is Miss Stoat,' he said, 'one of the teachers. She is to be billeted with the Wyatts.'

Miss Stoat read out the names of five children from her list. She had a mincing, refined voice. Poor Wyatts, thought Jane. Rather a thousand children than a teacher!

'Well now,' said Jane, when five children had been separated from the others and handed over to her. 'I'm sure we're all going to get along splendidly. They'll soon settle down,' she said to Mr Bonner, with an assurance she was far from feeling. Mr Bonner hurried on with the remainder of his flock, and Jane and Flora stood awkwardly in the drive looking at the five children. The evacuation had begun.

CHAPTER FOUR

'Agnes,' said Connie Aspinall diffidently, standing in the drawing-room doorway on the morning after their evacuees – a mother and two children – had arrived. 'Agnes,' she repeated more loudly, trying to make her voice heard over the noise of the Hoover, which Agnes was wielding with great energy and enjoyment.

'Yes, Connie, what *is* it?' shouted Agnes impatiently, brushing aside a small table and pushing the Hoover relentlessly into a corner.

'It's the *children*,' Connie shouted, her voice cracking with the effort.

'What about the children?' said Agnes with her back still turned.

'I don't quite know how to put it, it's something not very *nice*.'

Agnes looked interested but went on with her vacuuming.

'They've got things in their hair.' Connie was forced to say in a loud, harsh tone what she would have preferred to whisper confidentially.

Agnes turned round with a gleam of triumph in her eye. 'I

knew it,' she said snapping off the electric current with a decisive movement. 'Lice,' she added, with an emphasis which seemed to give the word a full and very sinister meaning.

Connie stood helplessly in the doorway, rubbing her hands together in a nervous gesture. 'We'll have to send them away,' she said. 'No one could expect to have children who were not clean in the house.'

'*Send them away!*' Agnes stood in the middle of the room, a magnificent figure with a newly lighted cigarette jutting aggressively from her mouth. 'My dear Connie, this is wartime. Go and get the Lysol out of the bathroom cupboard – I shall wash the children thoroughly in the scullery and their clothes must be dealt with too. And on the way up go and see if Mrs Dobbs is getting up – she may be tired after her journey, but she's certainly not going to spend the morning in bed.'

Connie walked upstairs with an attempt at briskness, but when she reached Mrs Dobbs's bedroom door she hesitated and the knock she gave was a very timid one.

'Come in,' called a loud unabashed voice. 'Oh, it's you, dear,' said Mrs Dobbs. 'I'm quite cosy, thanks.'

She certainly looked cosy, sitting up in bed in a pink nightgown of shiny artificial satin. She was a youngish woman, with a bold face and bleached hair, done up in a complicated arrangement of curlers. Connie looked down at the dark rug by the bed and saw that it was littered with cigarette ash.

'Yes, I was just having a smoke,' said Mrs Dobbs, producing a hand from underneath the bedclothes and revealing a cigarette, which she had evidently hidden on hearing Connie's knock. 'I thought you was the other one,' she said with an ingratiating smile.

'Wouldn't you like some breakfast?' Connie began, not liking to say what she had to say straight out.

'Well, that's an idea,' said Mrs Dobbs brightly. 'It would be ever so kind of you. A nice cup of tea and a bit of toast and I daresay I could fancy a nice boiled egg. You get nice fresh eggs in the country.'

'Well, if you like to get up, you can go down into the kitchen and cook yourself something,' said Connie ineffectually.

'Rightyho, dear, just as you like,' said Mrs Dobbs, settling herself comfortably among the pillows and obviously with no intention of getting up.

Connie stood there wishing she had Agnes's forceful personality. She lingered uncertainly in the doorway and went out of the room, murmuring words that sounded more like an apology for having disturbed her guest than a command to get up.

Later that morning when the children had been expertly dealt with by Agnes and Mrs Dobbs had reluctantly got up and gone out with the children to meet the other mothers and do some shopping ('I see you've got a Woolworth's,' she said condescendingly as she went out of the door), Agnes and Connie were tidying the kitchen when Beatrice Wyatt called. She sank on to one of the bentwood chairs at the kitchen table.

'I felt I had to come and see how you are getting on with *yours*,' she said.

'We're just taking it in our stride,' said Agnes heartily. 'A mother who won't get up in the morning and two children with vermin. I've just spent the morning bathing them and baking their clothes.'

Beatrice shuddered. 'Agnes, you are marvellous. I wouldn't know what to do at all. At least there's no danger of that with our teacher.'

'What is she like?'

'Very *dainty*,' said Beatrice. 'She's called Madge, by the way, and insists on Christian names. She's so thoroughly at home and somehow *patronizing*. And then, of course, she has to be with *me* all the time. I almost wish we'd had children.'

237

'Ours are sweet but not quite *clean*,' said Connie.

'Mrs Palfrey's got five – the vicarage is so big. I saw her in the town. Apparently they were up at six o'clock this morning running all over the house and garden, even in the vicar's study.'

'Well, we must get into town and do our shopping,' said Agnes briskly.

'I'll come with you as far as Woolworth's,' said Beatrice. 'I want to see if I can get any black paper.'

'Oh, there's not a sheet of that left in the town,' said Agnes confidently. 'Come along, Connie.'

Connie crammed a beige felt hat on to her head, pushed up a few wisps of hair and hurried after them. 'I feel such a mess,' she fluttered. 'Everything seems to have been such a *rush* this morning.'

'Oh well, nobody's going to look at us,' said Agnes, taking an old beret with a moth-hole in it from the hall stand and putting it on at a straight, uncompromising angle.

There was something almost comforting in the thought that she might be their contemporary, Beatrice decided. If I were that age, she thought, I shouldn't be thinking about Michael Randolph all the time.

Agnes marched into Woolworth's and made for the biscuit counter. Connie and Beatrice followed her more slowly. Agnes was thinking only of cheese biscuits at 3d a half-pound, but they had other things to occupy their minds. While Beatrice was trying to imagine herself in twenty years' time, Connie was darting furtive glances at herself in the mirrors by the door. She looked *awful*, such a mess, but, of course, they were hardly likely to meet anyone who mattered in Woolworth's.

'Oh, look, what pretty silk handkerchiefs,' she said, plucking at Beatrice's elbow. 'They look quite good. I think I will buy one.' She looked round furtively for Agnes, who would certainly have disapproved of such a purchase. She chose a pink one and was handing it to the girl with her sixpence when a voice behind them said, 'Good morning, Miss Wyatt, Miss Aspinall,' and there was Edward Wraye, looking unexpectedly older in khaki uniform. Beatrice and Edward were making general conversation about the war and what Edward was doing when Connie became aware that Amanda Wraye had come up behind them. She was accompanied by a tall, beaky woman.

'Oh, Miss Wyatt, I don't think you have met my sister-in-law Lady Nollard,' said Mandy in her usual vague way. 'I don't think you *can* have done because she hasn't been down here much, have you, Eleanor?'

'No,' said Lady Nollard rather grimly. 'I left London on account of the war.'

'How dreadful it must have been for you, Lady Nollard,' murmured Connie respectfully. 'You must feel like a refugee.'

Edward choked with laughter and Beatrice found herself smiling, too. But Lady Nollard saw nothing comic in this pronouncement.

'Yes,' she said, with emphasis, 'it has been *dreadful*. I have had to leave everything behind, of course, absolutely *everything*.'

'Well, Eleanor, you seemed to bring a great deal of luggage with you,' observed Mandy.

'I meant my furniture,' said Lady Nollard coldly. 'All my beautiful *things*.'

Mandy began an aimless conversation with Beatrice about the evacuee children and how sweet they were and how they must go now because she wanted to see them having their dinner. Meanwhile, Lady Nollard had found a most sympathetic listener in Connie and seemed reluctant to return to her unappreciative relations.

'I hope we shall meet again,' she said, smiling graciously.

'Oh, here you are! I wondered where you'd all got to.' Agnes came hurrying up to them holding two bulging bags of biscuits.

'Good morning, Lady Wraye. How do you do,' she said casually when she was introduced to Lady Nollard. 'Have you tried these Woolworth cheese biscuits – they're really marvellous.'

Connie felt that she must be quite scarlet all over with shame and mortification. It was just like Agnes to come and spoil everything. Coming crashing along and telling the whole world that she had been buying biscuits *here*. Whatever would Lady Wraye and Lady Nollard think?

But Mandy was enthusiastic and cried, 'What a marvellous idea! I never thought of it. Lyall is always saying that we must economize, especially now. I shall go and get some. I think it's *marvellous*,' she repeated, as though buying biscuits at Woolworth's was as extraordinary as picking up a Schiaparelli model at the local draper's.

'Well, darling, people *do* buy things at Woolworth's, that's what it is for. And anyway, you came in to buy some embroidery thread.'

'Oh, yes, dear, I know, but *biscuits* . . .' and Mandy darted off purposefully towards the biscuit counter followed by Edward and, more slowly, by Lady Nollard.

'Of course,' she said to Connie, 'one can hardly expect the biscuits to be of such good quality as Romary's, but I suppose we shall have to put up with that sort of thing in wartime. Fortnum's may not be able to deliver,' she added. 'We must all make sacrifices.' She nodded graciously at Connie and moved after Mandy and Edward.

'Fancy Lady Wraye not knowing about Woolworth's biscuits!' said Agnes when they were on their way home. 'She'll be glad that I gave her the tip.'

Connie was lost in her usual daydreams, but this time a definite figure had come into them. Lady Nollard was talking to Connie and saying that she had dreaded coming into the country and what a comfort it was to have found a really sympathetic friend. And in the winter perhaps they might go to a health resort together, Bournemouth or Torquay would be nice. And in the hotel there would be crowds of Lady Nollards and other people too, retired Army men, even Bishops . . .

'We've just been round to the fish and chip shop,' Mrs Dobbs was saying. 'I was quite *surprised* that you had one here . . .'

'Connie! Connie!' Agnes called. 'You've forgotten the side plates.'

'All right, dear,' said Connie mildly. 'I couldn't get everything on the tray.'

You must call me *Eleanor*, Lady Nollard was saying.

CHAPTER FIVE

'Well, Beatrice, you must go down to your supper now. Miss Stoat will not like to be kept waiting. It would not be polite to keep one's guest waiting ...' There was a gleam of amusement in Mrs Wyatt's eye as she lay back on her pillows anticipating her own meal, which was due to appear at any moment now.

'Oh, Mother,' Beatrice sighed. 'If only you knew what it's like to have her sitting opposite one at every meal!'

'I thank God I need not see her,' said Mrs Wyatt simply. 'But there is a war and we must all do our duty.'

Beatrice wondered how her mother proposed to do her duty.

The supper was brought, liver and bacon, with rich brown gravy, new potatoes and peas. Mrs Wyatt gripped her knife and fork firmly.

'I think I should like some Burgundy,' she said. 'Water is not much of a drink for an old woman. We must keep up our strength in wartime. It really is our duty to be as healthy as we can.'

'Miss Wyatt! Supper is ready!' a fluty voice came drifting up the stairs.

In the dining room Beatrice noticed that there was a pink

blancmange on the sideboard, a sweet she particularly disliked, with its cold flannelly texture and indefinite taste, but her mother was fond of it and she still ordered the meals – it was the one household task that she continued to do.

Miss Stoat pulled a pink angora cardigan round her shoulders. 'It's quite nippy this evening, isn't it?' she said.

Beatrice got up from the table. 'Perhaps it is,' she said. 'I'll go and get an electric fire.'

'Oh, don't bother for me,' said Miss Stoat. 'I'm as warm as toast in my woolly.'

Beatrice sat down again.

'Do you think the children are settling down well?' she began hopefully. 'It must be so different for them, living in the country.'

'I'll say it is,' said Miss Stoat, with a surprising attempt at an American accent. 'Do you go up to town much?'

'To London? Yes, sometimes. Not as much as I used to.'

'Oh, I love London,' said Miss Stoat. 'I'm fond of a bit of gaiety.'

'I'm afraid you won't find much gaiety here,' said Beatrice, not without satisfaction.

'Oh, well, I like the country too,' said Miss Stoat complacently. 'I'm sure I shall find plenty to do.'

They went on making rather strained conversation throughout supper. Miss Stoat was very fond of blancmange. She praised all the food and said how lucky she was to have such a good billet. Beatrice began to feel ashamed of her unkind thoughts and made a resolution to be more friendly and try to look for the *good* in Miss Stoat. After supper she went up to her room to get some sewing. After all, the war would probably last for years and Miss Stoat with it. They might even be good friends by the time it was over, she thought without enthusiasm.

'You haven't got a special chair, have you?' asked Miss Stoat as she came into the drawing room.

Beatrice had a special chair and Miss Stoat was in it. She had her feet up on a footstool and was settled in such a way that even the most outspoken and selfish person would have hesitated before asking her to move.

Beatrice remembered her resolution of a few minutes before and sat down in an unfamiliar and therefore uncongenial chair. She put her sewing on the floor. The little table she usually used was over by Miss Stoat. The light was wrong, too.

'I never mind where I sit,' said Miss Stoat comfortably, picking up a bundle wrapped in a silk square and unrolling it. It was the body – or rather the torso, for it had no legs – of a china doll.

'Whatever is it?' asked Beatrice, fascinated. 'What are you going to do with it?'

'I'm making a nightdress case. It's rather a cute idea, isn't it? A Victorian lady with the case in her skirt,' she explained. 'The mauve silk is for the skirt, a sort of crinoline really. I love mauve, don't you? I think it's so dainty in the bedroom.'

'Dainty?' said Beatrice. 'Oh, yes it is.'

'I wore a lot of mauve after Mother died. After the black, of course.'

There was a ring at the door and Beatrice went to open it. Outside was the muffled figure of Mr Bompas the Air Raid Warden. He was so confused and apologetic that it took Beatrice some time to realize why he had come, but at last she gathered that a bright unshaded light was blazing in one of the upstairs rooms.

'I wouldn't have troubled you, Miss Wyatt,' he said apologetically, 'but somebody happened to point it out to me, and you know how people are.' Mr Bompas was their local grocer and the Wyatts were good customers whom he did not want to offend.

'Of course,' said Beatrice. 'I'm so sorry – I'll see to it right away.'

She shut the door and ran upstairs to her mother's room, for she could guess where the light was coming from.

'Didn't Alice draw your curtains, Mother?' she asked, hurrying to the window and dragging them across. 'I told her to be specially careful.'

'She came to do it,' said Mrs Wyatt, 'but I did not allow it. It is more pleasant to have the air coming in.'

'But Mother, there's a war on. We aren't allowed to show lights. Mr Bompas, the Warden, came to tell me about it.'

'Mr Bompas must be civil,' said Mrs Wyatt grimly, 'or we shall change our grocer.'

Beatrice sighed. 'I'm sorry, Mother, but they must be drawn. Now then, are you quite comfortable?'

'I think I should like some cocoa and some biscuits.'

Beatrice went into the kitchen to tell Alice that on no account should she leave the curtains undrawn and to take some cocoa upstairs. As she came out of the kitchen she heard voices in the drawing room, Miss Stoat's shrill giggle and the deeper tones of a man. It was Michael Randolph.

She ran lightly up to her room, tidied her hair, powdered her face and made her entrance looking fresh, neat and suitably surprised.

'I didn't hear the bell,' she said. 'I didn't know you were here.'

'I'm afraid I startled Miss – er,' said Michael. 'I came round and tapped on the french windows.'

'Yes, he gave me quite a turn,' Miss Stoat said.

'Would you like some tea?' Beatrice asked.

Miss Stoat gathered up her doll's torso and the mauve silk.

'Well, I'll leave you two good people alone,' she said coyly. 'I expect your mother would like some company. She must be lonely up there by herself. So long!'

'Poor Beatrice,' Michael said, when the door had closed behind her.

'She's only been here a day,' she said. 'I shall get used to it.'

'But, surely you don't have to stay here if you don't want to.'

'Oh, really, how could I possibly leave Mother? After all, she is an invalid.'

The most unclergymanlike snort came from him and she found herself laughing.

'But you do see how it is?' she said.

'Oh, yes, I see quite well. You like to imagine yourself as an Edwardian unmarried daughter sacrificing her life to look after her invalid mother.'

'I wonder how Miss Stoat is getting on with Mother,' said Beatrice, changing the conversation awkwardly. 'I should love to hear their conversation.'

The conversation, in fact, consisted of a long monologue from Miss Stoat and occasional protests from Mrs Wyatt as pillows were whisked from underneath her, shaken up and put back in a new and uncomfortable way.

'I know all about invalids,' said Miss Stoat brightly but firmly. 'My mother was bedridden for ten years before she passed away last year.'

'What was her illness?' asked Mrs Wyatt with interest.

'Now, now, we don't want any depressing talk about illness, do we? I'm going to read to you. I always used to read to Mother. It's a nice little book, I shouldn't be surprised if it sent you off. It's little pieces, like poetry, only they don't rhyme. They're called *Fragrant Thoughts*.'

Mrs Wyatt lay back on her pillows and made a feeble gesture that Miss Stoat took for assent.

Miss Stoat opened the book with its pale yellow cover and began to read. She read 'Helping Each Other', 'Patience' and 'Tea by the Fireside' in her mincing voice. Mrs Wyatt groaned faintly. '"Catkins,"' announced Miss Stoat in a high, rather surprised tone. '"Have you seen the golden catkins, the dainty fairy bells ringing in the springtime in the shady woods and dells. Each catkin has a message of hope for you and me ..."'

'I want to go to the lavatory,' interrupted Mrs Wyatt.

Miss Stoat stopped reading and blushed. She was not used to such plain speaking. Mother had always managed to convey such a request in a more delicate way.

Miss Stoat looked about the room for something she did not name but indicated by a fluttering wave of the hand.

'Let me help you,' she said. 'I am used to invalids.'

'I will get out of bed and go to the lavatory,' said Mrs Wyatt, and, before Miss Stoat could stop her, she had swung her legs out of the bed, pushed Miss Stoat away with an impatient gesture and walked slowly but surprisingly firmly towards the door.

'Oh, do lean on me,' cried Miss Stoat. 'Your legs will be all wobbly!'

'My legs are not at all wobbly. I am not in my grave yet!'

'Mother, what *are* you doing?' called Beatrice from the hall. She ran up the stairs. 'What can you be thinking of, getting out of bed like this?'

Mrs Wyatt said nothing but indicated the door through which she proposed to go, went in and slammed the door res-olutely. Beatrice stood on the stairs too surprised to say anything.

'I was in the middle of reading to her,' explained Miss Stoat, 'and she suddenly said she wanted to spend a penny.'

Beatrice's eyebrows rose. That certainly seemed out of char-acter, but then, Mother getting out of bed in such a way was out of character too.

'Perhaps,' she said, 'we would all like a cup of tea.'

'Oh yes,' said Miss Stoat, 'that would be ever so nice.'

CHAPTER SIX

Flora woke up with a sinking feeling. Something unpleasant had happened. And then she remembered. It was the war. She thought it must be morning but her room was dark. The pretty rose-patterned curtains had been roughly lined with black casement cloth. In her mind's eye, Flora could see the long dark whiskers which hung down from the raw edges where she hadn't even had time to hem them. I must do that, she thought. It looks so untidy, it spoils the room. It must be time to get up. She became aware of noises outside her door – Mrs Palfrey calling to her husband that she had finished in the bathroom, Gladys using the Hoover somewhere, the voices of the children singing.

> 'Angels never leave Heaven,
> Angels like you . . .'

sang the children, but then, evidently unable to remember any more, turning to the more familiar 'Lambeth Walk'.

She put on her dressing gown and went to the bathroom. Outside the door she met two of the children.

'Good morning,' she said uncertainly.

They stared at her, giggled and returned her greeting.

From the bathroom Flora could hear the sound of the little boys rushing about in the garden shouting and quarrelling. When she went into the dining room she found her mother alone, sitting wearily at the table.

'Oh dear,' she said, 'Jimmy opened the little gate and let the chickens out. They're all over the garden. Your father's trying to catch them.'

'Little beasts,' said Flora.

'Oh, that's nothing,' said Jane. 'Something else has happened. Much worse. I was expecting it, but still . . .'

'What is it?'

'One of them has wet the bed.'

'Oh, *Mother*!'

'Gladys is very upset. I'm afraid we will have to do most of the housework to pacify her. She's talking about munitions factories in a very sinister way.'

'Oh, Mother!'

'I know, dear. It's not much fun for you. Still, I believe Edward Wraye is here,' she said brightly. 'Perhaps he will come and see you.'

There had been a mild romance between Edward and Flora for some years, but since he had been away at Oxford he seemed to have become more sophisticated and Flora had felt that she was no longer dashing enough for him. But she still believed herself in love with him since there was really nobody else to be in love with.

'Is he here? Who told you?'

'Gladys told me, as a matter of fact. She said he was in khaki.'

'Oh, he won't come and see me,' said Flora drinking up her unpleasantly lukewarm coffee. 'I suppose I'd better wash up.'

She carried the tray with the breakfast things out into the kitchen, where Gladys was cleaning shoes with a martyred expression. Jane and Flora hardly liked to have any conversation of their own and it was well known that it was useless to attempt to make conversation with Gladys when she was in one of her moods, so the work went on in silence.

At the sink Flora thought how ugly the orchid nail polish looked against her hands, which had become red with the too-hot water. It was chipping too. She would have to give up using it 'for the duration' – that was the phrase that people were using now. Gladys stumped out of the kitchen with her arms full of newly cleaned shoes. At that moment there was a brisk knocking at the back door. Flora dried her hands and went to open it.

'Good morning,' said Agnes Grote. 'I thought I might find you in the kitchen so I came round the back.'

'You do indeed find us in the kitchen,' said Jane, who was peeling apples rather too thickly. 'How are *yours*?'

'Oh, I'm managing them quite well. I had a busy morning yesterday. We discovered the children had *lice*.' She gave the word its full emphasis.

'Oh,' said Flora faintly, 'how awful. I hope ours haven't any.'

Agnes advanced further into the kitchen and surveyed the scene, absently tracing the letters A. M. Grote on the dusty surface of the dresser. 'I was thinking,' she said, 'that something should be *done* about these children.'

'Oh, I agree,' said Jane, 'but what? We really don't seem to be very good at coping with them.'

Agnes made an impatient movement with her hand. 'Communal meals,' she said, 'that's what they ought to have.'

'Oh, *yes*,' said Jane, 'but who would organize it?'

'It's up to us,' said Agnes firmly. 'I shall go and see all the hostesses and we must approach the school people *together*.'

Jane was silent in admiration. How useful Agnes's managing qualities were in wartime.

'I must go and see Lady Wraye,' went on Agnes. 'She has

quite a few evacuees there. I saw her in Woolworth's yesterday. Edward was with her,' she added with a glance at Flora, 'looking quite the soldier. I believe he is going off today.'

Flora bent over the sink and washed an already clean plate. Going today. Perhaps never coming back, and he hasn't even come to say goodbye. She hardly heard Agnes go, she was too busy working herself up into a fine state of emotion in which she had killed off not only Edward but all other eligible men of her generation and had doomed herself to a life of lonely spinster-hood, when her mother's voice cut across her thoughts.

'The children are supposed to have made their own beds – I've changed the one that was – well – wet, but you'd better go and tidy the others. I don't like to ask Gladys.'

The day passed in various tedious household tasks punctuated by noisy and messy meals with the children, and at three o'clock Flora had sunk exhausted into a chair in the drawing room, too tired to do more than idly turn the pages of her Boots' Library book, while Jane was frankly asleep in her chair. They were disturbed by the front door bell.

'Go and answer it, Flora,' said Jane, starting out of her sleep, 'but don't bring anybody in here.'

Flora opened the door and there was Edward holding a rather roughly put together bunch of flowers in his hand.

'Hallo,' he said, manipulating the flowers and something in a large envelope.

'Edward . . .'

'I've come to say goodbye. I brought you these flowers.' He thrust them towards her and she saw that they had been hastily plucked from the garden and were not bought ones.

Flora took the flowers. 'Shall we go into the garden?' she said, and led the way round the front of the house, round the side and towards the lawn. She glanced quickly back at the house and through the window saw Jane, looking agitated and dishevelled.

She hoped that her mother would be able to organize something in the way of tea. She tried to remember if there was a fresh cake.

'You look surprised to see me,' said Edward, quite forgetting those times in the past months when he had avoided Flora.

He took her hand and they walked up to the end of the garden and a large patch of cabbages. The sight of them seemed to inspire him for he suddenly burst out, 'I couldn't go away without saying goodbye to you. It's such a comfort to know one is leaving behind somebody who *cares*! I know we will think about each other a lot while I am away.'

Flora laughed. 'Oh, *yes*!' she cried fervently. It was as gratifying as it was surprising, this sudden change on Edward's part, especially when she remembered how obviously bored he had been with her in July. It was altogether just the situation she had always dreamed of between them, and yet, now that it was happening, she was conscious of a feeling of anti-climax. Surely he was not as *tall* as she had always thought him. He had a spot on his forehead and his manner was really rather *affected*.

He was now taking something out of the envelope he had been holding.

'I've had my photograph taken,' he said importantly. 'I thought you might like to have one. Actually, I think it's quite good,' he said casually, and Flora could feel him waiting for her opinion. She looked at the photograph.

'Oh, Edward, it's *lovely*!' she cried. And indeed it was. The clever Mayfair photographer must have known just how Edward wanted to look, a handsome young man in uniform with a stern, rather sardonic expression on the face that was normally boyish and smiling. The cunning shadows emphasized good points and concealed the weak.

'I expect you would like me to write something on it,' he said, looking very pleased at her response. 'Let's go and sit on this seat.'

Edward got out his pen and sat frowning with concentration as he wrote.

'There,' he said, 'I'm afraid the inscription is rather simple – I couldn't think of anything witty.'

'To Flora with love from Edward,' he had written in a large, rather childish hand.

He screwed the top on to his fountain pen and put it back in his pocket. Now there would be somebody in England loving him, he thought, somebody minding if anything happened to him.

'Let's go in to tea,' said Flora, who had seen Jane making signs from an upper window. They walked decorously back to the house, Flora carrying the flowers rather awkwardly and the photograph by a corner.

In the drawing room there was a very respectable display of food and Jane was sitting bolt upright in an armchair. She had changed into her best garden party dress, a navy crêpe patterned with indeterminate flowers, and was even wearing her new court shoes which Flora knew were too tight for her.

'Well, it *is* nice of you to come and see us,' Jane said warmly.

Flora murmured an excuse and disappeared. She returned shortly with her hair brushed, her nose powdered and a new, fiercely orchid mouth.

'I do hope your mother is well,' Jane was saying.

'Oh, yes, thank you. She's really very happy. She seems to enjoy having the house full of children,' said Edward distastefully.

'Edward has given me his photograph,' said Flora.

'Oh?' said Jane in a high surprised tone. 'That is nice. My husband will be so sorry to have missed you,' she added, as if following up a natural train of thought. 'But I hope you will be back home again before long.'

Edward shrugged his shoulders dramatically. 'One can't say – one can't make any plans for the future now . . .'

'Then live in the present and have another bun,' said Jane, rather spoiling the effect. Edward took one. Indeed, he ate so much tea that Jane wondered if the poor boy got enough to eat. She could easily believe that Amanda Wraye might be a little vague about meals.

After tea Flora and Edward walked to the gate. Edward would have liked to kiss her but he was a little doubtful about the orchid mouth, which did not look entirely indelible, so instead he kissed her hand, which Flora rather preferred, thinking it very charming and continental.

CHAPTER SEVEN

Lady Nollard looked up from the Obituaries in *The Times*.

'Lavinia, Viscountess Hinge,' she read aloud. 'Of course she had been ill for a very long time so it was not unexpected.'

Mandy looked up from her simple boiled egg. It was really splendid how economical they were now. Every time she came to breakfast and noted that the lavish dishes of kidneys and bacon and fish were no longer on the hotplate she felt quite a thrill of pleasure and satisfaction. It was only one of the many small but meaningful differences that the war had made in her life.

'I see that Lord Calyx's sister has died as well,' said Lady Nollard with gloomy relish. Eleanor's friends, thought Mandy, all had two things in common; they were all of aristocratic families and were all either dead or dying.

'I think I shall give a party,' said Mandy suddenly.

'A party!' Eleanor looked startled, as if she had suggested something disgraceful, or at least unsuitable.

'Yes, people need cheering up – all of them: Miss Grote and her cousin, Canon Palfrey and his family – Flora is a sweet girl – that nice curate . . .'

Eleanor's expression softened when she heard that the clergy were to be invited.

'I'll have it at the weekend when Lyall's down here. People would find it more interesting and he will like telling people all about the war. We'll have bridge and sell tickets for comforts for the troops.'

Eleanor marvelled, as she often did, that her brilliant brother should have married someone as silly as Mandy.

'Oh, I can hear the children,' said Mandy, her face lighting up. 'Eleanor, can you hear?'

'I could hardly fail to,' replied Eleanor with a shudder.

'I love Saturday morning when they don't go to school. I like to hear them laughing and singing about the house.'

'I doubt whether you would be quite so enthusiastic if you had to look after them yourself,' observed Eleanor drily.

'But I *do* help to look after them. I take them for walks and give them their tea and bath them and put them to bed. And I always say goodnight to them. They are so sweet – it's almost like having Edward a baby again. Better, really, because Nanny never let me do anything for him.'

'All this evacuation will only make them dissatisfied with their own homes,' said Eleanor severely. 'There was certainly no obligation on your part to purchase clothing for them.'

'It wasn't an *obligation*!' Mandy said. How could she convey to Eleanor that one of the happiest mornings of her life had been the one when she had taken the children shopping in the nearest large town. She had bought coats and shoes and trousers and dresses and berets and all the other clothes they needed, and even some that they didn't need – just for fun.

'Do you realize,' she said, 'that Jenny had never had a *new* coat before. Always something handed down or from a rummage sale! Imagine!'

But, of course, Eleanor could not imagine and Mandy was only just beginning to do so. She sprang to her feet.

'I must go and see the children,' she said. 'I promised to show them how to play Snakes and Ladders.' She went out of the room humming what anyone but Lady Nollard would have recognized as a rather silly song about the Siegfried Line.

Sir Lyall Wraye got out of the train, looking back into the first-class carriage to make sure he had all his belongings – his despatch case, his umbrella and his gas mask in a brown leatherette case. He wished now that he had telephoned for the car to meet him, as he seemed to have several things to carry and it was beginning to rain. It was dark, too, so that it was unlikely that anybody would see him setting a good example to his constituents – saving petrol and carrying his gas mask.

As he passed along the High Street, he noticed several chinks of light through the curtains. Really, things down here were very slack.

Oh, how marvellous! thought Connie Aspinall, hurrying along to the wool shop to get another ounce of wool for Agnes to finish her seaboot stockings. I shall meet him if he doesn't cross the road.

'Good evening, Sir Lyall,' she called out, shouting a little in her anxiety not to be ignored. 'It seems to have stopped raining, doesn't it? I was afraid it was going to be a nasty evening.'

Lyall switched on his politician's smile, even though she couldn't really see it in the darkness. The voice was familiar, though he couldn't put a name to it. Doubtless one of the many admirable women who had helped at the last Conservative Tea.

'It was raining in London,' he said. 'There was quite a heavy shower as I walked from my Club to the House this afternoon.'

'Oh . . .' Connie was almost speechless at being given this glimpse of life at the highest level.

'Everyone will be *so* glad that you will be back for the party,' she ventured.

'The party?' he asked.

'Oh, yes, Lady Wraye has very kindly asked some of us to a party at Malories tomorrow evening. It is in aid of comforts for the soldiers,' she explained, in case he thought it was simply a frivolous occasion.

Suppressing a feeling of irritation with his wife, Lyall said smoothly that he hoped he would have the pleasure of seeing Miss Aspinall – he brought out her name triumphantly from the recesses of his memory – among the company.

'Oh, *yes!*' Connie breathed, hardly able to contain her rapture.

He raised his hat and murmured good night, striding on in the darkness. She realized that she had turned round and, trotting along beside him, had come right out of her way. Now the wool shop would be shut. Whatever would Agnes say? But after the joy of her conversation with Sir Lyall she didn't care. Agnes ought to have got it herself, she thought. I don't care – I don't give a *damn*! she told herself defiantly.

A *party*, thought Lyall as he trudged up the drive; whatever was Mandy thinking of.

'Why, Lyall, I didn't expect you until tomorrow,' said Mandy, who was standing aimlessly in the hall. 'I hope there will be enough for dinner.'

'What on earth are you wearing?' he asked crossly.

She was dressed in the navy uniform of a Red Cross Commandant, but her black-stockinged legs ended, unexpectedly, in frivolous pink mules trimmed with ostrich feathers.

'They wanted me to be in this Red Cross affair,' she said, 'and I couldn't very well refuse. Not that they will let me do anything. Agnes Grote and Nurse Stebbings run the whole thing.

But it means that they can have meetings here and things,' she said vaguely. She looked down at her feet. 'I had to get some horrid heavy black shoes to go with the uniform, but they were so uncomfortable that as soon as I got home I took them off.'

She slip-slopped up the stairs in front of him, humming. '"South of the Border,"' she sang softly, '"down Mexico way."' She would change out of this drab uniform and put on her coral red dinner dress, something bright and cheerful for when she went to say good night to the children.

CHAPTER EIGHT

'I don't quite see what a clergyman has to do with comforts for the troops,' said Canon Palfrey, as they were getting ready to go to the party at Malories. 'Surely it means knitted garments and that kind of thing.'

'Well, I daresay, but there are always *spiritual* comforts,' said Jane doubtfully. 'Do I look the *complete* country vicar's wife?' she asked, searching among a tangle of beads in her jewel box. 'I had some Woolworth pearls somewhere. They might add something to this dress.' She rummaged unsuccessfully and then pushed the box into the drawer and stood up. 'Oh, well, I don't suppose anyone would have been deceived – still, a string of *good* pearls – I suppose they might have been left over from my girlhood.'

Flora was in her room, looking with satisfaction at her deep Burgundy red nails which she was waving about as they were not quite dry. Jane came in to hurry her along.

'Oh, Mother, you *can't* wear those shoes and stockings!' she exclaimed.

Jane looked down at her lisle stockings and comfortable boat-like shoes. 'Nobody's going to look at my feet and legs,' she said. 'I really can't be bothered to change them and it's a cold night.

You'll wear your rubber boots to go in, dear?' she suggested hopefully, glancing at Flora's thin sandals.

'Oh no! It looks so awful arriving with one's shoes in a bag!'

'I expect Agnes and Connie will be wearing theirs,' continued Jane. 'Agnes was telling me about some she saw in Pontings' catalogue, zipping up to the knees . . .'

'Oh, *Mother!*' said Flora in disgust.

When they got outside they found that it was a perfectly dry evening, so Jane felt that Flora had really got the better of her.

'I wonder if there will be any *young* people there,' said Jane optimistically. 'Oh, look!' She plucked at her husband's sleeve. 'Isn't that Michael Randolph and Beatrice Wyatt? You know there *is* something . . . Are we all going to the party!' she called out to them in a loud clear voice.

'Surely,' said Michael, 'nobody can be going anywhere else this evening.'

'Michael has just been telling me a piece of news,' said Beatrice in a rather shaky voice. 'He's probably going to be a chaplain in the Army.'

'I was going to tell you, sir,' said Michael to Canon Palfrey, 'but I've only just heard from them this afternoon.'

'And I was the first one to be told,' said Beatrice, still sounding confused, for the telling of this piece of news was not the only thing which the Palfreys had interrupted.

'It's been quite a day,' Michael said laughing. 'Do you know what amazing sight met my eyes when I went to Beatrice's house this evening?'

'Do tell us,' Jane said with interest.

'Mrs Wyatt. Sitting downstairs in the drawing room! It's the first time she has been downstairs for three years!'

'I really *must* come to see her,' Jane said, from force of habit, and then, realizing what Michael had said, added in amazement, 'How marvellous! You must be so pleased.'

'Oh, yes, I am,' said Beatrice. 'It's Miss Stoat who has done it really. She has been a splendid companion to Mother and has been encouraging her to get up a bit every day.'

Michael, whose private opinion it was that Miss Stoat had so exasperated Mrs Wyatt that she had been driven from her bed to the drawing room, smiled.

He was feeling quietly happy. On his walk with Beatrice that evening, he had proposed to her at last. Indeed, he had just been given his answer when the Palfreys interrupted them. It had not been Yes, but it had not been No. Beatrice still saw herself as the spinster daughter looking after her invalid mother. But now the situation had improved. Given the continuing attention of Miss Stoat, there seemed to be no reason why Mrs Wyatt should not go out. Let her but take up afternoon bridge and all might yet be as he wanted it, thought Michael. To use the phrase so often employed by his favourite Victorian novelists, Beatrice had given him to understand that she cared.

'I still don't understand about this party,' said Canon Palfrey rather plaintively. 'Nobody has really explained to me what we are going to do.'

'Some people are going to play bridge and some whist, and the proceeds from the tickets are going to buy wool for the working parties for knitting comforts for the troops,' explained Flora patiently.

'Here we are,' said Canon Palfrey, shining his torch brightly among the laurels round the front door of Malories.

'Now then!' said a sharp female voice. 'You really ought to have that torch covered with at least two thicknesses of tissue paper.'

'Ah, Miss Grote,' said the vicar, correctly identifying the author of this admonition. 'And Miss Aspinall?' he asked, looking round at the scurrying breathless figure behind her.

'Agnes goes so fast,' said Connie resentfully.

They left their coats and galoshes with Rogers, who was, as she put it to the other maids, glad to see a bit of life about the place at last.

'Come along,' Agnes's voice rang out, 'we're going to play bridge in the drawing room.' Connie, who had been bustled along by Agnes before she had had time to tidy her hair properly, arranged the lace modesty vest that filled in the vee of her maroon wool dress. She noticed with some satisfaction that Agnes's collar was half tucked in at the back.

As they entered the drawing room she saw Lady Nollard smiling most graciously, apparently at *her*, so that everything else went out of her head. She at once left the others and made for the corner by the great fireplace where Lady Nollard was sitting in a large, regal armchair, her feet in their long, buckled Langtry shoes resting on a footstool.

'Well, Miss Aspinall,' she said condescendingly, 'I hope you are in better health than I am. I have been quite *poorly*, you know. Yesterday I was prostrated by a sick headache . . .'

'I think it's *liver*,' said Mandy in her clear voice. 'I believe there are some pills you can take, but Eleanor won't try them. Now, shall we draw for partners? Lyall is in the other room arranging the whist.'

Connie was racked by indecision. She was not a good bridge player and enjoyed whist much more. But, on the other hand, Lady Wraye and Lady Nollard were here and Sir Lyall might only be *arranging* the whist. He might come and play bridge when he had got things settled . . .

'Well, well,' said Canon Palfrey. 'We seem to have made up our table.'

'I can't think why you people don't learn contract,' said Agnes, who was already dealing. 'Now then, Lady Wraye, you do play one club, don't you?'

Mandy swallowed nervously and picked up her cards. She

was not happy at the idea of having Miss Grote as a partner. She thought enviously of her husband playing whist, and even of the vicar playing auction. 'Oh yes,' she said bravely. 'I love one club.'

Connie was playing with Jane Palfrey and two other women, one of them the wife of the local draper – 'This war is a great equalizer,' Lady Nollard had said, and her tones had not been those of approval. But they were pleasant women and nobody minded when Connie dropped her cards so that her ace of diamonds fell face upwards and they had to deal them again.

'Funny, wasn't it, Mrs Palfrey,' said Mrs Horrocks, who had been playing the hand, 'how those spades went.'

Jane, who had slipped off her shoes under the table and was now trying unsuccessfully to locate the left one, came to with a start.

'How is your son getting on in the Army?' she asked.

'Oh, very well. He's putting in for a commission. He's not far from here, though I'm not supposed to know where. But he comes home on twenty-four-hour leaves. It would be nice if he could be at the camp here next summer.'

'Camp?' asked Jane, startled.

'Oh, yes, they're going to have a summer camp in the fields – just beyond here.' She waved her arm in the direction of the window. 'We shall be quite jolly, shan't we, with the soldiers in the district!'

It would be fun for Flora, Jane thought. There might be some nice young men she could be friendly with. Soldiers coming to supper. Jane's nimble mind leapt forward through the remaining months of winter and spring and she wondered what they could have to eat. She hoped that they might still be able to get the odd chicken – boiled, smothered with white sauce – or was that only for the clergy?

'Oh, Sir Lyall is coming in here,' breathed Connie. 'I wonder whether he will play bridge.'

He did not play bridge, but stood watching the tables, and when the break came for refreshments an admiring crowd gathered around him, asking questions about the progress of the war and begging for the inside story of Mr Hore-Belisha's resignation, which had been announced that week. He was admirably non-committal about both topics, though he hinted at secret knowledge which he could not reveal in public.

Agnes Grote declared firmly that Hitler couldn't face a long war. She had read in the papers about somebody in a neutral country receiving a letter from a friend in Germany which had 'we are starving' written under the stamp.

'But how did they *know* there would be something written under the stamp?' asked Mandy.

Sir Lyall volunteered the opinion that there might well be a revolution in the German Army by spring.

'We shall see a lot of changes when the war is over,' said Lady Nollard repressively. 'Miss Aspinall, I wonder if you could kindly pass me that plate of queen cakes. I believe I can take something plain.'

'Oh, I'm sure a queen cake couldn't do you any harm,' Connie fluttered. 'And these little lemon biscuits are *delicious*.'

'Perhaps I will have one of those,' said Lady Nollard graciously. 'There is no cream in them, is there?'

'Oh, no, they are quite plain. Perhaps they would be better than queen cakes. I mean,' she suggested diffidently, 'if you have not been well, currants might disagree with you.'

Lady Nollard beamed and nodded. 'Very thoughtful, Miss Aspinall. One does not come across thoughtfulness very much nowadays,' she continued, 'it seems to have gone out of fashion, like so many other little courtesies.' She raised her voice and glanced balefully in the direction of her sister-in-law. But Mandy

265

was laughing happily at one of Canon Palfrey's simple jokes and Connie and Lady Nollard seemed isolated in another world where little courtesies were observed and relations were careful for one's digestion.

So Very Secret
a spy novel

Note on the Text

This novel (227 pages) was begun in January 1940. A diary entry reads: 'Writing notes for my spy novel, also began knitting stockings for the Balloon Barrage', but she did not actually begin writing it until 1941.

August 26th. About 3.25 the sirens went! So off on my bike feeling rather foolish in my tin hat. I think I must write my spy story.

September 22nd. Did ironing and writing – the spy complications are difficult.

September 29th. After tea I wrote – rather well. It varies but it gets on if I make myself do it.

October 9th. It is getting rather involved and I don't quite know what I'm driving at – that's the worst of a plot.

October 28th. Writing. I have done over 190 pages and really should be able to finish it now.

October 30th. Did a lot of writing – over 200 pages now.

November 4th. The novel is nearly finished.

She seems to have finished it before she joined the Censorship in Bristol in December. From then until after the war Barbara wrote no more fiction.

This was her only attempt at a different kind of novel, and she was not happy with the need for a strong plot. She obviously only really enjoyed creating the characters and incidents that would have been more at home in her other books. The idea of an Excellent Woman as the heroine of a thriller is not as incongruous as it might appear; the Excellent Woman, after all, always copes when those around her (especially Men) are failing to do so.

So Very Secret

It would be just like Harriet to say that flowers in the bedroom were unhealthy, I thought, as I stepped back to admire the arrangement of delphiniums on the table. I would find the vase put outside the door tonight.

I was putting the finishing touches to Harriet's room when I caught sight of myself in the mirror and thought that anyone meeting me for the first time would know me immediately for what I am – Cassandra Swan, a country woman in early middle age, daughter of the former vicar and still living alone in the family home, quite comfortably off and reasonably happy. My life is filled up with the activities of a country village in wartime – Red Cross and canteen work, besides church brasses and flowers, relics of the time when I had been the vicar's daughter and one of the most important women in the parish. Not that my place had been filled, for the new incumbent, Mr Ballance, a tall, ascetic and rather gloomy man, had told Agnes Liversidge that he believed in the celibacy of the clergy. And there were other things too – incense, sanctus bells and even confessions on Saturday afternoons. But I was always busy at the canteen then, cutting thick sandwiches, poaching eggs and serving tea from the big urns. Sometimes when there was a lull in the flow of soldiers, I felt sorry for Mr Ballance sitting all alone in a little box, waiting for people to come and confess. Father wouldn't have liked it at all. I still thought of what father would have said, although he has been dead for five years.

I looked again at my dowdy appearance in the mirror. When Harriet came tonight, I would wear my blue marocain and silk stockings, with my patent leather court shoes. I'd put vanishing cream and powder on my face. I might even wear that lipstick I bought in Oxford the last time I went shopping.

But somehow, even when I had changed, I was not really satisfied with my appearance. My dress though 'good' was unfashionable, and my hair was dull, unlike Harriet's elaborate arrangement of curls. But then, it had always been the same, ever since we had been at school together. Harriet had always been outstanding: a brilliant career at Oxford and then into the higher reaches of the Civil Service. Now, since the beginning of the war, she had been working in the Foreign Office and her job had been so secret that I sometimes wondered if she herself knew exactly what it was all about.

The war had really made very little difference to my life. Our village was so dull that even our evacuees left us, although we think that we are almost a little town with our cinema and our hairdresser and our few shops. In 1939 a big militia camp was set up just outside the village, and that is where I help in the canteen.

Harriet arrived at tea-time in her little car. When I saw her expensive tweeds I felt all wrong in my blue marocain, as if I had changed into evening dress too early. I had arranged a little supper party for Harriet's first evening. I invited Agnes Liversidge and Miss Moberley, the sister of our late Bishop, both of whom Harriet knew from her previous visits. When they arrived they questioned Harriet about the progress of the war, though Miss Moberley was much more anxious to know about the bomb damage. She enquired eagerly about the more select districts of Belgravia and about Gorringes, her favourite London store. She had wanted to order a new velvet bridge coatee and wished to make sure that the shop was not even now in ruins. Harriet waved her fork in the air.

'Oh, yes,' she said, 'we now realize that the Finland affair was not an Imperialistic war. I think a great many people were misled at the time.'

I nodded my head in agreement.

'The vicar doesn't *care* for the Russians,' said Agnes, speaking as if they were a kind of wartime dish. 'He was saying on Sunday that the Godless Rule of the Bolsheviks is very little better than the jackboot gangsterism of the Nazis.'

'Did he really say that?' said Miss Moberley. 'Clergymen use such violent language now – one can hardly tell the difference between them and the politicians.'

'There certainly *ought* to be a difference,' said Agnes. 'I must say I was rather surprised myself. Though I have never agreed with some of his practices . . .'

'Romish,' said Miss Moberley, 'decidedly Romish.' She pursed her lips. 'I don't know what my brother the Bishop would have said. We always liked the Russians. As you know, we went on a visit to St Petersburg once. Of course the Revolution was dreadful – so bloody.' She used the word with a solemn, literal reverence.

'Most violent upheavals are bloody,' said Harriet calmly.

We all nodded wisely and then Agatha, my maid, brought in the cheese and biscuits and everyone was so delighted to see such a large piece that Russia was forgotten amid their cries of delight and astonishment.

'I have never been offered more than my ration,' said Agnes, cutting herself a generous portion, 'but, even if I was, I don't think I should accept it.'

'I don't think I have any choice,' I said hastily. 'The order comes every week and I never know what will be in it. It's like a kind of lucky dip!'

After Agnes and Miss Moberley had gone, Harriet and I sat and drank a cup of tea and talked of old times. She gave me news of Adrian, my love of 1912, whom I had not seen for many years. He was now a very important man in the Government.

'He is very well thought of,' said Harriet. 'If you had married him you would have had quite a position. Would you have liked to be a politician's wife?'

'I wanted to be *his* wife,' I said. 'But, of course, he wasn't a politician then. And,' I added, for I had always been truthful with Harriet, 'he never asked me, you know.'

'I feel you should have married,' Harriet said, 'although you make a very suitable spinster. You know, I sometimes envy you and your life.' For a moment she looked serious then we both laughed, for the idea of Harriet spending her life in a quiet village did seem most unlikely.

Harriet went up to bed and I went around the room, tidying up as I always do. I like to see that the doors are properly locked and that all lights are out, and never trust anyone but myself to do it. It has become doubly important since the war, especially as our Air Raid Warden is the grocer with whom I am *not* registered. As I went along the landing to the bathroom, I saw outside Harriet's door the vase of delphiniums.

The next morning was beautifully sunny and we were able to have breakfast on my little verandah.

'I don't know what you like to eat these days,' I said to Harriet. 'I always have some sort of cereal – though they're becoming difficult to get.'

Harriet picked up the packet of All-Bran.

'"For constipation",' she read. 'How very outspoken we are now!'

I laughed and told her about Miss Moberley, who had pasted a strip of paper over the indelicate words when she had a young clergyman staying with her.

'She's asked us to tea tomorrow,' I said. 'I hope it won't bore you to go.'

'No, I'm here to be bored, if you see what I mean,' said Harriet. 'I want a complete change. What I also want is to get my hair done. Have you got a good hairdresser here?'

'Well,' I said, 'we have a hairdresser. I don't know how *good* she is because I only have mine cut and marcelled. Would you like to ring up? You might just get an appointment for this afternoon.'

Harriet went to the telephone and came back saying recklessly, 'I'm going to risk everything and have a perm! They said they could do me at two o'clock.'

'Oh, I have to be at the canteen this afternoon.'

'That's all right – I don't expect I'll be back until about five or half past – it does take rather a time. I must take lots of things to read.'

'I don't know *what* is suitable reading for an afternoon at the hairdresser's,' I said after lunch when we were looking at books.

'Not poetry,' said Harriet, 'though Swinburne might go well with the scented hothouse atmosphere. Something light and romantic is best. Or short stories.'

I handed her Saroyan's *Daring Young Man on the Flying Trapeze* in a Penguin edition. 'You might like that,' I said.

She looked through it. 'Yes, I might. It doesn't look like your sort of book, Cassie.'

'No,' I agreed. 'I was really attracted by the title. I bought it when I was shopping in Oxford one day. And I read it on the train coming back. And, after I had read the first story, I closed the book and sat clasping my shopping basket on my knee, saying to myself, "Oh *dear* Mr Saroyan – how well I understand you!"'

Harriet looked at me quizzically.

'But in some ways he is so *like* me,' I said.

We walked along to the hairdresser's together, Harriet with her books and knitting in a despatch case and I with my blue canteen overall on my arm. When we got there Harriet stood for a moment looking somehow indecisive, unusually so for her. She regarded me earnestly as if she was about to say something, but then she hitched her despatch case more securely under her arm and said, 'Don't wait tea for me if you're back first.'

The canteen and club for soldiers was housed in our local assembly rooms, where in happier days dances and whist drives used to be held. The long room with its gold-framed mirrors at one end was now crowded with tables and chairs. But even when full of khaki, the rooms kept their old atmosphere, and there was a dim, greenish look about the air as if it was full of ghosts. Archdeacon Glossop, Rector 1892–1911, still looked down from the walls. Nobody had thought of removing his portrait; it was so large and cumbersome in its elaborate frame. I walked in, moving towards the mirrors. Whenever I did this I always expected to come upon my own reflection as it had been at my coming-out dance in 1912, with my hair piled up precariously and wearing the white flounced dress which Miss Dace had finished only an hour before the dance was due to begin, so that I sat waiting in my bedroom, my combinations tucked in all ready.

I had hardly got inside the door before Agnes was calling to me.

'Cassie, do come here. You're the only person who can cut the bread thin enough for sandwiches. We've got some lovely tomatoes the vicar sent from his greenhouse, and, of course, there's always lettuce.'

I have never been able to understand about meals in the Army. The men always seemed to be ravenous at any time of day. We were soon having to cut more sandwiches and put out more trays of cakes. I was feeling particularly hot and flustered when I saw that Mr Ballance, our vicar, had come in and was moving among the men, most of whom looked rather sheepish, though a few stopped eating and grinned in a friendly way.

'I have brought another helper with me,' he said. 'Mrs Nussbaum, an Austrian lady, unhappily exiled far from her native land.'

We all smiled rather stickily and Miss Gatty, the little dressmaker, voiced the thoughts of us all when she said, 'I'm afraid Mrs Nussbaum will find Distington very different from Vienna. Though, of course,' she added, 'we will do our best to make her feel at home.'

'Naturally,' said Agnes, who was rather annoyed that Miss Gatty had been so presumptuous as to speak first. 'I am sure,' she said graciously, 'we will all be very interested to hear about Vienna.'

'Cup of tea and two cakes, please, miss,' said a voice at the counter, and as I went forward to serve him I saw that Agnes was somewhat officiously showing Mrs Nussbaum how to make sandwiches. Mr Ballance was hovering about with a rather pleased smile on his face and, as we were very busy, I suggested that he might refill some of the rapidly emptying trays with buns, but he was so slow that eventually I did it myself.

When I went into the kitchen Agnes came up to me, carrying a lettuce.

'I'm afraid Miss Gatty is offended,' she said. 'She's gone home.'

'Oh dear,' I said, 'too many people have turned up.'

'Yes, Miss Gatty said that she could see she wasn't wanted and she had a lot of work to do at home.'

I sank into a chair. 'It will be too late to run after her, I suppose. When I go to try on that skirt tomorrow I'll have a word.'

But as I was walking home I met Miss Gatty coming out of the draper's so I stopped and made a remark about there being such a crowd of people in the kitchen that I had decided to come away.

'Yes, Miss Swan, that was just what I felt.' She looked up at me. 'It was that Mrs Nussbaum. She pushed me out of the way when I wanted to get at the toaster. Well, I wasn't going to stand for that. Not from a foreigner.'

'I wonder if I could postpone the fitting of my skirt,' I said hastily turning to more congenial topics. 'I have a friend staying with me and I don't need it very urgently.'

Miss Gatty said that it would be quite all right, and I wondered if I dared tell her not to add the two inches to the hips which she always did, regardless of the client's measurements. But I decided that as I had managed to smooth her down about the canteen I would be content with that. It would be so awful if she sniffed and suggested that I might perhaps prefer to get it made in Oxford – at Elliston and Cavell, pronounced with as much scorn as if it had been as out of my sphere as Worth or Molyneux.

It was Agatha's day out so I started to prepare tea myself. I filled the kettle and cut some sandwiches (Harriet would need something fairly substantial to eat after her perm), singing, as I usually do when I am alone, 'Immortal invisible, God only wise'. By the time I had finished it was nearly six. I covered the sandwiches with a plate and listened to the headlines of the news on the radio. Then I began to read the parish magazine, which had just come. I turned first of all to my favourite page of queries. Can a lay reader officiate at a christening? What is the origin of wafers at Holy Communion? Should cars be parked on consecrated ground? I became quite absorbed and came to with a start to find that it was half past six and Harriet had not yet returned.

Four and a half hours, I thought. What tortures women

endure to be beautiful. I decided to ring up and see if she had left, but the line was engaged, so I thought I would go out and meet her. I hardly admitted it to myself, but I was beginning to feel uneasy. I got to the hairdresser's when they were just closing. One of the assistants was sweeping up and the air was hot with the smell of ammonia, perfume and singed hair. Harriet must still be in there, for one of the cubicles still had its green curtains drawn.

I recognized the girl sweeping up. Her name was Gladys Price and she had, some years ago, been in my Sunday school class.

'I've come to see if my friend Miss Jekyll has finished yet, Gladys,' I said.

'I think everybody's gone,' the girl said, looking around her.

'She was having a permanent wave,' I said. 'She must still be here. She hasn't come home and I didn't meet her on the way.'

'I'm sorry, Miss Swan, but there's nobody here now. We haven't done any perms this afternoon.'

'But you must have done. She had an appointment for two o'clock.' I felt that my voice was rising and I made an effort to be calm.

'Her name is Miss Jekyll,' I said firmly. 'She is tall and rather stout, with dark hair going grey. She was wearing a striped silk dress and camel-coloured coat . . .'

'I'm sorry, Miss Swan,' the girl repeated, staring at me curiously, 'but there hasn't been anyone like that here. We haven't done any perms,' she repeated as if this would convince me.

'Harriet!' I called. 'Are you there?' I stumbled about among the driers and the permanent waving machines until I reached the cubicle with the drawn curtains. I ripped them aside. I don't really know what I expected to see, but the cubicle was empty. I stood there, leaning against the chair, my eyes fixed unseeing on the various objects – a bottle of shampoo, curling tongs on a little stove, a box of hairpins, two combs, a tattered copy of

Vogue, a paperback book with an orange cover. A Penguin edition of *The Daring Young Man on the Flying Trapeze*.

I turned to the girl. 'Now, Gladys,' I said sternly, in my best Sunday school manner, 'you're quite sure you didn't see Miss Jekyll?'

'Oh, no, Miss Swan. I came on at half past two and she wasn't here then. Marion might know. She was here before that, but she's gone home now. You know her, Marion Phillips.'

'I see,' I said. 'Is there a back way out of here?'

'Oh, yes. It goes out into the yard at the back of Hughes's.'

I looked out of the doorway – just an ordinary, empty yard with long shadows across it and the glint of the evening sun.

'Well, Gladys,' I said smoothly, 'I am so sorry to have kept you. I expect Miss Jekyll changed her mind and will be waiting for me at home.'

As she turned to open the door for me I snatched up the book and, concealing it under my coat, I left the shop.

When I got home the house was very still and silent. I took the kettle off the hob. It had almost boiled dry, but Harriet would not be wanting any tea now. I had no idea what I ought to do. Harriet obviously knew her own business. I couldn't imagine her being taken anywhere against her will. She was a big woman and there were other people about. I wished I had some sensible, sympathetic person to advise me. That nice police sergeant who had given us our ARP lectures and had advised us to be 'as prone as possible' in a gas-filled room would have been a comfort. Perhaps I should telephone the police, but then, if Harriet turned up with a perfectly reasonable explanation, she might not be best pleased. She might, I thought, with a flash of indignation as I remembered the large smoked haddock I had bought for supper, at least have left me some sort of message. I went to the kitchen and absently began to eat the sandwiches I had cut for Harriet. After I had finished them I felt better able to *cope*, as Agnes used to say.

I turned the pages of the Saroyan book, my only link with Harriet. To my surprise, I found at the bottom of one of the pages a scribbled note in Harriet's writing. My first reaction was one of irritation. I cannot bear anyone writing in a book, even a bookstall paperback.

'Cassie,' it read, 'keep quiet about this. Very important. Oxford – Sunday afternoon. Upstairs in small drawer.' That was all. I was so excited at having found this that for some minutes I imagined that the whole thing was over: I shouldn't have to ring up the police after all. Then I realized that there was still something for me to do and I went into the hall. As I was about to go up to Harriet's room, Agatha returned from her day out. She had been to see her sister in Oxford.

'Did you have a nice day?' I asked her dutifully.

'Oh, yes, Miss Swan, ever so nice. And what do you think, we saw Miss Jekyll on Oxford station. I *was* surprised. I said to my sister, Freda, I said, there's Miss Jekyll. She's been staying with us and Miss Swan didn't say anything about her going. Only just come she has.'

'What time was this?' I asked.

'Oh, it must have been about half past three, because I had just said to Freda that I could do with a nice cup of tea and what about going to Boffin's and she said Boffin's isn't there any more, so we had to go to Lyons.'

'Miss Jekyll was called away suddenly,' I explained, 'something to do with her job.'

'Jobs!' Agatha sniffed. 'Freda's youngest is going to be a bus conductress if you please!' She went into the kitchen shaking her head.

I ran upstairs and into Harriet's room. There was only one *small* drawer in the dressing table. I opened it and found, under some handkerchiefs, a few letters and a long foolscap envelope. One of the letters was from me, inviting Harriet to stay, another was a bill for books from Blackwell's. The third read as follows:

Dear Miss Jekyll,
    Any Sunday afternoon in term-time. We shall be so pleased to see you. We have tea-parties for undergraduates and anyone else who likes to come. Do drop in. Mark is always here.

Yours in haste,
Edith Kennicot

The address, embossed in heavy Gothic letters, was Gladstone Lodge, Banbury Road, Oxford.

That must be it, I thought. I felt relieved. I could certainly cope with a North Oxford tea-party. Maybe there I would find out what I could do to help Harriet.

As an afterthought, I opened the envelope. It contained several sheets of thin paper typewritten in a strange language which I imagined might be Russian. I supposed it must be important and I hoped I would not have to do anything about it.

The next day was Saturday and I decided to go up to Oxford a day early and stay overnight with my friend Jessie Cantripp, who was a don at one of the women's colleges. I spent the morning packing a few things and letting it be known that Harriet had been recalled to London and that I was going away for the weekend. Fortunately I managed to find someone to take over my canteen duties, though Agnes was rather scornful about people who did not take their responsibilities seriously in wartime.

I was a little worried about what to do with the Russian papers. I felt I ought to take them with me and yet I did not feel, somehow, that they would be really safe in my handbag. My glance fell upon a photograph of Bishop Moberley, which he had once given to us and which had to be displayed in a prominent position whenever his sister came to supper. It was not large and it was easy to remove the back, insert the papers between the photograph and the backing and reassemble it. It would look like a photograph of my father, for certainly nobody could have been expected to have loved this thin, sheep-faced clergyman unless he was a relation.

When I arrived at St Margaret's Jessie seemed glad to see me and fortunately vague about my reasons for wanting to stay with her. We made general conversation about Oxford in wartime and I commented on the curious dress of the Slade students who had been evacuated there, and the fact that half the College lawn had been dug up and planted with potatoes. I was glad to go to my room, one of the small guest rooms overlooking the gardens and the Chapel, a corrugated iron building rather like a garage.

I always like Oxford on a Sunday morning. The first church bells begin early and there are so many places of worship to choose from. I always find the University sermon rather heavy going and I was relieved when Jessie suggested that we should visit a North Oxford church.

'Mr Unthank doesn't even preach about the war,' Jessie said. 'His wife doesn't let him.'

The church was a notable example of Oxford's Gothic revival, with variegated brickwork and an interior of yellowish-brown woodwork and bright stained glass. I felt that there was an atmosphere of devotion, accumulated over long years. The outside world with all its violent happenings seemed far away. The congregation consisted mostly of elderly people and the sermon was, as Jessie had prophesied, a pleasant change from some of the fierce political perorations I have heard from Mr Ballance's pulpit.

After lunch, I sat in the College garden in the sunshine and must have fallen into a doze, for I woke with a sudden feeling of dismay to find that it was half past three.

'I'll be back for supper,' I said to Jessie and hurried to catch the bus that went up the Banbury Road.

Gladstone Lodge was also Victorian Gothic, with a small tower and slit windows. The front garden was overgrown with laurels and other sooty shrubs and the whole place seemed dark and uninviting. I stood with my hand on the gate when I heard a voice behind me say, 'Hello, are you going in too?'

It was a young, cheerful voice and I turned round, grateful that I was to have company. I saw a dark young man, with the air of an undergraduate, wearing a neat Sunday suit. He smiled engagingly. 'My name's Hugh Fordyce. I'm at Balliol.'

'I am Cassandra Swan.' We shook hands rather formally.

We had now reached the front door and Hugh was tugging confidently at an old-fashioned bell-pull. Through the frosted glass door patterned with stars I caught a glimpse of a hall paved with coloured tiles. We were shown into a room full of people and I was glad to be in his company. It made me feel quite affectionate towards this young man I had only just met.

I could see no sign of Harriet, but a tall, fair woman came towards us.

'You must be Miss Linksett,' she said. 'I'm Edith Kennicot, my husband Mark has been looking forward to meeting you so much.' She indicated a good-looking man with a beard who was standing with his back to the fireplace, holding forth to some young women and an Indian student who were sitting on a sofa.

I took a cup of tea and looked about me. Now that I had time to take in the occupants of the room, I saw that it was simply a typical Sunday afternoon Oxford tea-party. The food seemed of a higher standard than the usual wartime teas that I had become used to, but everything else seemed perfectly normal. I wondered why Hugh was there. It seemed a very dull way for such a charming young man to be spending a Sunday afternoon. He seemed to be making a good tea. Perhaps that was why he had come.

Gradually the conversation petered out and the guests began to leave. When Hugh left, he smiled at me in a friendly fashion and I had an impulse to run out after him. But Harriet had obviously wanted me to come here so I felt I had to see it through. Though what it was I could not imagine. When only the Kennicots were left, Edith Kennicot leaned forward and said, 'We were relieved to see you, Miss Linksett. The woman Jekyll has disappeared and we have not been able to find her. When you turned up we knew that it was all right.'

'Yes,' said her husband, 'Von Lebens is in Oxford now and will be going up to London tomorrow. All we need is your contribution – those papers – and then the whole thing is complete.'

I sat there, my knees shaking. My thoughts were wild and confused, but I knew one thing, I had come to the wrong place. This was The Enemy. What was I to do? What had Harriet meant me to do? I tried to pull myself together.

'Oh dear,' I said. 'There seems to be some mistake, my name isn't Linksett – it's Sinclair, Connie Sinclair. Miss Cavendish passed on your invitation to me. She must have confused our names.' I attempted a laugh. 'She has been *very* confused and vague since her sister died.'

'*We* seem to have made the mistake,' Mark Kennicot said. 'You must have wondered what we were talking about.'

I laughed nervously again. 'Yes, I was rather muddled.'

The fact that they made no comment about Miss Cavendish and her sister, obviously invented on the spur of the moment, made me realize that they suspected me. Well, they wouldn't find anything. Thank goodness I hadn't kept the papers on me.

I would try to appear as stupid and simple as possible, which would not be difficult, considering how much in the dark I actually was.

'I really must go now,' I said.

Edith Kennicot rose and for one wonderful moment I thought that I was going to get away with it.

'Yes, of course,' she said. 'But before you go, do come and look at my cactus plants – I believe I heard you saying how interested you were in the ones in this room. Those I have upstairs are even more rare.' She led the way up the staircase. For a moment I was tempted to rush to the front door and try to escape, but I knew that it would be locked and that my only hope was to appear to act naturally.

On the first landing there was a broad window-sill covered with spiky, prickly plants.

'How magnificent!' I said enthusiastically.

'They are rather unusual,' Edith Kennicot said. 'I keep the really special ones in the bathroom – the warmth, you know, most beneficial.' She led me into a room on the right. It was a lofty room, more like a chapel than a bathroom, I thought, with high Gothic windows decorated with red and blue glass. There was, indeed, a bath, encased in mahogany, with old-fashioned brass taps. A lot of cleaning, I thought, especially in wartime with servants hard to get.

I turned from my contemplation of the bath to find Edith Kennicot standing behind me with a towel in her hand. With a quick movement she placed it over my mouth and nose. There was a sweet sickly smell. It must be chloroform.

'Edith, you fool –' a loud voice boomed like a foghorn, then the voices came and went, near and far away. I was nearly off now. I found I was looking at one of the stained glass motifs in the window. It looked more like a rosette now, the little ribbon rosette that Mr Ballance, our vicar, wore in his black hat. What did it mean? Something high-church. There floated before my eyes Miss Moberley's long sheep's face and pursed lips, saying, 'Rather *Romish*, rather *Romish* . . .'

The next thing I knew was a cool hand pressed against my forehead and a blurred design of roses. Somebody was holding something for me to be sick into. Then I lost consciousness again. When I woke up, I felt almost normal and was able to note that there was still daylight coming through the window of the prettily furnished bedroom where I was lying on the bed. Beside the bed there was a small table with some photographs on it. One was of a woman whose face seemed somehow familiar, but I was too confused to remember where I could have seen her.

Edith Kennicot was sitting on a chair leaning towards me. I shrank back, but her voice sounded anxious.

'That *was* a nasty turn you had just now,' she said. 'We were so worried. I do hope you are feeling better now.'

So concerned did she sound that I began to wonder if I hadn't imagined the whole affair.

'I'm so sorry,' I said. 'I've been so much trouble. I must go now. My friends will be anxious.'

'Won't you stay the night?' Mrs Kennicot said. 'It's getting late. It's nearly ten o'clock.'

'Ten o'clock at *night*!' I cried.

'Yes, these light evenings are quite misleading.'

'Oh dear.' I swung my legs over the edge of the bed and was relieved to find that I could stand up. 'My friends *will* be worried.'

'We could telephone,' Mrs Kennicot said. 'Indeed, we did try to find an address or number in your handbag, but we couldn't find one.'

With a rush of gratitude, I remembered that I had used my

285

new handbag and had only put in it a clean handkerchief and a purse. That could not have told them much.

'Let Mark take you back in the car,' his wife was saying.

'Oh, no,' I protested, 'it is not far and the air will do me good.'

They made no attempt to detain me and I walked slowly away, resisting the temptation to look behind me until the house was out of sight. When I was sure that no one was following, I got a bus and returned to College. The portress who let me in looked at me suspiciously and when I caught sight of myself in a mirror I realized why. My hair was coming down at the back and my hat, which I had jammed hastily on my head as I came away, was on crooked. I looked thoroughly disreputable.

I went hastily into my room to make sure that Bishop Moberley's photograph was safe. It was still hidden among my clean handkerchiefs and when I took off the back the Russian papers were just as I had left them. But when I opened my handbag I noticed that the lining had been slit.

I went to find Jessie expecting her to be worried about my long absence, but I should have remembered how vague she was. She had been busy preparing a lecture and had not even wondered why I had not come in to supper. We sat and drank cocoa together and I was glad of the Petit Beurre biscuits which she found in a tin. She didn't ask me anything about my afternoon and evening. Instead, with that peculiar bitterness that scholars seemed to feel against each other, she complained about a man called Wrenn who had stolen, as she put it, her version of a disputed line in an Anglo-Saxon text. It was obviously useless to confide my story to her.

As I looked out of the window of my room I was reassured by the high walls round the garden, crowned with spikes, and felt safe. Temporarily safe, I told myself. I could hardly spend all my time in the sanctuary of a women's college. Tomorrow I must set out on what I was already thinking of as my quest for Harriet.

Just as I was falling asleep I remembered the photograph beside the bed with its teasing resemblance to somebody I had seen before. It was Mrs Nussbaum, the person who had pushed little Miss Gatty away from the toaster.

Next morning I rang up Agatha to see if there had been any message from Harriet. But there was none. 'A Mrs Nussbaum telephoned, though,' she said, 'to ask if you were away. I said that you would be back today. Was that right?'

'Yes, perfectly, Agatha. Though I don't think I will be back for a few days yet. I will let you know.'

Somehow, this morning I felt fit and well and ready for anything. I felt I might be almost anywhere and was quite exhilarated at the prospect of further adventures.

I told Jessie that I was going home and took my suitcase and left it at the Left Luggage Office at the station. I decided to leave Bishop Moberley's photograph in it. The papers would be safer there than hidden on my person.

I was walking down Broad Street not quite knowing what to do next when I saw a bearded man who, for a moment, I thought was Mark Kennicot. It was not him, but the jolt that it gave me reminded me that I did not want to be seen and recognized by any inhabitant of Gladstone Lodge, since I was not at all certain that I had succeeded in disarming their suspicions.

I stopped and looked at my reflection in a tailor's window, mirrored against a background of dark suitings. I looked perfectly ordinary, just like any other rather dowdy woman of uncertain middle age, but to me I was my own self and even my appearance was unlike that of other people. It is not easy to disguise yourself in wartime. I couldn't buy any new clothes because I didn't have my clothing coupons on me. But, I decided, I could go to a hairdresser and smarten myself up a bit. I could have my face made up and varnish on my nails and I could buy a new hat without coupons.

In the hairdresser's I felt just like Meg in *Little Women* as the girl applied the coralline salve to my lips and a little rouge to my cheeks.

'Oh, madam, what an improvement!' said the girl, when she had worked upon me for some time and was holding up a mirror so that I could see the back of my hair, now elegantly curled. I had to agree that I looked smarter, younger even, although I was not altogether sure that it was an improvement.

By the time I had got my new hat, prudently carrying away the old one in a paper bag, it was after twelve and I was hungry. It is a very odd feeling to be in disguise – you feel inwardly the same, but the consciousness that you look different makes you feel that you cannot still be yourself. As I walked into Fullers to have some coffee and whatever food they were offering, I felt that everyone must be staring at me. But the waitress, a tired elderly woman, treated me as all waitresses seem to, with a mixture of kindness and condescension, so my manner must still have been the same even if I did *look* different. As I was sitting in the window slowly drinking my coffee and occasionally glancing down into the street I suddenly saw a familiar figure hurrying along the other side of the street with a tall white-haired man. It was Harriet. I tried to call out, but embarrassment meant that only a thin sound emerged, which was obviously not audible to her. I rushed outside and into the street just in time to see her getting into a car which sped away towards the Woodstock Road. I stood irresolute on the pavement and then suddenly remembered that I had dashed out without paying my bill. I went in and found the waitress, mumbling some excuse about trying to catch a friend, but she seemed totally unsurprised and incurious. I went out into the street feeling very depressed. If only I could have spoken to Harriet. Indeed, if only I could speak to *someone*. But there was no one in Oxford to whom I could tell my story.

Suddenly I remembered the young man at the tea-party and how I had somehow felt comfortable in his company. He might do, I thought. Of course, he appeared to know the Kennicots, so I should have to go carefully, but I couldn't really believe that he was mixed up in anything sinister. There was something about him that reminded me of Adrian, when he had been an undergraduate. I felt I could trust him.

I turned into Balliol and asked the porter for the number of Mr Fordyce's rooms. I wandered around the dark Gothic quadrangles looking for staircase 25 and after venturing into a building that was obviously the chapel, although it smelt of cooking, I found it and knocked.

Hugh opened the door and I saw that he was working at a table surrounded by tottering piles of books. His face broke into a welcoming smile.

'How good of you to come and see me,' he said. 'I was just going mad with my weekly essay – you cannot imagine how welcome an interruption you are! Now let's have tea. I know it's a bit early – I do hope you're not one of those people who *won't* have it before four o'clock.' Babbling cheerfully in this fashion, he led me into the room and sat me down in an armchair.

I was slightly dashed for a moment. 'Did you recognize me, then?' I asked. 'I'm supposed to look different. I thought I had disguised myself!'

He laughed delightedly. 'Why on earth should you want to disguise yourself? Let me see. Your hair's different and you are wearing make-up and that *is* a different hat – rather frivolous, perhaps a new one? You see how observant I am!'

The scout came in with the tea and he poured me a cup.

'Are the Kennicots friends of yours?' I asked warily.

'You mean the people yesterday? Goodness, no. I went by

mistake, but there were so many people there they didn't seem to notice.'

Indeed, the Kennicots had filled their drawing room with a motley collection of undergraduates, so that it was not surprising that one more young man would be accepted without comment.

'But why there?' I asked.

'I was supposed to be going to *Palmerston* Lodge, not Gladstone! You know who lives at Palmerston Lodge?'

'No, I'm afraid I don't.'

He mentioned a name high up in Government circles.

'He's the uncle of a friend of mine and we thought he might do something for me after the war – I want to go into the Diplomatic, when all this is over.'

He seemed so genuine, but could I trust him?

'Lovely as it is to see you,' he was saying, 'I have the feeling you came to tell me something. What is it?'

'I don't know if I *can* tell you . . .' I began.

'My father is a *Member of Parliament*,' he said with mock gravity, 'if that's any recommendation. And I'll swear on anything you like.' He was laughing. 'On the *Statesman's Year Book*,' he said, picking up a heavy volume, 'or that mystic badge you are wearing.'

I glanced down at my lapel and saw that it was my WVS badge, which I always wear on my coat.

'I'll trust you,' I said, deciding suddenly. And so I began – first of all with Harriet and then my own muddled experiences that seemed to get more muddled as I recounted them. 'So you see,' I finished up, 'I've still got these papers. If only I could have spoken to Harriet, but she went so quickly – Goodness!' I exclaimed, 'perhaps she was being kidnapped!'

'Perhaps she was.' Hugh's eyes were sparkling. 'Fancy all this happening to you!' His tone was frankly envious, and I realized, rather to my surprise, that he was now taking me seriously.

'What shall I do?' I instinctively turned to him for help. He looked so like Adrian that I felt it quite painful to realize that I was not the Cassandra Swan of thirty years ago.

'I think you must go home and carry on as usual,' he said gravely. 'I will go to Gladstone Lodge and see what I can find out.'

'Do you think you can?' I asked hopefully.

'I usually manage to find out anything I want to,' he said with cheerful confidence. 'Write down your address and I'll get in touch with you when I have some news.'

He tore a piece of paper off a letter which he had obviously just started, and I couldn't help noticing that it began, 'Darling Angela — I have been meaning to write for ages, but you know how it is . . .' I wanted to say: You must write another letter, she will be so disappointed. I could imagine her waiting, as I had waited for a letter from Adrian. But, of course, I couldn't say anything, and young people seem to be so different these days.

We walked down into the quadrangle planted with beetroot. I felt rather flat and disappointed now that my adventure seemed to be at an end. But it would be nice to be home again. Tomorrow was Tuesday and I would be at the canteen in the morning and after tea there was bandaging practice at the First Aid Post.

We went out into the street and Hugh said that he would come with me to the station to see me safely on my train. It was a lovely evening and we walked down Beaumont Street. I looked up at the Randolph and remembered how I had had tea there with Mrs Moberley and her brother. In my mind I could hear his high-pitched voice telling us about there being no wash-basins in the Palace and all the water having to be brought up in brass cans. 'And to think,' he had said, his voice soaring with indignation, 'that we are living in 1925!'

Outside the Randolph a large black car was drawn up. I looked idly at it and suddenly the registration number seemed familiar: CYX 9935. It was, I felt sure, the car in which I had seen Harriet being driven away. I grasped Hugh's arm and told him about the car.

'Are you sure?' he asked. 'You can't have seen it for more than a moment.'

'Oh, yes,' I said, feeling rather foolish. 'I'm very good at noticing car numbers because I play a silly sort of game, adding up numbers to see if they are "propitious", so I always notice them automatically.'

'Right.' Hugh went over to the car. An elderly man was sitting in the back fussing over some papers. As we reached the car a man in a chauffeur's uniform came up and was about to get in when Hugh spoke to him.

'Wasn't it you who drove a couple up to London this morning?' he asked, making a wild guess as to the destination.

'Well,' the man said, and his manner was truculent, 'what if I did? It's a hire car, isn't it?'

'It's awfully important,' I said, and described Harriet as well as I could. The man listened impassively, and then to my delight, I saw Hugh press a pound note into his hand, just as they do in detective stories. The man's manner softened.

'Yes, I did take a lady like that, and a gentleman, to London. Druids Avenue, Maida Vale, number 35. Just got back. That's why I'm a bit late, taking Mr Lonks up to the British Museum. I'd better get on,' he added as furious mutterings came from the back of the car.

As they drove away, I looked at Hugh.

'I think I can find it.'

'You're going up to London, then?' I was amused to detect a note of admiration in his voice.

'Oh, yes, I must find Harriet.'

When we reached the station I fetched my case, which seemed to be intact, and walked on to the platform.

'Where will you stay in London?' Hugh asked. 'In case I need to get in touch with you.'

'I'll stay at the Jeremy Hotel, near the British Museum, in Bedford Square. I always used to go there with Father and they know me there. Do take care of yourself – at the Kennicots', I mean.'

'I'll be very careful,' he said. 'Actually, I'll be up in town tomorrow seeing a friend of my father's who's looking for a private secretary – I'll give you lunch, if you like. My train gets into Paddington at ten forty-five – see you there.'

For a moment I thought of Angela and wondered if he would indeed remember. But this would be Adventure and not mere Romance. I leaned out of the window as the train moved off, and he waved until we were out of sight.

When we arrived at Paddington I was feeling dazed. I had slept for a while on the journey and on waking found the whole situation a little unreal. I pulled myself together and thought. Maida Vale was not far from Paddington, so I would take a bus. For some reason I felt I couldn't trust a taxi. The bus swayed down Praed Street and up the Edgware Road.

Maida Vale is wide and somehow *noble*, I always think, in spite of the decaying grandeur of some of the houses. Now, with ruins from the bombing here and there, the nobility seemed accentuated, as if the ruins were those of ancient Greece or Rome. I got off the bus at the nearest stop to Druids Avenue, or so the conductress told me, and walked slowly, since my suitcase was becoming heavy and more unwieldy.

Druids Avenue was a dusty street with children, who ought to have been in bed long ago, playing hopscotch on the pavement. As I approached number 35 I saw a little group of people on the pavement. The house was indeed number 35. I spoke to a woman in an overall.

'What's happened?'

'Oh, the poor soul, such a dreadful thing. One of those Austrian ladies.' The woman looked upset but excited and she was obviously longing to pour out the whole story. 'They found her with her head in the gas oven. Her friend that lived with her had gone away, you see, so no one found her in time. There's nobody else that lives there now, except them two. No wonder nobody found her until that lady and gentleman came in the big black car.'

I looked at the house again. In the window was a notice which said 'DRESSMAKING. Hilde Nussbaum and Gertrude Linksett. Tailormades and Alterations Done at Moderate Prices'.

'Are they still there?' I asked the woman. 'The people who came in the car.'

'Oh, no, they left about half an hour ago.' The woman stopped and regarded me closely. 'You'll be Miss Swan,' she said.

I felt a moment's panic and then she went on, 'The lady in the car described you, but you've got your hair done different to what she said, so I didn't recognize you at first. She said to give you this note if you turned up.' The woman produced from her overall pocket a piece of folded paper. It was a page torn from a pocket diary. Looking round me to see that I was not being observed by anyone who looked like an Enemy, I unfolded it.

Dearest Cassie – So sorry about this. Oxford was a mistake, hope you managed all right. If all is still OK get the papers to Sir Gervase Harringey – *nobody else*! Don't worry about me. H.

I fumbled in my bag and found some coins which I gave to the woman, thanking her rather incoherently.

'That's all right,' she said. 'Are you all right?' She looked at me curiously, but the sight of the police coming out of the house with a covered stretcher attracted her attention and I was able to slip away.

I felt very tired when I finally reached the gloomy but respectable classical portico of the Jeremy Hotel. I was also a little apprehensive about getting a room, arriving as I was so late at night. But a hastily invented story about urgent family business seemed to convince old Mr Bridges, who had known me for so many years, and he found me a small but comfortable room at the back of the hotel.

'I know you always liked a *quiet* room, Miss Swan,' he said.

In my room I put my suitcase down gratefully. It was too late to find Sir Gervase tonight. Tomorrow would have to be soon enough.

I thought about poor Miss Linksett. No wonder she had not been at the Kennicots'. But what was her connection with them? And Frau Nussbaum? It all seemed so difficult and not the kind of thing my upbringing had equipped me to deal with. Worn out with all these problems I eventually fell into an uneasy sleep.

Next morning I woke at seven o'clock, feeling very much more my old self. I got out of bed and drew back the stuffy blackout curtains. It looked as if it was going to be a hot summer's day. I must not, I thought, present myself at Sir Gervase Harringey's house too soon. I had looked him up in a volume of *Who's Who* last night. Fortunately, the Jeremy was the sort of hotel which had such volumes in its lounge. Sir Gervase lived in Eaton Square. About nine o'clock would be a good time, I thought, before he left there. But perhaps he slept at the Foreign Office. I seemed to remember a picture in some magazine – *Picture Post*, I think it was – of the office of some Minister of the Crown, with a camp bed by the desk. But that had been at the beginning of the war when people were doing things more feverishly and ostentatiously than they were now. So I thought it would be best to go to Eaton Square.

In the dining room I made a good breakfast. Meals had been very erratic these last few days and I couldn't be sure that lunch would follow breakfast. I decided to leave my suitcase at the hotel and went up to my room to take out the papers. I removed them from behind Bishop Moberley and cast about me for a safe place to keep them while I transported them to Sir Gervase. Fortunately I had brought my ration book with me, so I slipped out of the hotel and bought a tube of glue from the stationer's nearby. I put the papers between the middle pages of the ration book and stuck them together. I hoped I would be able to get the papers out without tearing the ration coupons because it would be awkward trying to explain to the girl at the Food Office what had happened.

I took the tube to Piccadilly, planning to change there for Hyde Park Corner. As I sat rocking in the train with all the people going to work, I clutched my handbag to me and thought that soon now I would be free of all responsibility for these papers. I looked around at the other passengers and then I had a dreadful shock. At the far end of the carriage were two women. One of them was Edith Kennicot and the other, sitting beyond her, seemed to be Frau Nussbaum – her face was hidden but I could see her feet and large legs in their shiny artificial silk stockings and the imitation pigskin handbag resting on her lap. I shrank back in my seat, trying to hide myself behind the paper of the man sitting beside me. The next station was Piccadilly and I made a rush for the door, squashing myself, as best I could, between the other people getting out.

I rushed along the passages and on to the other platform and just managed to fling myself into another train going in the direction I wanted. It was only two stops and I hurried out of Hyde Park Corner station. I could not see them behind me, and surely they would not dare to do anything with other people about. So I walked as calmly as I could down Grosvenor Crescent in the direction of Eaton Square. As I crossed the road to go into the square I looked round to see if there were any cars approaching and to my horror I saw them coming up behind me. There was no one else about, the square was quite empty. I simply took to my heels and ran. I had got halfway round the square and had a terrible stitch in my side. Clearly I could not go on like this much longer. I looked at the great houses as I passed and suddenly I saw number 175.

175 Eaton Square was a number that used to be engraved on my memory, for it was here that Adrian lived. Although we had hardly met at all since our youthful romance, I had followed every step of his career with a consuming interest and, indeed, sometimes when I had been in London I had come to walk past the house, just to look at it, to see what the curtains were like and what flowers he had in his window boxes.

I cast a hasty glance behind me. My pursuers, obviously even less active than I was, had not yet turned the corner of the square and I was therefore hidden from them. I ran up the steps into the portico and was about to ring the bell when I saw that the door was open. Without hesitating I went inside.

There is something unnerving about the silence of a strange house, especially a strange house you have rushed into without invitation and which, for all you know, may be hostile to you. As I stood there Adrian came out of a door on the left, obviously the library.

'Who are you?' he asked sharply. 'What do you want?'

'I wanted to see Sir Gervase Harringey,' I stammered. He obviously didn't recognize me, though he still looked so very like the Adrian I had known. But then, he was only fifty-eight, the prime of life for a man. I couldn't bring myself to reveal who I was and our former acquaintance, especially since a neat grey-haired woman had come out of the library and was standing there with a notebook poised, obviously his secretary. She stepped forward eagerly.

'Oh dear, people do sometimes mistake the numbers. Sir Gervase is at number 195, quite confusing really.'

I stammered my apologies, saying to Adrian how sorry I was to disturb him when I knew how busy he must be. At that a charming, rather weary smile crossed his face, and I saw once again the Adrian I had known. Since I was obviously and unmistakably a respectable gentlewoman who had made an embarrassing mistake, he set out to be charming to me.

'It really is of no consequence,' he said, smiling once more. 'A perfectly natural mistake. Miss Dyer will point out the house to you. Now, if you will excuse me.' One more smile and he was gone. I stared after him. Was this the man whose memory I had cherished for so long? This blank, wooden personality with only a certain facile charm, which could be switched on and off as required? My thoughts were interrupted by Miss Dyer.

'Were you wanting to see Sir Gervase personally?' she was asking.

'Yes, I was.'

'Oh dear, well, I'm afraid he's out of London. Sir Adrian was supposed to be seeing him today but the meeting had to be cancelled because Sir Gervase has to go to his mother's funeral. There's a bit about it in *The Times*.' She picked up the paper from the hall table. 'Yes, here you are.'

The paragraph read: 'The funeral of Florence, Lady Harringey will take place at St Michael's, Champing Parva today, Tuesday June 3rd at 2.30 P.M. .... Train leaving Paddington at 10.00 will be met at Champing Parva station . . .'

'She was ninety years old,' said Miss Dyer solemnly.

'How splendid,' I said feebly. 'Where is Champing Parva?'

'It's in Shropshire.'

'Oh dear,' I said anxiously, 'I really do have to see Sir Gervase urgently – I must try to get to Paddington to catch the ten o'clock train.'

'I don't think you will be in time,' said Miss Dyer, 'it's a quarter to already. Perhaps if you could get a taxi ...' She swept me up and by some miracle of efficiency seemed to materialize a taxi outside the door. I thanked her incoherently and, without even looking to see if Miss Kennicot and Frau Nussbaum were anywhere in sight, urged the driver to make all speed to Paddington.

Alas, when I arrived, the train had already left. I felt near to tears of frustration and despair, so I went into the Refreshment Room and got myself a cup of tea. I sat at the green tiled table, waiting for the hot, bitter tea to cool a little and staring at the stained glass window with its motif of birds and grapes. I drained my cup of tea to the dregs, swallowing a mouthful of leaves, which seemed to emphasize my weariness. I went gloomily out to enquire about the next train to Champing Parva. The ticket collector on the platform the train would go from was talking to two people, a tall, stooping clergyman and a woman, as tall as he, evidently his sister. I was able to gather from their conversation that they too had intended to go to Champing Parva for Lady Harringey's funeral and that there was not another train until two o'clock that afternoon.

'Excuse me,' I said, attaching myself to them. 'Is that the next train to Champing Parva you are talking about? I have just missed the last one myself.'

'Yes,' replied the woman, 'it really is most provoking. Now we shall miss the funeral. It will look so peculiar in the papers,' she turned to address her brother with some acerbity, 'to announce that Father Boulding and Miss Boulding regret that they were unavoidably prevented from attending, when we've told everyone that we are going.'

'Well, Mildred,' said her brother, 'there is no need to announce our stupidity to the world!'

'I shall certainly send a note to *The Times*,' she said firmly. 'People will assuredly notice if *we* are not there. After all Lady Harringey always attended our church when she was in London, and you often used to hear her confession.'

I must have looked somewhat surprised for Julian Boulding said, 'I am the Rector of St Cyprian's, Eaton Square. My church is rather what you might call High. Were you going to the funeral, Miss – er?'

'Swan,' I said, 'Cassandra Swan. Yes, I was, I suppose, in a way.'

'Perhaps we could hire a car, or go by charabanc,' he said.

'Impossible,' his sister snapped. 'It's much too far, we would never get there in time.'

'Then short of hiring an aeroplane, there seems little that we can do. It would be exciting to arrive there by aeroplane, don't you think so, Miss Swan?' he enquired, turning to me with a rather pleasant smile. I had the feeling that he had somehow taken a fancy to me.

I laughed. 'Yes, it would be fun!'

A crowd of people getting off the Oxford train came surging along the platform near to us and I heard a voice calling, it seemed to me in relief, 'Miss Swan!' and there was Hugh. I hastily excused myself to the Bouldings and drew Hugh to one side where we could talk undisturbed.

'What did you find out at Gladstone Lodge?' I asked eagerly.

Hugh seemed unwontedly subdued.

'Nothing at all,' he said dejectedly. 'There was no one there, the house was all shut up.'

'I thought it might be,' I said and explained how I had seen

Edith Kennicot – indeed had been pursued by her. Hugh appeared rather put out by the fact that I had succeeded where he had failed. Had I succeeded, I asked myself? Certainly I still had the papers, and that was something.

I told Hugh I was going to Champing Parva to try to find Sir Gervase, and I feared the Kennicots would be there too. I half-hoped that he might insist – as Adrian would have done – that he would go instead, but all he said was, 'Look here, we really *must* disguise you properly this time – to give us a bit more chance with the Kennicots. Now, my aunt's more or less your height and build. She lives in Bayswater and is in the Red Cross. We'll borrow her uniform for you. Come on.' He swept me off in a taxi.

At an expensive-looking block of flats we took the lift to the top floor. The door was opened by an elderly maid.

'Oh, Mr Hugh,' she cried, 'Mrs Fordyce has gone out to lunch.'

'That's all right, Richards,' he said, patting her shoulder. 'We've only come to collect Aunt Bea's Red Cross uniform that she's lending to this lady.'

As Richards bustled off to look for the uniform I said to Hugh, 'But won't your aunt need the uniform?'

'I shouldn't think so. She only wears it when she's going to have her photograph taken for the *Tatler*.'

'I think Miss Swan had better change here,' Hugh said when the maid came back with the uniform.

I was shown into a luxurious bedroom. I had an impression of pink satin and white furniture and very soft, shaggy rugs. Feeling rather foolish, I changed into the uniform and the long dark blue coat and little cap to match. Then I called to Hugh.

'I suppose I look quite different now.'

'You look very nice,' he said quickly. 'You'll need something to put your own things into. Here, take this dressing case.'

He took down an elegant cream leather case and started to

pack my things into it. I reflected that this ruthlessness with other people's property was rather a good sign in a budding politician.

Hugh insisted on our having lunch at the Ritz, a place I would never have dared to enter, feeling I had no clothes worthy of such grandeur; but a Red Cross uniform always looks right in any circumstances. Outside he found a taxi with the air of someone who expects to do so.

'Look here,' he said, 'I've got to see this man. It's terribly important for me.'

I realized that for Hugh even Adventure must take second place to his career. I thought of Angela and wondered if she was in a position to help him too. Otherwise there seemed little hope for her. He really was very like Adrian. He put me in the taxi and paid the driver, for which I was grateful since my money was fast diminishing.

'You will take care, won't you?' he said, and once more gave me that charming smile. As the taxi moved off he was already turning into St James's Street.

At Paddington I settled into a comfortable sort of lethargy in the carriage, which I had to myself, but after a while I decided that I would like some tea, so I struggled through the swaying corridors to the restaurant car. The train had just drawn into Leamington as I was about to pour the tea and I was grateful for the stop. In the silence I heard a woman's voice raised above the general murmur of conversation.

'Now, Julian, you see I was right. We could have stayed in our compartment and then walked comfortably along the platform, instead of struggling along the corridor.'

Mildred Boulding strode through the restaurant car looking for a table for two, followed by her brother, who stopped beside me with an exclamation.

'Miss Swan, how nice!' I was disconcerted that he recognized me so easily in my disguise. 'And in nurse's uniform too. Do you mind if we join you?' He raised his voice and called to his sister. 'Mildred! There are two places here – with Miss Swan.' I wished he would not speak so loudly. Now everyone in the car would know that I was Miss Swan, though I hoped that it would not convey anything to them.

'You will be surprised to see us on the train, Miss Swan,' said Mildred Boulding, settling herself more comfortably, 'but I persuaded Julian that we should come. Even if we cannot be there for the funeral, there may be something that Julian can do for Lady Harringey's family.'

'There's not much I can do in general, except criticize the choice of hymns and inspect the messages on the wreaths,' said Julian rather frivolously. 'Still Mildred insisted that we should come.' He smiled at me in a conspiratorial manner to which I could not help responding.

At Shrewsbury the Bouldings and I changed to the little local train for Champing Parva, which seemed to stop at every station. Unfortunately we had to rely on hearing the names of the stations called out in unintelligible country accents, since, because of the Emergency, the station signboards had all been taken down, so that they could not help the enemy.

After an endless series of stops, Mildred voiced all our anxieties. 'We must surely be there by now, we must ask someone.' So at the next station she put her head out of the window and hailed a porter in an imperious tone.

'My good man, how far is it to Champing Parva?'

He regarded her with malicious pleasure.

'You've passed it, m'm,' he said. 'Three stations back. Up Callow, that's where you are now.'

We climbed out of the train quickly, just as it was about to move off. Mildred began to blame Julian for our misfortune, which I felt was very unfair. He, however, seemed unperturbed.

303

'It is a pleasant evening for a walk,' he said.

'Don't be ridiculous,' his sister snapped. But the old porter insisted that there was no train back to Champing Parva until nine twenty, and he was very vague about the possibility of a car. Something about no petrol and the Home Guard and road blocks – it was all very confused.

'Isn't there anyone we could telephone?' I asked, but the old porter told us with some satisfaction that the telephone wasn't working, and hadn't been all day.

'How far is Champing Parva?' Julian asked him.

''Bout nine miles. But you might get a lift.'

'Let's go,' said Julian. 'Anything's better than hanging about here.'

'Bear left outside the station,' said the old man. 'Then after about a mile you'll come to a crossroads. Take another left turn and go straight on from there.'

Leaving our luggage to be sent on (I thought nervously of Hugh's aunt's beautiful dressing case), we proceeded at a brisk pace and soon left the village behind us. It was a lovely evening and the road was lined with tall grasses, foxgloves and purple vetch. Julian and I walked together, chatting easily as if we were old friends, while Mildred kept up a continuous grumbling behind us.

We came to the crossroads and saw that we were on a main road where it seemed more possible that we might get a lift. There was the sound of a car behind us and a long, black, sleek vehicle passed and drew up a little ahead of us. We hurried up to it and the window was wound down and a pleasant voice enquired, 'Can I give you a lift? I'm going to Champing Parva.' It was Mark Kennicot.

Fortunately both Julian and Mildred were tall people and I had been standing behind them. I remembered Hugh had said that I looked quite different from the back in my Red Cross uniform. Perhaps he hadn't seen my face.

Mildred was talking to him. 'You really are a Good Samaritan!' she exclaimed. 'Most kind,' Julian added. I said nothing but climbed into the back of the car with Julian, while Mildred sat in the front beside Mark Kennicot. She was chatting away about Lady Harringey's funeral.

'Is there a comfortable hotel at Champing Parva?' Julian asked.

'The Lamb is quite good, I believe,' Mark Kennicot said.

'We had to leave our luggage at Up Callow,' Julian continued. 'They promised to send it on, but I am rather doubtful if it will arrive tonight. What do you think, Miss Swan, are you more optimistic?'

I held my breath and was sure that I saw Mark Kennicot stiffen, but he made no comment. Just then we were overtaken by a heavy army lorry and he stretched out his hand to adjust his driving mirror. When he had done so I saw that my face was reflected in the mirror and I knew then that he recognized me.

When we drew up at the hotel Mildred went in to see about accommodation and Mark Kennicot drew Julian to one side and appeared to be talking earnestly to him. For some reason I felt sure that he was telling Julian that I had escaped from a mental home and that he was a doctor come to fetch me back, or some such story to get me in his power again. I must admit that I was not thinking rationally and I panicked. I noticed a bicycle leaning against the wall of the hotel and while their backs were turned I wheeled it swiftly and silently round the corner and set off on it as fast as I could pedal. As soon as I had done it I realized that it was a foolish mistake but I pedalled on. I thought if I doubled back along the side streets of the village they might lose sight of me. I took a turning to the left by a little wool shop and was looking out for another turning to take when I saw to my horror that it was a cul-de-sac. The street ended in a large redbrick building I hoped might offer me some shelter and when I got up to it I saw to my relief that there was a bicycle rack full of bicycles. I slipped mine among them and hurried into the building by a side door. As I went in I saw the long black car hesitating at the turning into the road.

I found myself in a bare corridor smelling of polish and anti-septic. A plaque on the wall informed me that this was the Great Champing and District Hospital and that the foundation stone had been laid in 1924 by Lady Harringey.

I nearly laughed at my good fortune. My Red Cross uniform would excite comparatively little comment here. I came upon an open door and looked into a room full of women, several of whom were in uniforms exactly like mine. I hurried in as unob-trusively as I could and joined them. There were rows of chairs across the room and charts on the walls showing the circulation of the blood. Some of the chairs were occupied but most of the people were crowded at one end of the room. I joined them and saw that they were watching a demonstration of hospital bed-making and sheet-changing.

The lecturer was a middle-aged woman in a nurse's white cap and apron, whose stocky figure and determined manner reminded me of my friend Agnes Liversidge – suddenly a com-fort at a time like this. The 'patient' lying on the bed was a pleasant-faced woman of my own age, with blonde hair hanging in wisps round her rosy face.

'Now then,' said the nurse, 'we'll try it again. Who'll be the patient this time? How about you, Miss – er –' Her eyes rested on me.

'Yes, of course,' I said and stepped forward quickly and took off my cap and my coat. I got on to the bed and turned on to my left side so that my face was not visible to anyone coming through the door. It was just as well that I did so for hardly had two ladies, whom the nurse addressed as Miss Hope and

Miss Angus, begun to draw back the sheets, than there was a disturbance near the door and I felt sure that Mark Kennicot had come into the room. I listened to what followed with a beating heart, pressing my face into the pillow. But I need not have worried. Nurse Dallow, for such was her name, was more than a match for him.

'I really cannot have all these interruptions,' she declared in a loud ringing tone. 'I have already told you that your sister is not here. We are having a Home Nursing Class and I should be obliged if you will kindly leave us to get on with our work.'

'I am very sorry,' said Mark Kennicot in a creditably meek voice. 'I thought I saw her come in here.'

'Well you were mistaken,' said Nurse Dallow firmly. '*Now*, Miss Hope and Miss Angus,' she went on, dismissing him, 'you don't seem very sure where to begin. Tell them, somebody, what to do first.'

I gathered that Mark Kennicot must have gone for a buzz of conversation started up of which I heard only snatches. 'A *horrid* man,' somebody said. 'Most unpleasant for her . . . ' Nurse Dallow clapped her hands and called their attention back to the matter in hand. I lay silent and unprotesting while I was rolled backwards and forwards by the heavy hands of Miss Hope and Miss Angus, two strapping young women by whom I should not have cared to be nursed. At last, when the sheet was changed, Nurse Dallow consulted a small watch pinned to her bosom and declared that the lecture was at an end. 'Friday at the same time,' she said. 'Don't forget.'

The crowd began to disperse, leaving me lying on the bed, stranded like a fish, on the shore. Where could I go now, I wondered. It must be getting late and my courage was beginning to fail me. I sat up and swung my legs over the edge of the bed. Nurse Dallow approached me.

'You're coming back with me,' she said in firm but kindly

tones. 'You look quite done up. Such a nasty experience with that dreadful man.'

I stared at her in astonishment.

'As if I would believe that you had escaped from a mental home,' she snorted contemptuously. 'Why, I could tell the moment I saw you that a lady like you wouldn't be related to a man like him!'

This rather obscure remark somehow gave me confidence to get to my feet and murmur gratefully that it was very kind of her.

'You come back and have some supper with Lucy and me – that's my sister,' she explained. 'And then you can tell us all about it.'

I followed her meekly from the hospital and out into the now empty street. I looked cautiously about me, but there was no one in sight. Nurse Dallow stopped outside the little wool shop that I had noticed on my way in. Over the door it said 'Lucy Dallow' in neat lettering. She went into an entry beside the shop and let us in by the back door.

Lucy Dallow, a smaller, meeker version of her sister, was friendly and welcoming, and didn't seem particularly surprised that her sister had brought a complete stranger home to supper.

'This lady,' said Nurse Dallow impressively, 'has had a very nasty experience.'

'My name is Swan,' I said, 'Cassandra Swan. And I am most grateful . . .'

'Supper first,' said Nurse Dallow firmly.

I don't know when I've enjoyed a supper more than those fried potatoes and bacon, with bread and butter and a great many cups of good strong tea. And then Lucy leapt to her feet and said that there was that bit of gooseberry tart left. So we had that, too, with some custard and more cups of tea. I certainly felt a different person after it.

Looking at the two women I knew instinctively that I could

trust them with my story, so I began at the beginning and poured out my adventures of the past few days. When I had finished, Lucy's eyes were round as saucers and she made little tut-tutting noises and murmured, 'Well, I never!' at intervals.

Nurse Dallow pursed her lips and said vehemently, 'There! I knew he was up to no good. I never did trust men with beards!'

'Oh, but, May,' cried her sister, 'what about the vicar's father-in-law? *He's* got a beard.'

'Oh, yes, but he's an *old* man, so that doesn't count. So,' she said, turning to me, 'you're in the Secret Service then?'

'Not really,' I replied, rather taken with this description of myself. 'I am doing that sort of work at present, I suppose, but usually I just live at home in the village – quite near Oxford – and do ARP and canteen work.'

Sister Dallow seemed to feel that this made me practically one of the family and said, 'Now we must help you to get those papers to Sir Gervase.'

'Is the house far away?'

'About half a mile,' said Lucy, 'but there's a very long winding drive, which must be almost another half mile.'

I shuddered at the thought of the long drive, probably dark and shadowed with trees and shrubs, behind which who knows what might lurk. I should have to walk boldly, perhaps run, humming 'Onward, Christian Soldiers' to drive away the powers of darkness in the shape of Mark Kennicot.

'We must think of a plan,' said Nurse Dallow. 'After what happened you can't go alone.'

I sat there, content for the moment to have somebody else do my thinking for me.

'I know,' she exclaimed, 'the tandem!'

'You mean a bicycle?'

'Yes, you and I will ride it, Miss Swan. Come along, the sooner we get those papers to Sir Gervase the better.'

We went out into the hall and put on our hats and coats and Nurse Dallow slung her civilian respirator case over her shoulder and slipped on an arm-band with the words Civil Defence on it. 'You never know,' she said obscurely.

After the first few moments when I felt the pedals going rather too fast for me, I soon got into the rhythm and we went spinning along in fine style out of the village, since the road was slightly downhill. We must have looked a peculiar sight, the two of us in nurses' uniform pedalling along on a tandem. Indeed, when we passed a group of soldiers one of them called out, 'Hello gorgeous!' and some of the others started to sing 'Daisy, Daisy'.

'They're really very cheeky,' said Nurse Dallow, 'especially when there are a lot of them all together.' But I got the impression that she wasn't really annoyed, but even rather flattered.

'Now then,' she continued, 'here's the drive.'

We passed through the open gateway. The iron gates had gone for salvage but the gateposts remained, crowned with a pair of urns.

We pedalled briskly up the drive which was as dark and frightening as I had imagined it, and I was very glad indeed that I was perched up behind Nurse Dallow on a tandem and not walking on foot and alone. Suddenly we heard voices round a bend in the drive and there were Julian and Mildred, trailing wearily, still engaged in argument.

'I cannot feel that we will be very welcome at this hour,' Julian was saying, 'but we shall feel that we have done our duty. Personally, I feel that we have exceeded it.'

Nurse Dallow rang her bell and they started and jumped aside.

'Miss Swan, and on a tandem!' Julian cried. 'The long walk has been worthwhile after all!'

'We are on urgent business and can't stop!' Nurse Dallow called out and swept on, leaving them staring in bewilderment.

A few minutes later we reached the house. It was a large and imposing building, with a great many classical pillars giving it an impressive frontage. Nurse Dallow leaned the tandem against one of these.

'I'll wait for you here,' she said, suddenly seeming diffident when confronted by the local gentry.

I felt rather nervous myself as I approached the massive front door and rang the bell. There was a sudden confused noise of barking and scuffling and the door opened to reveal a youngish woman dressed in black restraining with some difficulty several lively dogs.

'I'm so sorry,' she said in a pleasant voice, 'they're a bit out of hand today.'

'I am so very sorry to bother you at such a time,' I said, 'but I have to see Sir Gervase on urgent business.'

She laughed. 'Gervase's business always is urgent. Do come in, so that I can let this lot loose.'

I stepped inside as she closed the door and the dogs went rushing off back into the large pillared hall.

'Gervase is in his study. This way.'

She led me up a curved staircase, opened an elaborately carved door, put her head round it and said casually, 'One of your urgent callers, Gervase.'

I felt feverishly in my handbag to make sure that the ration book was still there and went into the room.

Sir Gervase rose to his feet. He was shorter than he seemed in his photographs, but then I suppose people often are.

'Good evening,' I said. 'I'm sorry to have come at such an awkward time . . .'

'Not at all, Miss – er—'

'Swan. Cassandra Swan.'

'Ah.' Sir Gervase looked puzzled, as if he had expected to hear a name more familiar to him. 'I suppose you are one of Grampian's lot.'

'I'm not anybody's lot,' I replied. I was rather taken aback by my own boldness. 'I got into this all quite by accident.'

I tried to explain how it had all come about, but Sir Gervase did not seem to be listening very carefully.

I prised open the centre pages of my ration book and took out the papers.

'Did you hide them in there?' he asked curiously. He glanced at them and put them to one side with some other papers. It was all over. I felt a twinge of disappointment, even of resentment, that the papers which had given me so much pain and trouble should be put away like that, hardly even mentioned.

'Are they important?' I asked.

'Oh, yes, Miss – er – Swan. Very important. I must tell Grampian that you did a splendid job . . .'

'But I'm not . . .' It seemed too difficult to explain. Then something occurred to me. 'But the man Kennicot – what about him?'

'Oh, I expect Grampian's lot will see to it – not my pigeon.'

'But he's *here*, in the neighbourhood . . .' I felt I must make Sir Gervase understand and I leaned forward urgently, but his face was swaying oddly and seemed to come and go and suddenly everything was black and I knew no more.

I regained consciousness to hear familiar words.

'You've had a nasty turn . . .' But the voice was the reassuring one of Nurse Dallow and all around me were friendly faces: Lady Harringey, Nurse Dallow, Sir Gervase and hovering anxiously in the background, Julian and his sister Mildred.

'Well, you gave us quite a fright, going off like that!' Sir Gervase said and Lady Harringey passed a glass of water to Nurse Dallow who held it to my lips.

'Poor thing,' she said, 'you must be quite worn out, you really need a good night's rest. Better come back with me.'

'We can easily have a bed made up here,' said Lady Harringey helpfully.

'We reserved you a room at the Lamb,' Julian said. 'We thought you might be coming back.'

Everyone looked at me, waiting for me to speak, but it was Nurse Dallow who broke the silence.

'Well, just as you like, dear,' she said. 'I know Lucy will have made up a bed for you, but that doesn't matter . . .'

It was clear to me where my duty lay. Nurse Dallow showed all the signs of a person about to take umbrage. It was the same old story – Miss Gatty being pushed away from the toaster, Nurse Dallow's bed not being good enough to receive Cassandra Swan's weary body.

'Of course I am going with Nurse Dallow,' I said. 'But thank you very much for your kind offer, Lady Harringey. I feel I've given you enough trouble as it is.'

'Oh, no trouble,' said Sir Gervase. 'You've done an excellent job of work. I shall commend you to Grampian when I see him.'

'Don't do that,' I said. 'But do, *please*, do something about that man I told you about.'

'Kennicot,' said Sir Gervase. 'I'll make a note of it.'

I turned away discouraged and followed Nurse Dallow into the hall.

'I have ordered the car to take you back,' said Lady Harringey. 'After all it is practically war-work, so I think we are justified in using the petrol. I will send Frost down with your bicycle in the morning.'

We all got into the Daimler, Nurse Dallow ostentatiously getting into the front with the chauffeur while I sat in the back with Julian and his sister. The events of the evening seemed to have reduced them to temporary silence. As we progressed regally down the drive, Nurse Dallow suddenly gave a cry.

'Look! It's him, in those bushes!'

We all twisted round, but could see nothing in the darkness.

313

'Who?' I asked, knowing in my heart that she could only mean Mark Kennicot.

'That dreadful man who came after you! But never mind, dear,' she added soothingly. 'Don't worry, it's all over now.'

I supposed it was. But the thought of Mark Kennicot prowling around the house and the casual way that Sir Gervase had laid the papers to one side aroused my apprehensions once again. But that was Grampian's business, or Sir Gervase's; nothing to do with me. I leaned back comfortably and listened to Julian's amusing conversation, thinking how nice it would be to be back home again, when suddenly I sat bolt upright, jerking poor Mildred to one side and startling her considerably.

'It's Harriet!' I cried. 'I still haven't found her!'

And then I had to explain who Harriet was and how she had led me into this adventure and how worried I was about her disappearance.

'Oh, I expect she'll turn up, dear,' said Nurse Dallow, in that flat, reassuring voice which must have soothed so many patients.

Miss Boulding shuddered. 'Poor soul, I do hope she is not undergoing any *unpleasant experiences*.'

'Oh, come, Mildred,' said her brother, 'I imagine she is perfectly capable of taking care of herself. My dear Cassandra, you have done everything possible. You must just let things take their course.'

The car drew up at the little wool shop and Julian helped me out of the car. How kind everyone was, I thought. And he had called me Cassandra too. He was using my name again.

'Goodnight, Cassandra. I do hope you sleep well. Perhaps you will come round to the Lamb and see us tomorrow morning. Or perhaps we will call on you. It would be a pity to lose touch.'

Nurse Dallow hurried me into the house and Lucy soon had the kettle boiling. She was already prepared for bed and wore a blue ripple cloth dressing gown and her hair down in a plait.

The sight of her nightwear reminded me that my luggage was by now at the Lamb, but Nurse Dallow produced a blue cotton nightgown with a sprinkling of hand-sewn embroidery at the neck.

'Lucy's made up a bed for you in my room, dear,' she said, 'I thought it would be better for you to have company.'

'Thank you,' I said gratefully, 'I shall be glad to get to bed.'

I got quickly into bed and Nurse Dallow came in, dressed in a pink wool dressing gown, but still looking somehow as if she was in uniform. She carried a glass of water and a parish magazine.

'I don't suppose you'll feel much like reading, though,' she said.

I lay down and closed my eyes. I was so very tired but it did not seem that I could ever sleep with so much to think about. I ran through Eaton Square, I was face to face with Adrian again, I talked to the Bouldings on Paddington station, I had lunch at the Ritz with Hugh, I walked along a dusty lane with tall grasses and vetch ... and dark tunnels of rhododendrons ... and I rode on a bicycle and then I rode a tandem ... and there was a walk between pillars to a big house and the noise of dogs barking behind a closed door. They barked and they howled and wailed in a most frightening manner, going up and down, so that I woke in a fright and called out.

'It's all right,' came the reassuring voice. 'What a pity it woke you up. It's only the siren.'

'What time is it?' I asked, struggling to sit up.

'Half past one. They *would* come tonight. We haven't had a raid for over a week. Lucy and I have got to go to the First Aid Post,' she continued. 'I don't know if you would rather come with us or stay here.'

'Oh, do let me come,' I said. 'I'll only be a few moments getting ready.' I was soon ready in my Red Cross uniform as was

Nurse Dallow, who also wore a large tin hat which wobbled a bit on her head.

'I've got the food, May,' said Lucy, coming into the room. She too was wearing a tin hat and, rather surprisingly, navy slacks. 'But I'm not putting that block of chocolate in. You know what Miss Gurney's like. Never brings anything of her own and expects us to provide things for her.'

We went out into the street. It was a beautiful night, except for the sinister purr of enemy planes up among the stars.

'I expect it's Merseyside they're after,' said Lucy. 'It's terrible the damage. They say there's nothing left of Church Street . . .'

'Liverpool, oh, it's dreadful,' said a breathy female voice behind us.

'Oh, Miss Gurney, I've got that wool for you,' said Lucy. 'I brought it along with me so you can start it tonight.'

'Oh, thank you, Miss Dallow. I will knit if I can . . . it may be a *help* to me. One can do so little . . .'

'She never does anything,' said Lucy in an aside to me. 'Never offers to make tea or cut sandwiches. Thinks herself above things like that.'

By this time we had reached the First Aid Post, which was in a sort of annexe to the hospital where I had been once already today. It was surrounded by sandbags, which seemed to be filled with anything but sand, to judge by the dark, rich earth that was bursting out of many of them. Nurse Dallow opened the door into a hall which had two or three doors leading out of it. These smaller rooms were brightly lit and hazy with cigarette smoke and there was an air of cheerfulness and bustle. Everyone seemed to be laughing and talking as they went about their tasks. Women, in voluminous blue cotton overalls with ARP embroidered on the bosom in scarlet letters, hurried to and fro carrying large bottles and boxes of dressings. Men in navy blue boiler suits were filling water bottles and fetching blankets. A stout, good-looking woman nursed a long sandwich loaf in her arms and another followed her with a packet of margarine and two jars of potted meat.

We went through a door labelled Women's Treatment Room. There was a long scrubbed table covered with dressings and bottles and in one corner a conglomeration of crutches, wire mattresses, metal splints and other objects which I could not identify. It did not seem as if there would be much room for casualties.

'Now, dear,' said Nurse Dallow, 'make yourself comfortable.' And she handed me a couple of pillows in rather dirty white jaconet covers. Several people came into the room and made up makeshift beds – Miss Gurney, engaging in a complicated piece of knitting, a Mr Mariner and a Mr Long, both very jolly and full of jokes. After a while we heard the hissing of a Primus stove and smelt hot paraffin fumes.

'Ah, good,' said Mr Mariner, 'that means tea.'

Someone appeared carrying a tray with mugs of tea and thick triangles of bread spread with margarine and fish paste.

When we had finished eating we fell into a kind of lethargy. Miss Gurney leaned her head uncomfortably against a wall with an expression of martyrdom on her face and closed her eyes. Nurse Dallow and her sister sat bolt upright knitting and I wound some wool for Lucy. From the other rooms we could hear the hum of voices and the occasional laugh or a cry of 'Double four spades' or 'Having no hearts, partner'. But after a time there was almost complete silence so that when a plane came over everyone heard it and sat up. 'That's one of ours,' said Nurse Dallow triumphantly. 'It sounds as if it's chasing a Jerry.'

She had hardly finished speaking when the whole place seemed to shake and the glass rattled. Mr Mariner sat up and said, 'That was a near one!'

Everyone seemed to wake up now. Excited voices could be heard and great activity was going on in the hall.

'It fell somewhere near Cuckoo Grange ... there may be casualties ...' The stout woman burst into the room. 'The ambulance people have gone now.'

'Everything ready in here?' enquired a voice, which I recognized as belonging to one of the bridge players.

'Doctor Finn,' said Nurse Dallow, 'I do wish you would ask the authorities for more pillows. These are disgraceful!'

'Excuse me, Nurse,' said the doctor backing out of the room, 'I think I'm wanted.'

'You see – it's always the same. Impossible to get anything.'

'You should ask Mrs Moat,' said Miss Gurney.

There was a grim silence.

Nurse Dallow sniffed. '*I* shan't ask Mrs Moat for anything,' she said shortly. 'After the way she treated me over that oilcloth.'

There was a great bustle outside and a man burst in to say that a casualty was being brought into the Men's Treatment Room. We looked out into the entrance hall, trying not to appear curious, but all we could see was a muffled form on a stretcher. Nurse Dallow went out of the room with the light of battle in her eye.

'He's pretty badly hurt, unconscious,' somebody said.

'They ought to have taken him straight to the hospital if he's really badly hurt,' said Lucy. 'Oh, here's May, she'll be able to tell us.'

'Miss Swan, dear,' she said, sitting down beside me. 'It's someone we know.'

My heart leapt and began to beat sickeningly.

'It's that man,' said Nurse Dallow, 'you know ...'

'I know,' I said, feeling shamefully relieved. 'Mark Kennicot.'

'Strange it should be him. It seems rather like vengeance, doesn't it?' said Lucy.

'I don't know,' I said rather miserably, 'it's certainly very strange. I wonder how it happened.'

'From what I hear, a bomb fell on Cuckoo Grange – that's a house near here. It's been empty but we heard that strangers had rented it. It must have been him. And he was outside when the bomb fell in the grounds.'

'What was he doing outside at half past two in the morning?' Lucy demanded.

I could imagine only too well what he might have been doing.

'Was anyone else hurt?' I asked.

'Yes, they're bringing someone in – a lady,' said Nurse Dallow.

'Oh, they'll be bringing her in here,' cried Miss Gurney. 'We must be ready.'

Suddenly, from outside the door I heard a firm voice protesting, 'This is ridiculous. I can walk perfectly well.'

I flung the door open and there, on a stretcher, sitting up and waving her arms in protest, was my dear Harriet.

I don't suppose Nurse Dallow and Lucy ever knew a more triumphant moment than the one in which, under the eyes of everyone, they took me and Harriet away to the little wool shop. We were driven in state in the ambulance.

'Mrs Moat wanted to put you up,' said Nurse Dallow jubilantly, 'when she found out who you were!'

'But I'm not a celebrity,' protested Harriet. 'Cassie is the heroine of this story. And don't say, Oh, I did nothing,' she warned me, 'because I shan't believe you. We'll have the whole story in the morning.' And with that she dismissed us all to our beds – Lucy was going to sleep on the sofa and give Harriet her bed – like a queen finishing an audience.

In the morning, over breakfast, I asked Harriet the one question that had been nagging away at me from the beginning.

'Why did you disappear from the hairdresser's like that?'

'Because I saw someone coming in who had been following me. I caught a glimpse of her in the mirror and slipped out the back way.'

'Frau Nussbaum!' I exclaimed. 'There are so many things I don't understand.'

'God moves in a mysterious way,' said Harriet, 'and the Foreign Office moves even more mysteriously, when it does move!'

'The Foreign Office!' breathed Lucy. 'And now That Man is very badly injured, so he won't cause any more trouble.'

'What about Edith Kennicot?' I asked Harriet. 'Will they pick her up? I must say Sir Gervase was very casual about it all – I mean, he couldn't know that Mark Kennicot would be immobilized by a bomb. I expect he will say that capturing Edith Kennicot and the others is Grampian's affair!'

'Oh, Grampian!' Harriet laughed. 'He will be furious when he hears that Kennicot was struck down on Sir Gervase's doorstep, so to speak.'

I smiled. It seemed that some form of umbrage could be taken even in the higher reaches of Whitehall.

'What day is it?' I asked suddenly. 'So much seems to have happened that I've lost track.'

'It's Wednesday,' said Nurse Dallow vigorously. 'And my clinic is due to open in half an hour.'

'And I must go down into the shop, I suppose,' said Lucy reluctantly.

'And Cassie and I must go home,' said Harriet. 'I hope,' she said, turning to me, 'that it will be all right for me to finish my holiday with you.'

'Oh, Harriet, of course! I'm so glad you don't have to go back straight away. It would have been so flat just to have gone home on my own!'

We said goodbye to the Dallows with repeated thanks for

their kindness. There seemed no way we could repay them. Money was obviously out of the question. In any case I had very little left and Harriet, after all she had been through, had been hardly able to carry her handbag with her. But we felt sure that the excitement of the adventure they had experienced with us would probably be reward enough in itself.

We left Nurse Dallow on her way to the clinic where she would be weighing babies and distributing rose hip syrup with the calm efficiency for which I had been so grateful. Our last glimpse of Lucy was of her attempting to pile up unwieldy skeins of oiled wool and balance on them a notice saying NO COUPONS.

We called in at the Lamb and I left cordial messages for the Bouldings who were with Sir Gervase and Lady Harringey, presumably giving the comfort which they had been unable to give the day before. I hoped I might see them again. Julian had had a very amusing turn of phrase and was quite unlike any other clergyman I had ever met. I hoped, too, that I might see Hugh again, although he would probably soon be too busy. Nevertheless it seemed that I had made several new friends in the course of my travels.

But I was not to be allowed to forget my old friends, for when we reached home at last, there was Agnes on the doorstep.

'Cassandra,' she said sternly, 'we expected you back on Monday. It was very awkward at the canteen. Miss Brewer did the money and you know how flustered she gets. So now we are five and sixpence out!'

Short Stories

Note on the Text

'So Some Tempestuous Morn' (*probably written in the early 1950s*) *and* 'The Christmas Visit' (*1977*) *are both examples of the way Barbara 'salvaged' characters from her unpublished novels and used them in short stories. The first takes Anthea, Miss Morrow and Miss Doggett from* Crampton Hodnet *and presents them in slightly different circumstances, though their characters remain the same. The Aingers and Faustina were taken from* An Unsuitable Attachment *when Barbara was asked to write a Christmas story for the* Church Times. *This commission gave her great pleasure since she enjoyed quoting items from this publication in her novels. It was, in fact, a mutual admiration, since the* Church Times, *which did not normally review novels, made an exception for hers.*

'Goodbye Balkan Capital' *was written in 1941, inspired by a news item. From her diary: 'Heard on the six o'clock news that Mr Ronald Campbell and the staff of the Belgrade Legation are nowhere to be found! I wonder if J. is with them?'*

23rd April. After tea began writing a story about the Balkans and me (perhaps) which I thought might do for Penguin New Writing.

25th April. I finished the first draft of a short story Goodbye Balkan Capital.

23rd May. Finished my grey suit also the typing of Goodbye Balkan Capital.

July 4th. Three weeks have passed and I have heard nothing. Shall I ever succeed – I begin to doubt and now is a hopeless time to try . . . It seems that the best stories nowadays are more atmospheric than anything else – incomplete rather than rounded off – anyway they mustn't be too long as my things generally are.

Sadly, John Lehmann, editor of Penguin New Writing, *did not care for the story: 'September 19th. Did a little writing and washed my hair. Had 'Goodbye Balkan Capital' back.'*

'Across a Crowded Room' *was commissioned by the* New Yorker *and published in July 1979. Barbara was very gratified to be asked to write for a magazine of international standing and felt that this really confirmed her 'rediscovery' as a writer.*

As for the subject of her story – in April 1978 she had written to Philip Larkin

You say that you will be in Oxford 19th–20th April – is that by any chance for the Rawlinson dinner at St John's? Because if it is we may catch a glimpse of each other (across a 'crowded room', of course), as I have been invited to this as a guest . . . I thought I had better warn you, though in a novel one would prefer the man to be taken by surprise and even dismayed!

So, Some
Tempestuous Morn

A wet morning, thought Anthea sadly, listening to the rain which did not seem to go with the brilliant bird chorus. A wet morning in North Oxford, with its laburnums and flowering shrubs and strange architecture and her great-aunt's gloomy, solidly furnished house ... If she had opened her eyes for a moment, Anthea closed them again; she was not quite ready to face life yet. People did not always realize that even at nineteen one sometimes had to make an effort.

Anthea was a pretty, gentle-looking girl and her parents were abroad. 'My nephew has a *very* high position in the Colonial Service and is doing brilliantly ... ' – how often had she heard Aunt Maude make that remark to the dull people who came to the house. Anthea herself was vaguely 'studying English Literature'. She was not clever enough to go to one of the women's colleges, but there seemed no harm in her going to a few lectures chosen by her aunt or in her meeting the carefully selected young men, so 'suitable' and usually so uninteresting, who were invited to the Sunday afternoon tea parties. Perhaps their grandmothers had known Aunt Maude as a girl, or there was some ecclesiastical connection – Canon Bogle's son, Archdeacon Troup's nephew, or even some distant link with a bishop or titled person. All were carefully chosen and existed because of their impeccable connections rather than in their own right.

Anthea had never had a young man of her own; sometimes she admired particular undergraduates from a distance, but they never seemed to notice her and they never turned out to be the kind her aunt would ask to tea on Sundays. These might dart frightened glances in her direction through the forests of tables and china ornaments, but Anthea, in her perverseness, felt that she would only despise them more if they appeared to be attracted to her. It was the unattainable ones she pined for –

> The desire of the moth for the star,
> Of the night for the morrow,
> The devotion to something afar
> From the sphere of our sorrow . . .

She did not perhaps appreciate what a comfort English Literature was to her in her lonely state. She saw herself, three months from her twentieth birthday, growing to be like Miss Morrow, her aunt's companion, dim and not very well dressed; the kind of person who had no life of her own and who, in an hour or two, would be tapping at her door to tell her it was time to get up.

Waking at dawn, Miss Morrow heard the rain drumming on the laurels below her window, and no doubt dripping through the branches of the monkey-puzzle too, she thought, imagining it there in the half-light, coming too close to the window.

'This is a *front* bedroom,' Miss Doggett had so often reminded her. 'It is really one of the best rooms in the house. Not many companions would be given such a room. I happen to know that

Lady Victoria Nollard's companion sleeps in an attic on the same floor as the servants.'

'She is lucky to have servants as well as a companion,' Miss Morrow had said, making one of those unfortunate rejoinders which were so unexpected from one of her meek appearance.

'Lady Victoria Nollard is an Earl's daughter,' had been Miss Doggett's simple but magnificent reply.

After five years Miss Morrow had grown used to the room and even liked it. She lay now, listening to the rain, looking at her 'things', those objects that make one room a home, without really noticing them. She was so familiar with the faded photographs of her parents – the inevitable clergyman and dim-looking Edwardian lady – the school group, the little souvenirs from a holiday on the Italian Riviera or in the Highlands of Scotland, the prize set of Jane Austen's novels, and the Penguins with their orange covers looking a little garish next to the leather-bound poems of Matthew Arnold.

Matthew Arnold, ah yes, he would be able to describe this morning . . . Miss Morrow raised herself up on one elbow, imagining the drenched garden at the back of the house.

> So, some tempestuous morn in early June,
> When the year's primal burst of bloom is o'er,
> Before the roses and the longest day –
> When garden-walks and all the grassy floor
> With blossoms red and white of fallen May
> And chestnut flowers are strewn . . .

All that heavy rain in the night would have spoilt the flowers she was to pick for decorating the church this morning. She felt almost glad and lay smiling in bed, thinking of the vicar's wife in her silly raffia-embroidered hat and listening to the rain falling among the leaves. So, some tempestuous morn, indeed!

In an hour it was time to get up. Miss Morrow went to the window and, with a daring gesture, flung aside the net curtain that screened her doings from prying eyes. Opposite, through the dark spiky branches of the monkey-puzzle, it was possible to catch a glimpse of the theological college with its architectural extravagances, coloured brickwork, pointed Gothic windows and little towers. And inside – Miss Morrow's vivid imagination went rushing boldly in – were the theological students in their narrow cell-like rooms, all behaving in a devout and suitable manner. Or indeed, it is to be hoped that they are behaving in such a manner, she said to herself. There was certainly no sign of life now, but after a moment or two a figure on a bicycle appeared in the road and dismounted at the gate of the college. It was a strikingly handsome clergyman, not very young, but certainly not old, perhaps about Miss Morrow's own age which was the late thirties and really quite the prime for a man, though it could be many things for a woman and not all of them quite the prime.

As he stopped to open the gate and push his bicycle in, something must have made him turn and glance at the house opposite and upwards at the figure of Miss Morrow in the window.

Going to have breakfast with the principal, she thought. A hearty manly breakfast of mutton chops and beer ... no, hardly that, manly Oxford breakfasts were not what they were and perhaps men were not either. Tea and cornflakes, more likely ...

The rain had stopped now and the sun was shining brightly. A sudden impulse made Miss Morrow wave her hand at the clergyman. He raised his hat in reply and smiled; then he was gone through the gate, wheeling his bicycle round the side to the little Gothic bicycle-shed.

Miss Morrow laughed to herself and turned away from the window. Whatever could she have been thinking of to wave to

328

him like that? Still, no doubt he had thought it was 'one of the servants' and in any case he was probably accustomed to gestures of this kind as a rightful tribute to his good looks. She must hurry down now and help Maggie with the breakfast and call Anthea on the way.

Breakfast was already on the table when Anthea came down. Miss Doggett was pouring out the coffee, the sun was shining and through the french windows the lawn and the drenched herbaceous border could be seen.

'Well, Miss Morrow, I'm afraid the flowers are quite spoilt,' said Miss Doggett, almost with satisfaction. 'You will find it difficult to pick anything for the decorating. The peonies are all beaten down by the rain.'

'Yes, ravaged, aren't they?' Miss Morrow glanced indifferently towards the window. 'Ravaged, ravished, one might almost say.'

'*Ravished?*' repeated Miss Doggett, her voice puzzled as if there was something not quite right about the word, though she was unable to say exactly what.

'Ravished, yes,' repeated Miss Morrow firmly.

Anthea giggled.

'Really, Miss Morrow. I hardly think . . .' Miss Doggett's tone was pained but she did not want to have to put what she felt into words. Indeed, she hardly knew how to. The unsuitability . . . and Miss Morrow often had these little lapses. Quite well bred, Archdeacon Troup had given a reference, most glowing, really. It wasn't that she was unsatisfactory, exactly; there was nothing one could put one's finger on. It was these remarks she let fall, these unsuitabilities. Were they perhaps clues to what went on in her thoughts, her mind? Miss Doggett pursed her lips and fingered one of the gold chains which hung on the bosom of her purple dress.

'Anthea, you are late this morning.' Her tone was sharp. It

was a relief to turn from the darkness of her companion's mind to her niece's unpunctuality. 'And what are you going to do this morning? I expect they will want some help with the decorating, you might go along with Miss Morrow. I shall want some cakes from Boffin's, too. Quite a number of people will be coming to tea tomorrow.' She smiled, unable to stop herself at the thought of the Honourable Basil Fordyce, a Peer's son and bishop's nephew, taking tea in her drawing room. She had invited this particular young man on several previous occasions, but his charming replies had always put her off, regretting so much that he had another engagement, nothing would have delighted him more than to take tea with Miss Doggett. And tomorrow, feeling perhaps that he might as well get it over, he was really coming. She did hope that he and Anthea would take to each other, for, to give Miss Doggett her due, she was as anxious as her niece that love should enter her life, though, of course, she would not have put it quite like that. Anthea would marry, naturally, but it must be a suitable marriage. There had already been one or two disappointments, not only in Anthea's failure to impress the young men, but in the young men themselves. Canon Bogle's son had turned out to be a grubby young man in corduroy trousers; Lady Dancy's nephew was too small and apparently interested in nothing but archaeology. That had been a great disappointment; even Miss Doggett could see that there was little future in dry bones and fragments of pottery.

Miss Doggett rose from the table.

'Man goeth forth to his work and to his labour, until the evening,' thought Miss Morrow, going up to help Maggie with the beds. She supposed she would have to go into the garden and pick some flowers for the church and then stand by while the vicar's wife arranged them more tastelessly than one would have thought possible.

'I will go for the cakes, Aunt Maude,' said Anthea. It was a lovely morning now and she could take a long time over her errand and perhaps walk somewhere by the river, away from the depressing presence of her aunt and her companion. Perhaps it would be better to buy the cakes afterwards; she would not want to carry them into Christchurch meadows.

It was a pity she had not yet reached Matthew Arnold in her studies of English Literature for she would have found much in his poetry to enhance her enjoyment of the beautiful morning and the Oxford scene, but as it was she wandered by the river in a pleasant state of melancholy, wondering if she would have a romantic encounter this morning.

She had been walking for some time before she came upon him, the young man reclining in a punt with a book which he did not appear to be reading. He was anchored round a bend in the river, half hidden by the drooping branches of a willow, so that she came upon him suddenly and was so startled that she stopped involuntarily, for he was – and this seemed right and inevitable on such a morning – one of those she had admired from afar at Professor Lyly's lectures. She must have looked surprised, perhaps she even exclaimed, for he looked up as she approached and smiled.

'An encounter,' he said. 'What could be more suitable on a June morning, Penelope?'

'My name isn't Penelope,' she said stupidly. 'And you don't know me anyway, so how could you know my name?'

'But I *do* know you – sitting in a corner at old Lyly's lectures taking down every platitude that falls from his lips and never raising your eyes from your notebook.'

'I don't remember seeing you there,' she lied, but their glance had never met. 'And what's the use of going to lectures if you don't take notes?' He never did, she had seen him just sitting, looking bored and sometimes drawing on a sheet of paper.

'Of course you are not an undergraduette,' he pronounced the word distastefully, 'so it may be that you take the study of English Literature seriously. I imagine you living in some Gothic house in North Oxford, a fastness with horrid towers and dark trees, so much more inaccessible than a women's college and so much more intriguing.'

She smiled faintly. He was making fun of her, she knew, but how was she expected to respond? She had certainly not imagined their first meeting like this. 'I do live in North Oxford,' she ventured, 'and in a house rather like that, I suppose.'

'Why don't you come and sit down and tell me about it?' He held out his hand and she stepped on to the green velvet cushions in the bottom of the punt.

Once there she felt stupid and awkward. Whatever would Aunt Maude say? Why, this young man had just 'picked her up'; she could imagine her aunt's tone and pursed lips as she pronounced the words; it was most unsuitable.

'Tell me about your Gothic house,' he said. 'Do you live with your parents?'

'No, my parents are abroad. I live with my great-aunt.'

'Does she have Sunday afternoon tea parties?'

'Why, yes. How did you know?'

'All respectable North Oxford residents do. I have made a study of their habits. I really think I shall have to do some practical field-work and get myself invited to one.'

'Oh, dear,' Anthea stood up suddenly. 'I've got to buy cakes for tomorrow – I'd quite forgotten.'

'Surely the guests won't notice what they eat if *you* are there?'

'I wish you wouldn't say things like that. You're only making fun of me.'

'My dear, I assure you I'm not,' he said, really looking quite serious. 'What is the name or number of your great-aunt's house?'

'It's called Leamington Lodge. There's a monkey-puzzle in the front garden. It's opposite a theological college.'

332

'Perhaps we shall meet again,' he said gaily. 'You never know.' And taking her hand he kissed it lightly. 'Now run and buy your cakes.'

Anthea hurried away in a turmoil of emotion. It was only when she had got into Boffin's and noticed that the best cakes were gone that she realized that she did not know his name nor he hers and that he had made no serious suggestion about meeting her again. For a moment she felt a little cast down, but she cheered herself up by remembering the lectures. Now perhaps they could smile at each other and speak. He might even sit by her. She did not know how she was going to get through the days until the next lecture. Oh, she thought, carelessly choosing a dozen of any old cakes, it was fine to be young and in love on a lovely June morning – not like poor Miss Morrow, grey and in her thirties and decorating the church with the vicar's wife and all the other good ladies who were so patronizing to her.

The peonies, the ravished peonies, thought Miss Morrow, padding about among the wet plants in her galoshes. When she touched one all the petals fell off, but there were other flowers that would do quite well. She cut some syringa and irises. Purple, that was a Lenten colour, not really right for Whitsuntide. Still, they were lucky to get anything.

She hurried to the church and into the porch. The mumbling of women's voices with one or two raised in command told her that she was late. The sun was shining brilliantly now and the church seemed all the darker by contrast. The vicar's wife had her back turned as Miss Morrow entered and nobody noticed her come in. On a sudden impulse she laid the flowers down in a corner with the others already there, and tiptoed away. She did not feel like decorating this morning, handing bits of greenery to the vicar's wife up in the pulpit or filling jam jars with water.

She felt very free when she got outside the church – a whole hour of her own, what should she do with it? Morning coffee first, that sinful habit denounced by Miss Doggett as time-wasting and self-indulgent. 'When one has had a good breakfast and is going to have a good luncheon it is quite unnecessary to eat or drink between meals.' Where should she go to waste time and be self-indulgent? Obviously not to one of the places where she might meet one of Miss Doggett's less strong-minded friends. She would go to the fashionable undergraduate haunt of the moment, the café of a large shop, where up to now she had only peered from the cake department into the smoke-laden and vice-infested air. She found a table on the outside edge of the room where she could observe and remain inconspicuous, a dim figure on the fringe of the University melting away into North Oxford, she felt. It was quite alarming the decadence there must be among our youth today, she thought with amusement, noticing how full the tables were. Time-wasting and self-indulgent ... still, perhaps they had not all had good breakfasts or could not be so sure of adequate luncheons. Well, it was not really so very interesting, she decided, as she drank her coffee and ate a large sickly cake, and the coffee was not so good as that made by Miss Latimer and Miss Forge, two gentlewomen who ran a dull teashop frequented by Miss Doggett's circle. Still, it was something to have been here, an experience. There would be time to walk through the shop before she need return to Leamington Lodge.

It was here that she really came to grief, fingering a rail of printed summer dresses in gay colours and patterns. Perhaps it was her contact with decadence that made her linger and pick out a dress patterned with green leaves. The girl who helped her to try it on was so kind and encouraging. She said it suited her and it was such a nice day after all that rain early this morning, it really made you feel like buying a new dress.

Luncheon was rather an odd meal. Nobody except Miss Doggett seemed to be hungry. Anthea looked quite distracted, but Miss Doggett attributed her strange manner and lack of appetite to the fact that she had given her a severe talking-to for having bought such a poor selection of cakes.

'Bishop Fordyce's nephew – he's Lady Mortlake's son, you know – and the new chaplain of Randolph College are coming,' she wailed. 'I particularly wanted them to have a nice tea.'

'Perhaps clergymen don't notice what they eat,' said Miss Morrow demurely. 'One feels that they might not.'

'And you were a very long time decorating the church this morning, Miss Morrow,' said Miss Doggett, turning on her. 'I expected you back by half past eleven. Were there a great many flowers to arrange or were there fewer helpers than usual?'

'Oh, there were fewer helpers,' said Miss Morrow. 'Certainly one less than usual.'

Miss Doggett rose from the table. 'Well, we shall see tomorrow what the church looks like,' she said. 'I hope our flowers are in a good position.'

'Irises on the pulpit!' said Miss Doggett at luncheon the next day. 'Most unsuitable. The colour is quite wrong for Whitsuntide. I thought the altar vases were very badly arranged . . . did you do them, Miss Morrow?'

'Oh, no, I did nothing that could be seen,' said Miss Morrow quickly. It was a brilliantly hot day and she had decided to wear her new dress for the tea party.

'We might have tea in the garden, perhaps?' suggested Anthea. 'It's such a lovely day.' If only she could slip away somewhere by herself and think about *him*, instead of having to sit and make conversation with dull young men in a stuffy North Oxford drawing room.

'Tea in the garden? Oh, no, I'm afraid I should find the sun too much,' said Miss Doggett. 'Besides, people are not at their best in the open air. Conversation is so difficult and things blow away.'

'Wasps get in the food,' murmured Miss Morrow.

So they sat waiting in the drawing room which faced north and whose windows were obscured by the bottom half of the monkey-puzzle.

The first arrivals were two shy young men who came together. It seemed that they had met on the doorstep and were giving each other mutual support. One of them carried an umbrella which he seemed unwilling to relinquish.

'Ah, Mr Burden and Mr Monksmoor,' said Miss Doggett, 'I knew your aunts. Wouldn't you like to leave that umbrella in the hall? It will be quite safe.'

'I have a feeling it is going to thunder,' said one of the young men, addressing Anthea in a loud, nervous voice.

But she could not answer him, for at that moment a third guest was announced, the Bishop's nephew and Peer's son, and it was the young man she had met on the river yesterday morning.

'Ah, Mr Fordyce, at last!' There was a real welcome in Miss Doggett's tone. 'I am so much looking forward to having a long talk about your uncle.'

So he was the Bishop's nephew, Aunt Maude's young man, not hers. It was a sickening disappointment. Anthea could hardly bear to look at him.

'Please try to keep the conversation away from my dear uncle,' he whispered.

'Why? It will at least be something to talk about,' said Anthea indifferently.

'But he isn't my uncle and I'm not Basil Fordyce. I wanted to find a way of seeing you again and I knew Basil had an invitation to take tea in North Oxford this weekend, so I changed places with him.'

Anthea smiled. 'But we could have met some other way – at the lectures or in the town. You didn't have to come here.'

'No, but I wanted to be accepted by your aunt.' He gave her a bright-eyed wicked look that seemed to shut them off from the rest of the room.

'Where is Miss Morrow?' said Miss Doggett rather sharply.

'Here I am, Miss Doggett,' said Miss Morrow, coming in through the door in a new dress patterned with leaves.

'Miss Morrow and I have been in the garden,' said the handsome clergyman with her. 'I somehow missed the front door, and Miss Morrow found me wandering in the laurels.'

Missed the front door ... wandering in the laurels ... and Miss Morrow in that gay unsuitable dress ... Miss Doggett was bewildered. She sank down into a chair. This was the new Chaplain of Randolph College, a very good-looking man, perhaps a little free in his manner for a clergyman. He and Miss Morrow were actually laughing together. She was asking him if he had had a good breakfast, had there been mutton chops and beer ... what could she mean? Miss Doggett turned away in despair. She would have a little chat with Mr Fordyce about his uncle.

'Now, Mr Fordyce,' she began, 'how is your uncle?'

'Which one?' he asked brightly.

'Why, Bishop Fordyce, of course.'

'Oh, Miss Doggett, I've done a very wicked thing,' he burst out.

'Come now, Mr Fordyce,' she had to smile indulgently, he was really such a very good-looking man with those brilliant hazel eyes. 'I'm sure you can't have done anything so very bad.'

'Oh, but I have. I'm an impostor. I'm not Basil Fordyce at all. I'm Simon Beddoes.'

'Well, really, Mr Beddoes ...' Miss Doggett smiled again, but a little absently. There was a connection somewhere and it was quite a good one, though she could not remember for the moment exactly what it was. Something political or diplomatic, she fancied ... Bishop Fordyce had not been much of a man really, rather a dull stick, she had never particularly cared for him.

'You see, I wanted to meet your niece, and,' he added hastily, 'I had heard of your delightful tea parties.'

'Oh, well, I suppose I do manage to collect an interesting circle of people round me,' said Miss Doggett, almost purring. 'Do have another cake, Mr Beddoes. Now, Mr Merriman,' she turned to the handsome clergyman, 'I do hope my companion has not been boring you?'

'Oh, I am used to being bored by ladies,' said Mr Merriman lightly. 'There is nothing I enjoy more.'

'You must see the garden before you go,' said Miss Doggett, 'though I'm afraid it is not quite at its best now – that heavy storm yesterday morning ...' She paused. Yes, there had been something strange about yesterday morning. 'The peonies were very fine but the rain spoilt them. They look quite ...' what was the word Miss Morrow had used, something most unsuitable ... 'quite beaten down,' she said rather loudly. 'Mr Beddoes, perhaps you would like to see the garden too? And Mr Burden and Mr Monksmoor, I should like to have a chat to you about your aunts. We met in Malvern in 1923.'

She rose from her chair and the little procession wound its way through the furniture, out into the dining room and through the french windows on to the lawn.

After they had gone, Miss Morrow picked up a cake and devoured it in two bites. Then she too went out through the french windows and followed them solemnly round the garden.

Goodbye Balkan Capital

The six o'clock news blared out, crowding the already over-crowded little drawing room with all the horrors of total war in 1941. The photographs on the piano shook with the noise. The Archdeacon's face, or as much of it as was not concealed in his bush of beard, seemed to express distaste at the vulgarity of it all. Mrs Arling looked as she had in life, meek and resigned. Thirty years of her husband's thundering sermons had hardened her to loud voices and violent opinions. And anyway, all this that was happening was no concern of theirs. They had both died in the 1920s, when Hitler was writing *Mein Kampf*, and the Archdeacon, also a disappointed man, had turned to preparing a collected edition of his sermons as a consolation for a vacant Bishopric which he had failed to get.

The Misses Arling, accustomed to these horrors, sat quietly listening. Janet, the elder sister, was knitting a khaki sock. A cigarette jutted from her square face, and she held her head thrust up to avoid getting the smoke into her eyes. Her fingers went on mechanically with the knit two, purl two ribbing. There would be no need to look until she started to turn the heel.

Laura Arling was arranging some polyanthus in a bowl. She

was dim and faded, with a face that might once have been pretty in her distant Edwardian youth. It was an unfashionable face, but somehow nostalgic and restful in a world so full of brutality and death. If anyone troubled to look at her they might say that she had a sweet expression, if, indeed, that phrase is ever used seriously now.

She had spread a sheet of *The Times* on the round mahogany table, and the flowers, crimson, purple, yellow and creamy white, were scattered all over the Deaths column, so that as Laura picked up a flower her eyes would light on a death and then go all down the column, looking fearfully for the words 'by enemy action'. She wished Janet wouldn't have the wireless quite so loud. It must be because of her deafness, although she would never admit it. The words seemed to lose all their meaning when they were blared out like this. It reminded Laura of the police car which had come round on that dreadful September evening, telling them to get ready for five hundred evacuee children who had arrived at the station. Laura smiled as she remembered the sad little procession dragging through the garden gate, labels tied to their coats, haversacks and gas masks trailing on the ground. Janet had been so splendid. She had sent them all to the lavatory, which was just what they wanted, if only one had been able to think of it, for after that they had cheered up and rushed shouting about the garden until it was time for bed. It seemed such a long time since those first days of the war. The children had all gone back after a month or two and the house had seemed unnaturally quiet until April, May and June, when the distorted voice of the wireless had flung so many terrible pieces of news at them, that now, a year later, it seemed hardly possible that they had survived it all and were still here.

Now it was the Balkans, the *Drang nach Osten*, Janet said, and she always knew about things like that. At the beginning of the war she had got a translation of *Mein Kampf* out of Boots. Of course, as everyone said, the Balkans didn't seem quite so bad. They were further away, for one thing, and after the collapse of France one no longer had the same high hopes of other people. Also, it was mildly comforting to feel that the Germans were going in the opposite direction. Now, after the usual War of Nerves, German troops had begun to enter another Balkan Capital. But this time it seemed more real and important. Laura stopped arranging the polyanthus and listened. This was *his* Balkan Capital, her dear Crispin's. He was First Secretary at the Legation there, and they were saying that the British diplomats were ready to leave at any moment.

'You can't trust these Balkan people. No guts,' said Janet, brushing a wedge of ash off her knitting. She got up and turned the wireless off with a snap.

Laura did not protest. She was remembering Crispin at a Commemoration Ball in Oxford, when she was eighteen and he twenty-one. They had danced together an improper number of times, having somehow got separated from the decorously chaperoned party in which they had started the evening, and at six o'clock, when the dance was over, they had gone on the river in a punt and had breakfast. It had been like a dream, walking down the Banbury Road in the early morning sunshine, wearing her white satin ball gown and holding Crispin's hand. Even Aunt Edith's anger and her threat to Tell the Archdeacon had failed to terrify her, because she was remembering Crispin's kisses and the beautiful things he had said. It had been their first and last meeting, for she had never seen him again after that morning. She supposed that she must have been a little unhappy at parting, she must surely have longed for letters which never came, but her memory did not help her here. It had kept only the happiness, enshrined in all its detail like those Victorian paperweights which show a design of flowers under glass, and which are now sought again, in days when Victorian objects are comforting relics of a period when the upper middle classes lived pleasant, peaceful lives and wars were fought decently in foreign countries by soldiers with heavy drooping moustaches. Laura had never loved anyone else, not even in the last war, when officers used to come to supper on Sunday nights, and her poor mother had dared to hope that it might not be too late even then. Crispin had gone into the Diplomatic Service after leaving Oxford and it had been quite easy to get news of him. Laura had been able to imagine him in Madrid, in Washington, in Peking, in Buenos Aires, and now in this stormy Balkan Capital, where he had been First Secretary for several years. Indeed, she was expecting that he might be made Ambassador or Minister somewhere, although she feared that there must be a lot of unemployment among diplomats, with the Germans occupying so many countries.

Laura's imagination and *Harmsworth's Encyclopaedia* had helped to give her quite a vivid picture of the town where Crispin now lived. She could see its fine modern buildings, the streets all glass and steel and concrete skyscrapers, with brilliant neon lighting flashing out foreign words into the darkness, and the fine Art Gallery and Museum were as familiar to her as if she had really trudged round them on a wet afternoon. The British Legation was in the old part of the town, near to the famous Botanical Gardens. Laura often thought of Crispin walking there on fine spring mornings, perhaps sitting on a seat reading official documents, with lilacs, azaleas, and later, scarlet and yellow cannas making a fitting background for his dark good looks. For she could not think of him as fat or bald, the brightness of his hazel eyes dimmed or hidden behind spectacles, his voice querulous and his fingers, gnarled with rheumatism, tapping irritably on his desk. Devouring Time might blunt the Lion's paws; these things could happen to other people, but not to Crispin.

'I've got a WVS meeting tonight,' said Janet brusquely. 'We're going to divide the town into districts and get somebody to canvass each street.'

'What for?' asked Laura vaguely.

'Pig swill,' said Janet briefly. 'There's still far too much food being wasted, especially among the poorer classes.'

Laura studied her sister dispassionately. She was so formidable in her green uniform, or splendid, that was what one really meant, what everyone said. She was like the Archdeacon, firm as a rock, much more efficient than Laura, who took after their mother and was dreamy and introspective. Perhaps it's because I haven't got a proper uniform, thought Laura, who, as a member of the ARP Casualty Service, had only a badge and an armlet. Uniform made such a difference, even to women.

The next day the news was worse. The perfidious Balkan State had signed the Axis Pact, the British Legation was leaving, and there was a talk on the wireless about what happens when diplomatic relations are broken off. Laura now imagined Crispin in his shirt sleeves, burning the code books, stuffing bulky secret documents into the central heating furnace, a lock of dark hair falling over one eye. She was sure he would be doing something really important, for he had always seemed so fine and exciting to Laura, shut in then by the Archdeacon and North Oxford aunts in Edwardian England, and now by Janet and all the rather ludicrous goings-on of a country town that sees nothing of the war.

In the Balkans, in the dangerous places,
Where the diplomats have handsome faces ...

she thought, as she walked along with her shopping basket. But that wasn't right at all. It was the Highlands and the country places, and the Highlands brought her back to porridge and oatmeal. Lord Woolton had said that we must make more use of oatmeal. Janet had got some recipes from the WVS and they were going to have savoury oatmeal for supper tonight.

One couldn't honestly say that it was very nice, but it was filling and made one feel virtuous and patriotic, especially when eggs or something out of a tin would have been so much more tasty. But Janet had banned all tin opening and the eggs were being pickled for next winter, when they would be scarce, or *difficult*, that was the word she had used.

They had just finished supper when the siren went. Laura's stomach always turned over when she heard the wailing, although this was the fifteenth time this year, according to her diary. Still, it was eerie when it went at night, and one never knew for certain that the planes were just passing over on their way to Liverpool. Sometimes they sounded as if they were right over the house, and, as the Head Warden had said, not without a certain professional relish, two or three well placed HE bombs could practically wipe out their small town.

'What a good thing you've had supper,' said Janet, splendidly practical as always. 'I should change out of that good skirt, if I were you.'

Janet ought really to have been the one to go out, thought Laura, but she had resigned from ARP after a disagreement with the Head of the Women's Section. It had started with an argument about some oilcloth and had gone on from strength to strength, until they now cut each other in the street. And so it was Laura, always a little flustered on these occasions, who had to collect her things and hurry out to the First Aid Post.

She came downstairs carrying her gas mask and a neat little suitcase, in which she had packed her knitting, *Pride and Prejudice*, some biscuits, and a precious bar of milk chocolate. On her head she wore a tin hat, painted pale grey and beautiful in its newness. They had been given out at the practice that evening, but Laura had hidden hers in her room, wanting to surprise Janet with it the next time she had to go out.

Janet seemed rather annoyed when she saw it. It made Laura look quite important and professional. 'I should think it must be very heavy,' she said grudgingly. 'I'll leave a thermos of tea for you, though I suppose you'll get some there.'

'Well, expect me when you see me, dear,' said Laura, her voice trembling a little with excitement. Going out like this and not knowing when she would return always made her feel rather grand, almost noble, as if she were setting out on a secret and dangerous mission. The tin hat made a difference, too. One felt much more *splendid* in a tin hat. It was almost a uniform.

Laura went out and switched on her torch, being careful to direct the beam downwards. The bulb was swathed in tissue paper and tied as on a pot of jam, so that she wanted to write on it 'Raspberry 1911', as their mother used to. After a while her eyes got used to the darkness, and she could see that it was a lovely night with stars and a crescent moon. The planes were still going over, a sinister purring sound somewhere up there among the stars. Laura hurried on. Her tin hat was loose and heavy on her head, making it feel like a flower on a broken stalk.

'Liverpool again,' said a calm, melancholy voice behind her. She recognized the shape of a woman she knew.

'Yes, I'm afraid it must be. It's so terrible,' said Laura helplessly, wishing there were something adequate one could say. But there was nothing. It was of no consolation to the bombed that the eyes of women in safe places should fill with tears when they spoke of them. Tears, idle tears were of no use to anyone, not even to oneself. This oppressive sorrow could not be washed away in the selfish indulgence of a good cry.

At the First Aid Post everything was jolly and bustling. Stretcher bearers and First Aid parties in dark blue boiler suits were filling water bottles and collecting blankets. Women were hurrying to and fro carrying large bottles, dressings and instruments. An efficient girl was at the telephone and the doctor, stout and reassuring, was hanging his coat on a peg and looking forward to a game of bridge later on. Everything was ready for the casualties that might be brought in.

Laura put on her overall. It was of stiff blue cotton, voluminous and reaching to her ankles. It had full, short sleeves, a neat collar and ARP embroidered on the bosom in scarlet letters. She got out her knitting and sat down on the bed with the nurse and the friend she had walked up with.

At first they were jolly and talkative. These nocturnal meetings were a social occasion enjoyed by everybody. The most unlikely people were gathered together, people who would otherwise never have known each other, bound as they were by the rigid social conventions of a small country town. Conversation was animated and ranged over many topics, horrible stories of raid damage, fine imaginative rumours, titbits about the private lives of the Nazi leaders gleaned from the Sunday papers, local gossip and grumblings about ARP organization. Time passed quickly, an hour, two hours. The throb of the enemy planes was drowned with voices until everything was quiet, except for the chatter and the welcome hissing of the Primus from another room. When this sound was heard everybody began to get out their little tins of biscuits, rare blocks of chocolate were broken up and shared, like the Early Christians, Laura thought, having all things in common. At last somebody came round with cups of tea on a tray and thick triangular slices of bread and margarine, with a smear of fish paste on each. No banquet was ever more enjoyed than this informal meal at one o'clock in the morning. Whatever would poor Father and Mother have thought of this gathering? Laura wondered. Perhaps it was a good thing that they had not been spared to see it. Laura had always thought that the shock of a

Labour Government in office had hastened the Archdeacon's end.

After the meal everyone settled into lethargy. Conversation died down to a few stray remarks. The doctor's voice was heard saying, 'Double five hearts,' and there was a hum of voices from the decontamination room. The women knitted rather grimly, and the men, already tired after a day's work, dozed and smoked. The room was very hot and people were seen dimly through a haze. Laura thought longingly of rivers, pools and willows, of her own linen sheets, of plunging one's face under water when swimming, even of the inside of a gas mask, with its cool rubbery smell and tiny space of unbreathed air.

They had turned the light out now and the room was in darkness, except for the glowing ends of cigarettes and a Dietz lantern which flickered on the table. The scene would have made a good subject for a modern painter; there was nothing in Dali and the Surrealists more odd than this reality, the smoky room crowded with silent men and women, lying or sitting on beds, chairs or the floor, some covered with dark army blankets, others with coats, one or two faces with mouths a little open, defenceless in sleep, one man, surprisingly, for it was very hot, clasping a stone hot-water bottle with 'HMGovt' stamped on the end. As still life garnishings there were the tables covered with dressings, bottles and instruments, with all that their presence implied, long metal Thomas splints lying on top of a cupboard, heavy wooden walking sticks and crutches crowded into a corner. In a hundred years' time this might be a problem picture. What were these people doing and why?

Laura sat bolt upright, leaning against the wall. She closed her smarting eyes and tried to sleep. But she found herself thinking about Crispin in the Balkans, wondering what he was doing at this minute. He was probably lying down in a comfortable sleeper in a special diplomatic train, like the luxurious Nord or

Orient Expresses, which glide silently into stations at night, their dark windows shuttered, conveying their rich sleeping passengers with the least possible disturbance across a sleeping Europe. But Europe was never sleeping, and now less than ever. Things happened in these hours when human vitality was at its lowest ebb; bombers rained death between one and four in the morning, troops crossed the frontiers at dawn. Crispin was probably awake too, looking through important documents, perhaps even dictating to a secretary, while the great train, diplomatically immune from the inconveniences of *Zoll* and *Douane*, carried him eastwards to Moscow or Istanbul, further and further away from his Legation. Laura saw it as a large suburban house, built in continental wedding cake style, a magnolia tree, impersonal in its beauty, in bud in the garden, and inside all the desolation of a house whose occupants have had to leave it in a hurry. Drawers open and empty, out of date foreign newspapers on the floor, dead flowers in the vases, dust on the rococo furniture and the massive square stoves, their pretty majolica tiles cold now and stuffed with the dead ashes of the code books and secret documents. The keys had been left with the kind, homely American Ambassador, who had promised to keep an eye on the things that couldn't be taken away, like the valuable paintings and the stuffed eagle shot by the Minister on a hunting tour in the mountains, just as if they were going to the seaside for their summer holidays and would be back in a month. But it was 'Goodbye Balkan Capital!' and the train was rushing through the darkness to deposit its important passengers, blinking like ruffled owls in the early morning sunshine, on the platform of some other foreign capital, where Great Britain still had a representative to greet them. And then, after a cup of tea, so to speak, they would be pushed on to another train or boat, always on the move like refugees, except that they had their own country waiting for them at the end of the journey, houses in Mayfair or Belgravia and loving friends to welcome them, servants to put cool, clean sheets on their beds . . .

A beautiful note sounded through the room, piercing and silvery as the music of the spheres must sound. It was the All Clear. In a surprisingly short time the blanket-covered shapes became human and active, everything was put away and they walked out into the sharp, cold air, their voices and footsteps ringing through the empty streets. They were all much jollier and noisier than they normally would have been, because they were up at such an odd hour of the morning and they felt the glow of virtue which comes from duty done. There had been no bombs and no casualties but they had been standing by. They had missed their night's rest so that if anything *had* happened they would have been there to deal with it.

Laura let herself into the house very quietly. She went into the drawing room and sat by the dead fire, drinking the tea that Janet had left for her. It wasn't very hot and had that tinny taste peculiar to thermos tea, but Janet would be hurt if she left it. It did not occur to Laura that she could pour it away.

It was an exquisite pleasure to turn over in the cool sheets and stretch her tired limbs. She remembered some lines from Sir Philip Sidney:

> Take thou of me smooth pillows, sweetest bed,
> A chamber deaf of noise and blind of light,
> A rosy garland and a weary head . . .

It was as if she had never been really tired before.

Outside the first birds began to sing. It would soon be dawn. How thrilling one's first sight of Moscow must be, Laura thought. All those curiously shaped domes and towers, the Kremlin, Lenin embalmed . . .

Eventually, as Laura gathered from much anxious listening to the news, the Legation staff did arrive in Moscow. They were to take the Trans-Siberian railway back to England. This journey was so great and so amazing that even Laura could hardly conceive what it would be like. A journey to the moon would have been easier to imagine. She studied her atlas carefully, but it was all too vague to be real except for the ending, the eventual safe arrival in England on a sunny day in June, July or August – she had no idea how long it would take – with the plane trees in the squares in full, dusty leaf. She wondered whether Crispin had a house in London and where it was. She hoped that it had not been bombed, and even began the futile occupation of studying the addresses of people in *The Times* killed 'by enemy action' to see what parts of London might be supposed to be in ruins.

It was while she was doing this one day that she came across it, *his* obituary among the long, impersonal list. She read it through mechanically, attracted by the name Crispin, without at first realizing that it was anybody she knew. He had died at the house of his sister Lady Hinge, in a village in Oxfordshire. It didn't say anything else, but Laura discovered a small paragraph about him on one of the inner pages. 'Since leaving Oxford,' it said, 'he had been in the Diplomatic Service, retiring from it in 1936.' Five years ago! Laura was annoyed to think that she had missed that information, if, indeed, it had ever been mentioned anywhere. The paragraph ended with three dry words. 'He was unmarried.' Laura had somehow thought that he would not be married. Her reading and imagination had given her a picture of diplomats which did not include wives, although she had not been so unworldly as to suppose that there could not be substitutes which were just as good. And at the back of her mind there may have been a hope that he would one day come back to England and the romantic first meeting would happen all over again.

When she had recovered from the first shock Laura found herself grieving not so much for his death, as that could make no practical difference to her, but for the picture she had had of him. The remembrance of her wonderful imaginings about his journey made her feel foolish and a little desolate, when all the time he had been perfectly safe in an Oxfordshire village, his life as dull as hers. He might even have been an Air Raid Warden. She paused, considering this possibility for Crispin with amusement and dismay.

She cut out the notice with her embroidery scissors. It was sad to think that the only tangible souvenir she had of Crispin was the bald announcement of his death. And yet her memory had a great deal. She found it hard to look forward to the future and a New Social Order, when there had been so much happiness in the past, the bad old days, as she had heard them called. Surely *they* (by whom she usually meant people like Mr Herbert Morrison and Mr Ernest Bevin) would leave her that, her Victorian paperweight, with its bright and simple design of flowers? Perhaps she had already been punished for her self-indulgent dreaming by her disillusionment about Crispin. No dramatic 'Goodbye Balkan Capital!' but a quiet death in a safe part of England. It was even possible that *her* end might be more violent and exciting than his.

Why, she thought, when the siren went that evening, I might get killed by a bomb! And yet that would not be right. It was always Crispin who had had the dramatic adventures, and after all these years Laura did not want it to be any different. In life or in death people are very much what we like to think them. Laura knew that she might search in vain in the Oxfordshire churchyard among the new graves with their sodden wreaths to find Crispin's. But it would be easy in the Balkans, in the dangerous places. There would always be something of him there.

The Christmas Visit

On Christmas Eve Sophia Ainger's old tortoiseshell cat, Faustina, emerged from her basket by the kitchen boiler and began to take an interest in the icing of the cake.

'Ought she to be licking out that bowl?' Mark Ainger asked.

'It's all right – I've given her a bit of almond paste – she does love it so.'

'Is this all you're putting on the cake this year?' Mark picked up a battered-looking plaster Father Christmas.

'Yes, I forgot to buy new decorations, so we'll just have to put up with this old thing, looking like King Lear in the snow, deserted by his daughters. Many people *are* lonely and neglected at Christmas,' Sophia said, a serious look on her thin dark face, 'so perhaps this *is* suitable in a way. And isn't it about time you went to the station to meet Daisy?'

'So it is.' Mark looked at his watch, trying not to sigh. Sophia had always been surrounded by what he thought of as a kind of flotsam and jetsam of deprived relatives and friends, the kind of people who would welcome an invitation for Christmas, especially now that the Aingers had moved to a country parish with three churches. This year Sophia had asked

Daisy Beaver, a newly discovered distant cousin who lived alone in London, while Mark was expecting an old college friend and his wife.

'I suppose the Starlings' – Sophia could not yet think of them as Edmund and Isabel – 'will come later this evening?'

'Yes, they're driving down. It'll be good to see Edmund again.' Mark said this rather as if he felt he ought to express such a sentiment, for the old college friends had not met for nearly thirty years and Mark had not exactly invited him to stay. Edmund's ancestors came from one of the villages in Mark's parish, so he had suggested the visit and also a delving into the parish registers on Boxing Day.

Sophia finished icing the cake, found a frill from last year, and put it away safe from Faustina. Mark got out the car and went to fetch Daisy. In half an hour they were back.

'Daisy, how nice!' Sophia embraced the solid dumpy figure, seized her suitcase and led her up to her room.

Instead of a fattening tin of biscuits by Daisy's bed, she had added a copy of *The Ritual Reason Why* – relic of Mark's hopeful Anglo-Catholic boyhood – to the selection of paperbacks on the table, for Daisy was the kind of woman who was always higher than the vicar, whoever he might be. There was also an old *Crockford* in the bookcase, but that was too heavy even for the most eager researcher to read in bed.

'I suppose there *will be* Midnight Mass?' Daisy was asking.

'Oh, yes,' said Sophia, feeling a little guilty at not revealing that the service would be a little different from what Daisy was accustomed to.

'Of course, one does miss one's own church at these times,' Daisy said. 'Father Spode will be *so* busy today, hearing confessions right up to the time of Midnight Mass. He never spares himself.'

At that moment Faustina entered the room.

'I try to keep her out of guests' bedrooms,' said Sophia hopelessly.

The cat jumped into Daisy's open suitcase and began plucking at a folded garment.

'Now then, pussy,' said Daisy, as Sophia removed her. She was obviously displeased.

The cat was also passionately interested in the fish pie Sophia had made for supper, so she had to be shut away in Mark's study where she jumped up on his desk, settling herself down among the sermon notes he was sorting out for the various services. The largest of his churches had advanced as far as Series Two ('authorized for experimental use in the Church of England until 8 July 1972', Mark sometimes quoted to himself when he realized that they were still using it in 1978). There was to be a midnight service (not called 'Mass') here, and also a morning 'Family' service which was likely to be attended by some of the once-or-twice-a-year churchgoers of his congregation. The other two smaller churches were to have morning services at suitably staggered times, a retired elderly lay-reader assisting Mark at one of these. If only Daisy could have been a deaconess or even a woman priest!

'Ah, supper.' Mark came into the kitchen. 'Fish pie?' It was what they always had on Christmas Eve. 'Where is it they have carp at this time? Poland, I believe, perhaps Russia, I daresay.'

'This is not carp,' said Sophia, serving out the pie.

'Cod, I expect,' said Daisy.

Sophia did not reveal that it was not cod but coley, for fear that Mark might exclaim without thinking, 'Oh, but that's what you get for Faustina!' Economic necessity had made her aware for some time now that the pinkish-grey of the coley in its raw state could be transformed by cooking into a perfectly acceptable white fish.

'Edmund and Isabel would know about carp,' Mark went on. 'They've probably eaten it somewhere on their travels.'

'Have they lived abroad?' Daisy asked.

'Yes, Edmund was at Oxford with Mark – he's had a brilliant career, hasn't he, dear?' Sophia turned to her husband.

'Yes, he's done well in the Diplomatic Service,' Mark admitted, wondering why people often spoke of 'a brilliant career' in these circumstances, when a person achieved in the course of time and by gradual steps no more than was expected of him. 'I suppose you might describe him as brilliant,' he added, feeling that he was being ungenerous.

'Of course, one doesn't often hear of somebody having a *brilliant* career in the Church,' said Sophia. 'It might suggest something shady or not quite above-board. And who could be brilliant in a country parish?' She glanced affectionately at her husband, who was not altogether pleased. After all, though he could hardly point it out now, he and Edmund had started out equal after the University, it was only later that their paths had diverged. Could he perhaps work out a sermon on these lines, with some kind of a pay-off ending, though he had no idea what that was going to be, or even if it was at all likely that there would be one . . .

'I never draw the curtains in the kitchen,' Sophia said, seeing that Daisy was glancing over towards the window as if, as a town-dweller, she expected to see it shrouded in nylon or Terylene net. 'We aren't overlooked in the churchyard, after all. I chose this particular vicarage because of this view from the kitchen – Faustina can play among the graves safely and it will prepare her for her own end.'

'She must be quite old?' Daisy asked, thinking that even Sophia could hardly go to the length of having the cat buried in the churchyard.

'Yes, sixteen, which is over a hundred in animal terms. So different from a young girl of that age!'

'We both like this view,' Mark said. The old tombstones,

some carved with cherubs and skulls, with their worn lettering impossible to decipher, gave him a feeling of timelessness – life passing, going on and then renewing itself. One would hardly be surprised in this place and at this time to discern among the stones a figure from the past – the seventeenth century would have been Mark's choice – George Herbert, his favourite poet; Henry King, poet and Bishop; Anthony à Wood, crabbed antiquarian … How many Bishops now were also poets?

It seemed ridiculous, impossible, of course, but there was a figure moving among the tombstones, stumbling a little, as if impeded by the uneven ground, walking over the older unmarked graves in the dark. But there could hardly be anybody there now, unless it was vandals or even practitioners of black magic … Mark was instantly on the alert. He opened the kitchen window and called out in a stern voice, 'What are you doing there? You know this is consecrated ground?'

'Of course I know,' came a querulous educated voice. 'I'm trying to find the vicarage – we were told this was a short cut.'

Mark now realized that the figure was not alone. Behind him hovered what looked very much like a bear, on closer view a tall woman in a dark bushy coat. Of course, it was Edmund and Isabel.

'We left the car round by the church,' said the woman. 'Edmund wanted to inspect the graves.'

In the lighted kitchen Mark and Edmund, the old college friends, greeted each other. Mark saw that Edmund was still a handsome man, who had kept both his hair and his figure. He was certainly better-preserved than Mark who, although not fat, had a worn look about him, with thinning hair and an anxious expression – distinguished remains rather than conventional good looks. Isabel was large and expensively dressed, but their undignified entrance through the churchyard had put them at something of a disadvantage. A brilliant career, Mark thought, but now a rather ridiculous pair. He despised himself for feeling slightly pleased.

The midnight service went well. There was a large congregation and afterwards they all had soup and sandwiches in the vicarage kitchen. It was early morning before they got to bed. Mark had to go off at seven to take the first service of Christmas Day at the most remote of his three churches where he could expect no more than a handful of communicants.

In her room Daisy lay uneasily trying to get to sleep. It was not a good idea to leave one's own bed in winter, especially at Christmas, but Sophia's invitation had been so pressing that she had not liked to refuse it. She and Mark must miss their London parish and it was the least she could do to attempt to cheer them at this time. But whose need was greater, theirs or Father Spode's?

In the other spare room Edmund and Isabel talked in low voices. He had been dismayed at how Mark had aged and how poorly he and Sophia were living in this gaunt country vicarage, with that dreadful cat getting into everything. How did they endure *that*? Isabel wondered. She hadn't really wanted to come to Edmund's old friend at Christmas and regretted that unfortunate approach through the churchyard, another of Edmund's misguided ideas. Still, it was the least they could do, and she had unpacked her ruby-red velvet dress to wear for the festivities.

A splendid dress, Sophia thought, as she contemplated Isabel, positively upholstered in the ruby velvet, like some magnificent armchair. Daisy too was dressed – one could quite appropriately even say 'clad' – in a garment of flowered brocade, almost ecclesiastical in design, which looked as if it might have been material left over from an altar frontal she had been making for Father Spode. Sophia herself felt altogether inadequate in her dark flowered cotton, but it was the only long dress she had.

How good it was to sit here, not in the kitchen for once, preparing to enjoy their Christmas dinner, Mark able to relax after the labours of the day, Faustina safe in her basket, anticipating tit-bits from the bird!

'Which church is your favourite of the three?' Edmund asked. He did not yet know which one was associated with his ancestors so was unprejudiced.

Mark smiled. 'I can't have a favourite. It would be too obvious to choose St Mary's, with just a handful of farming folk gathered together in the early morning; or St Luke's, which is the best architecturally; or even All Saints', with its larger congregations and superior singing – I like them all in their different ways.' But, he reflected, he was not required to pick out his favourite *people* among the three congregations – that might well be another matter.

Boxing Day, St Stephen, of course. 'Double of 2nd Class with Simple Octave', Daisy read from her missal, but she feared there would be no service here. It would be good to be back in London again with Father Spode, and she couldn't help worrying about him. The services would have been splendid, but it was so cold in the clergy house, even with the paraffin stove in his study, and he was so ineffectual domestically that one did sometimes wonder if the celibacy of the clergy was altogether a good arrangement, and nowadays, with even Roman priests marrying, there was no knowing . . .

'Where in London do you live?' Isabel was asking, as she and Daisy took a Boxing Day walk over the sodden fields.

'West Hampstead,' Daisy told her.

'Ah, *West* Hampstead, I don't think I've ever . . . ' Isabel was at a loss. She had heard of Finchley Road, could even picture it, but anything the other side of it was beyond her imagining. Almost Kilburn, that would be? 'We have a flat near Victoria

Station when we're in London,' she declared, suddenly remembering, as she glanced at the leafless trees, that comforting glimpse of Westminster Cathedral from her sitting-room windows. She was not a great lover of the country, but Edmund had insisted. This desire to revisit the homeland of his ancestors, 'roots', you might call it, almost like that television series . . .

'Victoria Station,' Daisy repeated. 'That must be convenient.'

'Yes, in the days when we used to go on the Golden Arrow, but now of course one flies everywhere.'

'Of course,' said Daisy, who had never been in an aeroplane.

They walked on in silence for a while. 'Are you fond of cats?' Isabel asked at last.

'I must confess I'm really more of a dog person,' said Daisy. Her small flat had never been soiled, fouled or besmirched by any kind of animal, but there was something pleasing about the idea of a dog. 'Do *you* like cats?'

'No, I do *not*. If I had known – but how could one? I think I'm allergic to them. I'm the sort of person who *knows* when there's a cat in the room, even if I can't see it.'

This seemed a matter for congratulation and Daisy nodded sympathetically in the cold air. 'That cat is always in the kitchen, it seems to sleep there, and I do wonder if its hairs don't get into things. You'll be going back to London tomorrow, will you?'

'Yes, we have to get back. You too, I imagine?'

'Yes, I must. Though I've retired now and live alone I have a lot of things to do.' And Father Spode will need me, she thought confidently. 'The Aingers are very kind and of course Christmas in the country *is* delightful . . .'

Daisy sounded so very doubtful that there was no need for Isabel to comment further.

'We can go back over the churchyard – a short cut,' said Mark, smiling. 'Remember – the way you surprised us on Christmas

359

Eve? I didn't recognize you at first – for one wild moment I thought it was the Bishop – you're not unlike him, you know – about the same height, and he also has a good head of hair . . .' Mark felt he was talking almost excessively, chattering in a way he normally despised, but in this instance conversation of any kind seemed better than silence. As long as he avoided the subject of the parish registers and that shouldn't be difficult. Such a disappointment and a surprise – Edmund's ancestors not even gentlemen! And he had always understood that they had been connected with the manor house. Well, in a sense, they might have been, as gardeners or agricultural labourers; they had probably tilled the soil in some way, and even if it wasn't quite what Edmund had expected, what could be nobler than that?

'I *think* we shall have to start back this afternoon,' Edmund said, as they sat at lunch. What could it possibly be but cold turkey, with that cat eating all the best bits, crouched over what looked like a Crown Derby saucer laid on an old copy of the *Church Times*?

'In that case, I wonder . . .' Daisy began.

'We could perhaps give *you* a lift back to town,' Isabel suggested, an offer that was taken up with quiet satisfaction.

'Well, it would certainly be more comfortable for you, Daisy,' said Sophia, her heart bounding with most unsuitable joy, 'though of course you can stay here as long as you like. But I know what a busy person you are . . .' All that fussing over Father Spode, she said to herself.

It was dusk when they finally packed themselves into the car, Edmund and Isabel in the front and Daisy in the back with some of the suitcases. As they drew nearer to London, passing through suburban roads with lighted Christmas trees in the uncurtained windows, their stilted conversation began to flow more easily.

'You found what you wanted in the church registers?' Daisy asked.

'Oh, yes – some interesting facts came to light. I've often thought I'd like to have been a country parson,' Edmund said. 'A worthwhile job, that, meeting country people – the best type, after all.'

'And having three churches and a choice of vicarages,' said Isabel.

'I wonder if they made a *wise* choice,' said Daisy, 'that kitchen looking over the churchyard, and that cat playing among the gravestones.'

'That *cat*,' said Isabel feelingly.

The three did not know each other well enough to lapse into open disloyalty to their host and hostess, so they sat in a comfortable silence until the time came to drop Daisy at her flat. They had not taken to her sufficiently to suggest keeping in touch, but if they ever did chance to meet again, they would have quite a lot in common.

'I suppose it *was* a good idea,' Mark said doubtfully, 'but I can't help feeling there might have been other more suitable people we could have asked.'

Faustina slept in her basket, replete with cold turkey, and Sophia was beginning to wonder about supper. 'Oh, Daisy is a *dear*,' she said firmly, 'and Edmund and Isabel are probably dears too when you get to know them better.'

Of course Mark was right, they were not the kind of people she had imagined inviting for Christmas, not what one thought of as deprived or 'disadvantaged', even with the revelation about Edmund's ancestors, but perhaps it was selfish to expect people to be at the receiving end of a benefit, as if wanting to feel good oneself, surely not the true spirit of Christmas at all.

'Boiled eggs and coffee and more Christmas cake? Will that do for supper?' she suggested. The cake had been cut into on

Christmas Day so that King Lear now seemed to be standing on the edge of a precipice.

'I really will get some new decorations for the cake *next* year,' Sophia said.

Across a Crowded Room

The hall was candlelit, as might have been expected on the occasion of this anniversary dinner, this 'feast', held every year in this particular Oxford college, to commemorate the seventeenth-century worthy who had left his bones in the college chapel. The candles, the portraits of past Rectors and benefactors high up on the walls, and then the Latin grace (how much had she remembered of her Latin?), rendered by the fresh young voices of the singers in the gallery, contrasted with the scene below, which was not, on the whole, fresh and young.

She had been invited as a guest, one of a scattering of five or six women among eighty or so men. It was certainly an occasion, the kind of thing that might have demanded a new dress had not her sense told her that something dark and unobtrusive would be the most appropriate wear for a woman of her age in such a setting. So she was in her old black with a gauzy Indian stole round her shoulders, the whole thing blending in with her surroundings.

Avocado pears, cut up and dressed in some special way, was the first course awaiting them, with a glass of dry sherry. On her left was the man whose guest she was, 'dear old George', kind and bumbling, who had thought she might like an evening out, given her rather dull life in the country. And of course she *was* an Oxford graduate, might even have become a person of distinction had her life taken a different direction. But George, having invited her, needn't bother to make much conversation with her, but would be talking shop – he was a professor of history – to the man sitting on his other side. She would have to concentrate on the person on her right, a youngish fair-haired American (perhaps not quite so young as he appeared at first sight), a professor of English Literature at a small respectable New England college. She had read English too, all those years ago, so perhaps as the evening progressed they might find that they had something in common.

The avocado was replaced by a clear dark soup; perhaps it might even be turtle, but, not wanting to put her glasses on, she had not studied the menu.

'Turtle soup,' said the gnat-like voice of her American neighbour. 'How very English that seems! The Lord Mayor's Banquet and that kind of thing.'

'Yes, one doesn't have it every day,' she agreed.

'I'm lucky to be sitting by one of the few ladies here tonight,' he went on.

She glanced at him in surprise. It was so very much a mechanical compliment from one who, as was evident from his whole demeanour, was interested only in women of his mother's generation. But of course she *was* of his mother's generation and long past the age when she might have expected a real compliment.

'Do you know many people here tonight?' she asked formally.

'A few. I'm a sort of visiting professor; you know the kind of thing.'

'I believe your subject is English Literature?'

'Oh, have people talked about me? Have I been singled out?'

'Well, my friend who invited me tonight did tell me something about you.'

'What did he say?'

She was hardly a match for his eager enquiry, for George hadn't said all that much, only that her neighbour would be an American who was here doing something connected with Eng. Lit., he wasn't sure what.

'That I was an American called Ned and that my subject was Keats?' He took advantage of her hesitation to fill in the gap.

'Keats,' she repeated, hoping she could do something with that. Keats, the young girl's poet, as she had read somewhere, but perhaps hardly appropriate as a subject of conversation here. She could only think of the 'Ode to a Nightingale', 'Isabella' (or 'The Pot of Basil'?), and a poem about a dove which seemed totally unsuitable. But then she remembered Keats's house in Hampstead and a visit there, one day long ago with somebody she had been in love with (or fancied she had been in love with). 'Of course you must have been to Keats's house,' she said. 'Very charming and sad, isn't it?'

'Yes, I remember the first time I went – 1968 or '69 it must have been – a wet day and certain tensions in the air.' He smiled.

It was difficult to do much with that, she felt, the kind of remark accompanied by an intimate smile that hinted at things she couldn't possibly know about. She could hardly ask him what the 'tensions' had been. 'We did have some wet summers in the late sixties,' she ventured. 'When *I* went there, it was spring and the blossom was out.' In April, the cruellest month, immortalized by a great American poet . . .

'How very suitable,' he said, in a mocking tone that made her wish she hadn't said it, spring and blossom being inappropriate to a woman of her age.

The next course came. It was salmon, and a white wine was

poured into one of the tall glasses on her right. She turned her attention to the fish, enjoying it. After all, salmon, like turtle soup, was not a food of every day. The young American – must she think of him as Ned? – was talking to the man on his other side.

'All right?' George asked kindly.

'Fine, thank you,' she said, and finished her salmon in contented silence.

Now a meat course was brought to the table. Venison, George informed her; otherwise, without her glasses, she wouldn't have known. The dark rich meat was unfamiliar to her. A picture came to her mind – deer leaping in the Wychwood forest, or Wordsworth's poem 'The White Doe of Rylstone', such was the effect of Eng. Lit., but she remembered nothing of the poem. Ned had turned to her again, and there was an expectant silence. 'I live near a forest,' she began.

He inclined his head politely. Her remark must have seemed a total *non sequitur*. 'I was thinking of deer and forests because of the venison,' she explained.

'It's *venison* – this meat?' There was a kind of horror in his tone. He put down his knife and fork, for he had not yet started to eat it, in what she thought of as the American fashion, cutting up the meat and then eating it with the fork.

'Perhaps it came from the Wychwood forest, which is near here,' she said, but this was evidently no encouragement or recommendation. Perhaps Americans couldn't cope with things like venison, she thought. She was about to make a remark on these lines, bringing in something about Red Indians and hoping it would come out as light, frivolous and witty, but by the time she had finished framing it in her mind he had turned away, and as George was talking to the man on his other side she was temporarily abandoned, as it were, though this seemed too violent a way of describing her situation. She took advantage of this lull to look around the hall, to glance towards the high table even, to see whether there was anyone she knew – unlikely though this seemed – for she had not studied the guest list. George had guided her to her place, and she knew that when they changed their places for dessert he would guide her again.

It was interesting to observe the few other women present on this occasion, to speculate on who they might be – not just the wives of Fellows, she was sure of that (*they* would no doubt be sitting at home watching television) – and whether they were persons of distinction. One, at the high table on the Rector's right, wearing an MA gown over her black dress, looked like a female academic, the kind of person one might have difficulty in making conversation with. She was sitting next to a grey-haired man with a rather nice face. He reminded her of somebody she had once known a long time ago, but was it, could it possibly be, the same person? She must ask George or look at the table plan.

'You can bring yourself to eat *deer*?' Ned was saying.

'Do you know who that man is, next to the woman on the Rector's right?' It was just possible that Ned, being Eng. Lit., might know.

'Oh, I think it's one of those grey English dons from one of the other colleges or even a red-brick university.'

A red-brick university. She knew he had not ended up here at Oxford, though she had not followed his career all these years, and they had been a good many, over thirty, since she had last seen him. Gervase Harding, the name came back to her. It had seemed a romantic name in those days . . .

Strawberries in wine, served in tall glasses with whipped cream on the top, was the next course, and with it a delicate white wine, Vouvray perhaps, one of the few wines whose name she knew and which she remembered having drunk on holiday in the Loire.

'Strawberries,' said Ned, with evident enjoyment. 'Would they be grown locally?'

She didn't knew and her concentration was divided now, for she was thinking about Gervase, stealing surreptitious glances, remembering. Words from one of the numbers of a popular musical of a few years ago came to her, something about seeing somebody across a crowded room on an enchanted evening: something like that, hadn't it been? But that song had been about meeting somebody for the first time, surely, not being suddenly confronted by a person one had known forty years ago, now both old and grey?

'What are you smiling at?' Ned's gnat-like voice broke in.

'Only that I've seen somebody I used to know a long time ago, and his hair, which used to be fair, is now quite grey or white – hard to tell exactly at this distance.'

'"His golden locks Time hath to silver turn'd,"' Ned quoted mockingly. 'Do you know that poem?'

'Peele, isn't it, or one of those minor Elizabethans.' She did remember.

'And there's a line about his helmet now making a hive for bees. Would that apply, too?'

'I hardly know – not having kept pace with his career, whatever it may have been ...'

They now rose from the table and left the hall for the tables to be cleared and rearranged for dessert. She found herself in a chilly passageway and drew her fragile Indian-gauze stole more closely round her shoulders. A thin, meagre-looking clergyman was by her, not as easy to talk to as the young American had been.

'What happens now?' she asked. There was a stack of bicycles in a corner, which seemed an unusual note.

'Happens?' The clergyman was evidently unaware of anything out of the ordinary.

'These bicycles.'

'Oh, those. I expect they belong to the domestics.'

Certainly there was a clatter of crockery and the sound of voices, 'rough' voices almost, so they must have been near the kitchens. She was looking out for Gervase, but there was no sign of him. Through the open window a few people could be seen walking about in the still evening air. All in the April evening, she thought, remembering another tag. It was a song – something the clergyman might know, she felt – but he was unresponsive when she asked him, and looked at her as if she were mad. Elderly women quoting poetry was something to be avoided, to run a mile from. Would it be possible to approach Gervase before the evening was out, to have a few words with him? She had not prepared herself for anything like this, and now began to think what she would say to him, how she would greet him after all this time.

'This is the new quadrangle you can see from the window,' the clergyman said, as if making amends for his failure over the April evening. 'There's been a good deal of controversy about it.'

She looked out at the stark buildings, blending unhappily with the ancient mellow stones of the earlier work. They reminded her of something a child might construct from his box of bricks. In the centre there was a piece of modern sculpture – hardly a statue – which seemed to resemble the lower half of a torso, as far as she could make out in the dim light.

'It's good to encourage modern artists,' she ventured, with an attempt at a charitable approach which she felt the clergyman might expect. But he evidently did not expect it, and said briefly that he thought the work hideous. On this note the crowd began to move into the hall again and she became separated from him.

'All right?' George was at her side, solicitous for his guest.

'Yes, fine, thank you. I've seen somebody I used to know.'

'Really? Perhaps I can bring you together again.'

'I don't think you'd know him – he's a guest here, I think.' She spoke Gervase's name, but met with no response.

'You're sitting on the Rector's right for dessert,' George said. 'You may not find him very easy to talk to,' he added, on a warning note. 'And on your other side . . .'

Of course it was not Gervase on her other side; that would have been too much to expect, too much like a romantic novel, though fiction now tended to be rather more realistic than life, she felt. The young man on her other side was so very young, with his fresh cheeks and soft fair hair, that he might have been chosen in piquant contrast. It would be many years before time turned *his* golden locks to silver. A brief polite enquiry on her part brought forth the information that he was a junior Fellow, newly appointed, and that his subject was computers. She was at a loss for a moment and then made some fatuous remark about computers threatening to rule our lives, an observation he treated with the polite contempt it deserved. In the silence that followed he turned to his other neighbour and she found herself invited to take port with the Rector. Or take something else, a golden liquid whose name she didn't catch in an elegant eighteenth-century decanter . . . . would she prefer that? No, she would take port; that was surely more correct, the kind of thing one ought to drink on this kind of evening. And now the Rector indicated a huge golden pineapple and invited her to partake of that ('partake' was the word that came into her mind), and there was no need to be daunted, because it was already cut into slices, all neatly put together again to make the whole fruit. So she took a slice of pineapple and the Rector asked her where she lived.

'I live near a forest,' she said, using the same bit of talk she had brought out for the young American, Ned.

'Ah, the Wychwood forest?' said the Rector, and he smiled a kind of secret smile.

'You know it?' she asked.

'I *did* know it, once, many years ago.'

It seemed to be that kind of evening, with its reminiscences of old unhappy far-off things and battles long ago. But of course she could hardly quote that, either to the Rector or to the young computer expert on her other side. So she let the Rector's observation fall, as perhaps it was meant to, without comment, while she cut the rind off her slice of pineapple. Having successfully dealt with this, she looked down into the body of the hall to see if she could find Gervase again. And now she saw that he was sitting at the table just below hers. He was much nearer than before and she was able to observe him more closely. He had taken port and, like her, a slice of pineapple. There was something pleasing in the idea of their choice being the same – 'Great minds think alike', that old childish joke. There was no doubt that he was still a good-looking man and people would probably say that he had worn better than she had, if there was ever a question of comparison, which there obviously never would be. He had married, of course, quite soon after going down from the university. Had she ever known his wife's name? She must have and now she tried to remember it. Something beginning with 'M', she believed – Mary, Margaret, Mavis, Madeline, Millicent; or a more exotic name, Mélisande or Morwenna – but nothing seemed quite right. Perhaps it was not 'M' at all.

'Memory plays such curious tricks.' The Rector's voice came to her, as if echoing her thoughts. So he was still on about the Wychwood forest, she realized, and had perhaps been disappointed by her lack of response.

'Yes,' she had to agree, 'it certainly does.' Now she cast about in her mind for an example, something to embellish that bald statement. 'All that wonderful weather of long ago, summer and springs!' she said.

'I think of the forest as being always covered in bluebells, and a little later sheets of wild garlic. Is it still?'

'Well, at the right time of year,' she said cautiously. 'In a few weeks from now it will be just like that.'

Now she looked away and down the hall again to where Gervase was sitting, and it seemed to her that he looked in her direction, that their eyes met. If he had indeed recognized her, they were now coming nearer to a meeting. Well, hardly that – there had been nothing romantically Byronic about their last meeting. Things had just fizzled out, so either he would remember her or he would not. She must be prepared for a blank look of non-recognition – men were expert at that.

They rose from the table for the final grace. The dinner was over, but the evening was not yet at an end. George was by her side again. They would go into a common room for coffee and liqueurs, brandy or whisky, whatever she felt like. Ned, the young American, came up to her. She could feel his curiosity as he asked, 'Have you met up with your friend?'

'Not yet.' That sounded as if it was only a matter of time before the meeting with Gervase, and that was by no means certain.

Now the atmosphere of the evening was subtly different, and not all that subtly, either, she thought. A group of younger Fellows were crowding round the table, helping themselves to drinks. It was like a mass of young animals, tomcats in their prime. She noticed the young computer expert among them, less inhibited now. Many of the older Fellows had left after the dinner, returning decorously to tall North Oxford houses where wives waited grimly. Yet there would have been nothing for them to be grim about, unless it was the superior food and drink and possibly higher level of conversation.

George was offering her brandy or whisky, but she would

drink nothing more. Instead, she took a crystallized fruit from an exquisitely arranged box – a beautiful apricot glistening with sugar.

At this point, just as she was about to bite into the apricot, she heard George's voice saying, 'I believe you two know each other,' and Gervase was standing at her side.

So it had *not* been a romantic glance of mutual recognition, she realized, meeting his response of polite surprise when George introduced them. Her name did not appear to mean anything to him. *She* would have to fill in the details, explain that they had met all those years ago when they had both read English at Oxford. She was about to embark on this with mechanical politeness, in the way that nice women so often find themselves doing, but then she suddenly thought, Why should I? Perhaps she had been given courage and independence by the drink, though 'drink' was a crude way of describing the measured succession of civilized and appropriate wines with which her glass had been filled. Anyway, something had got into her, made her remain silently smiling at George's introductory words, 'I believe you two know each other'; so, taking pity on Gervase's air of puzzlement, she said at last, '*Used* to know,' and let him make what he would of it.

'Then I'll leave you to talk over old times,' George said, moving away.

'"Old times,"' Gervase repeated, obviously trying to gain time. She imagined him casting about in his memory, thrashing around, trying to remember what these 'old times' could have been. It was strange the way she had found herself getting nearer to him as the evening went on – first the distant glimpse, then the closer view at dessert, and now so close that she was looking up into his face, noticing the lines and the golden locks turned to silver but still, she could see now, with some gold in them.

'This wasn't here in those days,' he said, indicating the new quadrangle through the open door. 'Would you like to stroll outside? It's such a warm evening.'

Not as warm as all that, she thought, drawing her Indian stole more closely round her shoulders, but of course men's clothes were thicker and warmer.

'Do you like this new style of architecture?' she asked formally. 'It seems not to go very well with the rest.'

'No, I don't like it in this setting. It reminds me too much of my own university, built in a less gracious age.'

'I suppose one must move with the times, even in Oxford,' she said. Can you think of nothing better to say? she asked herself. They were now standing by the modern statue, seeming to contemplate, even study, it. Some intelligent comment was called for here. 'I suppose the texture of the stone is the most satisfying thing about this,' she said, placing her hand on it.

He sighed. 'In my university this would have been defaced, I'm afraid – the form is rather asking for it, isn't it?'

She looked at the lumpish mass again doubtfully, and saw that it was possible to give it a certain interpretation; if one's mind worked that way, she amended, and perhaps the minds of provincial students in the 1970s did work that way. It was not a conversation that could usefully be extended or continued, but he was obviously hoping that in the course of it she might give him a clue about the old times they were supposed to be recalling. And now she began to relent; she decided to throw him a crumb.

'Do you remember Professor Ransome's lectures?' she asked. 'Wasn't it at one of those we first met?'

'Of course, that was it!' he said gratefully, though she might have been any one of several other girls he could have met at those lectures, she thought. Some detail was needed, some convincing detail – something she had worn, perhaps, but a man could hardly be expected to remember something like that.

374

'On the Elizabethans,' she said. 'Don't you always think of the way he used to recite Peele?'

'Yes.' Gervase smiled. '"His golden locks Time hath to silver turn'd."' He glanced at her own grey, neatly-set-for-the-occasion hair. She was startled at his quoting that, to think he seemed almost to be applying it to her as she had applied it to him. 'I wouldn't have said that my hair was ever golden,' she remarked. But now their reminiscences threatened to become too intimate. It was unsuitable and faintly ludicrous for people in their sixties to recall what colour their hair had been forty years ago.

'I've been trying to remember your wife's name,' she said, in a louder, more social tone. 'Something beginning with "M", wasn't it? Not Mary or Margaret . . .'

'My *wife*?' He seemed startled. Perhaps she was dead and the recollection too painful. 'But I had no wife. I was never married.'

She looked at him in amazement. It *was* Gervase; there had been no case of mistaken identity, but in some way her memory had been at fault. He had never married! An abyss seemed to open before her, and their conversation came to a full stop. Standing by an ornamental pool, they suddenly had nothing more to say to each other.

A group approached, others strolling in the warm air – all in the April evening, indeed. Ned was among them, and she heard his unmistakable tones drawing attention to a dead pigeon lying in the water round the statue. 'It ought to be removed,' he said. 'Somebody should take it away – otherwise it will putrefy.'

She wanted to laugh at his choice of the word 'putrefy', and would have introduced Gervase to him, but then George came out, looking for his guest, judging that she had probably had enough talking about old times.

'Are you staying in college?' he asked Gervase politely. 'Or can we give you a lift anywhere?'

'Thank you, but I'm staying here.'

'Is it comfortable?' she asked.

'Tolerable – I only hope there'll be a bedside light in working order.'

'Yes, that's a great thing,' she agreed.

'It's been so nice renewing our acquaintance,' he said, turning to her.

'Yes, it has, even if we've had to revise our memories a little.' She smiled, picturing him going back to his northern university, unmarried. Perhaps he had had a mistress, then, but it was too late and she was too tired to speculate further. It would puzzle her in the watches of the night, that name beginning with 'M'.

They all said good night and George fetched her fur cape. 'Quite an evening,' he said. 'I do hope you enjoyed it.'

When he got back home, his wife, cosily tucked up in bed rather than grimly waiting, would ask him how the evening had gone, what they had eaten, who had been there, and whether his guest had enjoyed herself. He would be able to tell her that she did seem to have done that. She had got on very well with that young American and she had even met an old flame or something – he wasn't quite sure what.

Finding a Voice: a radio talk

This was recorded on February 8th 1978 for a BBC series and transmitted on BBC Radio 3 on April 4th.

I've sometimes wondered whether novelists like to be remembered for what they've said or because they've said it in their own particular way – in their own distinctive voice. But how do you acquire your own voice or indeed any kind of voice? Does it come about as inevitably as your height or the colour of your eyes or do you develop it deliberately, perhaps in imitation of a writer you admire?

I've been trying to write novels, with many ups and downs, over more than forty years. I started as a schoolgirl, when I used to contribute to the school magazine – mostly parodies, conscious even then of other people's styles. Then in 1929, when I was sixteen, I discovered Aldous Huxley's novel *Crome Yellow*. I came across this sophisticated masterpiece in the wilds of Shropshire, through that marvellous institution Boots' Library, now, alas, as much of a period memory as the seven and sixpenny hardback novel. I was a keen reader of all kinds of modern fiction, and more than anything else I read at that time *Crome Yellow* made me want to be a novelist myself. I don't suppose for a moment that I appreciated the book's finer satirical points, but it seemed to me funnier than anything I had read before, and the idea of writing about a group of people in a certain situation – in this case upper-class intellectuals in a country house – immediately attracted me, so I decided that I wanted to write a novel like *Crome Yellow*.

And so my first novel – unpublished, of course – was started in that same year, 1929. It was called *Young Men in Fancy Dress* and was about a group of 'Bohemians' – I must put that word in quotes – who were, in my view, young men living in Chelsea, a district of which I knew nothing at that time. The hero wanted to be a novelist and, as one of the characters put it, 'If you want to be a proper novelist, you must get to like town and develop a passion for Chelsea.'

Reading the manuscript again, I detect almost nothing in it of my mature style of writing, except that the Bohemian young men aren't taken entirely seriously, and that there's a lot of detail – clothes, makes of cars, golf, and drinks (especially descriptions of cocktails – which I'd certainly never tasted). I've always liked detail – in fact my love of triviality has been criticized – so perhaps that was something I developed early. And obviously at that time I read a lot – if a bit indiscriminately. In this early novel all the 'best' or at least the most fashionable names are dropped, from Swinburne and Rupert Brooke to D. H. Lawrence and Beverley Nichols.

When I was eighteen, I went up to Oxford to read English. Most aspiring novelists write at the University, but I didn't, though I *did* start to write something in my third year, a description of a man who meant a lot to me. I tore it up, but this person did appear later in a very different guise as one of my best comic male characters.

There was nothing comic to me about him at the time, but memory is a great transformer of pain into amusement. And at

Oxford, as well as English Literature, I went on reading modern novelists.

I particularly enjoyed the works of 'Elizabeth', the author of *Elizabeth and Her German Garden*. Such novels as *The Enchanted April* and *The Pastor's Wife* were a revelation in their wit and delicate irony, and the dry, unsentimental treatment of the relationship between men and women which touched some echoing chord in me at that time. I was learning; these novels seemed more appropriate to use as models than *Crome Yellow* – perhaps even the kind of thing I might try to write myself.

It must also have been about this time – still in the 1930s – that I was introduced to the poems of John Betjeman. His glorifying of ordinary things and buildings and his subtle appreciation of different kinds of churches and churchmanship made an immediate appeal to me. Another author I came across at this time was Ivy Compton-Burnett – I think *More Women than Men*, her novel about a girls' school, was the first I read; then *A House and Its Head*, one of her more typical family chronicles. Of course I couldn't help being influenced by her dialogue, that precise, formal conversation which seemed so stilted when I first read it – though when I got used to it, a friend and I took to writing to each other entirely in that style. Another book we imitated was Stevie Smith's *Novel on Yellow Paper*, a fantasy, written with all the humour and pathos of her poems.

So *all* the writers I've mentioned played some part in forming my own literary style. But of course I'd also been reading the classics, especially Jane Austen and Trollope. Critics discussing my work sometimes tentatively mention these great names, mainly, I think, because I tend to write about the same kind of people and society as they did, although, of course, the ones I write about live in the twentieth century. But what novelist of today would *dare* to *claim* that she was influenced by such masters of our craft? Certainly all who read and love Jane Austen may *try* to write with the same economy of language, even *try* to look at their characters with her kind of detachment, but that is as far as any 'influence' could go.

The concept of 'detachment' reminds me of the methods of the anthropologist, who studies societies in this way. The joke definition of anthropology as 'the study of man embracing woman' might therefore seem peculiarly applicable to the novelist. After the war, I got a job at the International African Institute in London. I was mostly engaged in editorial work, smoothing out the written results of other people's researches, but I learned more than that in the process. I learned how it was possible and even essential to cultivate an attitude of detachment towards life and people, and how the novelist could even do 'field-work' as the anthropologist did. And I also met a great many people of a type I hadn't met before. The result of all this was a novel called *Less Than Angels*, which is about anthropologists working at a research centre in London, and also the suburban background of Deirdre, one of the heroines, and her life with her mother and aunt. There's a little church life in it too, so that it could be said to be a mixture of all the worlds I had experience of. I felt in this novel that I was breaking new ground by venturing into the academic scene, although in many ways that isn't unlike the worlds of the village and parish I'd written about up to then.

I admire those people who can produce a new book regularly every year. I've found it more difficult as time goes on. I suppose it's easy for anyone to produce their first novel – it's all there inside you and only needs to be written down. Also a second and third may be just under the surface and comparatively easy to dig out. After that it becomes more difficult, unless you're prepared to go on writing exactly the same book with only slight variations, over and over again. And people are always very ready to tell you anecdotes from their own experience – which, in their opinion, would be just the thing for one of your novels. Readers who *don't* like your kind of story sometimes suggest plots or subjects for you in the hope that you may write something different. And sometimes, especially when things aren't going well, it's tempting to give it a try.

In the early 1960s I sent my seventh novel to my publishers. And to my horror they wrote back saying they didn't feel they wanted it. I offered it to several others but the manuscript still came thudding back through the letterbox. One publisher said, 'We think it's very well written but there's an old-fashioned air about it.' Another thought that it wasn't the kind of book to which people were turning – I wasn't quite sure what he meant by that – while a third said curtly that their fiction list was full up for the next two years. I had never made my living as a writer so I still had my job, but my books had been published regularly and now it seemed that nobody wanted them. It was an awful and humiliating sensation to be totally rejected after all those years, and I didn't know what to do about it. I did seriously consider trying to write something different – perhaps a thriller or a historical novel – but I never got very far with the idea.

Maybe it was too late to change my voice. I wrote two more novels in my own style and sent them round, but they still came back with the same kind of comments. Then, when I was on the verge of retiring from my job at the African Institute, the idea for my last novel, *Quartet in Autumn*, came to me. And again, I started writing it with no real hope of getting it published. It's about four people in their early sixties – two men and two women – working in a London office. During the course of the story, the women retire and one of them dies. I wanted to write about the problems and difficulties of this stage in one's life and also to show its comedy and irony – in fact I'd rather put it the other way round: my main concern was with the comedy and irony, the problems and difficulties having been dealt with almost excessively, one might say, elsewhere. I think some readers have been disappointed in this novel because it seems less light-hearted than some of my earlier ones, yet I enjoyed the writing of it almost more than any of the others, perhaps because I felt that I was writing for my own pleasure with no certain hope of publication at that time.

But then, at the beginning of 1977, both Philip Larkin and Lord David Cecil wrote of me as 'an under-rated writer' in *The Times Literary Supplement*. As a result of this, *Quartet in Autumn* was accepted for publication, and two of my earlier books were re-issued. It was marvellously encouraging to be brought back from the wilderness. But it was disquieting too. I wonder how many other novelists have suddenly been told their work is not fashionable or saleable any more, and never been lucky enough to have the generous praise I had from the right people in the right place.

And this leads me on to the question of why we write at all. Is it enough just to write for ourselves if nobody else is going to read it? As Ivy Compton-Burnett said in a conversation with her friend Margaret Jourdain, 'Most of the pleasure of making a book would go if it held nothing to be shared by other people. I would write for a dozen people ... but I would not write for no one.' This is what I feel myself – it is those dozen people that spur me on, even when it seems that I'm writing for myself alone. So I try to write what pleases and amuses *me* in the hope that a few others will like it too.

So I did go on writing, even in the face of discouragement. For the last thirty years or so I have kept a series of notebooks, like a kind of diary, in which I also write down all sorts of other things – possible scenes or turns of plot for novels, quotations that appeal to me, occasional overheard scraps of conversation, anything, in fact. Doing this is often more of a pleasure than the actual writing. To jot down an idea for a scene and then to imagine it filled out is immensely satisfying, but, as everyone knows, the final result invariably falls short of the original conception.

I'm fascinated by the notebooks of great writers – Hardy, for example. Let me quote this entry for Sunday, February 1st 1874: 'To Trinity Church, Dorchester. The rector in his sermon delivered himself of mean images in a sublime voice, and the effect is that of a glowing landscape in which clothes are hung up to dry.' Or another entry, for October 25th 1867, more likely to have inspired a poem: 'Martha R –, an old maid whose lover died, has his love letters to her bound, and keeps them on the parlour table.'

To descend from these heights, here's an example from my own notebooks. In September 1948 I described a visit to Buckfast Abbey:

> ... much commercialised, teas, car park etc. shop full of Catholic junk as well as books. Abbey very clean and new looking, inside bright and light, tiled effect; incense smells almost hygienic. Not thus would one be sentimentally converted to Rome, though perhaps rationally. Very young priests in the parties of sightseers, mostly in pairs like little beetles, from the seminary in Paignton. The herds of people – the monk showing us round says: 'I don't suppose any of you are Catholics' and explains about Our Lady – makes one feel inferior.

This passage seems to have found its way, very little changed, into my novel *Excellent Women*. At about the same time I noted down something seen from the top of a bus – 'A woman and a clergyman sitting on chairs (hard) in the Green Park and talking with animation' – and this gave me the idea for an important twist in the plot of that same novel.

Sometimes, on the other hand, the novelist will seek his material more deliberately. Robert Liddell, in his book A *Treatise on the Novel*, describes the experience of Flaubert who went to a funeral. 'Perhaps I shall get something for my Bovary,' he wrote to a friend before he went. But when he got there, all he met with was a bore, who asked him foolish questions about the public libraries of Egypt, a country which he had lately visited. Whatever Flaubert had hoped to gain from experiencing the funeral was quite put in the background. So in this way we may not always get what we expect or hope for from an experience, but we shall probably get something, though I don't know whether Flaubert ever made use of that bore. Ivy Compton-Burnett, on the other hand, claimed not to have the notebook habit, but admitted that some sort of starting-point is useful and that she got it 'almost anywhere'. This starting off, the point where to plunge in, as it were, is often more difficult than might be imagined from the finished work. I usually think of several beginnings and try them out before the right one emerges. I find it's sometimes necessary to go further back in the story or to look at things from a different standpoint.

Perhaps I've been influenced by something I was once told about Proust – that he was said to go over all his characters and make them worse. Regrettably – I think, and I daresay others would agree with me – it's more interesting to write about people's less admirable qualities than to chronicle their virtues.

After having published seven novels and written a great many more, I suppose I can be said to have found a voice of sorts. I hope so, anyway. But whether it's a distinctive voice must be left to others to judge.

One of my favourite quiz games on television some years ago was that one in which panellists were asked to guess the authorship of certain passages which were read out to them, and then to discuss various features of the author in question. There were no prizes for guessing, no moving belt or desirable objects passing before their eyes, just the pleasure and satisfaction of recognizing the unmistakable voice of Henry James or Henry Greene, or whoever it might be. I think that's the kind of immortality most authors would want – to feel that their work would be immediately recognizable as having been written by them and by nobody else. But of course, it's a lot to ask for!

EXCELLENT WOMEN

Barbara Pym

Introduced by Alexander McCall Smith

'I suppose an unmarried woman just over thirty, who lives alone
and has no apparent ties, must expect to find herself involved or
interested in other people's business, and if she is also a clergyman's
daughter then one might really say that there is no hope for her.'

Mildred Lathbury is one of those excellent women who are
often taken for granted. She is a godsend, 'capable of dealing with
most of the stock situations or even the great moments of life – birth,
marriage, death, the successful jumble sale, the garden fête spoilt by
bad weather'. Her glamorous new neighbours, the Napiers, seem to
be facing a marital crisis. One cannot take sides in these matters,
though it is tricky, especially as Mildred has a soft spot for
dashing young Rockingham Napier. This is Barbara Pym's
world at its funniest and most touching.

'I'd sooner read a new Barbara Pym than a new Jane Austen'
Philip Larkin

'Barbara Pym is the rarest of treasures; she reminds us
of the heartbreaking silliness of everyday life'
Anne Tyler

A GLASS OF BLESSINGS

Barbara Pym

Introduced by John Bayley

'My favourite writer . . . I pick up her books with joy, as though
I were meeting an old, dear friend who comforts me, extends
my vision and makes me roar with laughter'
Jilly Cooper

Wilmet Forsyth is well dressed, well looked after, suitably
husbanded, good-looking and fairly young – but very bored.
Her sober husband Rodney, who works at the Ministry, is slightly
balder and fatter than he once was. Wilmet would like
to think she has changed rather less.

Her interest wanders to the nearby church, where she can neglect
her comfortable household in the more serious-minded company
of three unmarried priests, and, of course, Piers Longridge,
a man of an unfathomably different character altogether.

'[Pym] makes me smile, laugh out loud, consider my own foibles
and fantasies, and above all, suffer real regret when I reach the
final page. Of how many authors can you honestly say that?'
Mavis Cheek

'Barbara Pym is the rarest of treasures'
Anne Tyler

**You can order other Virago titles through our website: *www.virago.co.uk*
or by using the order form below**

☐	Excellent Women	Barbara Pym	£8.99
☐	A Glass of Blessings	Barbara Pym	£8.99
☐	Jane and Prudence	Barbara Pym	£8.99
☐	Less than Angels	Barbara Pym	£8.99
☐	No Fond Return of Love	Barbara Pym	£8.99
☐	Some Tame Gazelle	Barbara Pym	£8.99

The prices shown above are correct at time of going to press. However, the publishers reserve the right to increase prices on covers from those previously advertised, without further notice.

Please allow for postage and packing: **Free UK delivery.**
Europe: add 25% of retail price; Rest of World: 45% of retail price.

To order any of the above or any other Virago titles, please call our credit card orderline or fill in this coupon and send/fax it to:

Virago, PO Box 121, Kettering, Northants NN14 4ZQ
Fax: 01832 733076   Tel: 01832 737526
Email: aspenhouse@FSBDial.co.uk

☐ I enclose a UK bank cheque made payable to Virago for £ . . . .
☐ Please charge £ . . . . . . to my Visa/Delta/Maestro

Expiry Date ☐☐☐☐   Maestro Issue No. ☐☐

NAME (BLOCK LETTERS please) . . . .

ADDRESS . . . .

. . . .

. . . .

Postcode . . . . Telephone . . . .

Signature . . . .

Please allow 28 days for delivery within the UK. Offer subject to price and availability.

PENGUIN BOOKS

THE CATHOLICS OF ULSTER

'A major study by a historian unafraid to take on a subject whose
parameters are both wide and problematic, and to make it her
own. She triumphs by judicious use of evidence, ability to
understand and re-create historical atmosphere over the centuries,
and a deep-rooted empathy' Roy Foster, *Irish Times*,
Books of the Year

'An excellent new history . . . it is safe to say that Elliott will
offend the right people, on both sides . . . One hopes that she will
be widely read not only in her own countries but also in America,
where a certain sentimentality often contorts the understanding of
Irish affairs . . . If there is anyone in the new Bush administration
who wishes to break with the tendency, and wants to be informed
about the northern Catholic experience in all its complexity,
Marianne Elliott's book is the best place to start' Brendan Simms,
Wall Street Journal

'An honest and important book, one that deserves a wide and
careful readership' Ray Ryan, *Guardian*

'Reading it is like standing beside a turf bank and seeing all the
layers, the centuries of history stacked on top of each other, from
the very bottom to the present day . . . strong, disturbing, emotive
and in a peculiar way liberating' Denis Bradley, *Irish News*

'A formidable achievement' C. D. C. Armstrong, *Daily Telegraph*

'Marianne Elliott's history combines original scholarship with a
strong sense of her own identity . . . Her discussion of the 1798
rebellion is masterly, as is her analysis of the role of the Catholic
hierarchy in education . . . enlivened by Ms Elliott's use of folklore
material and regional writing to shed light on the intricate and (to
the outsider) baffling ways of life and thought of the Ulster people'
Economist

MARIANNE ELLIOTT

The Catholics of Ulster

A HISTORY

PENGUIN BOOKS

PENGUIN BOOKS

Published by the Penguin Group
Penguin Books Ltd, 80 Strand, London WC2R ORL, England
Penguin Putnam Inc., 375 Hudson Street, New York, New York 10014, USA
Penguin Books Australia Ltd, 250 Camberwell Road, Camberwell, Victoria 3124, Australia
Penguin Books Canada Ltd, 10 Alcorn Avenue, Toronto, Ontario, Canada M4V 3B2
Penguin Books India (P) Ltd, 11, Community Centre, Panchsheel Park, New Delhi – 110 017, India
Penguin Books (NZ) Ltd, Cnr Rosedale and Airborne Roads, Albany, Auckland, New Zealand
Penguin Books (South Africa) (Pty) Ltd, 24 Sturdee Avenue, Rosebank 2196, South Africa

Penguin Books Ltd, Registered Offices: 80 Strand, London WC2R ORL, England

www.penguin.com

First published by Allen Lane The Penguin Press 2000
Published in Penguin Books 2001

1

Copyright © Marianne Elliott, 2000